SPOTSWOOD'S JOURNEY

with The KNIGHTS of the GOLDEN HORSESHOES

300 YEARS AGO

A HISTORICAL FICTIONAL NOVEL ABOUT THE JOURNEY

OF LT. GOVERNOR ALEXANDER SPOTSWOOD

OF VIRGINIA 1710-1722

BY ROBERT G. TAYLOR

.1

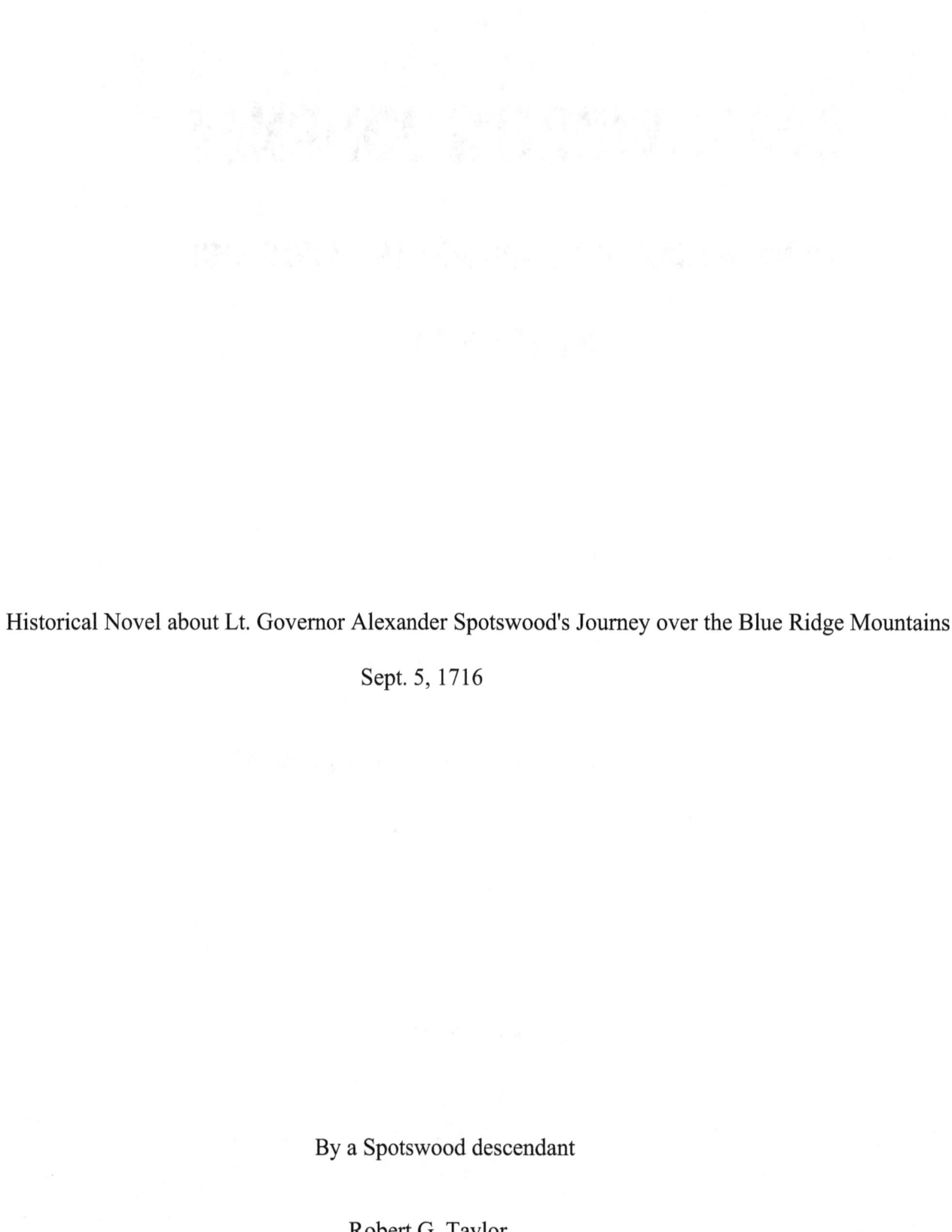

Historical Novel about Lt. Governor Alexander Spotswood's Journey over the Blue Ridge Mountains

Sept. 5, 1716

By a Spotswood descendant

Robert G. Taylor

dedicated to Becky, Christy, Erica, and Chloe

May 1. 2015

ISBN 978-0-692-72052-3

This is simply an attempt to celebrate a journey of Lt. Governor Alexander Spotswood of Colonial Virginia which he accomplished in August and September of 1716. It is not to be taken as historically accurate. Although many of the historical names and facts may be somewhat correct, I will leave it to the real historians to determine the importance and the accuracy of the recorded historical events. Throughout the years there have been many tales told about Alexander Spotswood and his distinguished band of landed gentry and servants achieving a successful expedition with a somewhat romantic, adventurous, and lively trek to cross over the Blue Ridge Mountains. Not only for adventure's sake, but for sensible, economic, political, and for military defensive reasons, the journey was significantly important for the growing population living and arriving in the colony and for a necessary expansion westward. As a result, Virginia and the other colonies grew quickly and strengthened the British Empire's stronghold in the New World, with the assistance of his merry Knights of the Golden Horseshoes.

The real Alexander Spotswood is my 7th generation grandfather in the line of descent. I am very proud of his many noble accomplishments for his Maker, his family, his government, his country, and for his own honor. This novel is in no way to distract from his respectful characteristics or actions. It hopefully neither embellished his achievements nor diminish his immeasurable worth to his family nor discredit in any way, his abilities in life. The same effort was made to tell about the interesting journey by using historical facts sparingly, also holds true for the other characters in the novel. The readers should judge the characters in the novel and not assume they are the same historical figures in English and Virginia history.

Alexander lived on three continents and a brief possible travelogue what his surroundings may have been liked, have been included. If the novel only helps us remember his name in history and becomes a wish list for many to visit Tangiers, Africa; London, England; Williamsburg, VA ; Germanna, VA; and for the Shenandoah National Park, then it has partially accomplished its goal.

There have been many informative and factual books written about Alexander Spotswood, the Lieutenant Governor of the Virginia Colony from 1710 to 1722. There are many court and legal letters in courthouses throughout Virginia, but mainly concentrated in Orange County and Spotsylvania County, Virginia. There are even books that have been published of some of the official letters written by Alexander Spotswood while he was in office. There are many factual books written about his administration at Germanna College and the Virginia State Library. The real historian will be able to discern the facts from the fiction and the real history from this fictional story. There have been many tales told about the Journey over the Blue Ridge Mountains by Alexander Spotswood and his Knights of the Golden Horseshoes. What really happened on the journey will be a mystery and only that which was shared with us by Fontaine, Byrd, and Hugh Jones who all accompanied the Knights on the expedition in 1716. Many a search for the source of some of the stories included in the overall story proved futile.

Very little information has ever been shared or even known about the boyhood of Alexander Spotswood in Morocco. Also, there is very little knowledge about his education, his life in London, and his military life of 16 years. There is no known information about the relationships between different members of his family including very little information about his wife and children. There has been no established historical evidence of any relationship with any of the kings and queens or royalty of England. How he was chosen to be Lt. Governor is not known to the writer. There are no known relationships with the Churchills and any members of Parliament, or any of the other prominent citizens in this story. There are certainly no known writings about the relationships with the Brayne Family and with the Knights of the Golden Horseshoes. It is documented that Alexander Spotswood did appoint Benjamin Franklin as a postmaster. It is documented that he gave the order to capture Blackbeard, the notorious pirate. Again, the best source of factual information is from the history books of Virginia and not this historical novel.

In ever writing that has been read by the writer of this story it has been established that the real Alexander Spotswood was a capable and able government official, superb military officer, friend to the Indians and the citizens, and saw to the improving of the belfry at Bruton Church, completing The Palace, and assisted in the improvements of William and Mary College. He was a learned man, skilled in writing and speaking, a man determined to improve the beautification of Williamsburg, and he was an excellent family man. May another 300 years come and go, and the name of Spotswood is remembered in the land.   May 2014

Contents

The next historical book in the series will be *The Spotswood Patriots*, Copyright 2019 TXu 2-155-456

ISBN 978-1-5136-5807-0. It tells of the Lt. Governor's grandchildren as they prepare for the Revolutionary War.

.5

Journey in Morocco

Once upon a time, a very long time ago, in Tangier, Morocco, a baby boy was born in 1676 in the year of our Lord and Savior The baby would be named Alexander Spotswood and would be destined to be one of the most influential and well known men in the history of Virginia in the New World, thousands of miles away. This influence and fame would also be many years in the making. For now, Alexander's parents had been assigned to the British garrison in Tangier on an order by King Charles II of their native England. Alexander's father, Robert Spotswood was a surgeon assigned as a doctor to the naval garrison in Tangier. This rugged but beautiful city of Tangier was much harder to raise a family in than London, with all its amenities, but Robert thought it would be a temporary and important assignment and enthusiastically welcomed the new addition to the family. Alexander would carry on the male Spotswood line, and Robert and his wife Katherine would raise their baby boy as best they could in this antiquated but strategic British colony many miles from their English home.

Morocco, a predominantly Berber country in the Northwest corner of Africa, is bounded by the grayish-blue waters of the Atlantic Ocean to the west and the crashing waves of the Mediterranean Sea to the northeast. Due north of Morocco is a body of water that is the entrance to the Mediterranean Sea and the straits of Gibraltar. Gibraltar and Spain are the ancient land masses north of the straits. Algeria is to the east of Morocco and the Great Sahara Desert is to the south of Morocco. On a clear day, Robert Spotswood could stand on a scenic overlook on the rugged Rif Mountain at Jebul Musa or better known as Mt. Moses, the highest point on the Moroccan coastline and look about fifteen miles to the north and see the Andalusian Mountains near Tarifa, Spain. The ancient city of Tarifa was well known for charging docking fees at the seaport to captains of cargo ships carrying treasures from the Arabian countries to Europe. The captains jokingly called them tariffs after the city. The city of Tarifa was strategically located at the entrance to the strait of Gibraltar at Cape Spartel. Cape Spartel was a rocky, craggy mountain about thousand feet above sea level and located about fourteen miles west of Tangier. Robert would walk up their sometimes just to feel the cool breezes of the Caves of Hercules which were located at the bottom of the Cape. These caves contained long massive tunnels which had been explored for thousands of years. Explorers and adventurers would tell tall folktales about the tunnels being used for pirate hiding places, resting places for invading armies, homes of Greek gods and goddesses, trade routes from Spain to Africa, and many other unbelievable tales. Over the years these stories circulated in the town square about the cave and tunnels at Cape Spartel.

Robert was a tall thin man with attractive features, dark blonde hair, and had piercing blue eyes. He smiled a lot even though his working conditions were more modest and frustrating than he had hoped for when he had arrived in Tangier with the Navy. His soldier's pay verily covered the family's expenses, but he was thankful to the Lord for his hard-earned provisions. Robert was physically fit and used his long, lean, and muscular body to take hikes and mountain climbs around the trails in the Medina and mountains that surrounded Tangier. He did sometimes fear for his safety because the native Berbers, usually peaceful, did resent the English presence. He kept a watchful eye and stayed behind the safety of the garrison walls at the first signs of trouble. For the most part, the Berber merchants in the souk marketplace welcomed the money that the English spent in their shops and did not bother the garrison soldiers.

Since Robert had lived in the garrison for a few years. he undoubtedly had heard of the local legends about the Barbary macaques, the grayish monkeys that lived and roamed around on the steep, red, jagged cliffs in the coastal town of Tangier. The stories passed down from the Berber natives that the macaques immigrated to Morocco centuries ago underneath the straits of Gibraltar in the tunnels at the Caves of Hercules that connect Morocco to Spain. The local Berber families called these macaques monkeys *llanitos* and would take them to their homes and care for them as pets. They made for great pets except occasionally the monkeys became mischievous in the local souks or marketplaces and cause some minor damages by playing sport with the merchants and their wares.

Gibraltar, sometimes referred to as the Rock of Gibraltar is a two-mile square land area at the entrance of The Mediterranean Sea across the straits of Gibraltar and is bounded by The Andalusia Mountains of Spain to the north. The mountains, steep cliffs of Tangier, the ocean, sea, and straits were the surroundings of the Spotswood family. Their living at the British naval garrison protected them from the dangers of the warring Berbers. Tall fortified palisade walls surrounded the English garrison. There was also a stone fortified sea wall at the edge of the coastline and garrison that help prevent warring tribes and pirates from attacking directly into the bay of Tangier along the front of the garrison. All these walls made them feel secure. Robert and Katherine and their newborn son, Alexander were in a scenic area of North Africa in a strategic coastal city protected by the British navy, the strongest navy in the world. Every trade route coming out of every part of Africa led to Tangier. Throughout history, whoever controlled the city, controlled the trading and wealth of Africa and the Middle Eastern Arabic countries. By this control, this governing system became the dominant empire of the world at that point in history. Tangier was a city of Roman walls, stadiums, and grand architecture. It was a city of Spanish cathedrals and Muslim mosques and had sturdy built stone buildings and structures that remained from every empire that had controlled the city from its beginning. Tangier, only eight miles from Spain, the hated enemy of the English, had remnants of some Spanish influence. An attack from the Spanish did not seem eminent at the present time. As for the Spotswood family, they would make do for now and enjoy the comfortable, year-round Mediterranean climate. From their rooms at the garrison's barracks, the Spotswoods could see the blue turbulent and therapeutic waters of the straits of Gibraltar from the hills above the walled fortifications below. In addition to the many sailing vessels, fishing boats, and cargo ships sailing to ports all over the world, the Spotswoods would occasionally see the diving antics of the dolphins and whales in the waters of the straits.

During the months before his departure from England to Morocco, Robert had spent many hours studying the history and culture of Morocco. He knew that he would be living and working in a mysterious land much different than England and Scotland where he had been raised. He had attended the best schools in Scotland and had mastered English, Irish Gaelic, Scottish Gaelic, and Latin while studying to be a doctor He was curious about the origins of the Berber people, Muslim culture, and historical events. In his studies of Morocco, Robert had learned that many ancient civilizations had claimed Morocco for their king and country. It was a land of Berber nomads and many different Muslim tribes with Arabic origins. In the beginning, Morocco was called the Land of God by the Arabs Muslims under King Manzer. The Muslims had taken control of these original Phoenician colonies that had been created by traders and Phoenician soldiers six centuries before the birth of Christ. This Arabic influence was short-lived because the Romans took control of the land as part of the powerful Roman Empire six centuries after the birth of Christ. After the Romans lost control, Morocco was controlled by the Byzantine Empire, the Visigoths, the Vandals, Spain, Portugal, and the Arabic Empire. Robert had also learned that Morocco was predominantly a Muslim nation and most of its citizens were made up of members of the Berber Nation. The Berbers lived in the mountainous regions of Northwest Africa and were largely unaffected by all the political changes. All the previous empires had left their mark on Morocco. There were remains and ruins of Roman walls, bridges and roads. Now the English would occupy and fortify the city and leave its mark, also. Dr. Robert Spotswood believed that Tangier would be the most strategic seaport in the North Atlantic for the British Navy, because it was situated on the mountains at the entrance of the Atlantic Ocean and the Mediterranean Sea. He also believed that the country that controlled the city would control the wealth and power on the shipping lanes to Africa, Southern Europe and the Arabic countries east of Africa. Undoubtedly, Robert was thinking what he could for his part in helping grow the British Empire. He was not thinking how he could acquire personal wealth or gain. His main job was to take care of the sick and wounded soldiers.

Robert's wife, Katherine, had been married once before to George Elliott in London. Katherine had been raised in Scotland at Cardoness Castle on the sea near Dumfries. She had later moved to London with her parents, Reverend and Mrs. William Maxwell when the reverend took on a new assignment in the Aldergate Ward. She had married at a young age to her first husband, Dr. George Elliott in 1660 in the year of our Lord and Savior at St. Olave on Hart Street by the Thames River. They had a daughter, Margaret, and a son, Roger named after his grandfather Roger Elliott. When George Elliott, member of the British Navy was assigned to Tangier, Morocco with the Earl of Teviot's Regiment as Chirosurgeon, Katherine and Roger also went on the assignment and stayed in the Barracks at the garrison at a place called Above the Mole. Margaret stayed behind in England to finish school and get married. Tangier was one of the few British garrisons where family members were allowed to live with their British navy officers. Katherine, Roger, and George found the tropical climate and modest living conditions comfortable enough in Morocco and became busy in his work and assignment at the garrison. After about four years into his assignment, George became ill with a fever and died at the young age of 32 and was buried in the naval garrison's cemetery. After a short period of time, the widow, Katherine married her second husband, Robert Spotswood, who had been George Elliott's assistant at the garrison. Robert who was now about 38 years of age and Katherine who was about 35 years of age made an attractive couple in a very unpretentious but sacred marriage ceremony by the navy chaplain. Roger was happy that his mother had married a man a lot like his father.

Bethia Spotswood, the servant for the Spotswoods, was also a younger sister to Robert. Robert had been named after the father and Bethia had been named after their mother. Bethia came to Morocco to perform the domestic duties for Robert. Their parents had died many years ago. Robert and Bethia had looked out for each other since living with their uncle Alexander at Darsie Castle in Scotland. Robert and been schooled by Doctor Longholtz in Edinburgh. Bethia had a good education at Rosefriar's grammar school and loved reading when she wasn't performing her servant duties. She spent most of her time out of sight reading her books and writing letters.

Bethia was a short round-face blondish gal with short cut hair. She wore the simple clothes of a servant usually with a dainty apron while she cleaned, mended, and washed clothes. She cooked many of the Spotswood's favorite dishes and kept everything very organized and tidy. She could bring in firewood after cutting down a tree and then chop it up and saw it into firewood. She also had a gentle and meek quality which made her perfect to take extremely good care of Robert and Katherine.

 A few years went by and Robert and Katherine announced to their friends at the garrison, that they were going to have a baby. Roger was the happiest one of all. Roger who was now 11 could have a younger brother or sister to share his time with when he got bored at the Mole. Life could get pretty routine at a navy barracks. Robert, whose father had died when he was 17, was insistent that it was important for a father and son to spend a lot of time together. Roger liked going to school at the garrison and was extremely fond of his teacher, Dr. Mercer. Robert and Roger spent lots of time together, talking and working on reading, writing, and arithmetic. For fun, they would hike up to the nearby Atlas Mountains, or the Cave of Hercules, and go boating and fishing on the ocean and sea.
They would sometimes go to the cemetery and visit the grave of Roger's father. Roger missed his father and Robert missed his former friend and supervisor. Robert also talked to Roger about military life and that maybe someday, Roger would be a military man like his father.

Katherine was so proud of her husband, Robert for being a good husband and father. She had written letters back to her daughter, parents, and friends back in England that she had been doubly blessed by the good Lord for giving her two good husbands. Katherine was proud and happy she gave birth to a son, Alexander, and hoped he would be like his father. Bethia, servant and proud aunt, would be happy to use her caring nature to help with the baby. Bethia's loving care and attention to Alexander would make life much easier for Katherine.

The Spotswoods lived at Above the Mole, a set of barracks on a hillside above the Bay of Tangier and above the mole fortification. The Mole was a quarter mile long and thirty-foot wide stone pier that went from the coastline of Tangier and jutted out into the bay where the navy ships could dock. The mole was high enough to keep the sea water from doing damage to the garrison. The mole was built by Bill Rutherford, Earl of Teviot and his regiment. It was designed by Henry Shere and Hugh Chomley to protect the English troops at the Tangier Garrison from the warring Muslim tribes who resisted and resented the English occupation at Tangier. This mole would be similar to the one they designed and built at Whitby, England. They knew it would work and brought forty stone masons with them to build the mole and surrounding walls. This mole in Tangier would cost the English government two million pounds over 15 years to maintain. King Charles II of England had sent Earl Montagu, the 1st Earl of Sandwich, to claim the king's dowry prize of Tangier after Charles II had married Katherine of Braganza.

 The new English masters of the politically hot city of Tangier caused the last Portuguese Governor of Tangier, Louis Almeida to recede back to Lisbon. Admiral Montagu took possession of Tangier and helped safeguard the city and garrison by his regiment, the 2nd Regiment of Foot, the Queens's Brigade. Later the regiment was reinforced with troops from Dunkirk, Ireland. This made the troop strength 500 horse soldiers and 2500-foot soldiers protecting the garrison from the warring Berber tribes. When Teviot built the mole around the garrison, the English felt more secure. The local shop keepers at the souks like the gallantry, charm, and extravagance of Teviot for he was good for their economy. There were many times that the troops could come and go from the barracks without any notice or bother from the local tribes. Although Teviot seemed strong against the Berber tribesmen, his troops said he slept with a gun and saber in case he got attached in the night by a wandering angry Berber. On one occasion, Teviot got the courage to take 500 of the soldiers out of the garrison to the outskirts of town. This ill-conceived adventure ended on bad terms with the local tribesmen. A leader named Ghailhan and his warriors caught Teviot's regiment off guard and killed all of British troops except nine soldiers who would live to tell the tale.

The Spotswood family continued to work at building a good life and contribute to the building a strong regiment by providing excellent health care and service to the sick and wounded.

It was 1680 in the year of our Lord and Savior, and Alexander was now an inquisitive toddler. Roger was at the age he could join the British Navy with the 2nd Regiment of Foot as an Ensign under Lt. Col Percy Kirke, who had been recently promoted just a few months earlier. Little did they know that this would be a year of many changes and be a turning point for the Spotswood family. Katherine was busy being a mother, wife, and doing domestics duties at the garrison. Robert was busy as the doctor, but he was weary and not very healthy. The tiring work at the garrison in an unforgiving country was draining him of his strength. Many of the soldiers he had come over with from England had died in the Muslim and Berber tribesmen's wars or die from the fever that seem to plague the barracks.

Alexander Spotswood was now 4 years old. He stayed close to the rooms his parents were staying at while assigned to the garrison. The rooms were cherry and open. A view of the Tangier Bay and the Strait of Gibraltar could be seen from the arch shaped window from his bedroom. He had some other children to play with in the compound. The mothers took turn watching the children. Roger was home today resting from wounds he received in a skirmish with some Berbers and had decided to take Alexander down to the docks where the fishing boats were anchored. Once they got down to the craggy and rickety old docks, they sat down and watched the ships going through the straits of Gibraltar from the Mediterranean to the Atlantic Ocean.

Alexander asked inquisitively, "Where are the ships going, Roger?"

Roger replied, "They are merchant ships carrying goods and supplies to ports all along Africa and Persia like the ships coming to Tangier from Europe and England.

Alexander asked, "Where is England?"

Roger chuckled and said, "I know you have heard of us talk about England a lot. It is where your mother, father, and I were born. It is many hundreds of miles away from us in that direction," as Roger pointed north.
Alexander taking advantage of Roger's good nature, kept asking, "Will we ever get to go to England?"

Roger replied, "I believe you will get there some day because of all the family we have there, and you never know what may happen to you in life."
Looking puzzled, Alexander said, I want to go there with Mother, Father, and you, Roger."

Some storks and a flock of birds were flying in the sky above in such great numbers it was difficult to ignore. They numbered in the thousands.

 Alexander asked, " Why all the birds?"

Roger said, "Because the birds are migrating and flying south to the tropical weather for the upcoming winter. They are coming from northern Europe where England is located."

Alexander proudly said, "That means they came hundreds of miles from there". As he pointed to the north. Roger laughed and said, "Good boy, you listen well. You will be a smart one at school."

There was silence for a while as they strolled along the beach walking on the hot sand and gathering shells. After a while they sit on the sand and stared at the sea.

Roger reluctantly had to tell Alexander some bad news. He began slowly, "Alexander, there is something your mother and I must tell you." Roger hesitated. knowing that they must go to their mother for this particular announcement. Roger continued, " We must go to our quarters and see mother and have her explain something to you."

Alexander listened intently and knew that something was dreadfully wrong. They began walking from the beach up to the quarters by a winding set of steps that led up to the hillside to the garrison.

In a few minutes, their mother, Katherine was standing at the doorway looking down at the sandy courtyard in front of their rooms waiting for their return from the outing. She had been crying, but she tried to muster a smile for the boys. Once inside, she told then to sit down on their cots, and she began to tell them what she was feeling. In a calm voice, she said, "Alexander, your father is dying with a fever and there is little hope of him getting well. Do you understand? "

The four-year old seemed to understand what that meant since he had seen patients brought in the infirmary and never get well. He said," Mother, I think so, but Father must not die."

Alexander said," Mother, when we pray each night, we pray for our family's safety and health and for the Lord to help us."

Katherine said," Yes. That is right and we also pray for God's will to be done."

Roger was sitting close by listening to each word but was in deep thought. His stepfather Robert Spotswood had always been good to him and affectionate to his mother, Katherine.

Alexander said, " Mother, did you not say all things were possible through Christ. He will not let Father die." and he began to cry.

With a very caring smile and loving motherly look. "Why, yes, it is God's will, and sometimes things happen that we do not understand, but you know that your father loves us and does not want to leave us." She hugged Alexander and looked at Roger to make sure he was handling this bad news as best as he could.

She looked at Alexander and said, "You have heard us talk about Roger's father, my first husband, George ,who was a very good man like your father. He got sick, too, and overworked, and overwhelmed, and we prayed that the Lord's will be done. His prayer was answered and not to our way of thinking either, but in God's way. George's work was complete in this life, and he moved on to the next life to be with the Lord. Do you understand? "lovingly she stated." It was hard on Roger and I. " Roger nodded his head in agreement.

Alexander, asked timidly, " May I see father?"

Katherine said, "Certainly, he has been waiting to talk to you."

.12

They all walked into Robert's bedroom, and one could barely recognize Robert's face, as he had been heavily perspiring and was breathing deeply almost as if he was having seizures.

Alexander walked up slowly to his father's bed.

A big smile came on Robert's face when he saw Alexander and he said, "Son, I love you, Alexander and that is all you need to know for now."

Alexander was puzzled with what to say or do, but he managed to say, "I love you."

Later, that day, Robert Spotswood died at the age of 43 in his bedroom and in a world that was far different than his Scottish ancestral home which was far away. He would leave letters to his wife and sons that he had written shortly before he died, explaining his love for his family and country. He also had a letter of his last will and testament. One special letter was marked for Alexander to be given to him when he became of legal age and was old enough to read and understand the contents by himself.

Roger, Alexander, and Katherine hugged each other and cried as some soldiers took Robert Spotswood's deceased body from his bedroom in the barracks to the hospital to prepare the body for burial. Roger did his best to calm his distraught mother. Alexander looked lost and confused. He had never seen his mother upset and crying. He hoped she would be stop crying and be herself again.

The memorial for Robert Spotswood was held at the chapel at the garrison. The service was led by Charles FitzCharles, 1st Earl of Plymouth who had been appointed Governor of Tangier by his father, King Charles II of England. He had the Royal Coat of Arms on his cloak and shield with a baron sinister overlay. Charles now 23 had been elevated in peerage in his youth as Baron of Dartmouth, and he would manage affairs wisely if he pursued the paths of virtue. Charles was also known affectionately by the soldiers in the navy as "Don Carlos" when he picked up the nickname while he completed his studies in Spain. By Charles side was his wife, Bridget, who was the daughter of Thomas Osburn, 1st Duke of Leed, the treasurer of England. Several hundred of Robert's fellow navy officers and soldiers were also in attendance.

Katherine, Roger and Alexander were staring sadly at the casket in front of them and didn't seem to be pay much attention to all the pomp and circumstance surrounding the ceremony. It was now sinking in that he was losing the companionship of his father. His mother had told him that his father was in Heaven and that no matter where we go in life, we are always comforted by our Heavenly Father who is always there. Alexander did not think about the future as long as his mother and Roger were there with him.

Charles FitzCharles began the service by saying the following remarks.

We are here to remember a friend and faithful English soldier, Dr. Robert Spotswood in the English Colony of Tangier. He held a responsible and unique position in the British Navy, 2nd Regiment of Bath, as Surgeon where he took care of the sick and dying. His compassion for others and love for England cannot be questioned. He gave his life for service to his country and God. For this we are grateful for those who knew him. His service and our memory of him will last forever. Robert was born in Scotland into an ancient and noble family. His father and father's father were faithful to England and Scotland in the military and in the Church. Robert came to Tangier on an assignment by my father, King Charles II of England with his friend John Middleton, 1st Earl of Middleton who preceded me as a colonial governor of Tangier and died a few years ago. The King has directed me to express his personal sympathy to the wife, Katherine and sons, Roger and Alexander. The kingdom of England was made stronger because Robert assisted the weakest in their time of most need. It is the kingdom of England's loss and the Kingdom of Heaven's gain. God, rest his soul. God save the King, so he reigns long over us. Amen.

The traditional church service continued for a while but soon ended with a benediction. As part of the memorial service, several soldiers fired a volley of musket fire into the Moroccan sky to pay their respects to their comrade. Many thoughts were racing through Alexanders head. He knew that he would never see his father again, and life would not be the same. The wooden casket of dogwood was soon buried under the Moroccan soil. Alexander knew that he would not forget his father's smile, the sound of his voice, the earthly and heavenly advice, nor forget the memories they had made in the barracks, at the beach, in the caves , or anywhere else they had traveled together.

Roger on leaving the grave site, was also deep in thought. He had stopped briefly to visit his father George Elliott's grave, which had been placed their 12 years earlier. Roger was about the same age then as Alexander was now and vividly remembered the kindness and face of his father. He remembered how grief stricken his mother, Katherine was that day. His thoughts turned back to his stepfather, Robert. Robert had been a kind, religious man and had expressed his love for him. He had been treated fairly and with respect by his stepfather. How would Alexander deal with all this? Roger wondered. Roger knew he would return to his assignment in the military service and would not have as much time to spend with his half-brother and mother.

After the memorial service, Katherine shook hands with all the friends and the Governor and his wife for paying their respects. She grabbed Roger's and Alexander's hands, and they all headed back to their home. Bethia, mourning at the loss of her brother, trailed behind. Robert and Bethia had always been close. The death of her brother at a young age reminded her of their father's death by beheading at a young age. Bethia's other brothers and sisters lived in Scotland, and she would send them a letter describing the fate of their brother and her uncertain future. For now, she could still be the servant to Katherine and her family if Katherine still wanted her to be. It would take a while for Bethia to adjust to the loss of her brother. It would take a while for Katherine Maxwell Elliott Spotswood to adjust to the loss of her second husband. Alexander would never forget the smile his father gave him the last time he had seen his father alive.

Katherine and Alexander attended the chapel service faithfully every Sunday. Katherine would read the Bible every night to her son. Robert had owned a small collection of books of stories of knights, and a book of animals and plants and a book of geography which fascinated young Alexander. One of the books, "The Plants at Fort Tangier" had been written and published by his father, Robert. The pictures of all the books stirred his imagination and seem to help Alexander get back to the routine of everyday life and help keep his mind off the loss of his father. Bethia would also try to comfort Alexander by telling him about his father's early life and all about the Spotswood family in Scotland and England.

One morning, Alexander was out on the veranda staring at the Mediterranean Sea. Bethia thought that Alexander might need some company. She said, to him. "I bet you are thinking about your father. He was a fine man. I know that I still miss him being here with us. Do you want to hear a story about the Spotswoods?"

Alexander said, "I would like that Aunt Bethia."

Bethia began the story," The Spotswood name was a well-known and honorable name in Scotland. The men had served the king and church with distinction since the time of King David of Scotland. The wives of the Spotswood men all came from the noblest families in all of Scotland. My grandfather, John Spotswood was an archbishop in St. Andrews Parish in Edinburgh and help write the prayer book used by all churches in Scotland. He bought a castle near his church named Darsie. When he died, he willed it to our uncle Alexander. When our father died, your father and I went to live in Darsie Castle with our uncle. He was good to us. Our new home at the castle was a beautiful old 3 story stone tower house along the River Eden. It was a beautiful place with lots of rooms and gardens to play in. There was a labyrinth maze parterre garden behind the house which had been built by a gardener of the former owners. Your father and I would play in the maze which was a path that led into other paths and we would follow the paths and try to find the center of the parterre. At the center was a stone bench where we could rest. There was also a little pond for the birds so they could fly down and get water to drink. We would watch the ravens fly from the nearby mountains down to the pond, drink, and the raise their wings and fly across the waters. We wondered how far they flew when they went away. Then we thought the ravens would come back again. My grandfather liked to watch the birds at the pond for it seem to make him feel better. It was so much fun for us to go from the pond back to the castle as we would try to follow the paths of the maze and find the entrance to the castle. There were so many pretty lawns, gardens, and meadows on the land surrounding the castle. There was a row of lime trees at one place. Your father and I would be careful when we went down to the river to swim or catch fish. Usually Uncle Alexander would be there to watch out for our safety and well-being. Also, the castle had a vaulted cellar below the castle where wine and cheese and other food were stored. We used to play hide and seek down in the cellars but we had difficulty lighting the lamps so Uncle Alexander would come down and play with us. It was wonderful growing up at Darsie Castle. My grandfather had always said that when he died that he wanted to be buried at Darsie or at the Old Darsie Church, but he ended up being buried in Westminster Abbey in London, England because he was a friend of King James I. He had been such an important person in the service to the King and popular with the people of England and Scotland. Before he died, he wrote a History of the Church of Scotland which can be found in every library in Scotland. I know Alexander that you may not know what all these words mean, and when you get older you will like the Spotswood family and be proud of them."

Alexander who had been listening politely as a four year could listen asked, "Aunt Bethia, did you say that my father and your father like to play in the castle?"

Well my father was named Robert Spotswood and he was killed by the King's men because he followed the orders of another king. He would be your grandfather, the father of your father. He was not at the Castle much because he went away for nine years to school. He was a good student and learned law and several languages. He traveled for King Charles I and became an important person in the kingdom. He was a Knight and had shield, sabers, and swords. Your father and I were very proud of him. One day he was captured in a battle and was tried for doing wrong by the new king and found guilty. They showed him no mercy for his doing all the good things for the old king. I know I should not tell you, but I love you and want you to know the truth. Many people liked your grandfather, but he was put to death for his service to his country."

Alexander curiously asked, "How did they put him to death?"

Aunt Bethia hesitated with tears in her eyes, "I should not tell you until you or older, but the mean people cut off his head by a thing called the maiden. The maiden is like an ax that you use to chop wood."

Alexander began crying, "No, that is not good. He should not be put to death." Alexander snuggled up close to Aunt Bethia, and he sobbed for a few minutes.

Aunt Bethia comforting Alexander, "Alexander, It's all right. It was a sad day for the Spotswoods when your grandfather died. All chances for the Spotswoods to have fame and fortune were lost that day. Your grandfather was gifted and could speak several languages including the Hebrew of the Bible and the Arabic of the Muslims. He traveled for the king over England, Ireland, Scotland, Europe, Asia and the Holy Land. He was appointed by the king of England to be Secretary of State for Scotland and President of Lords and Sessions which were well known and well-respected positions of power and prestige. Of course, your father and I missed our father, but through the years we remembered him as a good and decent father who loved us and that was important. We did not like the punishment of beheading for our father because of his loyalty to God and king. He did what he thought was right for his family. Everything is well now. It is up to you one day when you get older to keep the Spotswood name honorable and respectable"
Alexander lay in the comforting arms of his aunt.
Bethia said, "Alexander, if your father hadn't got sick, he would have kept the family strong and made the Spotswood name one to be proud of. Right now, there is no rank, no privilege or no power attached to the

Spotswood name. Maybe you will be able to change this and find favor with the new king and queen. "

Alexander, "When I get older, I want to be in the navy like my father, and I will make my name proud."

Aunt Bethia, "I know you will, Alexander, you are a good boy. "

After a while of sitting quietly with Alexander, Bethia said to Alexander, "You know that I do not belong here in this beautiful but dangerous country. I should be home in Scotland. I came with your father so I could take care of him. You, your mother, and Roger are all the family I know except for your cousin, John in Scotland. Maybe I will return home if you all don't need me. "

Alexander, "Aunt Bethia, please don't leave me. I like you, and I like your stories. Don't go."

Aunt Bethia told Alexander, "You don't belong here either, but God has a great plan for you. You will need to listen to his calling."

Alexander was puzzled by the remarks, but he knew and felt that his aunt wanted the best for him.

A Poem by Mikhail Lementov, warrior poet who claimed to be a relative to the Learmonth family who were previous owners of Darsie Castle in Scotland.

Yearning,

Why I am not a bird, the raven of the steppes
That just flown above me?
Why cannot I hover in the skies
And freedom alone adore?

Westward, ever westward would I fly
Where flourishes the lands of my forbears,
Where in an empty castle , on mist clad mountains
Rest their forgotten remains.

On an ancient wall their ancestral shield
And rusty sword hang.
Over the sword and shield I would fly
And flick away the dust with my wings.

A Sottish harp string would I barely touch
And a sound would swell up in the vaults.
By rapture alone aroused ,
As it rose so it would subside.

But in vain are my hopes, in vain my entreaties
Faced in the unbending laws of fate.
Betwixt me on the hills of my native lands
Spread the billowing seas.

The last offspring of gallant warriors

Lies withering amid alien snows.
Here was I born, but I do not belong here in my soul,
Oh! Why am I not a raven of the steppes?

The weeks after Robert's death started to go by quickly. Katherine managed to work some for the officers at the garrison to supplement the family income. She would hear some of their conversations and get uneasy when the officers talked about the Berbers and the Moor warriors wanting to oust the English from their country. The officers' wives and children also heard some of the chatter from their navy men about the local enemies. The Berber tribesmen wanted the English out of Tangier. They did their best to cooperate with the English, but every so often, the Berber's frustration would be manifested into an attack on the garrison. Just a few months before Roberts death, Ismail Moulay, the local leader was able to place a crippling blockade at the seaport in front of the garrison.

A year quickly passed and again, the Berbers made another crippling attack on the garrison. The Berber tribesmen's weapons were primitive and not as sophisticated as the weapons that the English navy possessed. They had only hand-made spears, knives, and stones to launch against the British Navy. They only had a few guns or powder to add to their arsenal. One day, in the fall of 1680, in the year of our Lord and Savior, Moulay and his warriors ambushed a troop of British soldiers on a routine patrol on the outskirts of Tangier. The battle was fierce, and many Berber warriors and English soldiers were killed. The English retreated behind the safety of the garrison walls. Later, that day, Moulay, had his warriors behead 119 English soldiers and stuck the gory and bloody heads on top of the wooden staves and poles that made up the palisade around the garrison and mounted the severed heads on top of the garrison walls. Moulay thought this would show his disgust for the English navy and scare the Englishmen in hopes that the English would abandon the garrison and would leave his country. This made the British even more determined to stay at the garrison. The Governor, Charles FitzCharles requested more reinforcements from his father, King Charles II, which was quickly approved. Charles FitzCharles died of dysentery, before the troops were sent. The dysentery was an illness which seemed to plague the garrison. FitzCharles was quickly replaced by another capable governor, and the English would stand strong against Moulay. They did not like the fact so many soldiers had been beheaded. Charles II always referred to Tangier as his Crown Jewel of the English Empire, and he was not about to secede it back to nomadic tribesmen. He appointed Edward Sochelles to be the Governor, and quickly the peace at the garrison was restored. However, it was rumored in the garrison that the cost of maintaining was draining the English budget, and there was a real concern on just how long the garrison would be kept.

Katherine was unable to explain to Alexander about the attack that day. She was relieved that her son, Roger was not in the Patrol and was still safe.

Alexander asked his mother, "Why did they enemies put the soldiers' heads on the wall?"

Katherine still in shock because she knew some of the soldiers said, "I don't know why. The Berbers have good people and they have bad people. Only bad people would do this. Nothing is explainable about war. It seems necessary sometime so we can live in peace, but this is just a barbaric act."

Alexander said, "This is not right. When I get old enough, I want to be like my father and Roger and punish the bad people. " His mother comforted him with a hug.

Later a detail from the garrison went to the walls and took the remains to the cemetery where the soldiers were given a Christian burial in the garrison cemetery which seem to be adding bodies too quickly.

After a few years went by, it was time for Alexander to go to the garrison school with the other children in the garrison who fathers served in the regiment. Now 6 years old, Alexander was attending the garrison school. His teacher, George Mercer, took a liking to Alexander, because of his seriousness about school and because of his inquisitive nature. Alexander liked writing and showed a fondness for history topics. Alexander made good grades and his mother read scriptures from the Bible every night in the candlelight. It was the King James Version in English. Charles II's grandfather, King James I of England, encouraged book makers to translate the old Latin Bibles from Hebrew and Latin into English. His mother encouraged him to memorize Bible verses as her father, William Maxwell, a pastor, and Robert's father had encouraged them when they had been Alexander's age. One of Alexander's favorite verses, was "I can do all things through Christ who strengthens me." That verse seemed to allude to receiving extra power and insight into doing good things with the help of the Devine.

As George Mercer showed more interest in Alexander's progress in School, Katherine showed more interest in George. He was a well learned man and a gentleman in every sense of the word. He had learned most of his teaching skills in London schools and joined the navy to be able to see the different seaports in the world and had been assigned to Tangier for many years. Katherine approved of his manners and charm, and they began seeing more of each other. Katherine would invite George over for supper, and afterward George and Alexander would begin their tutoring and studying, Alexander would ask him one question after another. There was nothing that George didn't know about English and Scottish history, the English Civil Wars, or the monarchs of England. After a while of seeing each other often and a short courtship, Katherine Spotswood and George Mercer would marry at the garrison chapel. George would be Katherine's third husband. Alexander was delighted. Roger was also pleased with the marriage and hoped they all would be happy. Roger was not at home as much now, because he was doing guard duty at the hillside forts out in the Atlas Mountains. Katherine and George Mercer would now work together to see that Alexander Spotswood would get the best schooling and church training of any student in the garrison. In fact, George would see to it that Alexander would read the Bible and accept Jesus as his Lord and Savior. They would read Bible stories together and talk to each other about the Bible characters. Alexander still missed his father and occasionally would visit his grave at the cemetery. He now knew a lot of his future success would be determined by his own achievements and dreams as he could not rely entirely on the honor and good standing of his family name. Sometimes Bethia would accompany him to the cemetery, but she mainly did her grieving and reminiscing in the servants' quarters.

Periodically, Alexander's half-brother Roger Elliott would reflect on his happy home life with Robert Spotswood and had admired his loyal service to the navy garrison. Roger was engrossed with the navy and was determined to prove his skill as an ensign in the Tangier Regiment of Bath. His newly appointed Colonel was Percy Kirke who had proven his military expertise in the Oxford Blues, part of the Household Guard of the army at Bristol. The Blues had served with distinction in the French Revolutionary Wars. Col. Kirke also had fought under General James Scott, 1st Duke of Monmouth , a Knight of the Garter, and an illegitimate son of King Charles II of England, which also made him half-brother to Charles FitzCharles, the former governor of the colony of Tangier who died in office. Roger remembered Charles FitzCharles as giving the nice eulogy at Robert Spotswood funeral service. Charles's half-brother, James was just as skilled as a military leader as his brother. The wars that had the most meaning for James Scott and Percy Kirke was at Maastricht and the Tuerene campaign when they tried to keep King XIV of France from taking over the Spanish Netherlands. It was a victory for the French and Col. Kirke had lost 300 of his men in the battle. Percy's father, George Kirke had been in the court of King Charles I of England and his son, Charles II. His loyalty to England was never in doubt, and since Charles II had put so much time and money into Tangier, the Crown Jewel of the Empire, Col. Percy Kirke would expect the best of the Tangier 2nd Regiment and protect the colonists and soldiers in the garrison. Roger was inspired by Percy, and he would do his best to improve his skills as a soldier. In his off-duty time, Roger would practice his rifle shooting, practice his horsemanship, and read about military strategy and public service. He wanted to go up in the ranks as high as he could go and make the best of his military career. This training and desire went on for a while until one day he met up with one his fellow soldiers, John Cutts, who had recently graduated from Cambridge University. John wanted to learn the practical side of life in the military because of his love for the military. He came from the gentry class and had a fondness for poetry and writing. The fellow soldiers had given him the nickname, "Salamander" because of his reciting the poem, "Ode to a Salamander", which he liked to delight any audience that would listen. He was a tall gangly, good looking and playful fellow and on one occasion decided to play sport with Roger.

Looking directly at Roger, Salamander Cutts asked him, "So you think you will get promoted in the ranks because you are a cousin to Col. Kirke? It will not be because of your honor as a soldier and a gentleman."

Roger was flabbergasted and became extremely upset and frankly did not know what to say. He was quickly thinking that getting into a fist fight or shouting match would only escalate the attack.

Roger angrily said, "He is not my cousin . He is my leader. I will show you what honor is. I will challenge you to a duel. I will get my father's dueling pistols, and we will see who has courage." Roger must have thought that bluffing Salamander would make him withdraw from the conversation and retreat.

Salamander quickly responded, "I accept your challenge on my honor as you amaze me with your brashness!"

Roger and Salamander had gathered a large crowd, and Colonel Kirk came out of his quarters to see what was causing all the commotion and what was drawing a growing crowd of yelling soldiers.

Col Kirke was looking at Roger and asked, "What is this all about, Ensign Elliott?"

Roger replied, " I challenged Salamander Cutts to a duel because he attacked my honor, sir."

Col Kirke looking at Cutts, asked, "Is this true, Ensign Cutts,"

"Yes, it is. I apologize as I was making fun of Roger, sir." Salamander answered.

Kirke looking disgusted said, "For your honesty, Ensign, your punishment will be that you serve 6 months in one of the outposts in the forts, and your duties will be assigned to you later."

Roger was looking down at the ground in guilt. Col. Kirke was looking at him and was hesitating what to say for a short moment, but the Col. finally spoke. "Ensign Elliott, you will be suspended from service in the 2nd Regiment of Foot and cashiered for violating one of the British military laws for unacceptable conduct. You will be sent to England as part of the cashiering and your future service will be decided by a court in London. Do you understand the charges and cashiering?"

Roger replied quickly, "Yes, sir, I do, and I also apologize, sir. "

Kirke replied, "You may go, and instructions will be sent to you. Godspeed to you."

Roger was more upset with himself than with Cutts for falling into the sport with Cutts. Roger knew he had to control his emotions in all situations in order to be an officer. He felt scared now about a scar on his career as he did not know what his future held. He could stay with his older sister and her husband in London. They had a favorable rank in society because of their father's peerage. He would miss the companionship of George and Alexander and would regret not seeing his mother as often. This was a setback in his career but also a lesson he needed to learn.

In a few days, Roger got his instructions and he would board the *Diamond*, the English Navy's HMS Destroyer and sail back to England. On the day he departed, his mother, Katherine, cried as he was walking the plank to get on board. She was worried about his fate. Alexander and George were waving farewell for now. They were hoping and praying that this trip to England would go well for Roger and that he would be sent back to Tangier soon. The uneasiness of not knowing the young man's future in jeopardy made them wonder, why do things happen the way they do?

Alexander stared at the huge grey *Diamond* sailing way in the blue waters of the harbor on Tangier Bay. In a few minutes, Roger and the destroyer would disappear over the slashing, billowing waves and distant horizon as they headed toward England, the country Roger vaguely remembered from his boyhood.

As Roger Elliott was heading for England, Katherine, George and Alexander headed for home. They turned away from the sea and looked toward the fortified walls of the city which seemed more than just protection from invading Berbers. They seem to add to the beauty of the riads and homes. The homes had white and blue rooves in the middle of the courtyards. The pretty scenery included the tall mosques and minarets oi the Berber faith jutting above the palm tree and the green of the Andalusian gardens. They left the pretty fishing docks and started climbing up by banisters made out of jute ropes that went up alongside of the steps to the streets of Tangier on the hillside above the sea. Once they got up to the market square, they smelled the aromatic mixture of spices and carpets being displayed by the vendors.

George said, " This has been a big day. Let 's eat at one of the cafes."

Katherine, I don't feel like eating much, but I would like some tea. I guess we can thank Queen Catherine of Braganza for introducing tea to the English."

George replied, "Yes, dear. Tea will calm your nerves and you won't worry about Roger's fate so much." Katherine nodded as if in agreement with her husband.

Alexander chimed in, "I'm hungry. I want some couscous and some fruit pastry."

They entered one of the doorways of the outdoor cafe where some British soldiers were already partaking of the spicy Berber cuisine. A Berber cook who spoke very good English said," You may sit over here." He pointed to some seats that were facing to the beautiful views of the Tangier Bay and the Mediterranean Sea. The list of foods a person could order included mutton, pigeon pie, and a variety of fish dishes. The Berbers only had goat milk and fruit juices as they would not drink any drink that contained alcohol and spirits.

Katherine ordered some mint tea and some pastry and almonds that had just been brought up from an orchard in the fertile coastal plains next to a city in the foothills of the Atlas Mountains. George ordered some chicken baked with many spices. Alexander ordered some couscous and a fruit pastry and a tropical fruit drink made from the juices of a dozen fruits. The man was wearing the traditional Berber attire. Red tarboosh hat or sometimes called fez typed hat, a tan colored djellaba over a long tan caftan with no collar. His slippers called debouches were comfortable looking. He could also speak some French and was very proficient in speaking Spanish. The Mercers and Alexander were doing their best not to worry about the fate of Roger. They had prayed that he would be able to get back into the Navy and maybe after some time had passed, he could reapply and get approved for re-entering the service. After the meal, they started on to their home in the barracks.

George and Alexander spent a lot of time together the next few months studying, reading, and questioning each other about their study materials. Alexander was an eager student and had a great thirst for knowledge. One day after about three months of Roger's absence from Tangier, the Mercer family received a letter from Roger, now settled in London with his sister Margaret and her husband.

Katherine was ecstatic with joy as she opened the envelope to read the letter. George and Alexander hoped he hadn't got into any more trouble and wondered what Roger was doing in his free time.

The letter read as follows:

_____

My dearest Mother, George, and Alexander,

I have finally had the opportunity to write after these few months. I hope you will get the letter without much ado because of the great distance between us at the present time. I am visiting with the court officials within a month to see when I can get back to service in Morocco. It took us almost 5 weeks to sail on the Diamond to Plymouth, the Navy shipyard. The captain said because of unfavorable winds and something called the Atlantic Drift impeded our speed. We were at the mercy of the wind and the current. I was surprise that I did not get sick from all the slashing of the ocean waves and the cramped conditions on the vessel. We had fermented drink instead of water as it was rationed. Our food was mainly bread and beans. I was very happy to depart in England and stay at sister Margaret's house. It has been pleasant weather and it is not always dreary here. Her husband has been very accommodating and asked about you all and Morocco all the time. They want to meet George and Alexander, too. I went to the home where I was born in the Aldergate ward, but really didn't remember the neighborhood from the days in my youth. There have been several fires in the ward that have altered the looks of the neighborhood. Margaret reminded me how our family survived The Great Fire of London in 1664 and the bubonic plagues that caused the death of many of the neighbors. Margaret is working for Richard Jennings, an accomplished businessman and a member of The House of Commons. I saw the graves of Grandfather Elliott and Grandfather and Grandmother Maxwell. In my spare time, I have been reading a book by John Milton, called "Paradise Lost". It is interesting book about life like it is in Morocco. The news has been fascinating. There was a law called habeas corpus written a few years ago. It basically says that a one cannot be imprisoned without a trial. This law is constantly being challenged in some counties because of unscrupulous sheriffs locking up innocent people in jail and throwing away the key. I was fortunate to see King Charles II, but I could not get close to him or his guards to greet him. The day I saw him, he was in front of Winchester Cathedral performing the treatment of scrofulous, a skin disease which George can tell you about and describe its symptoms to you. It is also called the King's Evil. King Charles II was touching the sick people one right after another who were suffering with the King's Evil. He was giving each person a small gold angel piece of jewelry which is worth about 6 shillings and makes a nice get-well gift. There were hundreds of people touching him, but he looked very tired and not very well. In some others news, a scientist named Isaac Newton has been proposing theories why things fall from the sky to the ground. Most of critics say that that is the way it has always been so why try to study this. I took a tour of a new museum that has opened called Ashmolean Museum on Oxford Street. The benefactor, Elias Ashmole has donated some of his antiques and artifacts from all over the world. There are books, maps, engravings, and ceramics from the Americas, Asia, Africa, and from all over Europe. The exhibits would be great for Alexander to see. The biggest story is about the Rye House in Worcestershire. It was a place where some of King Charles II enemies in Parliament were going to ambush him and his brother James, when they would be coming back from the horse races at Newmarket. The house is a fortified mansion surrounded by a moat on the toll road on the way to London. The perpetrators would hide on the grounds as they thought the king would stop there and rest and then they would ambush him and kill him and his party. What the men didn't know was that the town of Newmarket had a fire before the race and that nearly half of the town burned down. The horse races got canceled as a result of the fire. The King and his party left early and returned to London safely. The word had leaked out to the King about the plot and he ordered an investigation. Many members of the gentry and Parliament were involved. The courts have had many trials and it is still the talk on the streets around the Palace. The court found most of the men guilty of treason.   You may have heard of some of them. One of the men executed for the Rye plot was Thomas Walcott and another one was Algernon Sydney of the Cinque Ports. William Russell was beheaded. Thomas Armstrong of Parliament and Henry Cornish, the sheriff of London was hung by the rope and then drawn by the horses and quartered. A lady named Elizabeth Gaunt was burned at the stake alongside of Archibald Campbell, an Earl of Argyle with ten other conspirators. Patrick Hume and John Locke fled to Holland. The Kings own illegitimate son, James Scott, that had led Col. Percy Kirke in battle was implicated and was obliged to go to the Dutch Republic for his safety. The entire plot has been a bloody mess causing a separation in allegiance to the Kings and politicians labeling themselves as Tories or Whigs. Other news includes the King ordering the Royal hospital to be built at Chelsea for the old soldiers to stay when they need assistance. Some ladies proclaimed to be witches were hanged at Exeter for making statements against the church and for their practicing spells. I was able to talk to a delightful fellow, Edmund Halley who explained how comets streak through the sky at night. When I get back to Tangier, Alexander and I will have to go to the mountains and watch the stars and constellations. The stars have all kinds of meaning and significance. There is some news about a man named William Penn that was given a special charter involving thousands and thousands of acres to form a sectarian colony in the Americas. Can you imagine what it would be like to be in control of that much land especially after the small quarters in the barracks and the cramped condition on the ship. In my spare time I have been reading a new book, *Absalom and Achitophel* by John Dryden which is a political satire. In a few days, I will be going to a play on the *History of King Lear* based on Shakespeare's *King Lear*. Life in London is pure entertainment.

One more thing; there was a man from Bristol named Teach that got drunk and thought he could take a British Navy destroyer and go out on the North Sea towards the West Indies. He had some training on sailing in the Navy and was from a wealthy family. Everyone is wondering what caused him to think he could get away with such a crime. Most everyone agrees that it is his liquor speaking for him and that they put him in the city jail to sober him up. He seems a little mad. I like London. It has its good and not so good places. It also has some good and not so good people. I remember only a few things from my childhood here. I miss the warm weather in Tangier. It has been uncomfortably chilly here and most old timers believe that this winter will be the coldest winter in England's history. Don't worry. We are well stocked and wishing for a frozen Thames so we can have an Ice Fair. I can hardly wait to see you all again. Say Hello to Bethia. Roger

---

Katherine said, "That is a beautiful and interesting letter. I hope he is all right. "

George said, "I remember hearing about some of the people he mentioned, but it has been so many years ago since I lived in London. It has always been a busy and interesting place. I know that the habeas corpus to the people will be a popular doctrine. It is unfair to hold someone and not telling them about the charges against them. It is thrilling to see that there are laws changing for the good of the people. "

Bethia was busy as always working but couldn't help but hear the reading of Roger's letter and added, "It was nice of Roger to say hello to me. He is such a polite and well raised young man. "

Alexander didn't say much but started dreaming about the museum, the books, the people, and the comet. He read the letter repeatedly. He asked George a lot of questions about the words Roger used and what they meant so he could get a better understanding of what the life in London was like. One of the stories about Mr. Penn taking care of all that land made him think about America and wondered if that country was like Morocco. In his mind, he questioned what it would be like living in a world like America in the New World. After all, Alexander had never explored much outside the confinement of the garrison in his seven years of being in Tangier. It would be a more adventurous traveling hundreds of miles in unexplored country in a frontier like America.

Roger applied for re-in statement into The British Navy and after a few months, the Lord of Military Affairs William Coventry, approved his reassignment back to Morocco. Roger had to state that he would be court martialed out of the army if he violated any military rules of conduct within a year. He promised he would look at the position more seriously and professionally. A few minutes of anger had caused him many months of anxiety, and he had felt like he had learned an important lesson. He would strive to rise through the ranks and try to re-establish his family's good name. Soon, Roger was back on a destroyer headed for home, his family, Alexander, and Morocco.

Now that Roger was back from England, he could spend more time with Alexander. Roger would answer all his questions about London and his family and help Alexander with his homework. They would occasionally play some cricket, croquette, or some other ball games out in the courtyard. Roger was 12 years older than his half-brother, but they got along very well. Roger knew that Alexander would be coming of age soon, so he thought about planning a hiking trip up to the highest peaks on the Atlas Mountains.

One day Roger said, let us go down to the beach along the Atlantic. They packed some water in a navy canteen and food in a basket and headed for one of the long stretches of white sandy beaches along the many miles along the North Atlantic. These beaches were bordered by part of the sand colored mountains covered by fertile and forested mountain plains. The young men were enjoying the warm Mediterranean climate with cool breezes that was like summer temperatures in the dead of winter. Soon they found a spot to rest and camp.

Roger smiling," All we need to wear here in winter is cotton clothes and maybe a sweater. Do you know if we were in London it would be an ice storm? It is so cold and dreary there this winter that the ground gets frozen like ice. The River Thames, that goes through downtown London, is frozen and has hampered the shipping and sailing and that is all the seaman are talking about at the garrison. I am glad to miss all that."

Alexander replied, "I am glad you are back, Roger. I have read and learned a lot about your travels to London from your letters. I wish I could go there."

Roger, "I could bet that will happen one of these days. You can't say anything to our parents, but there was a rumor that the garrison may be closed here in Tangier and moved elsewhere. The cost of maintaining this Crown's jewel is draining the English budget, and there has been little improvement in the English economy because of it."

Alexander asking inquisitively, "Would the King move it to the New World?"

Roger laughed. "Maybe, but not likely. There are a few settled colonies there, and the King has his hands full there, too. Don't worry, we will be reassigned elsewhere, maybe London."

Alexander; "I won't say anything to mother, but it has been peaceful here. For the last few months, there has been no invasion from the tribesmen from the sea, no trouble at the mole, nor even any pounding on the garrison walls from the Berbers."

Roger, "Not even the Barbary pirates lurking out in the waters have tried to invade, steal, and plunder at the mole."

Alexander; "The soldiers would take care of them and put their heads on staves on the garrison walls."

Roger" You do remember that day, don't you?" referring back to the day the enemy tribesmen had slain some of the soldiers at the garrison and cut their heads off the soldier's bodies and mounted the bloody and gruesome heads on the poles of the garrison walls.

Alexander: "Yes, it was scary and sad."

Roger was now trying to get the young boy's mind on a cheerier subject, "Do you see that cargo ship coming up from the east? I guess they could be carrying exquisite goods, jewelry, spices like coriander and paprika, rum, olives, dates, and other items from Persia or the Mediterranean merchants along the southern European coastline. The Europeans like the Persian rugs that are woven there as much as the pretty rugs that are woven here. "

Alexander added to the conversation, "Some of the Berbers trade slaves, domestic servants, and concubines for cloth from each other."

.23

Roger, "How do you know about concubines?"

Alexander, "King Solomon in the Bible had several hundred concubines and he was one of the wisest kings that ruled Israel and Judah. "

Roger laughed again, "You got me there, little brother. He wasn't so wise if he had to take care of that many people if you ask me. But he was blessed by God, and he was rich. I see you have learned a lot about the world and about the Bible and about the cargo ships and the trade routes."

Alexander, "Our step-father, George has taught me a lot at school and at home. He said that all the roads that lead out of Tangier in all directions are trade routes that go to every corner of Africa. These roads go through jungles, deserts, plains, and mountains and they trade all kinds of things. They were trading goods even hundreds of years ago before the Romans and even before the birth of Jesus Christ. "

Roger, "You are learning a lot from the school master. I am glad to see you are getting along with him. You are very smart for your age. Do you know that? I like George, too."

Alexander looked as if he did not know how to take a compliment, but went on to say, "These routes are very dangerous and some of the tribesmen on these camel caravans try to take each other goods. It is no safer to haul cargo on merchant ships on the seas because of the greed for stolen goods that the pirates possess."

Roger, "We could provide the caravans and the merchant ships with military assistance so they could travel in safety."

Alexander explained, "George says that the pirates have thousands of islands where they can hide from the navy. Some of the Berbers thieves are chased by rival tribes and the thieves flee up into the mountains and go up the winding trails to hide or fight. "

Roger," And some of the Berbers make money selling dates and nuts. Some of them farm and grow tobacco, barley, and wheat. Some work in salt mines, and they make big blocks of salt which weigh 80 pounds, and these blocks are worth their weight in gold and silver."

Alexander added, "Many of the tribesmen raise cattle and chickens and sell cheese and eggs."

Roger said, "They live in these little houses in villages surrounded by protective walls. Many of the houses are connected in a single row. These houses have several rooms with very little furniture and may contain several families in one house. The homes are constructed of mud, stones, and clay and held together with the wheat straw or barley straw. Most have dirt floors. The rain and winds off the coast do not seem to affect the sturdiness of these houses. The houses usually surround a courtyard. There are lots of these little villages in the foothills and up in the mountains. The Berbers for the most part are very religious and peaceful Muslims, and they will be kneeling and bowing to Allah, their God, at least five times a day. They are mainly a peaceful people, but they sometimes get the wrong leaders that stir them up." Alexander nodded yes, as if he could picture the villages in his mind.

After eating their sandwich and drinking the water, Roger said, "Speaking of mountains, how would you like to go on an adventure and see the top of the Atlas Mountains. I know you are tired of seeing the red craggy Rif mountains back at the garrison. The views from Mt. Toubkal are spectacular there. I know because some soldiers and I went on patrol there before. We will have to get some horses at the barracks and make sure their horseshoes are good for the rocky trails.

Alexander excitedly, "Sounds like a fun adventure and I wondered what some of the countryside looks like. Will we be safe from the Berbers?"

Roger smiling, "The Berbers, that live in the country and mountains, will leave us alone. We would not be safe if we appeared to be a threat like a platoon from the garrison. I can tell when they are gathering for an attack, and we can outrun them by horseback to the nearest English fort if we sense danger. None of them have horses and would have to pursue us on foot. "

Alexander satisfied with the answers went on to say, "I have wanted to see the trees that my father wrote about in his book about plant life in Morocco. He wrote that there were walnut, almond, poplar, and juniper trees. He says there are virgin oak and pine forests in the lush valleys. He said there were forests of cork, olive, and date trees. He wrote the country was full of herbs, roses, flowers, and thickets full of broom, rosemary, and chrysanthemums, and sage and thyme. "

Roger exclaimed," I am proud of you, Alexander! Your father wrote all this down, and you know all about it?"

Alexander answered, "Yes, and then George has shown me other books from the school library that explained the plants to me."

Roger explaining, "I have heard about people trading tea, cotton, tobacco, sugar cane, and sunflower seeds."

Alexander adding, "Yes, they grow those crops here because of a long and warm growing season. "

Roger asking, "You won't be afraid of the wild animals we will encounter, will you? I will have a rifle and plenty of ammunition."

Alexander speaking as if he was an expert on the subject, "No, I don't think so. There are large lizards and harmless snakes, and big monkeys called the Barbary ape. We won't see any lions or tigers, but we will see foxes, jackals, and gazelles."

Roger was daydreaming about some bird hunting as there are so many birds in this part of Morocco. He became alert again and said, "There are supposed to be over 400 hundred types of game birds including pigeons, turtle doves, quail, wild ducks, and grouse. If we are not successful hunting, we will still have our packed food along with us."

Alexander smiling, "You are sounding like a school master like George now. It is good that you are home and we are planning a trip to the big mountains. "

Roger, " I am glad to be back. I have enjoyed this day. You are getting older now and we will use this trip to celebrate your stepping from boyhood into manhood."

They left the warm and beauty of the white sandy beach after spending several hours there. They headed for the two-hour walk back to the garrison. On the way home when they got to the marketplace in Tangier. Roger stopped in front of a hamman, the public bath house in the middle of a courtyard close to the souk and marketplace. Roger asking, "It has been a long walk and a hot bath would be good! Do you want one?"

Alexander still thinking about a trip to the mountains, said, "No, I will bathe when I get home. However, the hammans are supposed to be nice. Maybe another time."

Men and women have their own separate sections, if you are scared you might see a concubine." Roger laughed as he was trying to encourage his little brother. Roger was acting more like a caring big brother. Roger continued his selling of the idea. "They have sabot beide which is a unique black olive soap. Some of the baths have hassoul which is a lava clay that scrubs the skin, and you use a kiis for a scrub glove, and it doesn't cost that many dirhams."

Alexander watched Roger as he went onto the steamy bath house. Alexander staying firm in his decision, said, "I will go on home from here, but you can get a bath if you want."

As Roger disappeared into the bath house, a beautiful young Berber woman about twenty years of age with black hair and hazel eyes caught Alexander's eye. Her suntanned body and black hair were still wet as she was coming out of the ladies' section of the bath house. She had to be one of the prettiest girls in the city. He couldn't help but stare as she was clothed only in a thin bath towel. She started smiling at Alexander, and he was able to greet her by saying, "Hello." She said something which Alexander did not understand and was motioning for him to come towards her. Alexander realized that she was flirting with him or teasing him, and he became scared. He started running for home, and he could hear the young half-dressed woman laughing behind him. He would not tell Roger how embarrassed he had become about the antics of the young woman, and he definitely did not want to tell his mother. He knew he was not ready to talk to young women just yet.

The day finally came when Roger and Alexander saddled their horses and checked on their mounts' horseshoes, packs, and blankets. They would need a lot of supplies in their packs because they would be gone several weeks. The terrain was slow going and treacherous as the roads were rocky. Roger had paid close attention to the gear and the saddles. He also checked each horseshoe because they would protect the horses' hooves and would keep the big steeds from slipping and stumbling on the slippery trails ahead. And as Roger had promised, he brought his rifle and plenty of ammunition. Their parents were a little reluctant for Alexander to go on the trip to the mountains, but they knew Roger was a skilled soldier and also was a caring brother to Alexander, and they would protect each other. Alexander was making the transition from boyhood to manhood anyway so this would be a good experience for him. After all, Roger had promised Robert Spotswood that he would help look after his son, Alexander after his death and would hold some letters and papers for Alexander until he was old enough to understand and appreciate them. They rode for many miles the first day and finally made camp and pitched their tent. They had seen a lot of lush countryside and a few villages but didn't see that many Berbers or animals in the woodlands, plains, or meadows. They felt safe and built a small campfire after gathering some dead limbs in the forest. Alexander ate a little bit, but he was excited about seeing Mt. Toubkal. He asked Roger a thousand questions about worldly affairs and also about mountain climbing and how to make camps. He also asked all about horses and horseshoes. Roger did his best on trying to answer the barge of questions. The horses rested comfortably tied to a lower branch of a big old oak tree. There was some moonlight in the sky at night and the stars seem a lot brighter in the foothills where they had pitched the tent than down below in Tangier.

Roger to Alexander, "You know that I have tried to answer your questions tonight around this campfire. Many business deals and stories have been discussed amongst travelers on journeys around campfires ever since man could talk and fire was invented. Storytelling just makes life more interesting. I got to tell you this story I heard from one of the men in the barracks. In a Moroccan village, a sultan, which is like the king, had a small family with only one daughter. She was a beautiful and a charming princess named, Hiday which was his treasure. When she became 16 years of age, the sultan and his wife decided they did not want any of the young men in the village to see Hiday. They would marry her just because she was beautiful. They wanted Hiday to marry a prince in a nearby village. The parents wrapped up her face in a cloth so all that could be seen were her beautiful green eyes. They had concluded that if she married a boy in their village, she would have a miserable life. She would most likely be forced to accept a married life of work and poverty. For example, if Hiday married a miller, she might have to grind grain at the millstone every day. If she married a farmer, she might have to feed goats and pigs, every day. If she married a fisherman, she would clean smelly fish all day. If she married a basket maker, she would be weaving baskets all day long. On the other hand, if she married the handsome, rich prince of the neighboring village, she might become wealthy. When the prince's father would die, the prince would become the sultan, and she would be waited on night and day by the servants and slaves. The princess had no knowledge of her parents' plan, and the prince was busy learning the ways of a warrior and would be able to defend attacks on his village someday when the need arose. The prince was ambitious and did not know that the neighboring princess even existed. The prince's father said to his son, "Please do this one thing for me. Go to the neighboring village and find the sultan and wife and bring them back to me alive. I hear they have much treasure." The Prince named Jamail always strived to please his father and said that he would bring the neighboring sultan and wife to his father. After a full day's ride on horseback, the prince entered the neighboring village and captured the sultan and his wife. The sultan had heard his approaching hoof beasts and hid Hiday in the nearby woods on hearing that they were being invaded by Jamail and his warriors. The Princess, Hiday, was concerned about her parents' whereabouts. Through the trees in the woods, Hiday saw Jamail taking her parents away to his village. The sultan and wife kept quiet about having a daughter. Hiday feared that Jamail might find out about her, so she ran deep into the woods. Hiday hated the young prince for kidnapping her parents and didn't want to have anything to do with the handsome prince. She ran further and further into the woods and stumbled onto a herd of gazelles grazing on the forest grass and drinking the water from a nearby spring. She seemed to be drawn to their beauty and charm of the gazelles and the gazelles seemed to like Hiday. She stayed with them. There were fruits and nuts and herbs she could eat from the plants and trees in the forest. The trees and grass were so thick and tall that it was hard for anyone to see here, even the gazelles. It wasn't long before Jamail took control of Hiday's village and presented everything to his father as a gift. Jamail's father was well pleased with his son even though there was no treasure. In the meantime, Hiday was getting along well with the gazelles, the deer, and the other forest animals. She took off her veil and cloth that was covering her face and the turban on her head, and let her long shiny black hair unroll and drop down to her ankle. She had always washed her hair in olive oil and made it thick enough so she could use it as a cloak to help keep her warm on chilly nights. An old woman, who would come to the forest to gather the herbs for medicine came to the same creek that the gazelles came to for the refreshing themselves in the cool water. The old woman had to take a second look as she couldn't believe what she thought she had just seen. She thought she was seeing a scantily glad young woman with black hair and green eyes in the middle of a herd of gazelles. She could not believe how beautiful this girl was and wondered how did she get in this situation? The old woman ran back to the Prince's village and said that she saw a brilliant light and a dark cloud. The Prince ordered the old woman to come to her senses and asked her to explain herself. She said that the sultan has made it clear that he wanted his son to find a princess.

The old woman said to the prince, "I have found the most beautiful woman for you, your lordship. This girl has the shine and brilliance of the moon in her face and the most beautiful black hair and green eyes of any woman in the kingdom. If you promise me that I no longer have to pay taxes, I will take you to meet her."

The prince said, "Alright. You have a deal. You have my oath and word on that. The Prince led his warriors and followed the old woman to the place where she saw the beautiful girl was hiding in the tall bushes. Their plan was to capture the girl with the brilliant light and black hair and see if she would eat some food, they had brought with them. The gazelles soon came down to their usual drinking pool of water in the stream. The cooks who had come along with the prince put down two bowls of couscous. One bowl had salt on the meal and the other one did not. Hiday who was hungry from not having a cooked meal in a while chose the bowl that had the salt. This proved to Jamail and the old woman and the cooks she was human and not a gazelle. The warriors took the Princess back to the sultan's home. She did not know that she was the subject of a wife hunt. She finally got introduced to the Prince and asked him what he had done with her parents, because she had seen him carry them away from her village. The Prince told her they were safe and would be kept that way, if she would marry him. Hiday said that she loved her parents and didn't want anything to happen to them. But she told the Prince that she did not know him and knew that she did not love him. At that moment, the gazelles entered the Prince's village even though they had never done that before, even with the dogs and villagers howling and the horses rearing up on their hind legs. One of the deer fawns who tagged along come up to Hiday and she petted the little deer. The fawn then walked over to Jamail and begin to lick the Prince's hand. Jamail said that the fawn was a friendly and cute little animal. The Prince began to rub the fawn's back showing his fondness for the little animal. Out of the crowd, Hiday's parents came from the crowd and hugged their daughter. They said they had been treated very well by the Prince and his father. The sultan invited Hiday and her parents for supper. They ate well and Hiday's father went on to explain that Hiday and his wife were his only real treasure. The sultan said that indeed they were real treasures. Hiday was glad that her parents had not been put to death as is the custom.

The Prince went up to Hiday's father and said, "I will make your daughter happy if you and your wife will give me her hand in marriage. The father looked at Hiday and said that he was happy and that she could be, too. Hiday said she could marry the Prince because if he could show affection to a fawn, he could be capable of making me happy, too. The Prince and Princess got married and lived happily ever after. The most handsome couple had a beautiful home had a lovely garden. The gazelle and deer stayed around the village. Prince Jamail said that anyone who would kill or hurt the hair on the head of the deer and gazelles would be executed, and their head would be hung from the sultan's wall. Jamail's father died shortly thereafter and Jamail became sultan. Jamail had received all his wishes. He had a beautiful wife, many children, many gazelle and deer, and many slaves and servants to take care of them as they grew old.

Alexander said, "I see what you mean. That is a great story. Could you believe anyone could be that friendly with deer and gazelle?"

Roger answered, "Animals are not that much different than man. If they are treated correctly, they will act more correctly. It is time for us to get some sleep. Say your prayers, and maybe, someday, you can marry the most beautiful girl in the kingdom and that she likes animals. "Roger and Alexander chuckled and then quickly fell to sleep.

The horses and the two young men got plenty of rest that night and the next morning they started back on the trail towards the peak of the mountain range where Toubkal was located. Roger had a map and compass to keep them on course. Sometimes, they would see a village or an abandoned English fort that had been used as an outpost once to keep track of the tribesman and for the safety of the English soldiers. The forts seemed to attract more problems than to solve problems. The mountains of Morocco were dramatic and steep with beautiful green colored slopes with tall peaks and deep gorges. The two young men saw lush mountain valleys where Berber families would raise their sheep, goats, and mules because of the abundance of brush and shrubs. The air was pure with a combination of the moisture from the ocean mists and the tropical heat. In summer, the Berbers for centuries had been taking up their sheep and goat flocks to the higher elevations of the mountains and let them graze on the greener and longer grass on the plateaus and mountain valleys. Then in the fall, the Berbers would bring down their flocks to the warmer temperatures for the winter. This migration back and forth was like clockwork.

Roger and Alexander kept traveling toward Toubkal for several days. One morning they came upon a camel caravan that was headed in the same direction as they were just outside of a village, which on Roger's map looked like Marrakesh. They had just passed a large waterfall coming down a big mountain slope called Oussad which was a landmark on Roger's map. It was shown on Roger's map as the grinding of grain falls in Berber language and there were lot of mills on the river called the Slaves' River before the Falls.

Roger rode up to the owner who was an English speaking Persian, and said, " Do you mind if we follow you for a while for company and we would like to ask you some questions about navigating around the mountain passes. The owner seemed relieved that Roger and Alexander were not bandits who were infamous for attacking camel caravans in the hopes of stealing some valuable cargo. He said," Yes you can but we are not traveling that fast because we have many passengers and a heavy load and have a long distance to travel. We do not want to lose any more camels from working them to death or rushing them."

Roger asked, "Where are you going?"

The owner answered, "We are going down this part of the Silk Road to the Great Sahara and then headed east and will eventually get to Cathay or some travelers call the land, China. We will be stopping at a caravansarai south of Marrakesh that will end our stage today. Ride in the back of the train and we will visit there. If you stop in Marrakesh, you can join us in the morning on this trail, and the resting place is only a few miles south of town. "

Roger said, "That sounds like a splendid plan. See you at the rest stop."

After several more hours winding through a valley and mountains on both sides, the two young men were getting tired. They had passed kasbahs one after another which were fortified buildings with tall walls surrounding the building. Most of the kasbahs did not have any windows and were used by the more affluent Berbers for defense. They were constructed mostly out of stone and blended in with the sides of the mountains. There were groves of beautiful roses and flowers all along the valleys and orchards of palm, dates, and figs. The terrain was getting rockier and sandier. Just before dusk, the boys entered the village of Marrakesh. It was a curious place with mosques and a medina with souks of all kinds. In one part of the medina was a woodworking souk, a souk for leather, a souk for copper, and a souk for the aromatic spices and teas whose savory smells filled the air, and a souk for carpets that were all displayed neatly folded on a big marble table. The homes of the villagers were in long rows of about 30 rooms that held about 8 families. The homes had flat rooves and were huddled together by courtyards to look like a fortress, and they seemed to always blend in with the mountains behind them. Alexander could see into the almost empty rooms. They had low couches that were used for sleeping and a few tables and chairs. From the dusty streets and trails, Roger and Alexander could see there were gardens, pools, hammans, and courtyards. The local farmers were selling their dates, nuts, wheat, herbs, and other produce. It was a busy marketplace with or without the newly arrived caravan and the two young men. The place was clean and many of the houses and their courtyards were at different levels on the terraced hillside of the city.

Roger said to Alexander, "Let's stop here, for the people seem friendly enough," He politely waved to the caravan owner as he was continuing to head south to the caravansarai. The owner waved back as if to acknowledge that they would meet again later.

Alexander said, "Lets walk awhile down the street and walk the horses to the watering stations. "The horses drank the cool water. Then they started walking again and soon came in front of a mosque.

Roger said, "This is a landmark on the map and is called Mosque of the Booksellers or the Koutoubia Mosque which the Berbers use for worship, and it has all these elaborate columns and walls. It has long been said that the church or mosque in a place should be the best kept and most beautiful building in a town. Look at all the rose gardens that surround the mosque and the beautiful minaret on the tower above the mosque. Over there must be the Saadian tombs where the Berber princes and kings or buried. There must be about 100 mausoleums covered with the zelige tiles overlaid on the stones. "

Alexander asked, "What's zelige stone?"

Roger replied, "It is terracotta stone in yellow, blue, green, and red that is hand carved and covered with plaster that is made into chips of geometric patterns that are used by the Berbers to ordain their buildings. They use them on their walls, tables, floors, pools, and courtyard walls for ornamentation and beauty. "

Alexander said to Roger," Let's catch up with the camel train. I want to learn about the camels."

Roger agreed, "There is not that much else to see here and we will be safer with the caravan. That's a good idea, little brother."

They mounted their horses and headed south out of town. It didn't take them long to get to the caravanserai, and the camel pullers had finished unpacking the loads from off the weary camels. The caravansarai looked like a large fort with a very large center courtyard where there was enough room for the 150 camels in the train. There were individual stalls for each camel so they could lay down and rest for the night and enough room in the stall to place their loads there by the camel pullers. The camels had been given fodder and barley to renew their strength. Fodder was the customary camel diet. The next morning the train would be headed east. The camel pullers also had some dried peas stored in the loads if they needed it for the camels. There were usually mountain streams or wells in the central courtyard or compound in pools so the hot animals could refresh themselves. The camel pullers who usually were responsible for 8 to 20 camels in a file had their own rooms which they would share with the two or three cooks on the caravan. They would dine on oats and millet and drink tea at their meals. This specific train had 8 camel pullers and one cook. The owner was named Amir, and he was in customary Arab djellaba and turban. He also had a warm working cloak on that Alexander later discovered had been woven out of the hair of some of the camels. It looked like a very expensive cloth as compared to the cotton breeches and cloaks that Alexander and Roger were wearing.

Amir came over to the young men and said, "I see you all must have taken the grand tour of the village and didn't find it to be that welcoming. "

Roger said, "Yes, sir. Forgive me, but I am Roger Elliott from the British Navy and this is my brother, Alexander. We are on a holiday and wish to conquer the highest mountain, Mt. Jebel Toubkal in northern Africa. "

The caravan owner stated, "I am Amir from Persia, and I have been to England many times to get cargo to load on ships and send to Tangier. There, I put the cargo on my camels to take over to parts to Babylon, Calcutta, Asia, and China or anywhere I can earn some gold or silver. I like seeing other parts of the world even though it takes many months to make a journey. We will be passing by very close to Toubkal. It is probably an enjoyable view from the summit, and you must think the effort and work to get there is rewarding enough. "

Roger, listening carefully, "We do."

Amir continued by saying, "We travel with our loads through the mountains, valleys and deserts thinking that the risk of getting robbed by the bandits is less than the risk of getting attacked and hijacked on the open seas by pirates. Any ways, merchant ships costs lots of sterling and pounds. My father owns many properties, but he has many wives and many children, and he cannot afford a ship. For me, the camels hold many loads and don't cost much to obtain and keep going. "

Alexander curiously asked, "What kinds of loads do you carry?"

Amir politely answered, "We are not so particular. Mostly silk, cloth, carpets, spices, fruits and sometimes bananas if it is a short trip because bananas, coffee, and tea are usually are only bought by the wealthy in Europe. We have also carried copper goods from Algeria and salt from Timbuktu. We have on occasion dug up the graves of fallen princes and Arab travelers when they have died far from home and carried their remains back to the Arab world for burial in the family tombs."

Roger explaining his views, said, "Interesting! It hasn't been that long ago since I was in London and what you are saying is true. Most people only eat porridge and not that much meat because of poverty and lack of work. Only the yeoman class, gentry and royalty can afford the luxury of bananas and tea. It has been just a short time ago that most people started using forks." Alexander listened intently as he was thoroughly interested in the informative discussion.

Amir continued to explain his daily routine, said, " We rise with the sunrise and start feeding the camels and the camel pullers will start loading the camels and adjusting their harness. The travelers can engage in storytelling at the morning meal and start again from where they left off the conversations the night before. They will talk about anything, previous safaris, philosophy, religions, ideas for inventions, history, and their social life. Many of them will talk about their previous life in the military or time at sea or their schooling. Sometimes we meet other camel trains here at these places or at the oasis and we exchange ideas about the traders and business. Each day we call a stage of the trip. We travel as fast as a man walks each day which is about 25 miles to a stage depending on nature, wind, cold, sand, deserts, food, and shelter. Day by day is as far as we think ahead sometimes. We do not know what friend or enemy we may meet, but we have to have faith in each other and Allah."

Roger asked, "That is interesting. A Berber friend in Tangier gave me this map and said to approach Toubkal from the Imlil valley after having gone through the Azadene Valley by way of the Aguelzim Pass. Is this the correct route to the peak? What is your assessment?" It is a moderate climb from what I have been told and this will put you at the base of the southern rim."

Amir smiling at Alexander, said, "You will have to be careful in climbing straight up to the peak. I assume the young boy is up to the challenge."

Alexander said," With all due respect, sir, I am fit for the challenge of going to the top of the mountain, because I have already come farther than I had first assessed I could. My stepfather has said, "Do not be afraid for the Lord your God, will be with you wherever you go."

Amir, smiling, said, "Your stepfather is a very wise man. You are very learned and well spoken. Forgive me of my suspicion about a possible lack of your preparedness for the task ahead."

Alexander replied, "My stepfather is wise, but those words he merely remembered from his reading in the King James Bible. I need to believe that the words will guide me in all my tasks."

Amir nodded in agreement, "I worship Allah and you worship your Lord. We are both blessed and guided by a higher power. I believe it is time for me to check on the animals and men and get to bed on the straw in the stall. It has been great conversation. Good night to you, Englishmen."

Roger said, "I will check on the horses, and then I will also retire for the evening. Indeed, it has been a good day and for meeting you. Good night."

Roger said good night to Alexander, "Now don't go dreaming about some Persian concubines or belly dancers or girls at a bath house." Roger chuckled. Alexander tried to ignore the comment and thought that Roger must have heard the Berber girl at the bath house a few weeks ago laughing and teasing him. Alexander soon moved away from his thoughts about the bath house beauty and was now in deep in thought about his own future.

Alexander could see the starry sky when he lay down on the straw in the stall in the courtyard. This makeshift bed had to be better than sleeping on the ground and rocks that he had been getting use to for the last several days. He looked up in the night sky and saw a full moon and millions of stars. He saw a bright star in the west which seemed like a good omen. He began praying for Roger's and their travel plan, and gave thanks for his mother, and George. He was thankful about meeting the owner of the camel train, because it made him think of a bigger world outside of the home that he had at the garrison barracks and prayed that he could least learn about the reasoning and beliefs of others.

The next morning the animals all started stirring around at sunrise and all the camel pullers started waking up and preparing for the daily stage. The camels started eating more fodder and the camel pullers started cleaning the waste from the stalls to leave it satisfactory for the next train. Alexander ate a breakfast of some rolls and cherries that Roger had picked off some trees in one of the valleys the previous day. After Roger gave the Berber attendants at the caravansarai some dirhams for some hay for the horses, Roger and Alexander started to mount the horses.

Amir, with a friendly greeting came over to the two young Englishmen. "You know, I like your company, and you are well versed on your mission. I would not mind it if you want to stay with the train, but we will only slow you down. If you ride fast and take care of your horses, you could get to the valley of Imlil tomorrow evening. It will take the train 4 days to get there. My only advice is that you do not stop at the Palais de Badi. You will see it in the next valley. It has been partially destroyed by the ruler, Ismail Moulay, who has been trying to get the British out of Tangier. You will see crumpled stones and big pillars and a foundation that would have over 300 rooms. It used to be a royal Arabic palace. It has many sacred writings on the ruins, and it has inlays of gold from Sudan, a country in another part of Africa. The Berbers keep a watchful eye on this. Trying to get the gold there is not worth losing your lives. Just avoid it for your continued good health. Ismail Moulay has been quiet, but he wants to be known as The King of Morocco. He is very dangerous and has destroyed complete villages of his neighboring tribesmen and cut off the heads of more than 20,000 warriors and mounted them on his Royal palace walls. He has fathered over 600 children and more to come. He is to be avoided at all costs."

Roger said, "We had dealings a few years ago with Ismail Moulay. He killed over a hundred of our soldiers at the garrison in Tangier about three years ago. He had no regard for the soldiers and beheaded them and displayed the heads on top of the garrison walls. It was awful. We will be careful. Thank you for your hospitality and friendship. May the God of the East and West be with you. We will leave now. Hopefully you will continue to have a safe journey."

Alexander, "Thank you, sir. We have had an enjoyable visit." Amir smiled as if he admired the young man's courage and tenacity for adventure.

Roger and Alexander came on the ruins of Badi later that day that Amir had warned them about, and a few Berbers curiously looked at them, but Roger and Alexander left them alone and the young men obliged the Berbers by leaving quickly and peacefully. They continued to see orchards of apples and cherries, which had fruit for them, but the walnut groves were just getting green walnuts on the trees. They arrived at several passes and Roger believed they were on the right trails to Toubkal as they passed the falls at Ighoulidem, and it was on the way to the Imlil valley. After they had traveled though the valley, they rounded a corner near the end of the valley and crossed a shallow mountain stream and let the horses drink for a short time. They started riding carefully through the rough terrain and came up on a village with a shrine which had the name, Charouch. The shrine was in a middle of a rocky pathway surrounded by boulders and a few flat-topped Berber houses. There was no grass or trees anywhere. There was a trail leading to a mountain trail that was an ascending climb to a very tall mountain range that was barren of any plant life.

Since this was getting to the end of the second day after leaving Amir, the young men thought these must be the mountains that are part of the Atlas Mountain range where Mt. Toubkal is located. The further they rode the horses, the higher they were getting to the top. They were seeing less green, and they were seeing more craggy stone-faced bare mountains with some white snow caps on some of the mountains. After they started to leave the mountain trails, they could see deep gorges and the valleys below that they had just left behind. They would ride a little bit further and sit up camp. This time they would unpack their army tent and pitch it behind one of the big boulders for a windbreak. The higher they went up the mountain, the windier and colder it was getting. They allowed time to set up camp and more time to gather a large pile of wood for a large campfire to cook some wild ducks that Roger had just shot earlier prior to their setting up camp. The young men would need a large fire because it was getting chillier in the higher elevations as they were headed to the top.

Roger, stirring the pot of delicious duck meat, said "I bet you are hungry enough to eat some wild duck."

Alexander started to eat the tasty looking duck meat, "It is good, but it would be better if I was a little warmer."

Roger replied, "That reminds me of a story about an archer cooking a wild duck and getting it warm. There once was an archer who shot a wild duck and put it in his cooking pot, once he concluded the long ride of his hunting trip. He kept putting wood onto the fire underneath the pot but after several hours, the bird was just as stiff and raw as when he started cooking it. The archer believed that it must be a holy bird from a nearby monastery and thought that he must have committed the unpardonable sin. His sin was that he let the bird get stiff and waited too long to prepare the bird, so no matter how hot the fire, the duck would not cook correctly and was wasted." Looking at the east, Roger exclaimed, "By the way, the Great Sahara Desert is to the east of us, so we are getting closer to Toubkal." They ate their supper of wild duck and were getting more anxious and excited about finishing the journey.

Roger looking very serious, "I want to tell you something., Alexander. You are very smart and of age where you understand right from wrong, what's fair and unfair, and so on. I promised your father that I would comply with his wishes for you when the time seemed right, and you were old enough to understand his intentions. Our mother and I think that time has come."

Getting closer to the fire, Alexander was better able to see Roger who was pulling letters out of his saddlebag. Roger confirming, "Your father had written a Last Will and Testament when he died which had several provisions. Most of that was taken care of right after his death. It included the disbursements or giving away of his personal property which was not that much. There was a financial provision on how mother and you would have money to live on. He was not rich, but he did not have any debts. One of the provisions of the will was for me to give you letters and to give you a few of his personal possessions which your mothers has stored away in a safe place. The letters I brought with me so I could present them to you as God is my witness. I can read them to you."

Alexander, looking pensive, said, "Please" and wondering back to the day his father had smiled at him, while Robert was dying and being a little bit uneasy not knowing what was about to be read.

Roger said, "This is one of the letters."

:

My dear son, Alexander,

I will be departing this life soon because of my illness. I truly regret that you may not know me as a son should know his father and that I will not be with you as a father should be with his son, and that I will not be there to see you bring the Spotswood name back into its glory. I leave you in the gracious and loving care of your mother, Katherine Maxwell Spotswood who will provide for you until you are of legal age. I will be going to Heaven soon as promised by our Lord and Savior, Jesus Christ in his Holy Book, The Holy Bible. One of my personal gifts to you is the Bible passed down to me, by my father, Robert Spotswood, who died when I was a young boy. The Bible had been given to him by his father and my grandfather, John Spotswood, who was a well-known, well respected and a well-loved Archbishop in Scotland. I charge you and pray that you live your life by this book. Many of the men in the Spotswood clan gave their very life so this book could continue to be read and followed until Christ comes again. The Bible explains how to choose pathways and journeys that are pleasing to Christ and why he died on a cross for all of us.

My grandfather passed a letter to my father that stated that the family of Spotswood was an honorable ancient name that can be traced to an early period in the county of Berwick, Scotland. Robert de Spottiswoode, Count Burgh was in adherence to Edward I, King of all England in 1296, had much land and respect in Berwick. A William Spotswood was at proceedings in 1309 AD at the Royal Abbey in Holyrood involving the Knight Templars in that kingdom, and he was also present according to witnesses, Walter de Clifton and William de Middleton as Bishop of St. Andrews in Edinburgh. The Spotswood Estate and barony passed to my uncle, Alexander Spotswood in Scotland, and our branch of the family has been in the courts of the King of England or in military service to the kingdom. I will give you my father's sword that he used to fight bravely and victoriously at Kylsington. Use this weapon wisely to defend your name and defend your religious freedom. Know well that even though my father was a Scottish Knight and had faith in God, fate could not prevent his murder. If you do not know and respect the achievements of your noble ancestors, you may struggle in your attempts to achieve your personal goals and less likely to be remembered by your descendants. I cannot leave you many material things, but I pray you will see the value of making the Spotswood name a well-respected and well-known name in history as those that came before you. Please, keep the Bible, this letter and the sword close to you always to remind you of your importance to our family. I will close with our motto; "Patior Ut Potiar" which means "I suffer that I may obtain". I love you affectionately. See you in the next life. Robert Spotswood. 1680 AD

Roger paused a minute after reading this letter. He may have been consumed by the gravity of the moment or having flashbacks to the man, Robert Spotswood, that he also loved and respected and also had served as his father for over half of his life. After a few moments, he put some more wood on the fire to get more light from the fire.

Roger looked over to Alexander as if he saw him in a new light and said, "I will see that you get your great grandfather's Bible and your grandfather's sword and your father's letter. I will help you anyway I can. If you want to elevate the name of Spotswood all over the empire, I will help you there, too. We are after all brothers. I think our mother would appreciate this. "

Alexander sensed the importance in this stage of life after the revelations about the family name." I will do my best to please God and bring honor and respect to my father's name. I understand my father wishes. Thank you, Roger for reading the letter and your offer to help me." Alexander could hardly sleep that night thinking about what journeys and pathways he would choose. The next morning Alexander woke up and ate some dried fruits and dried meats with Roger. The natural beauty of the majesty of the stone covered and snow-capped Mt. Toubkal being the backdrop of their campsite.

Roger said, "After we break camp, we will go the rest of the way to the top of the mountain and claim it for Spotswood and Elliott. Here are the rest of the letters I have with me for you."

Alexander said with a little chuckle, "We have come this far so we just as well see what's up there."

They bridled the horses but Roger said that it would be best if the horses stayed there and graze while we go over to a nearby farm, and see if they could get some sure footed mules to take their packs up to the top while they walked on foot. Roger said, "We will follow the steep, rocky, and the winding trail that will get smaller and steeper, and we don't want our horses to get hurt by slipping and falling. The Berber mules are used to coming up here in the summer and are used to the trek. It is only a few hours walk up there. "

Alexander looked at one more of the letters. It was a description of the family history and a line of descent from Alfred the Great and Robert Bruce. It looked kind of interesting although he didn't know who they were. He thought he would read while Roger was watering the horses and preparing the back packs.

Roger went over to the village and the families seemed accommodating and friendly. The Berbers lived there during the warm months of summer and attended their goats and sheep flocks that grazed on the lush vegetation of the mountain valleys. The Berbers were happy to loan him some mules. It only cost Roger a few dirhams, and it would let the horses have a chance to rest up for the descent later.

Alexander looked at one of the letters copied in easy to read calligraphy.

_____

notes for John Spotswood. Lived 1510 to 1585

-second son of William Spotswood, killed at Battle of Flodden in 1513
-mother, Elizabeth Hop-Pringle daughter of Henry of Torsconse
- University of Glasgow in 1534
-MA degree in 1536
- London 1538, Archbishop Cranmer admitted holy orders
-employed by the Earl of Lennox in negotiations with Lennox and King Henry VIII regarding Lennox proposed marriage to Margaret Douglas, the king's niece.
-1547 presented to parsonage at Caldor, friend of John Sandilands and John Knox
-1558 accompanied James Stewart, Regent Moray to wedding Queen Mary of Scots to the Dauphin of France
-1560 appointed ecclesiastical superintendent to Parliament representing Lothario and Tweed dale
-1560 assisted in drawing up "First Book of Discipline"
-placed the crown on James I of England in 1567
-Superintendent of the Scottish Church in Scotland
-married Beatrix Crichton, daughter of Patrick Crichton of Lug ton and Gilberto
-one daughter, and two sons, John lived 1565 through 1639, Archbishop at St. Andrew and James, the Bishop of
-Glover, Ireland lived from 1567 to 1644
-died 5 Dec 1585

notes for John Spotswood lived 1565 to 1639

-born 1565 in mid Calder in west Lothario, Scotland
-died in 1639
-buried in Westminster Abbey
-built a castle near Edinburgh
-sold Spotswood's lands and barony in 1620 to the Bell family
-placed a crown on King Charles I in 1625
-MA University of Glasgow 1581

-Privy Council 1605
-Chancellor of Scotland 1635
-Historian of Scotland
-Wrote "The History of Scotland"
-married Rachel Lindsay, daughter of David, Bishop of Ross

notes for Robert Spotswood lived 1596 to 1646

-born in 1596 at Dunipace in Stirlingshire
-1613 MA degree from University of Glasgow 1613

-studied at Exeter College in Oxford under the famous rector, Dr. John Prideaux, who had been a chaplain to prince Henry, King James I, and King Charles I, and had Dr. Prideaux had married Ann Goodwin, granddaughter of Rev. Rowland Taylor, a Christian martyr under Queen Mary
-skilled lawyer, wrote "The Law Practices of Scotland"
-married Bethia Morrison, of Presten Grange d.1639
-Privy Councilor 1622
-appointed a Scottish Knight by King James I
-Lord President of the College of Justice
-granted lands and barony at New Abbey and commissioned Lord of Dunipace
-1638-Secretary of State for Scotland
-prominent role in "Athenae Oxienses"
-after college, traveled extensively for nine years learning law and theology in Italy, Germany, and France
-returned the Black Book of Paisley from Rome to New Abbey after it had been confiscated by the Covenanters
-could speak, Hebrew, Arabic, and three of the European languages, and Scottish, Irish, and English.
-had son, Robert born 1637, British Navy Chirosurgeon
-had son John died unmarried in 1650
-had son, Alexander who lived in Darsie, Scotland
-had daughter, Bethia born 1637
-close adherent of Charles I and appointed Earl of Montrose as Commander -in-chief of English forces
-captured at Philipaugh during Scottish Civil War, tried for treason, found guilty and beheaded
-died Jan 17th, 1646, and buried at St. Andrews Churchyard
-A wealthy citizen of Edinburgh, Mr. Scrigemour, saw Robert's blood on the Maiden after the execution and fainted. Later died as he was carried home. He had been a servant to Robert's father, the Archbishop.
-last words, "Merciful Jesus, gather my soul unto the saints and martyrs who have run before me in this race."

Alexander put the letter away in his traveling bags. He recognized his father's birth date and the birth year of his Aunt Bethia. There were several pages, and he knew he would not be able to study them like he wanted. He had a couple more letters to read, but he would do this later. it was now time to go up to the peak. Roger would soon be ready to start up the path to Mt. Toubkal. Alexander wondered what his father meant by his referring to regaining the name back to being well known and respected. His father had been a doctor that paid more than most jobs. Alexander thought his father must be thinking about his father's family as having castles and owning land, master's degree, rank, privilege, and having been leaders in the church and state and had special ties to the kings. After all, his Spotswood family had no land in England or Scotland and the only family he knew didn't even live in either country. They lived in a remote colony that didn't seem to be very popular with the English people. Alexander's mother's family, The Maxwells were well to do, but were not of the privilege class either. Grandfather Maxwell was a minister at a local church and did not inherit any money or property. Alexander started to think he would need a plan to get ahead in life. Maybe Roger would have some ideas for his future.

After getting prepared for the excursion to the top of the Mountain, Roger exclaimed. "All set! Let's go and see the top and what's down below from the peak. It will take some hard climbing and walking on the rocky trail and ledges, but it doesn't take a lot of skill. It just takes a lot of determination." They soon winded their way and trekked to the top. They saw a wild boar running down one of the ravines. Roger exclaimed, "Many people come out here hunting for boar, but we don't have the time to butcher a hog and cook the meat. It might draw some unwanted visitors like a Berber war party or some jackals and there would be too much wasted meat. Now if we see a fox, we can skin it and say we were fox hunting like the rich people do in England."

Soon they were at the top. "All you see are mountains and valleys below." said Alexander.

Roger said, "You know ,it is a clear day and if you look to the far west you see that little patch of blue , that is the Atlantic Ocean, and if you look to the east you see that small patch of light brown in the distance, that is the Great Sahara desert."

"I don't see the camel train anywhere ." Alexander said as if he were looking for the camels that they had followed part of the way from Marrakesh. "

Roger chuckling about those remarks," We are at the highest point in Morocco. Not many Englishmen have had the chance to get here. That makes us sort of unique. I am proud of you for climbing this mountain with me. You will have many mountains to climb in life. Some of them will be physical mountains like Mt. Toubkal, others will be in your mind, maybe obstacles that you will have to overcome. There may be times when you are the only one who may believe the way you do. Do you understand?"

Alexander was puzzled why Roger was talking this way but said, "Yes, I do." Alexander continued, "Big brother, why are you explaining this to me?"

Roger: "You are almost eight years of age and entering manhood soon, and you must begin thinking and acting like a man. You must have plans, and goals, and assume responsibilities as a man. We were not born into wealth or privilege. We must take charge of our own lives. You will win fortune and fame by your own abilities and judgments. They will not be given to you by the gentry. You will get ahead by your own choices in life. Not everyone will understand your journeys in life. It's not their journey to make sense of. It is yours and up to you to make it work. Also remember what our stepfather George said that the Psalmist wrote in the Holy Book. O God of our salvation, who art the confidence of all the ends of the earth, and of them, that are afar off upon the seat which by his strength sitteth fast the mountains, being girded with power, which stilleth the noise of the seas, the noise of the waves, and the tumult of the people. The Lord got us up here, and he will guide us down to Tangier, and guide us for the rest of our lives. This is a special moment that you will remember for the rest of your life."

They came down from the mountain top, and again, they were able to stay warm by a fire and look up at the starry sky at night even though it was extremely windy, and the fire was flickering and was barely staying lit.

Roger asked, " Do you remember the time that I wrote to you from London about seeing a comet with Edward Halley in London? I hope a comet comes across the sky tonight."

Alexander said, " Yes, I remember, and that would be great. Do you know that I have read the parts in the Bible about stars, and have you ever asked, why are there stars? The stars do not give off light or heat like a candle in a dark room would. Are they just there for their beauty?"

Roger who was yawning, "Sailors and explorers use the stars all the time. The ships at sea sometimes use the constellation or group of stars to navigate by. I know some people believe they cause things to happen in certain ways. For centuries, the Greeks and Romans have tried to explain their importance. "

Alexander exclaimed, " I see this star in the western sky, and it seems brighter than any other star. Do you see it?"

Roger, "I see millions of stars. I don't see it unless it is that star with the flashing points."

Alexander, nodding, "Yes, so this is the brightest star in the sky as he pointed to the flashing star. I guess, it is twice as big as any other stars. I will call it Sothis. When I feel like when I am in the most need in life, I will call on
.37

the name of the Lord, and he will never forsake me. Sothis is one of his creations that will remind me of his power and light. It reminds me of one of the things George also said that light is always associated with goodness of the Lord. In the Sermon on the Mount, the Lord said, "Let your light so shine before men, that they may see your good works and glorify your Father which is in Heaven." Roger, what do you think?" Roger had already fallen sleep in his cot in the tent on the tall mountain and probably would have thought the same way as Alexander did about the stars being the Lord's handiwork.

The next morning after a good night's sleep, they woke up with the sun coming up from over a nearby mountain top. They enjoyed the cooler Moroccan breezes in the mountains which were a relief from the tropical heat at Tangier. The air was thinner than their seaport home. They also enjoyed the quietness of the mountains except some occasional noises from the forest animals and birds. The two climbers were eager to get back to the garrison so they could tell their mother and George about their adventures and their achievement. They quickly ate some more of their grub and packed the tent and blankets on the backs of the mules. They took the mules back to the Berbers who were glad to get their mules returned in good condition. Roger and Alexander got their own horses and got back on the trail. They would take the same route back to Tangier that they used coming down to the Inlil Valley. It would take several hours to get down the mountain, but all the hours of preparation and any discomforts of the trip were worth the pleasure they got by climbing the tallest mountain in Northern Africa. They rode the horses all day arriving at a group of silver birch tree and an empty kasbah along the mountain side by the edge of the valley trail. They were about three hours ride south of Marrakesh. This would be a good place to set up their tent and build a fire. After their meal, Alexander wanted to read some more of the letters. He could ask Roger about what some of the words, and why the letters were so important to his father? Alexander asked about England, Scotland, the Knight Templars, the Scottish Church, the Anglican Church and the kings, and the wars. Some of the letters contained a history of the Spotswood, Lindsay, and the Bruce family of Scotland. Roger did his best to answer the questions from his own experiences, and it had been many years ago when he had grown up in London and learned about most of it in grammar school.

Roger explained, "Your father was proud of his heritage and envied it. He had a respectable position, but he never received the fame and fortune of his predecessors, but he died with the hope and faith that you would restore the family name, and you would achieve success in the military, church, and government. He wanted you to be important, live comfortably in wealth, and be respected by everyone."

Alexander puzzled by the wealth of information, said, "My great grandfather had all the power of Scotland in his hands and his son, my grandfather, had all the power of the law and justice in Scotland and had much wealth, but they left nothing of value to their family when they died. "

Roger replied, "They died for their beliefs and thought it always best to side with the royalty at the time, and unfortunately they could not count on the royalty to save their lives when it came down to that test of faith. They made the right choices for them at the time, but it cost them. We need to stand for something, Alexander. I am a military man and I believe that when you disagree on religion, territory, and pride you may be drawn into battles and wars. It usually doesn't settle much or change how men think but establishes an order of who is in deciding the affairs for a while until someone else comes along and wants to change everything. Sometimes we get on the losing side of events. I think you will be a great military leader and learn how to fight for what is right. You may become a general in the majesty's army."

Alexander was fascinated by all the new revelations about his family and heritage. The young brothers talked for hours and the howling and increasing velocity of the and cold night air did not hamper their zeal for talking and learning. Finally, after Alexander was satisfied with the answers to his questions, he said, to Roger. "Thanks, Roger. for getting me down here to the mountains. It was splendid seeing all the mountain views today. Did you see that Sothis is still with us?"

Roger asking, "What is Sothis?"

Alexander answered, "You were falling asleep when we were naming the brightest star in the sky. I called it Sothis."

Roger replied, " It will always be there when you look up to the sky in the evening. Good night, Alexander. We have nine hours of riding every day for probably the next nine days before we get home. We will probably wear out the leather on our boots and the horses will wear out their horseshoes."

"Good night, Roger"

Alexander said his nightly prayer for their safety in returning to the garrison. He prayed for strength and wisdom to know what he should do with schooling, the military, his family, and thanking God for the Toubkal Mountain experience. It would leave an impression on him for the rest of his life. He soon fell asleep and was getting the rest he deserved under the starry skies on a homeward bound path in Morocco.

Several days later, Roger and Alexander came through the doorway at their home and was warmly greeted by their parents. George was just smiling as he was happy the brothers made it home without incident. The young men had been gone about three weeks on their adventure of a lifetime. Alexander was excited to see his parents and began telling them about all the mountain scenery and the camel train. He told them about Marrakesh and the donkey ride to the base of Toubkal. He told them about the palace that had been destroyed by Ismail Moulay. He told them how they had hunted for game and had fruits and nuts from the orchards and trees along the way plus what his mother had packed for them. He told her about sleeping under the starry sky and Sothis.

Alexander's mother listened with pride and said, "I am glad you had a wonderful time, son." and she curiously looked at Roger.

Roger anticipating a question, "Yes, mother, I gave my energetic and curious brother, the Spotswood letters, and told him about the sword and the Bible."

The mother said, "I am glad you had a great time together. Roger, you have done a fine job of watching over your younger brother and teaching him survival skills. I was so worried that something bad could happen to you both. She looked at Alexander after George had retrieved the items from a big trunk under their bed. One of the items was Robert Spotswood family Bible that had been handed down to him from his father, and he had inherited from his father and a sword that had been used by Alexander's grandfather. Alexander pointed to the golden "S" that was inlayed on the handle of the sword symbolizing the Barony of Spotswood.

Alexander, admiring the sword and the very rich looking Bible said, "I will always take care of them."

Mother said, "Live by this book like your father lived by the word of God."

Alexander, "I promise I will."

George said, "I am glad you both got to see many beautiful things, and Alexander, I am glad you are getting your real schooling on the real conditions of the world. We will talk more about it later, but we have some very good news. We are leaving this garrison in a few months and going back to England. The Governor made the announcement that the garrison will be closing and Percy's Lambs, the 2nd Tangier regiment will be reassigned somewhere in England when they first arrive there."

Roger exclaimed, "That is good news. After all, this is a dreadful place with many disadvantages and all the frequent and irritating noise from the musket fire and the Berber attacks. The military support from the Royal Scot soldiers and grenadiers may not hold the enemy at bay much longer. I will not miss the lack of supplies. Besides, it is not always dreary in England. "

Katherine exclaimed, "It is good news, but Alexander, you don't know what to think, do you? You have never been there and only have heard us talk about England?"

Alexander said, "I have a pretty good idea, I think. I will be happy to be with you wherever we go. There will be a better life out there for us. After all, England and Scotland are the previous home and workplace of my father's family and my mother's family."

George said, "Amen, son, that is spoken like a true Englishman."

Mother said, "Yes, Alexander, although you are young in age, you are a young man now."

The George Mercer family, Roger Elliott, and Alexander Spotswood now started making plans to leave the garrison and had many good memories to take with them from Tangier.
They would have a few weeks to get ready. There was not much to pack except for their clothes and books.
Katherine still had some money and property in England from her first husband, George Elliott's estate that she could use if she wouldn't be able to live in the barracks. Alexander would certainly have a better choice for grammar school and tutors and a wider curriculum of subjects.

After a few days, Roger came to the Mercer home to repeat what he had heard at the captain's quarters. Roger informed the family that this garrison has cost the English government 200 million pounds to fortify and maintain, and it is extremely unpopular with the British people. The garrison was costing `13 % of the English budget yearly to maintain and they needed to use more of the budget for the Americas, for Calcutta, and for the West Indies. The people see the garrison as an army supporting the merchants and traders on the seas and trade routes rather than as a garrison for royal defense and empire building. King Charles II gave Admiral Dartmouth as secret order to close the garrison at Tangier at once.

Roger said, "Dartmouth has left Plymouth, England already to coordinate the evacuation of the garrison with Governor Percy Kirke and Colonel Cutts, my fellow soldier from the dueling episode. Dartmouth and Kirke are to level this fortification so no other kingdom will take over the garrison using English fortifications to their advantage against the Berbers, Moors, and pirates. Percy will lead the roughly 2000 troops to destroy the harbor, Mole, and garrison by post-hammers and picks to break up the stones, stakes, and walls instead of demolishing the garrison by explosives. This will take several months and has to be completed by next spring. We will leave on the *Diamond* next month on the 23rd of October for Plymouth. We are in the ship with the sick soldiers and the wives and children of the 2nd Tangier Regiment. I don't have any more details. I know that it is very secret, but Ismail Moulay has been camped at the outskirts of town by the Caves of Hercules. He must think that the soldiers are going to escape through the underground tunnels to Spain. He may think we are preoccupied with the destruction and mount an attack. He will be watching, and I hope we can get out safely from the bay area. Moulay will not fight on the sea."

George said, "The Lord God is our strength and refuge. We need not to fear Moulay, but only fear the Lord himself."
Soon the post-hammers and picks started their annoying hammering noises and the harbor was being disassembled. The soldiers began the backbreaking work of destroying the Mole breaking up the stone walls full of spikes and stone. It was hot working in the Moroccan sun even though it was late October. Many of the men would be given some of their pay in the form of lands and animals in the New World, West Indies, and Jamaica in the Caribbean, and other colonies of the British Empire. One of the men, Tangier Jones, a fondly loved soldier

had a knack for storytelling which the men enjoyed as a sport, was given thousands of acres in a place called Long Island which was close to New Amsterdam in the New World. Alexander and his family were happy to get away from the Moors and the Berbers and were not thinking about any vast domains of land and thinking about the open sea and getting home to England. Alexander had just begun his education of wide-open spaces of land on his recent journey to Toubkal, and now he would be taking his first journey on the water.

Katherine and her first husband had been one of the first families assigned to Morocco in 1661 in the year of our Lord and Savior some twenty-two years earlier. She would be one of the first to leave. She had mixed emotions about the garrison. She had witnessed the burial of two of husbands who she deeply loved, and they were buried in the garrison's cemetery. She did not want to leave them behind. She was in love with her third husband, George, and she would follow him, unconditionally. Tangier had so much natural beauty surrounding it and was the setting for a very romantic and mysterious place. She had seen her two boys grow up here and had watched them play cricket, nine pins, pelle melle and other outdoor sports. She had watched them fish for mackerel, herring, and haddock off the coast and had taught them swimming at the beach. They had spent many hours birdwatching and dolphin watching from the beach and walking along the hot sand of the Moroccan coastline letting the sand slip through their toes. She reminisced about the boys enjoying their schoolwork and their twitching and squirming at the Sermon and hymn singing in the garrison church service. She would miss the aromatic smell of the rose gardens that surrounded the courtyards and the smells of the spices in the souks. She would miss looking out her window and seeing the cargo ships out in the harbor and on the seas and wonder what remote place they were sailing to and imagining what rest of the world looked like. There had been all types of ship to daydream about such as the schooners, shallops, and slave ships. Maybe because she had been married to knowledgeable and skilled doctors who were also navy sailors, she had taken the time to learn about the smaller and faster sailing vessels, especially the settees, misticos, and trabaccolos launched from the Mediterranean seaports all along southern Europe. . Tangier had been a busy seaport with many merchant ships and fishing ships. She would remember the activities in this foreign land that had consumed many years in the prime of her life. She hoped to get back to the familiarity of London where her daughter lived with her husband that she had never met and would like the opportunity of getting to know. Katherine's father had died in London in 1655 and her mother had since died, too, after George Elliott and her had moved to the garrison. She hoped to get reacquainted with some of her former neighbors, family, and church friends when she got back to England.

George hoped to get back to England where he hoped to get into a teaching career at a grammar school instead of a navy school. It also had been many years since he had been in his homeland.

Roger was looking forward to getting back to London and advancing in his military career. He was now about 20 years of age and hoped he would have a bright future.

Alexander, now going on 8 years old had just completed one leg of a journey of a once in your lifetime dream. He now had a new focal point in his life. He would now start having to make choices that not only allowed him to survive but make him strive for a better life. He had a new appreciation for his family's destiny and wanted to perpetuate the family honor. This would be a turning point in his early stages of life, and he would drive to make himself succeed with the help of his loving parents, a half-brother who was his best friend, and the help of the Lord God Almighty.

The day finally came when they started out of the harbor to England on the *Diamond*, and Katherine started waving back at friends on the dock. A large part of the harbor lay in ruins. Katherine was crying out of happiness or sadness? Happiness is what Alexander had prayed for anyway. The family had climbed many mountains in Morocco. George and his stepson hugged Katherine out of their love for her not knowing exactly what the future held. They trusted God and was thankful for their years in Tangier not knowing whether they would ever return there again. The English were leaving Morocco, and this family would make a fresh start in England.

II. JOURNEY TO ENGLAND

The day came in October 1683, in the year of our Lord and Savior, that George and Katherine Mercer, Roger Elliott, and Alexander Spotswood boarded the ship, *HMS Diamond* for Plymouth, England and said good-bye to Tangier. Bethia Spotswood, Alexander's aunt who also served as the Mercer's servant also was glad to leave. As usual she remained in the back and quiet and almost unnoticed. Katherine looked up at the terraced hillsides of the city to view their modest quarters that she had lived in for the last 22 years. It was a low flat roof building still standing above the Mole and garrison areas that were being destructed by the soldiers. It would take several more months to destroy the Mole, garrison, and harbor docks of the English.

Katherine may have viewed it as one door shutting and a new door opening in her life and she had mixed emotions. As a wife and mother, she had acquired fond memories of a happy navy family, but also hesitant about restarting a new life in her native country. Undoubtedly much had probably changed in England and Scotland, but they had been her first home. Many of her family members and friends there had been adversely affected by the disease and sickness of the bubonic plagues. Many of the homes had been affected by the Great Fire of London that happened shortly after she had arrived in Northern Africa at the British garrison with her first husband, George Elliott. Almost a third part of Central London where she once lived had been rebuilt with new streets, new homes and gardens, new churches and schools, and new shops and parks. This gave her hope that her new life would be better with George, with Roger who would be continuing his military career, and with Alexander who would be attending grammar school. On the ship from the gun deck, Alexander waved at some of his friends on the dock and Roger was busy checking on the other passengers as part of his naval assignment was to be in charge of the safety and conduct of the other soldiers and their families. On board were 30 members of the 2nd Tangier Regiment and their wives and children which there were 50 in number. Also, there were 10 passengers who were wounded or sick and they were being evacuated first.

It was a cool sunny day and the wind which was normally gusty was almost still, but breezy enough for the ship's crew to set the sails for launching the ship. The fore lugs were flopping about as the wind picked up and the fall of the halyards taken to the Captain and the sails were set and drawn properly by the strength of the navy sailors. The sailors were precise with the cut and set of the sails. In a matter of moments, the *Diamond* was sailing in the water and leaving the dock. The bluish water was a little turbulent, but the passengers and crew soon got use to the flapping of the sails and the rocking of the ship up with the waves of the waters in the strait of Gibraltar and the Mediterranean Sea. They were headed northwest and was sailing by the stretch of water between the Mediterranean and the North Atlantic Ocean. From the deck on the southern side of the ship, they could see the sunny coasts and Atlas Mountains of Morocco, and from the deck on the northern side of the ship, they could see the Andalusian mountains of Spayna. They could also see the English Ensign Flag flying briskly and proudly, high in the sky above the Mole. They were traveling at first in waters that had several fishing boats and vessels as this part of the ocean was well known for fishing and was even known in the courts in Europe. One of the fishing boats, named the *Brisse* from Dutch Holland, and many of the boats contained the fishermen from England that used trawlers to scoop up fish in nets. There were lots of smaller coastal fishing boats of all shapes and sizes. There were merchant fishing boats that fished for mackerel, sardines, pilchards, tuna and anchovies. It was a busy shipping lane though the straits of Gibraltar. They would also observe fast moving clipper ships, sea rovers, brigantines, cogs, and frigates. They would be headed to the open water of the Atlantic and hope to get on the ocean drift called Islas Canaries which would enhance their sailing speed to Plymouth. It would take several weeks to get their destination if the winds and the weather were in their favor. The families prayed daily that their voyage would be safe and that they would arrive in England with their lives and body intact. Roger and his mother and stepfather had sailed long distances before. This was a new adventure for Alexander, and he was excited about traveling and learning about new countries and sailing.

After a few days on the ocean, Roger took Alexander aside and started talking to him about sail boats. Roger started to show how to identify ships when they would see them at a distance in the oncoming waters. Roger described the dogger was a fishing boat that could carry up to six tons of fish, 3 tons of salt to preserve the fish, and a ton of supplies. The dogger had a storage cabin and cooking area, living quarters on the forward deck and aft deck and the shipped sailed by a rudder rather than steering oars. There was a myriad of wooden ships on the high seas including schooners and Spanish galleys that had oarsmen. There were smaller vessels like the sloop and ketch. The sloops were often used by the pirates for rowing to their ports or to the coasts. There were also smaller boats that were seaworthy. Roger showed Alexander a ketch and explained what the bowsprit and two jibs were used for. Alexander was learning about top sails and main sails, foremasts, main masts, mizzens, lugsails, and spars. Roger hoped that Alexanders curiosity might lead him later in life to be a British sailor.

One day after they had been on the Atlantic Ocean west of Spayna and having left the Islas Canaries drift they were on the main channel of the Atlantic drift which would allow them to have better wind and sailing conditions. The captain, on the crow's nest, noticed a sea rover or sloop headed their way and alerted the sailors. He said they have raised a black flag and it is positively a pirate ship and not a phantom ship. The pirate stopped their approach and lay still. Likewise, the captain ordered the crew to back sail and stop their boat so as the two ships would not collide. The two sailing ships were now broadside of each other.

Roger said, "We will see what they want. If they try to fire or come aboard, we will let them have as much fight and firepower as they can take. Sailors, you stay hidden in the lower deck and protect the women and children. If I give the signal, come on the upper deck and began firing when I give you the order. It makes no sense that a pirate ship would attack a British warship." Roger was determined to keep the passengers safe and didn't want to get in a battle with the pirates unless they charged first.

The sailors slackened the main sail and dropped the main anchor and followed the orders.
The Captain of the *Diamond* said, " I see a pirate waving a white flag. He has some kind of bright yellow suit with long flaming red hair and red braided beard tied with ribbons. He has a metal claw for a hand and a wooden leg. The crew is very rough looking and are armed to the teeth. They have swords, pistols, cutlasses and knives ."
Roger gave an order, "Let them get a closer since the flag is raised."

The pirate yelled, "Ahoy, matey. What are you doing out here all alone, far from England? I have noticed your red ensign as your colors. You must be headed there?"

Roger asked, "Who wants to know?"

Pirate yelled, "Forgive me for my manners, Lieutenant. I am Redbeard and this is my son, Edward, who is 4 but learning the business, and my associates, the Pirates of Okracoke." Redbeard, chuckling, was amused at his own remarks. His son, Edward, unlike his father with red hair, had black hair and a dirty face, but looked well fed and happy. Redbeard continued, "My ship is the "Queen Katherine" named after the present Queen of Merry Ole England. The boy's mother was hung there for crimes. We hail from Bristol, England, but haven't seen the likes of that place for years. We have been getting bigger and bigger ships over the years as our business improves. I now have a crew that can sail anywhere for any reason. We sail by the North Star and use the ends of the Big and Little Dipper to point to the North Star and our compass of 32 points. We have no planned rutters. We will be headed for Hell in the long run. "

Roger said, "I am Lt. Roger Elliott of the British Navy. I am headed for England and charged with the duty of getting the passengers there safe and sound. "

Redbeard laughing," Aye, Matey, where are your passengers? Are they hiding with their muskets as if they want to harm us if provoked? "Redbeard thought that the passengers must be really all English soldiers. He was trying to estimate how big and dangerous the upcoming battle would be between the two ships.

Roger answered, "They are not hiding. They are enjoying their sailing holiday."

Redbeard, "If I was a betting man, I bet you are leaving Tangier as they are closing the garrison. We will move in and take control of the business when all the English leave."

 Now it was Roger's turn to laugh at the scallywag, "You will have to stand in line because every country in the known world of the 7 seas will want to take control of Northern Africa."

Redbeard getting a little bit annoyed," I see you like to parley so let's parley some more. What do you have on board of value that I may risk my own life, my son's life, and the lives of my crew? I know that you could have about 60 soldiers hiding down below in that bilge rat. They will be no challenge to us."

Katherine came up from below deck with George. She exclaimed, "There is only women and kids down below. Leave us alone and be on your way in a forceful and direct tone."

Redbeard, "Maybe you are telling the truth, but is hard for me to believe there is just one soldier defending all these people. We can use them for shark bait, and they can walk the plank."

Alexander who had been told to stay out of sight came upon the deck carrying his grandfather's sword. "He is not alone. I am defending them also." Alexander raised his sword.

Redbeard, laughing," So I see, little buccaneer. You are also learning a trade. This is a most amusing, I am discussing an attack on a ship of the English with a child. Is that not a true land lubber?"

Alexander said angrily, "I am not a child. I am a man who will defend my family and my honor." Roger looked at his half-brother, half angry, half amused, and surprised that he was that serious. Maybe Alexander had grown up on the trip to Toubkal or maybe he knew he came from a long line of fighters, fighting for their beliefs. Whatever it was, Alexander was not backing down and wanted no harm to come to his mother, stepfather, aunt, and half-brother.

Redbeard now was smiling, "Aye, I see. Well. Let's don't get to hasty. Let us see if we can reach an agreement. Do you have any booty, gold, silver, or precious jewels on board?"

Roger quickly said, "No!"

Redbeard asked, "How can I rob you if you have nothing to plunder? Do you have food?"

Roger answered, "Only enough to get to the next stop on our trip to England. There is no surplus."

Redbeard paused, "I need a mother for my boy and a wife to cook and clean for me."

Roger quickly answered, "All our women are married and have kids. We do not have maids on board."

Redbeard, looking straight at Katherine Mercer, "How about you pretty, Gracey O'Malley?" Gracey was a beautiful Irish pirate from long ago whose reputation for piracy was renown".

Katherine replied, "I have a husband who serves the Lord and he is all I need."

Redbeard, looking a little jealous, said, "I see you have a fiddle attached to the spar on the mast."

The Captain of the *Diamond* said, "I will give you the fiddle if you will let us be on our way."

Redbeard, sternly in a demanding tone, "Play something or I will kill the young man with the sword that is bigger than he is."

The Captain began to play an old English hymn, *The Water is Wide*. The pirate looked melancholy and said "Enough! Enough! It is too beautiful. Let's be on with it! You have no workers on board that I can sell for slaves? Nor rich persons we could hold for ransom?"

Roger standing strong and talking emphatically, "We do not have any slaves. No rich people. We are paid very little by the Royal Navy. "

Redbeard losing his patience, "How about deeds to land?"

Roger emphatically, "No, we are in the navy and have no property except the clothes on our back."

Redbeard said, "I don't need your land as I have castles almost at every port on the 7 seas. I even have Islands in the 7000 islands of the Caribbean and some land on an island called Okracoke. I find this kind of sporting, but I am getting bored and my associates want to see some blood and treasure. I would seize your frigate for the cannons, but it is too easy a ship to spot by your British Navy, and I would probably get mistaken for a British soldier and get attacked by the Spanish and French, which hate your English guts. I want to show you something that will make you wonder for the rest of your lives for I am putting a curse on you since I cannot get anything from you." He pointed to Alexander. "The only thing that will break the curse if this young man's sword is retrieved from a sinking ship. And the sword will somehow be returned to him."

Alexander raising his voice and getting angry, said, "I am not giving you my sword. My father gave it to me, and it belonged to my grandfather who was a Scottish Knight."

Redbeard, grinning with joy, "That makes it better for me, for then the spell will work better. "In a flash the pirate clapped his hands together and there appeared to be a puff of smoke in front of him. The sword came out of Alexanders hand and over the ocean from the English ship to the pirate's ship and landed in the pirate's hands.
Alexander and everybody that witnessed the flying sword gasped in amazement.

Redbeard said, "I have the sword now. Your curse is that everyone who has spoken to me this day will become beautiful, rich, and well known in all the land. They will be cursed with these afflictions until the sword is retrieved from a sinking ship or you die first. You will see that this curse is worse than being poor, ugly, and unknown."

Alexander speaking bravely," I will come and get my sword. My grandfather's spirit will haunt you."

Redbeard perplexed, "Are you cracked in the head? The sharks will eat you if you swim to me boat, Matey. I have more power than you, your father, and your grandfather. There is no chance of this ship sinking so that you will get your sword returned to you. If everybody dies on the sinking ship carrying your sword, you will not get your sword back. It is nearly impossible to break the curse. I see the S on the handle. Is it for silver, because this blade is pure silver? On with the show. I will now impress you with a demonstration."

A matey brought out a full skeleton of old bones and a small sack from the pirate's cabin. One of the pirate's crew tied the skeleton to the foremast and handed the sack to Redbeard. He opened the small sack and it had something shiny in the sack and Redbeard said, "This is silver dust that could buy you food, clothes, shelter, lands, and other nice things, but I will sprinkle it on the skeleton. Redbeard took his headband and put it on the skull of the skeleton. He then began to sprinkle the silver dust on all the bones of the skeleton. To everyone's amazement, the skeleton formed the body and face of a handsome young man and the skeleton came to life. Redbeard said, "From dust to dust, this man was cursed. He is now free to go because his curse was to be bound on a pirate ship and only would be freed if someone brought a pure silver sword on board that ship. This is that ship, this is the cursed man, this is the silver sword, this is the day he is free."

Red Beard looking at Alexander, "Aye, laddie, your life will not be easy. This sword may be your condemnation, or it might be your salvation. You will make the choice. Good quarter guaranteed. You, the prey is spared! Ho, Ho, Ho!" With that said, there was a loud explosion and a cloud of smoke came between the two ships. The cloud was like a heavy fog in which it was hard to see your own hands. When the fog lifted, the pirate ship had vanished. There was nothing but space. There was no trace of the ship anywhere, and it could not have sailed out of view that far away that quickly.

The Captain of the *Diamond* in awe, asked, "Did we all see the pirate ship and is it not so that we were talking with Redbeard a few minutes ago? Is it a dream, a hoax, a magic trick, or an illusion?"

Roger also in disbelief, said, "Yes, no, yes, I mean we all saw what we saw. It was no Phantom ship. The pirates were real as far as we know. The ship was there, and the pirates were there. Nothing else makes sense."

Alexander said, "I am angry. They took my inheritance. I don't believe in the curse. They were trying to scare us away. They were bluffing and playing tricks."

Katherine looking relieved, said, "You all are so brave!"

George, also relieved, said, "I am glad there was no fight. The soldiers can come up from below now but let us figure out what just happened and tell them later about the pirates. Let us get back on our journey before the pirates might come back."

Alexander, looking distraught, said, "I am sorry mother. I am sorry Roger that I lost my sword."

Roger, in a comforting tone, said, "It is alright. There is no such thing as being put under a curse."

Alexander said, "I hope not but, in a way, I would not understand why it would be a curse to be rich, handsome, and well known."

Roger, doubting his eyes and mind, said, "Let's hope we find out if it is really a curse. What kind of pirate or magician can make a man out of bones? Did you see it? I am not seeing things at sea which really aren't there, am I?"

Pretty soon, the rest of the passengers and sailors came to the upper deck not knowing what had happened. Seems like the people below deck had all been sleeping and resting unaware of any pirate activity between two ships at sea. Had they somehow been put under a spell by the pirates so there was no exchange of musket fire and cannons between the two ships?

Roger explained, "Dead men tell no tales and sleeping men tell no tales. Some things are better left unsaid." The crew soon pulled up the anchor and reset the sails. The wind started them back on their journey.

Alexander had returned to his bunk and started thinking about what he had just seen. He knew that he had been advised by a lot of different people, and he believed in God, and he now knew that the devil was real. The pirates spared them. He knew he should be thankful for the day's outcome. Later, he woke up and went up on deck with some of the others. There was Sothis, his personal star, was blinking bright in starry sky as if to confirm that everything was back to normal. He went back down to the cramped living quarters to be with the rest of the family. They were still up trying not to disturb any other passengers and still talking amongst themselves about the day's activities.

Roger exclaimed, "This is some tale if we tell it the way we saw and heard it. The last of the witchcraft and activity was finished in times past when the three witches were hung in London. It may have not been witchcraft for the sword to have been thrown in the air and be caught by Redbeard."

George added his remarks, "And what a tale about the silver dust and skeleton! That looked real!"

Roger agreed, "That was real!"

Katherine said, "I had a heard a tale about something like this when I was a girl in Scotland before we moved to England. I didn't know if I believed it then, but I am more inclined to believe it now after today. There was supposed to be a gold mine under a hillside in Green Largo Lo, an area in Scotland. All the local shepherds noticed gold spots on the sheep and thought it might be a result of the sheep grazing the grass on this hillside. The local shepherds were told by a stranger in a long dark cloak that was passing by on the road by the hillside that the Devil was buried there. The shepherds told the traveler that they had heard that gold was buried there but had never destroyed any of his grassy meadows where his sheep grazed to find out if that was true. The traveler said that there was no gold buried there pointing to the hill, and he could prove it. The devil makes people think that there is gold there to attract them here and to snare them into his kingdom. There will be a ghost here after the rooster crows and after the horn is blown so the cattle will know to go from their barn to the pasture. The next morning at the light of day, the rooster did crow, and the shepherd blew the horn so the cattle would go to pasture. Sure enough, the ghost was there at the base of the hillside next to a red oak tree. He said, "Dig up this ground, and treasure you will find, and if you tell someone what you've found, someone will vanish in due time." The ghost disappeared in a flash. The shepherd marked the spot with a stick and went to get his shovel. He returned to the stick and began to dig up the ground by the big red oak tree. Soon he dug across a stone coffin and there were parts of a knight's armor. There was a helmet scabbard and the upper breast plate. There were no lower parts of the armor or a sword. The parts seem to be made from pure silver. The shepherd thought that this will make me rich and this must be the treasure. Suddenly, the shovel flew out of his hand and landed on the ground on the other side of the red oak tree. The shovel started moving up and down on its own power as if it wanted to dig up the ground. The shepherd started digging, and he uncovered another stone coffin and inside the coffin was the rest of the armor; the lower part of the suit, the shield, and the sword. It appeared to be made of the same pure silver. He gathered up the parts of the armor, loaded them in a horse drawn cart and headed for the silversmith shop in the nearby village. He was so excited about his newfound treasure, he told the silversmith the entire story about the place, the ghost, the shovel, and the coffins. Intrigued, the silversmith said that he would smelt the armor down and change it into silver dust. Now it would be easier to carry, store, or hide from robbers and thieves, and more suitable for trading. The shepherd told the man that this was a good idea and that while he was working with the silver, he would go back to his home and check on his sheep and cows. On the way out the door of the shop, the shepherd dropped dead on the spot. The silversmith had just listened to the story and thought that he must take the shepherd back to his home and see if there is any more treasure. He loaded up the dead shepherd in his cart and put the armor in and body under a blanket so no one would suspect anything and tied his own horse back of the cart. The silversmith went to his house and told his wife that he had a shepherd from Green Largo lo he had to meet, and he had to exchange some armor for silver dust. He would be back in the afternoon. He then headed for the hillside in the cart. When he got to the place, it was laid out as exactly as the shepherd had said. There were two open coffins on either side of a large red oak tree. He figured he would bury the shepherd in one of the coffins and then would cover up the second coffin and take the horse drawn cart with the silver armor and his horse back to his shop. When the silversmith looked to see if there were any more gold or silver in the coffin and cover it with dust, he fell into the coffin and died. That night, the wife of the silversmith went to the constable to tell him she was worried about her husband, because he had not returned from Green Largo lo in the afternoon as he promised. The constable told her that a traveler had come to his office earlier in the day in a long dark cloak and said that while traveling by the road in Green Largo lo and he came across a ghastly scene. The traveler said that two men must have gotten in an argument over some armor laying by two graves. The stranger said that I don't know how the graves or stone coffins, or armor or men got to this place. He said each man was laying down in his own coffin. He said he went over and covered their bodies with dust so they would not be disturbed by birds and animals. The traveler said he thought he would stop by the closest constable office, but he had to hurry to get to Edinburgh for his business. Seeing that he broke no laws, I let him go. The Constable said that he was planning to go out to the place in the morning to investigate the incident. By the next morning, the word had spread in the village that two men had been killed, and a few men and the wife accompanied the constable to the hillside. The party arrived at the murder scene and the constable found the two freshly covered graves just as the traveler had reported the day before. Two men that had tagged along took the sheriffs shovel and alternated digging the dirt. One of them soon came across a stone coffin and opened it up. Inside was the deceased silversmith. "That is my husband", she cried, "Please take him to the cemetery at the kirk in the village." The sheriff found a volunteer to dig up the other coffin and soon they came upon another stone coffin. There is no body in this coffin. There is only a rusty old tin piece of armor and some old bones. There was a piece of wood that said Leave this hillside alone for there is no gold. Around the skull was part of a woolen hat. The sheriff said, I have seen enough and asked the volunteer to cover the grave. The constable did not know what to do or say. Some of the shepherd's neighbors had come over to see what was going on. The constable asked if they had seen two men fighting over armor and a horse cart and a horse. They replied that they had seen nothing at any time at Green Largo Lo. The constable asked them if they knew who the hillside belongs to. They replied that they had seen a shepherd on the hillside with his flock, but they had not seen him for a long time, and the sheep go unattended on the hillside. The constable seemed confused but maybe the traveler did not see but one man as he was in a hurry and seemed weary from his travels. Since there seems to be no murder, and the man must have died of natural causes, and no laws have been broken, this investigation is closed. To this day there is no horse cart, no silver armor, no shepherd, no traveler, no horse drawn cart, and no talk about gold. There is only sheep grazing on the hillside and a mystery of what the devil did at Green largo lo."

Alexander said, "That is a great story, mother. There seems to be some of the same unknowns that we saw today. I feel that I will fight the devil if I have to, to get my sword back."

Roger said, "I heard that in Scotland there are all kinds of strange disappearances that involves, witches, Satan, kelpies and warlords."

Katherine said, "I think they make great stories to pass the time on the open sea. Can you find any of these stories to be true? Better yet, will you all be able to sleep tonight? We are very fortunate that the pirates didn't start shooting at us today and our regiment must use the cannons through the gun port to fire back. They could have killed many of us and put us in Davy Jones Locker. They could have sunk the ship for meanness. I thank God for our safety and for Roger's and Alexander's bravery."

Roger said, "There are many things that happen that just can't be explained. Some are good and come from God and some are bad and come from the devil. Look at what happened today. We cannot explain that to anyone without them thinking we have lost possession of our minds."

George, "It is the devil himself trying to get to everybody to join him, so he won't be alone in Hell. Red Beard is definitely one of his converts if he stays on course."

Alexander concluded, "Satan is real just like God is real."

George explained, "A lot of people have trouble making the choice between the two."

Roger, standing boldly at the seemingly endless ocean and horizon in front of him, simply stated," It is better to follow God."

The next morning the sun was shining brightly, and the skies were clear and light blue and hanging above the bluish gray waters of the Atlantic. The sails were flapping and the English flag on the top mast blowing in the slight wind. The Captain of the *Diamond* was hoping to make up loss time from the unscheduled stop and unwelcome encounter with the pirates from the day before. The passengers on the ship were not getting any closer to enjoying the voyage. They had little amounts of bread and food each day. Water was rationed to them every day. There were cramped living conditions in the lower deck; cramped like sardines in a fisherman's net.

Some of the sick had died and their remains were tossed overboard as a too familiar and long-standing practice. There were usually a prayer and respectful memorial service given by the captain on these untimely occasions. He would make an entry into his journal to make a record so later he could notify the family of the deceased when the ship would arrive at port. Alexander witnessed a few of these memorials which somehow reminded him reminded of his own father's funeral service. He must have wondered and questioned who these men were that had died before the allowed time of seventy years. Why had they decided to go into the military? How had they liked Morocco? What were their homes like? What will their families think about the knowledge of not seeing their loved ones again and not knowing the unknown place of their watery grave? Alexander was learning about the uncertainty and sometimes seemingly unfairness of life. He had been taught at the garrison school and church that every day we should rejoice and give thanks for what we do have. He still had his family and the hopes of having a happy homecoming at the end of their destination.

The ship had been on the waters for a few weeks now and off the moors of Spayna. The ship was coming close to an inhabited island where they might could get some fresh supplies and stretch their legs on the Spanish controlled land. The ship pulled up along the moor where there was a stone and sand dock jutting out into the bay. The islands received supplies by cargo ships from all over the world and was frequented by slave ships, schooners, fishing boats and all kinds of sailing ships. The Mercer family got out and enjoyed walking out on the island looking at all the heath, grass, and trees of which they had not seen any of this kind of scenery for a couple of weeks. Alexander was pleased to get as much water as he wanted to drink. After a few hours, the *Diamond* set sail northerly again for the island of England. Alexander was probably hoping they would not be attacked by any more pirates and have any more curses put on him and his family. He had not seen any effects of the curse yet. He was secretly hoping that he might get wealthy enough to have enough food and water and build a capacious house after feeling the depravity of the close confinements of the ship's lodgings.

After they returned to the small confines below deck and the island was fading in sight behind them, Alexander asked Roger, "How do you think the pirate ship disappeared so quickly a few weeks ago?"

Roger answered honestly, "I don't know for certain. There was a soldier from Scotland at the garrison that told me about witches making things disappear and disrupting good folks' lives. He said that the local story goes that the devil, Satan, was carrying a load of rocks and some witches thought they would scare him. He dropped the rocks to the ground and formed a rocky mound near the sea. Satan, angry about the witch's' mischief, started a witch hunt and caught up with one of them and turned her into a rock. He then placed the rock with the ones he had dropped. The local folks thinking that the devil was finished with the hunt and the rocks, took the rocks and made a kirk or church. They used the church to escape from the witches and Satan. They called Satan, Ole Clootey or Auld Nick and when they died, they asked to be buried on the north side of the church to ensure their safety into the next world."

George remarked, "That reminds me of something I heard once about the rocks being brought to Scotland by the Vikings when they tried to invade Scotland and take possession. Some of the boulders are 40 feet high and it seems unlikely that the Vikings, even with their brawny arms, could have pulled off this gigantic feat. How could they have hauled the rock in their longboats? I think the rocks were already there before creation."

Roger said, "I can't say for certain, but the same soldier, nicknamed "Roa" told me the following story. He said, there is a rock standing about 40 feet tall at Culross, Scotland that has a witch's footprint embedded into the rock. The local citizenry believes there was a witch that was on a long trip and stopped there to rest and then flew away on a broomstick for a faraway land to wreak her havoc."

George commented, "Roa did tell some great stories at the garrison. The only one that could out talk him was "Tangier" Jones, the governor who by the way is headed for the New World. Maybe he will talk the House of Commons into giving him governorship of New England. Anyway, the two storytellers tried to compete to see who could tell the best story. There were some tall tales as a result."

Alexander remarked, "That was a good story about Green Largo lo, Mother. Do you have more?"

Katherine replied, "I have a rock story. There is a rock that is about 3 miles west of At. Andrews church. The rock is embedded in a hillside by the edge of the Darsie valley is about 8-foot-tall and 6 foot wide. St. Andrews is the church where your father's grandfather was bishop for the church. Long before he got there however, the parishioners decided to put a four knock-it steeple on their church. There was a giant from Duncarro that didn't like this idea. He didn't want the church to be built. He decided to get a rock and sling and knock the steeple down. The giant used his sling in a similar way as David slew Goliath, the giant. The giant used his mother's apron for the sling and as he was tossing it around and round, the sling broke, and the rock headed directly for the church but fell short of the target and landed in the hillside where the rock still stands. The people in the area think this was a good omen because the church and people in the church were not destroyed. In fact, the Scottish lads will ask their favorite lassies to marry them on this stone so that their marriage cannot be destroyed."

Alexander asked, "Is this where grandfather asked grandmother to marry him?"

Katherine answered, "I don 't know how they came to know each other."

 Bethia commented with a puzzled look, and spoke, "I never did hear what caused my parents to meet and marry," Alexander and Katherine smiled. As if to say, it is better that we do not know.

George, commented," There are good things that happened because of the holy water from the holy wells made from the rocks gathered from the mountain surrounding St. Andrews church. These wells have special unexplained powers that most of the folks debate whether the powers come from the devil or from the good Lord. In 1649 in the year of our Lord and Savior, the Scottish General Assembly came up with a writ to abolish the celebration of the Holy Wells which the parishioners over all Scotland celebrated every year since the reign of King Robert the Bruce. They never did figure out the spiritual source of the water so they said the assembly cannot allow the celebration until it is explained to their satisfaction. All I can say that what is told is that the holy well near St. Andrews has water in it. If you dip out the water and place that water on the eyelids of a blind person, that blind person will be able to see. There is a holy well near Darsie that is used for bathing, and people who bathe there will never have wrinkles on their face. I think these are miracles from the Lord. The devil would not care about you or if you have wrinkles. There is a well in Dumferline where the people plant flowers around the well and sing praises to the holy well so they will always have a blessing and scares away the witches, ghosts, and the devil from their families."

Roger added, "I have heard about a wishing well where your wishes will come true."

Alexander asked," Can we find this well and remove the curse? I wish that I could get my sword returned to me.
"

Roger commented, "It would be a blessing for you to get your sword returned. That reminds me of another tale that was told to me by Roa. There was a well called Seven Wells near Sterlingshire that had 7 springs that had seven corresponding openings to each well. The water was very pure and was good for making tea and drinking. People from all the neighboring counties would come by the wells and bottle up the water. And the people would get many bottles, jugs, canteens, and barrels of the water and take the water back to their homes. One Scottish Clan, the Andersens, decided they had enough of travelers and strangers coming to the wells and being careless with their animals and pastures and destroying their crops. The clan built a fence around the wells so that no one would benefit from the blessings of the well. This action angered the other clans that traveled many miles and spent much time getting to the wells only to be turned away when they arrived there. The king at the time was James II of Scotland and he told the people and the clans that the wells legally belonged to the Andersens and they needed to find another well or dig their own well. The advice worked for most of the clans and they left the 7 wells alone. However, there were some clans that had a problem with this advice from their king. They had grown accustom to helping themselves to the well and drawing the water to be used for medicinal purposes and for the waters purity to drink and to make tea. The clans would come to battle the Andersens and take the wells for themselves.

In every case the clans would be defeated by the Andersens and they would slay every member of the challenging clan. After the battle, the Andersens would wash the blood off their hands and swords. This happened time after time. They won every battle they fought. King James II of Scotland got reports about all the slayings at 7 wells. He said that I must travel there myself and see what the fuss is all about. He thought if he had the water, he could win every battle against the English or Danes or any other enemies of the Crown. He traveled to the wells in Sterlingshire. The king and his traveling party was greeted by the clan leader of the Andersens who hoped he didn't have to fight the king's army. The leader asked the king to drink the water since he traveled many miles and was probably very thirsty. Every time the king would touch the water, it turned to a bloody color He washed his hands in a barrel full of the water and his hands turned to a blood red color.

The king exclaimed, "Is it suitable for drinking?"

The leader told him to help himself. He drank from the well and the king became immediately ill, and the stomach rejected the water and he vomited profusely. He soon became well and headed on to his royal palace in Perth.
The king would not forget his trip to 7 wells. The Clan Andersens still drink the water and wash their hands after every tribal battle. Most of the clans now have the good sense to leave them alone."

Alexander remarked, "That was another good story."

Meanwhile, the ship continued to sail smoothly towards Plymouth. The Mercer family listened intently to each other's collection of stories and tales like they were used to doing at the garrison. This seem to entertain them on their long boring voyage. Alexander enjoyed their company and asked about the places and stories and wanted to know if they were mystical and magical events or did it happen. He did say his prayers every night for the safe journey, and he would go up on the sundeck to see if the starry sky contained the Sothis star and the star was always in the sky seemingly to lead and to follow as a guideline. He knew that he must not get too focused on the stories or on the stars as this took his time away from the Lord. He knew that to be a follower of the Lord, he shouldn't get involved or immersed in witchcraft or astrology.

Katherine continued the storytelling, "Alexander, before your father and I were married he practiced medicine in Scotland and had to be a doctor to many superstitious patients. Some of the people would not take their medication and spirits unless it was a certain phase of the moon. He would not be able to mend some cracked or broken bones on them unless a witch's chant was ministered to them ahead of time. Many other patients wanted the Lord's Prayer read before they were examined. Some told him they had to put polluted water that had been standing in a tree stump on their skin and this would cure their rashes. Some took a mixture of honey, egg white, and finely ground oats to put on their face to clear up their complexion and eliminate wrinkles. One man thought that using the dry skin of a chicken gizzard would cure baby's diarrhea. I don't know If it worked, but some patients thought earwax cured boils. Your father was a very patient and caring man. Some of his patients had some home remedies made from flowers and herbs. Some people thought if they sniffed rosemary flowers, their memories would improve. Some thought if you cut some slips of the mountain ash called the Rowan tree and hang it from the threshold of the front door with some red thread on their house, they would keep the witches away that caused their sickness. They also believed if these same rowan slips and red thread was put on the barns and sheds, their flocks of goats and sheep would not be harmed, either. I am truly glad your father does not have to deal with the superstitions, anymore. As far as understanding a curse, as you already know, that my father was a preacher in England, but he was originally from Scotland, and my brothers and sisters and I were born in Cardoness Castle.

He would tell us a curse that was put on the castle by a feudal lord in the time of King Robert Bruce of Scotland and King Edward I of England. It appeared that the feudal lord had been chartered the land from King Robert, but The Bruce chartered it to someone else. This made the lord angry and he put a curse on the land saying that whoever lived there would never prosper. The next three owners went bankrupt. Then a man name Cardoness got the land and lived there 20 years. He had nine daughters but wanted a male heir. He was so obsessed with this that he threatened his wife to have a son. He further claimed if she did not have a son, he would get rid of her and the entire family so he could remarry a woman that could deliver a son. She did deliver a son, to celebrate, the family went on the frozen lake by the castle to jump around and skate on the ice. The ice broke and the family drowned except for one girl. She was taken to her aunt so she would have family to live with. When she was of legal age to inherit the land, she got married to a man named Lynn. He received his money from selling cows, hogs, sheep, and goats and kept the castle in fair shape. He eventually sold it and they moved to Fairbourn, and the castle went through many families' hands, and the castle kept deteriorating until my grandfather Maxwell agreed to repair it, if he could live there for a small fee every year. He raised his small family there and was guardian of the castle. My father told the story that when he was a small boy residing in the castle, he would be awaken at night by the loud and awful screaming of girls splashing and screaming as if they were in the black waters of the nearby lake.

 Later one of the servants came to the castle to tell him to go home to attend his wife who was having a baby. On the way home he saw flickering lights along the banks of the Lake but neither neighbor nor servant could explain what they were seeing. They got to the servant's cottage. The neighbor went inside his cottage. When the servant finally entered the home and opened the door to his wife's bedroom, he saw several green elf-kins dancing around the baby's crib or so he thought as the wife had already delivered the baby. The elf-kins disappeared in the twinkling of an eye. His wife was sleeping in a clean bed. He looked in the crib, and there was a cute little baby boy wearing a green cap that matched the color of the elf-kins. His wife had a new green scarf around her neck that matched the color of the baby's cap. He was bewildered by the experience but had questions about the sparkling lights on the banks of the lake and the elf-kins presence at the cottage. Later the neighbor made testimony that the servant had drank no liquor and there seem to be no ill effect of the visions that evening. The castle is now in fact one of the most beautiful castles in Scotland. As far as the curse goes, I believe it worked for a while at the Castle Cardoness, but there was something that broke the curse, and it would be safe to visit again. It might have something to do with the birth of a son of one of the owners, in the number of owners the castle has had.

Roger, Alexander, George, and Bethia had all listened intently and heard the waves splashing along the gun ports of the ship. The kitchen fire in the quarters of the aft deck was dimming, and the moon was high over the horizon, and it felt like everything was progressing as planned on the journey. The families on board were getting far from Tangier with each ticking of the captain's clock. It was nine in the evening, and Alexander wanted to hear one more story.

Katherine said to Alexander, "Your father was in possession of many good luck charms that the other doctors in Fife and Dunfunshire had sent him. The other doctors had given him a list of the uses of the charms. The list included the practice of putting amber beads on a baby's bed to keep the fairies from keeping them awake and making them cry with the colic There were ointments ground up with herbs and greens to keep one's digestive tract in good health. Using some salts from the sea would promote the healing of cuts and wounds. If someone wanted to be safe from fire, they would burn the heart of a cow in their fire in the chimney or coal stove. If an owner took a key and put it in their Bible and really listened, they could learn the secrets of the house. If a tribal chief put an arch of mountain ash over the gate post to the farm, it would keep his lands safe from witches' attacks. One family believed that there were 31 verses in the 31st book of Proverbs would predict their future, if they looked at the number of the verse that correspond to the number of the day of the month they were born. Another belief was that if someone put a knife under the door threshold, that this would keep witchcraft from a home. There were lots of beliefs that had been handed down from generation to generation, and a lot of them were based on superstition. One of the good luck charms was the simple horseshoe."

Alexander, listening carefully, said, "Like the one the farrier had put on our horses to go to Toubkal?"

Roger answered, "Yes, we had good luck that day! The horseshoes kept our horses from slipping on the rocks and sometimes snow on the narrow rocky trails on our journey to Toubkal. The shoes also protected the horses' hooves from splitting."

Alexander, "I didn't know they would bring us luck."

Katherine, explaining her knowledge about lucky horseshoes, said, "Many a wooden Scottish ship had a horseshoe nailed to it for good luck and a safe voyage. Many Scottish and English houses had a horseshoe with the two points pointing up to the heavens, nailed to the house, above the front doors to keep ghosts, witches and the devil from entering. Horseshoe nails used on walls help improve luck to stop the plagues in a home. There were all kinds of thinking about the horseshoes. It was very lucky if a man found an old horseshoe thrown from a sprightly horse along a trail. To have more luck, the old horseshoe had to be a used horseshoe and had to be found and not taken out of someone's barn or shed. It is good luck for the owner of the shoe and not the finder. Horseshoes on cobblestone pathways will throw off sparks, and if a horseshoe is thrown and is found later, the owner will have more power and strength than before he found the shoe. The more worn a horseshoe is, the more power and luck it possesses. It takes 7 nails to hold one horseshoe to each hoof of the horse and 7 is the luckiest number because 777 is the numerical number associated to the Lord. A faithful servant of the Lord is correct in saying that there is no such thing as being lucky, but all things happen because of destiny which has nothing to do with luck. Your father was well respected for his patience with the sick and listened to them about their superstitious beliefs, but he really thought everything was controlled by the Lord. "

George explained, "Where this superstition started about horseshoes bringing luck, started in England when St. Tottenham accidentally nailed a horseshoe to the devils foot and Tottenham said he would only remove the horseshoe if he left the people alone, and if they had a horseshoe nailed over their front doors."

Alexander was curious about why there no horseshoes on the ship and asked Roger if they would have bad luck?"

Roger said, "We will have neither good luck nor bad luck. Just have faith and everything will be just fine."

George said, "Horseshoes were introduced in England by a Norman, William the Conqueror, who became King of England after the Battle of Hastings in 1066. He may have got the idea from Emperor Nero of Rome, who put solid silver horseshoes on his mules, and Emperor Pompey who put horseshoes of pure gold on his horses to have a brazen footed steed. Childeric , King of the Franks , body was dug up from a family plot to be put in a Royal Cemetery about 30 years ago after having being buried for 1200 years, and the only thing left in his grave was his bones and the horseshoes that he was buried with. About the nails in a horseshoes' importance, there is a saying; "As the horseshoe nails goes, so goes the country. The nails keep the horseshoe in place and keeps the horse steady, the horse keeps the knight mounted safely, the knights defend the maiden and the castle, and the strength of the castles and the castles armies keep the country strong." Can you believe what would happen if even one horseshoe nail is broken or missing in this chain of the knight's actions. When we get to England, we can take a trip out to Lancaster. One of the king's sons, known as the Black Knight, had a horse that threw a horseshoe when they marched through town after a battle. A townsman hung the horseshoe on a tree in the town square. Every 7 years, the townsfolks have a festival and replace the old shoe with a new one thus ensuring that they have 7 more years of good luck."

Roger added, "We even saw firsthand in Morocco the Moors who had some skulls of cattle with horns nailed on their houses to keep away evil spirits. And across the narrow passage of the straits of Gibraltar in Southern Spain, the Spanish of the Andalusian Mountains would use any type of animal's horn tips and put pure silver on the tips and wear them as an amulet around their neck by a braided cord made from the black hair of an Andalusian horse. They thought this would keep them from evil spells and allow them to live a long healthy life. Even some of the Berbers that Alexander saw on the way to Toubkal were wearing fossilized shark teeth, they had gathered from the dried-up valley lake beds in the Atlas Mountains. They believed this would help them be better fishermen. When I was in England a few months ago, I saw the shark teeth in pubs, churches, and taverns all for the purpose of bringing good luck. I would have said this was all a bunch of poppycock or rubbish until I heard this story. There was a doctor who was walking on Westminster Bridge and came across a horseshoe on the bridge, picked it up, and took It to his laboratory as a potential lucky omen. He suddenly got the brilliant idea to make a powder that would cure aches and pains, and he sold the idea to a factory and he made a fortune."

George retorted, "Could be a coincidence?"

Roger replied, "Might be, but what do you say about a preacher in Aldergate who had his parishioners put a brand that looked like a horseshoe on their animals. All his parishioners escaped death during the Black Death Plague 15 years ago, and when the Great Fire of London destroyed a third of the central part of the city, the wind shifted and the church and most of the houses of the church goers there were spared, because of the brand. How do you explain that?"

George rebutting those remarks, said," Maybe it is good fortune, but keep your thinking pure , because also the horseshoe was a symbol used by the heathen and pagan leader, Wodun of Saxony in Old England. And it is never been discerned why the Egyptians, with all their sky and earth gods, thought that the horseshoe in their hieroglyphics was used to signify the mystical door of life. Again, what you think might be good fortune is a snare for the devil to get you away from your real faith."

Katherine, grinning with pride, said, "Well said my love. Alexander, it is time to go to sleep."

Alexander, "Mother, I like all the stories about horseshoes and luck. Tomorrow, maybe you can tell me about London and Cardoness Castle." The idea of a preacher, kings, and lords from these places having so much influence over people fascinated him. He would have to ask more questions about the superstitions associated with ghost, witches, bones, teeth, dust, and horseshoes.

Alexander went up on deck and the wind was picking up at night. Sothis was faithfully there as if to confirm that some things in the heavens are visible and believable. Alexander must have been thinking that more knowledge is better, but one must carefully study somethings that are not so visible and believable. He had to ask himself, what is truth and is there such a thing as luck. Did some of the his newly acquired learning contradict with the Bible learning he had been accustomed to at the garrison from the first time he was able to read? These biblical truths also had been shared to him by his parents. After a few minutes of daydreaming on the gun deck, Alexander retired to an old cot in a small, cramped space in the hull, and said his prayers for his caring family and a safe journey. He quickly fell asleep. Bethia came to check on him to make sure he had plenty of blankets.

The next morning , Alexander went up on the aft deck, and Roger, an early riser, was already checking on the other soldiers' health and well-being. Alexander, yawning as if he was not fully awake yet, "Roger, can you tell me about ghosts and also about sailing by following the North Star?"

Alexander 's curiosity and appetite for learning and exploring was phenomenal. He wanted to know all about the stars and moon . The discussion about luck and witches made him wonder about all kinds of scary creatures.

Roger, telling his plans, said, "Only after breakfast, can I meet you and mother. I must earn my keep on this Brigadoon, you know. You never forget anything do you? I thought you had forgotten about the pirates, all ready and that episode."

Alexander said, "No, in fact I have been scouting for them at the lookout at the top of the main mast pole."

Roger, "Very good. So, we must train you to be an English soldier so you can fight the pirates at sea."

Alexander said " The only thing I saw from the lookout was hundreds of birds flying around the boat. *Do* you think they are headed to Tangier? "

Roger answered, "Maybe, they are headed in a southerly direction, alright. That reminds me about the North Star and directions. The best person to show you the North Star is the Captain of the ship. I will see when you can ask him all the questions you want. He has had much experience and he is a good navigator."

Alexander went down to the lower deck to see his mother and George. The other passengers were all awake now and were getting ready for a new day at sea. The sun was rising just over the horizon and it was slightly breezy, so the sails were filled, and under the ship at the waterline by the prow there were bubbles of ocean and foam signifying that the *Diamond* was making good speed towards England. Alexander had a breakfast of some fruits and nuts that he had gotten at the last island seaport.

George, teasingly, " Alexander, I am glad to see you alive and well. I was afraid we had talked you to death last night with all the witch and horseshoe stories."

Alexander replied, "The stories were very interesting, and I would like to hear more. Roger said he would tell me about ghosts after breakfast, and after he was finished morning inspection with the other soldiers."

George remarked, "You certainly do have a quest for learning new things."

Alexander quipped " And old things, too."

George, wanting to tell stories, too, said," Before I get all the children on the ship together this morning to teach English history and read prose to them, I can tell you about my favorite ghost story. It is about the commonly agreed on connections between ravens and ghosts. Ravens seem to make some eerie sounds and have some unexplainable habits. They seem to be at cemeteries, guillotines, town squares where there are quarters being drawn on prisoners, old battlefields, and old castles. There were hundreds of ravens that flocked around the 13 towers of the Old Royal Tower in London and were quite mischievous as if controlled by the devil himself. They agitated the visitors at the Tower, as if they were protecting some long-lost treasure. They built their nests on some of the steps and corners of the towers. The king at this point in history was King Bryan II, who threatened to kill all the annoying ravens from the tower and courtyard. One summer day, the king visited the Tower to make sure that one of the potential successors and threats to his kingdom was beheaded for treason against the Crown. Besides there being a large presence of townspeople at the tower to witness the beheading, there were several ravens that flew in a circular ring like group above the guillotine, the instrument of death. The beheading went on as scheduled and just shortly afterward there appeared to be white shadows with human shapes that were sitting by the ravens' nests. The ravens stopped their circling, appeared agitated, and made awful screeching sounds. The ravens became quiet and flew over to their nests, and or rested on the steps to watch the king. The 4 white shadows started to form images which scared the king and the onlookers. They appeared now to be kings with crowns and unknown to the crowd. Then an unexplainable event happened. The black ravens then turned white in color. Then the 4 kings went back to their former forum as white shadows. One raven flew over and landed on the arm of the king's chair. The raven looked directly at the king. The king received a message in his mind which was a poem that he later recited.

If the ravens you kill,
 that will not be all,
 kings' graves will unfill,
and your kingdom will fall.
If anyone tells what they see,
 Death will come soon to thee.

 The king told the crowd to be silent about what they had seen, or he would have them imprisoned and tried for crimes against the kingdom. The 4 white shadows disappeared in air as quickly as they had come to the scene. The crowd left bewildered, dazed, and confused by what they had just seen. The white raven flew away soon over the tower and then disappeared out of sight. The remaining ravens changed back to their black color and became very quiet. The king went back to the castle and asked his spiritual adviser what was the meaning of all this?

The adviser stated, "The 4 white shadows you describe are ghosts. You have threatened to kill all the ravens. A supernatural raven is telling you that if you keep your word and do this , the 4 former kings will come out of their graves to ensure your son will not inherit the English kingdom, and it will be ruled from someone outside the kingdom. If someone tells about the ghosts and ravens, you will most likely die by the guillotine. He went on to see at least 4 kings had been put to death on the guillotine, and many royal family members had been put to death. Also, many commoners had met their fate at the Tower. Many days, months, and a few years went by after the raven incident. Now and then, you would hear someone say they had seen a ghost in the tower's belfry, or they had seen some ghosts at the nesting area of the ravens, and the ravens would get agitated. King Bryan II became deathly ill and thinking that he was dying anyway , decided to get rid of the ravens except for 7 ravens which would have their wings clipped so they could not fly away. On his deathbed he told his son that he would leave him a very important letter. He told his son not to open or read the letter until 7 years after the king's death, if he wanted to be the king. King Bryan II died, and his son became the king. The son was faithful and did not open or read the letter for 7 years. The son called in his spiritual adviser for the reading of the letter and asked him what this poem meant.

Ravens you only need 7
for your royal tower to keep,
will send 4 kings to heaven,
and keep me in resting peace.
Our word we kept until the end,
and you knew from my pen.

The spiritual advisory tried to explain the poem and letter as best he could. The letter explained a mournful day in the land when there was a beheading of a future king who had threatened the father king's kingdom and the retaliation threat of the ravens and the 4 kings. The ravens and kings requested that the father king of this kingdom and the witnesses of the beheading that they would keep their word and would not tell anyone about the threats, or the father king would lose his kingdom. The father king had threatened to kill all the annoying ravens that were in the Royal Bell Tower. He killed all but 7. If he had killed all the ravens, then the ravens would use the reincarnated power of 4 previous king to help destroy the kingdom and likely fall into enemy hands, and the son of the father king would not be king. When the father king knew that death was intimate, he knew his son would have to keep his word and be trusted for 7 years and not to read this letter which explained the ghosts and the ravens so the son would keep his kingdom. The father king and the son king both kept their

.58

word. What the father king did was to keep his word by not telling his son man to man which did not violate the agreement He was very wise and informed his son anyway by writing a letter with the royal pen ensuring that the his son would inherit his kingdom. The father king is resting in peace in Heaven, and if there are ghosts in the Royal tower, they are not the 4 kings and certainly not the father king. The son king went out to the tower and saw the seven ravens and yelled at them. I have a great earthly father king in Heaven who loved me here on Earth. I have a Heavenly Father who is with me now. "The ravens remained quiet, and there were no ghosts that appeared."

Alexander liked the ghost story. He said that they were hard to believe, and he liked hearing the stories in the Bible even more. He felt that some of the stories were fun to listen to, but he believed that The Lord would guide him, and he would avoid the devils and the witches. George told him he was proud of Alexander putting the Lord first in all things.

George went on to deck where some of the young students had gathered to learn more English history. None of the children had ever seen their parent's homeland of England. They liked learning about the place they would soon call home. George had religiously been teaching them very valuable information and grammar school lessons every day since they had left Morocco. He wanted the garrison school to be well respected and be known for high academic achievement. Alexander had been a primary beneficiary of the school. He was poised to attend an excellent grammar school in England. He hoped to find a school that would begin to satisfy his insatiable quest for learning. His main concern now was to find Roger, and have Roger introduce him to the Captain about the North Star and sailing.

The time finally came when Alexander and the Captain of the *Diamond* spent a few hours together. The Captain was an authority on sailing and ships and came from a long line of sailors. One of his ancestors had followed a map that had been found in Alexandria, Egypt and had been translated from Arabic to English. This map had shown the sailing routes from England to the southeast corner of Asia at Cathay by going East around the southern tip of Africa easterly to the Indian Ocean and then further East to Cathay. This map was like the one Marco Polo used for a land route from Europe to Cathay on his journey. The land journey went through France, through Prussia, through the Turkish lands, through the upper Persian lands, and then easterly through land of the Mongols, and then over the mountains to Cathay. The journey went though many villages and large empires. The sea route to Cathay was much faster by several months but not any less dangerous.

 The captain proudly pulled out his course map for this voyage. It showed the short trip from Tangier to England and there were only a few days that they would lose sight of land or be that far away from the coastline. There were many well established seaports along the way where they could stop weekly to restock their supplies. The winds were usually predictable unless there was a severe storm. There were many marks all over the map.

Captain said, "I hear, young man, that you want to learn about sailing and the North Star. I can tell you many stories about that, but they might be boring. I think if you join me in tea and cake, you may find some useful knowledge."

Alexander excitedly and politely as he shared the meal, "Thank you very much."

The Captain, started, " I used a Jacobs staff, an instrument that has a crossbar and points that is used to measure the angles of the Sun to the horizon during the day and the angles from the North Star to the horizon at night. These angles could then be used to show latitude and longitude on this map. The navigators will do this periodically to adjust their course and stay on course. The trouble with this is that you don't always see the Sun and the North Star because of clouds, storms, or changes in the constellation maps, depending on the month of the year. It is also hard to get an accurate angle on the horizon when the ship is bouncing upon the waves and shifting to and fro. The North Star can be found by the Constellations named Big Dipper, Little Dipper, and the

Great Bear Constellation. The tips of the dipper constellations point to the North Star. A navigator and mapmaker must be able to find every bright star and constellation, so they can improve their accuracy in sailing a big ship. The moon also helps the navigator by guiding them by showing which direction is east and which direction is west. If the moon rises before midnight, then the illuminated side indicates west. If the moon rises after midnight, then the illuminated side indicates the east. If you can draw an imaginary line through the tips of a crescent moon towards the ground, it will point to the south. Most sailors and many nomadic people know this as they travel to keep their senses."

Alexander. "This is very interesting."

The Captain continued, "I use a compass and a device called a quadrant and astrolabe to stay on course. I put on marks on my map so I am usually pretty much on course, but I try to chart a map from the rutters, a detailed map which use the winds, the stars, the constellations to get the most speed from the sails. These marks are considered a mark plotting system passed down from previous sailors and geographers to be used by those who come later to make better judgments in their course selections."

Alexander, " Does it ever get so cloudy for a long time or the map so confusing that you just sail in circles and get lost?"

The Captain laughed, "Not likely young man. I know that most new sailors fear is that they will get seasick or being blown overboard to a watery grave by the winds, or that they will run out of food and water and die of thirst and starvation. This rarely happens. Most good sailors worth their salt could tell you exactly where they are located at any moment on the journey. The days of relying on a Genoese needle to point to the North Star are over and a captains sixth sense is just as good. The days of a sailor following a bird thinking that it is headed for land or following a cloud thinking that it is headed east are over."

After spending a few more hours looking at maps of England and Africa, the sailing Map of the World , a sailing map of the routes to the British Colony to the America and West Indies, and the charts of the constellations, the Captain said he had to resume his duties. In closing, the Captain said, "The *Diamond* has been tossed around by the turbulent sea but it is large enough and sufficient enough to handle the gale winds, running before a trade wind, and sail fairly close, and hauled back by adverse winds. I have marked the trade winds currents on the map for now. You will probably be a fine sailor, if you follow your big brother's footsteps in the Navy."

 Alexander thanked him, and he felt more confident about sailing. He knew he was not ready to think about being a sailor for now but enjoyed the stories the Captain told. They were sailing now so far away from land that the ship was centered on a blue ocean under a light blue, cloudless sky. The sun was bright, and the sea was calm.

Alexander went back to where his mother was located. She looked fatigued and was resting. "Mother, the Captain told me all about sailing and the North Star and how to point out the North Star and some other stars. It was fascinating."

Katherine nodded, "That is good, son." She was very tired was trying to force a smile.

 Alexander, "I feel free like the wind that is moving the ship. There are no garrison walls to protect me and no keeping me locked inside. I feel that we are drifting along on an adventure without any thoughts of time and place. We are on holiday with plenty of food and water. The Captain says we will be in Plymouth harbor soon in a few days."

Katherine smiled and said, "That is good news son. It will be good to be standing on ground again. Go wash up
.60

for supper."

It was getting near second dog watch when the sailors would be seeing the first stars at night. Alexander quickly grabbed a bucket of ocean water from letting a rope and bucket down to the waterline and pulled the bucket back up to the deck. He unhooked the bucket from the grappling hook and poured the water into a ceramic wash pan and washed his face and hands with lye soap. He then tossed the soapy water overboard. When he was finished washing his hands, nature called. Alexander would go to the jardine that was conspicuously out of sight on the main deck.

The Captain had set precise times for the evening meals. After prayer, the passengers and crew would line up for the meal. Tonight, the cook was serving fish that had been freshly caught and prepared earlier that day. It was served with moistened bread and vinegar water. There was not always fresh drinking water, so the shipmates relied on ale, beer, or a fermented drink to keep from getting dysentery or scurvy. After supper, Alexander listened to a few more stories to be amused. He said his nightly prayers and he remembered his mother saying, that no matter how small the prayer or how small the person's voice, The Lord will always here us. Bethia pulled the covers over the boy to keep him warm from the night's chill.

In a few days the ship pulled into Plymouth harbor. Standing tall in the harbor stood Eddystone Light House. It had prevented many disasters at sea because of the warning of shallow water and rocks it gave to unknowing sailors. The proud Captain stirred his rudder away from the lighthouse and pulled up to the quay and set anchor. The passengers soon disembarked. George and Katherine Mercer and Alexander and Bethia would have a new beginning. Roger would continue his orders and sail back to Tangier to finish his assignment of getting all the soldiers and their families out of Tangier and bring them back safely to England.

 Roger had told the Mercers that Plymouth was the largest naval shipyard in England and maybe anywhere else in the world. It was fortified for about four miles along the coast of the North Sea . There were close to 100 battleships anchored at the twenty-five berths ready for battle on the king's order. It was well fortified, and the French and the Spanish had not tried to attack it . There were enough cannons there to destroy the entire Spanish Armada. There were many navy men on the docks to help the new arrivals find their way. George and Katherine would be assigned to the garrison post in Deal on the eastern coast. After several days at Plymouth and after getting there few belongings off the *Diamond*, the Mercers would take a smaller ship to the harbor at Deal. The Mercers soon became preoccupied with the new scenery and surroundings. It was good to have something that seemed extremely solid under foot after having traveled for the last few weeks on wavy and billowing ocean water.

Roger continued to say that about 200 years earlier the Mayflower ships had been built here at the British docks in Plymouth, so the king could use the ships to send some colonists there to settle and colonize the new land in the New World which the enemy ,the Spanish, called America.

Alexander asked curiously, "What is America like? Is it like Tangier?"

Roger smiling, "Not at all. It is more like England than Africa. It is a very large land area and some of the first English settlers were given grants of land of ten to twenty thousand acres of land which is bigger than Tangier, Marrakesh, Casablanca, and Rabat land area added together. Most of the English are wealthy landed gentry with big houses and many servants . The natives of the land are called Indians and are primitive dark-skinned hunters. The Indians live in crude huts made from tree limbs and animal skins. They use tools for farming made from sharpened flint rock and hunt game with bows and arrows. An English explorer named Hilton traveled three weeks up a river from the Atlantic coast and found many fair and deep rivers. The land was suitable for farming and raising horses, cows, and pigs. He made favorable comments about the fish, wildlife, and game. There were large meadows suitable for planting wheat, barley, and oats. There were cypress swamps close to the sandy swamps, but he also noticed that oak, ash, and pine were in abundant supply and good for

homesteading and farming. He recommended to King Charles II, that they settle this part of the new world called Carolina quickly, before they would have to fight the Spanish or French for possession."
Alexander, "Sounds like it would be easy to get a vast amount of land."

Roger, looking impressed, "Before you build your empire, little brother, you had better finish your schooling."
Alexander chuckled.

Roger, sadly, "Before I leave again for Tangier, and you leave for Deal, I want to say farewell for now. I will write you letters."

Katherine, hugging Roger, "I love you , son. Take care of yourself."

George, shaking Roger's hand, said, "Goodbye for now. Looking forward to seeing you the next time. Good luck with Ismail Moulay. Excuse me, I should say, that I pray the Lord keeps you safe from Ismail Moulay. "

Bethia hugged the man she had served faithfully for all the years. She said to Roger as he departed, "I am looking forward to hearing more of your adventures. "

Alexander said, " I will miss you, Roger. You have been more than a brother. We have had such great times together. We walked the beaches at Tangier, we climbed the highest mountain in Northern Africa. You stood up to the pirates who stole my sword. You have taught me so many things. You have taught me how to ride and shoe a horse. Because you, I have learned to avoid ghosts and witches. I want you to keep writing letters to me, and I will write letters to you. Keep watching the stars and have a safe voyage back to the garrison."

Roger said, "I will miss you, too. I will write." Roger started walking down the quay where he would get on the ship headed back to Tangier with supplies. He turned around and waved goodbye. The Mercers and Spotswoods waved back and headed for Deal. They were at least only a little over 200 miles from London and Katherine knew that she would see her daughter Margaret in a few weeks after they got settled. It was late in November and maybe in a month they could see her family at Christmas in London. It would be the winter of 1684 in the name of our Lord and Savior, and it was forecasted to be a very frigid holiday season.

After a few days and getting their feet used to solid ground again after so many weeks at sea, the Mercers and a few other Navy families were transported to Deal by a frigate out of the Catwater Bay using the easterly winds to go to the eastern coast of England to Deal. It was the strongest navy seaport fortification on the English Channel and was used by the English to defend themselves from an attack by their enemies; the Spanish and the French. King Henry VIII had ordered a rose shaped castle to be built there during his reign. He also had ordered defense castles built at Dover, Wilmer, Calshot, Camber, and Sandown. These were villages that were near to Deal. Many armies would find it hard to invade England from the eastern shore. These defense castles were ordered by King Henry VIII in response to how easy Julius Ceaser had invaded England in this area centuries earlier. Even the Romans would find it hard to invade now. The sea was not very deep at the bay in Deal and large ships had no harbor in which to dock their ships. The ships were anchored about ½ mile out in the English Channel and passengers and supplies had to be transported from shore to ship or from ship to shore by smaller vessels. It was very time consuming getting on shore at Deal, but it was in such a strategic location that it seemed worth the trouble for the Navy. There was a sizable army and navy presence at Deal. The Mercer family would adapt to Deal in the following way. George would be the head school master. Katherine would be a happy housewife. Alexander would finish his schooling and pursue a career in the navy. Bethia Spotswood would continue to be a servant in the Mercer household.

The Mercers would get settled in their new home in the garrison. Deal was a very small fishing village in contrast to Tangier which was a large, bustling seaport that was on every trade route in Africa. Alexander would spend his time walking the sandy beaches of Deal , going to the Castles at Deal, and exploring the white chalky cliffs of Dover, a treacherous place to explore high on cliffs overlooking the English Channel. The views were spectacular of the seas, skies, and adjoining green meadows. Alexander would spend many hours thinking about his time in Africa, the knowledge he had gained from Roger and all the stories his mother would share with him. He missed the mysterious and rugged life surrounding the garrison in Tangier, the Atlas Mountains, and all the fishing and hunting trips that he had been on with Roger. He did not miss the constant attacks by the Berbers and Moors on the walls of the garrison in Morocco. He saw the sharp contrast of the nomad tribes in Morocco trying to raise crops in sandy soil to the feudal lords raising bountiful crops on beautiful green covered farms by the English countryside. He found the stories very interesting that were told by the lords when they came to Deal for supplies. He saw plowmen, harrowers, the shockers, and other farm hands explain their plight in life. They seem to be family oriented, and members of the church of England. Alexander liked to hear stories and he found the feudal lords' tales to be informative. He had always lived a sheltered, structured life, and the only fear was being overcome by a renegade Berber warrior. Here in rural England he found that people really had to work hard, plan much, and be weary of everyone. He saw that any failure to learn the lessons out in the fields could cost a person their very life. Hopefully this information would be as valuable to him as the subjects he was learning at the garrison school. Lot of the lords had to be strict despots to get their farm work done in the feudal estates. This needing to survive and thrive went from the noble lord at the top of the estate to the lowest level of dusty farm worker in that they had to do their share of the work for the estate to be successful and survive. One of the first decisions that the country folk around Deal had to decide if their land was out of the swamp moorlands, out of the rolling forest lands, and were lands that were even suitable for farming. If one of the elements of the lord and servant relationship was broken, there could be dismal ending to that estate and those servants. When lords left the estates, the servants and workers even at the lowest levels of the system might become slaves and servants at other feudal estates, but many times if they were not needed, their best defense was to try to escape. This could result in death or starvation. Alexander noticed that cattle were treated the same way. If the lords did not have enough food and hay for the cattle they were often slaughtered, and the meat was seethed to feed the soldiers at the barracks in Deal.

None of the meat of the slaughtered cattle was wasted. One of the lords told Alexander about how they would skin the cow and the skin would be stretched over a fire by the 4 legs tied to 4 stakes with the fur side down. Water would be added to the top or fatty side and would boil because of the hot fire below and when the boiling water mixed with the drippings of the fat making a broth that could be the meals for all the workers in that household. The Lords also told Alexander that winter was a brutal season for the lords and workers on the farms. Many of the farms tried to be self-sufficient in winter as roads and traveling was difficult, especially down on the moorlands. They might have a frozen deer staged on top of a roof of their huts so the wolves, which were their biggest fear, would not get to the meat before the lord and servant had a chance to have a good meal. Many times, hogs and cattle were slaughtered to keep the household going in the winter months. Trying to keep a fire going in a rock- built hut was a tremendous chore. People in the feudal system lived and died by their own efforts. There were distinct chores for everyone. In his case, he said he would set at the tallest and head table. Then there were tables of differing heights, and who sat at those tables depended on what level the workers ranked in the system. The household servants were at the lowest tables. From several lords, Alexander would learn that some of the feudal lords were well educated, or good warriors, or good writers of letters. Some of the families would be well educated as the Lord would hire a cleric to keep the estates books and teach and tutor the lord's family members. Deal had a communal house with a great hall where the different lords and workers would come and exchange stories , laugh and relax. The plowmen seem to have the best understanding of how the other workers felt but usually would not discuss any complaints to the lords who preferred to dine privately away from the noise of the great hall. Each estate had a variety of workers who were specialists and every person completely understood their rank and tasks in the scheme of the system, and they knew exactly what their rights were. Except the slaves which had few rights if any. There were roofers, bed makers, washers of clothes. There were cooks, pantry workers, shepherds, waggoneers, nurses, marshals, stablemen, garners, embroiderers, tenants, free men, indentured servants and clerics and so on. Two servants carried rushes and loads of water in baskets from the water sources to the estate by carrying the water in baskets on a cowl's staff or a big wooden pole between the servant's two shoulders. Every task had an assigned worker, who was made accountable, and they were told their duties and their rights.

One night when Alexander went to the communal house, one of the lords told him about a monk at one of the churches had special knowledge of finances of shipping and trading. He knew every lord in the community and even could tell almost every time where the produce, grains, or animals had been produced, and by which Lord. It had become known as the Cain effect. If a lord took good care of his fields against weeds or took good care of the animals, it would result in higher money being paid by the traders. They would get a better price when they shipped it and traded it for goods in other countries. The monk in turned would ask the lords for bigger donations to the churches and monasteries because of their getting higher prices for the grain. Consequently, if a farmer had a lot of weed seeds in with his corn, or thinly animals for sale, he would get little pay or no pay for his goods. This reminded Alexander of the camel trains in Morocco, and how the shippers and traders had made a lot of profit buying and selling of goods. The monk would get the information about markets, politics, and general information by the king's messenger service. The king had many swift lads who carried letters in a cane so they would be identified as messengers and were usually not harmed. The lads ate and slept little and crossed the many paths of the English island from coast to coast. They would usually run or walk briskly and made a decent living as a messenger. Most were very athletic, and the monk said that would cross the ditches and dykes and small streams by vaulting across to the other side. Many of the king's messengers used horses to carry larger bundles of mails in boysters attached to the saddles in a way that the rider had to be dismounted from the horse before the boyster could be taken from the saddle. This kept it from getting lost or stolen. The monk would sometimes get sensitive information about markets over in other countries so some of the messengers would know several languages, be available for travel, and be able to keep confidentiality . The Lord also told Alexander that some of the lords used this service to get information to other family members in other parts of England. Alexander thought this system would be a good way for his mother to get information to her daughter, Margaret Elliott that lived in London so he would tell his mother about the messengers. The lord told Alexander that the lords try to keep tract of everything going on in their manors and estates, just like the monks trying to help the lords get more money for their produce.

The lord said that there were laws of conducts in how all manor workers would take care of the ponds, the churches, the parks, dove houses, conygarths, and streams. There were rules the shepherds had to follow on how they must take care of their flocks, be accommodating to the miller, must keep his sheep sheared for wool in the summer, and must sleep in the fold with his sheep and sheepdogs. If the shepherds attend wakes, go to taverns, attend church, go to horse races, wrestling matches, cricket games, fairs, or markets, he must make adequate arrangements for someone else to watch the flock while he is away. The dairymaid has her own rules. She must be of clean and honest mannerisms. She must milk the dairy cows every day and make cheese and butter as needed . She is to make cheese and salt cheese twice daily in summer, and make sure the cows get to pasture and get plenty of hay. The plowmen must know how to sew all types of grains and fix plowshares. They are also to be able to light fires for protection against peril and keep the fires burning which is a necessity for the manor. He must be able to take care of the oxen which pull the plow and be able to stay in the barn to be able to keep watch over these big beasts. One of the most important tasks and rules are for the wagoneer who must get all loads of crops to the markets. He must be able to take care of and curry the horses. He must be able to repair their harness, saddle, and bridles. He must be able to fix horseshoes for the horses to protect the horses from split hooves. He must be able to sleep in the stables with the horses and see that the manure is taken care of in appropriate manner. Alexander listened to story after story the different men would tell. He had such an inquisitive nature and the lords treated him as one of their own. Alexander thought about the trading of goods and the markets. Was this the kind of profession that he was destined to be in? Was this the way he could make a fortune after he got out of school and military service? The men seemed to take a liking to Alexander's interests in their work.

The Christmas season was fast approaching, and this would be Alexander's first Christmas in England. He would rush home and tell his mother about getting a message to Margaret, the daughter of his mother, Katherine

Maxwell Elliott Spotswood Mercer. Margaret had invited them to London for the holidays, and Alexander was anxious to meet his half-sister. Roger had told him that Margaret and her husband lived in a very upscale place in England and had become friends with some of the most powerful and wealthiest people in England. Katherine soon got a reply ready to send to Margaret stating that the Mercers and Alexander would be leaving Deal and coming to London on the 24th of December. Bethia would be staying in Deal as she had been sickly and still had not recovered fully from the voyage from Tangier.

The day finally came when the Mercers got the team of horses ready and checked the rigging on the horse drawn carriage. Beginning at the daybreak and the wind was cold from the north, they soon were on their way to London. The road was well traveled, and the way was well marked, and the path was not wider than the carriage and the four-horse team pulling the carriage. The road was sometimes dusty, sometimes muddy, sometimes smooth, and sometimes with deep ruts from previous coaches going to London. The carriage and horses were moving at a brisk pace, and they wanted to make their destination by dusk. Along the way, the Mercers saw some beautiful meadows, rolling hills, and woodlands of the ancient forests of southeast England. They enjoyed the colors of fall that were adjacent to their road. Many of the meadows were dotted with cattle , horses, and sheep. The meadows usually spread with wildflowers, now had patches of autumn leaves that were being shuffled by the breezy winds that were getting stronger. In the summer, the fields were covered by cowslips and marigolds. In the marshes, there were no marigolds or bright lilies of the valley flowing in the woods. In the fence rows there was some hedge crown and white thorn mixed with the rowan and the hawthorn that grew freely and spread over the landscape. Occasionally, they would meet and greet an approaching carriage headed for the eastern shore. The Mercers certainly were riding through the best of God's handiwork in the English countryside. They must have thought how different it was to be riding over the bridges and canals that usually were lined with the prettiest wildflowers, blue corn cockle spurs, bittersweet, mallory, rush, meadow sweet. The harsh wintry air was about all they could stand. Snow was lightly coming down and this was the first time that Alexander had seen white crystals falling from the sky. There might be a white Christmas in London after all.

George began talking about the herb gardens that the farmers and country folks. George knew that Alexander liked reading his father's book on plants and their uses. Sometimes the farmers would sell their herbs to help them with their living expenses. Some of the herbs were dyers whine, soap wort, broom, and lavender. Around a doctor's office you could see an herb called onset and an herb called wild comfrey used to mend bones. Hoar hounds were used for sore throats. Horseradish mixed with cooking grease made a soothing ointment for sores. Rushes were used for scourging. Alexander's dad, Robert Spotswood had always said nutrients come from numerous minerals in the soil which when eaten can help provide needed calcium and sulfur for the healing process and for strong bone growth. Watercress especially was a plant that contained much iron which is good for the body.

The Mercers and Alexander saw many huts and houses along the way to London. Some were made sturdily of stone and rock and brick. Sometimes they were made of timber and wattle and daub used as mortar between the timbers of the walls. The huts were usually small and just tall enough for a man to stand up inside the house . They were usually wide enough so a man could stretch out on his bed from wall to wall. Usually there was a hole in one side of the roof to let in fresh air and a hole on the other side to let air out. This drought type of heating system let the smoke out from the fire below to keep the families warm, keep the foods dry, and for drying wet clothes from the winter rain and snow. These huts were crude but adequate to protect the residents from adverse weather conditions. The Mercers came across an abandoned castle made from stone walls and that was all that was standing. The roof was now just a blue sky overhead and the original roof lay in piles around the stone walls. The once beautiful floors of the castle were now dirt floors with green grass growing in the courtyard and the main ballroom floor. The trees surrounding the castles were growing from where once stood tall trees that undoubtedly had been used for the now rotted floor, floor joists and supporting beams.

Along the way the Mercers stopped at a resting spot on their journey. They ate some of the fruits and biscuits they had packed. They watered the horses in a stream along the side of the road and let them eat some grass to regain their strength. There was a wooden sign that said Maidstone. They knew the town must be close by. Up ahead they could see a huge castle out on a small lake. George said that it was Leeds Castle and once the home of King Edward I. It was now owned by Lord Culpepper and taken care of by his niece, Katherine Culpepper, his only heiress and her husband, Lord Thomas Fairfax. He went on to say that Lord Culpepper was a very wealthy man and was well liked by King Charles II, because of his loyalty to the king during the English Civil Wars. When they arrived at the entrance gates to the castle, the gatekeeper said that Lord Culpepper had been in The New World in the Colony of Virginia for the last two years. He was serving as a colonial Governor. He was not expected to return for several years. Lord Culpepper was taking care of 5 million acres of land grants in northern Virginia in the New World. If Lord Culpepper could get some of the English people to settle these lands, then these new landowners would be more loyal to the English crown. Alexander must have been thinking that this Castle must be the loveliest castle he had seen in his nine years on earth. Alexander was in deep thought about what all the 100 plus servants were doing in the castle, as they performed their household and business duties. Alexander could see at least 12 archers on top of the roof of the castle keeping their watchful eye out for friend and foe. Alexander must have been thinking what it would be like to control 5 million acres of land. After leaving the castle gates, the Mercers preceded on to the village of Maidstone which was conveniently on the way to London. It was a picturesque city on the banks of the River Len. Many people stayed in town overnight on their pilgrimages to the convents and Anglican churches on the East Coast of England at the Cliffs of Dover. There was a church on every corner of the town square. There was a military fort here at Maidstone which was used as a defensive outpost guarding against invading forces which try to capture London. Maidstone was considered a farming and fishing village just like Deal but was more developed , more organized, and cleaner.

The white snow made the Mercers reminisce about the good ole days. A couple inches of fresh winter snow had already fallen in London at The Golden Square where Margaret Elliott Andrews's home was located. The snow made for a winter wonderland and was coming out of the dark gray December sky. In a few more hours the Mercers would arrive safely at the Andrews House on Silver Street close to the Golden Square. There the Mercers could rest, get warm, relax, and getting reacquainted with the Andrews. This snowy white winter wonderland gave a fresh clean look to the countryside and cities. The temperature was getting colder, but the Mercers were happy about seeing Katherine's daughter, Margaret, and they had verily noticed the chilliness in the air. Alexander must have been thinking about all the sights he would see in London. He was seeing an array of grand castles, tall multi-story buildings, wide streets, and thousands of busy holiday shoppers. He could see thousands of homes in which the people of London called their home. It was approaching darkness in the early evening and the candle lanterns that were shedding some light on the streets. They were tired now, as they had started their journey almost 12 hours earlier. Alexander was very tired, but that all changed when his half-sister came out from her doorway to greet her mother, stepfather, and Alexander. She had been anxiously awaiting their arrival. Margaret stopped to hug her mother, George, and Alexander.

Margaret, "It is so good to see you all . Come into the house and get out of this bloody cold."

Katherine, "Yes, dear, and I almost said child. You are now a grown young lady."

Margaret, "Our servants will take care of your horses and carriage" They all went inside and were glad to leave the snow and cold outside. Margaret and her husband had acquired this big old brownstone house down on Silver Street. It had a spacious hallway with staircases that led to three stories, and a door that led into a very large and elegant parlor. On the one side of the room there was a large and welcoming fireplace and mantle with several logs burning to give warmth and charm to the family gathering. One look at Alexander's smiling face, and one could sense that the fire was a cozy necessity. The room was cherry and bright, and Margaret pointed out some fabric covered chairs and Alexander respectfully sat down after a servant took their coats and boots to the hallway closet.

Margaret explained, " We will have dinner in a little while. We dine around 8 o'clock. I hope you will like veal and potatoes and that it will meet with your delight."

George," That will be splendid. Do you mind if we say a blessing on the meal? "
George said a simple prayer, " Dear Lord, Thank you Lord for the great day and the safe journey. Thank you with this reunion with Margaret and her family. Bless this meal and those who prepared it. Thank you for Christ's birth and his resurrection. Thank you, Lord, for all our blessings. Forgive us our sins in Jesus name. Amen."
They all said Amen.

Margaret, " I want you to stay for several days . We have so much to talk about. I want to hear about your life in Morocco, about father's life at the garrison, and your plans. I want to really to get to know Alexander." She could scarcely take her eyes off the young lad.

Katherine looking for approval from George, " We can stay if it is all right with George."

George said, " It is a fine idea. We can spend Christmas together as families should."

Margaret looking at Alexander, "You are a very handsome young man. Roger said that you are a good student and very smart and curious. He also said you descend from an honorable and ancient Scottish family from Scotland."

Alexander respectfully said, " I trust your judgment on the handsome part. I like the companionship of Roger and I think of him as my older brother."

Margaret, smiling, " I want also to be treated like your big sister. With your good looks, you will not have any trouble in being successful in life."

Katherine, explained, " He is getting a good education for now in the garrison school in Deal. George has shown him a lot of books and taught him many subjects. We plan on getting him some tutors to give him some new areas of learning. He likes learning about everything. Someday I want to enroll him in a good college."

Margaret looking again at Alexander, "Roger said that you will probably go into the military like he did and be a courageous soldier like your father and grandfather."

Alexander proudly, "I most likely will."

Margaret, curiously prodding, said, " Mother, you must tell me about Morocco. We hear very little about Tangier except through military friends at church. They say it is a beautiful place of mountains, forests, and deserts but it is a mysterious and dangerous place. "

Katherine responding, " That is true. We came close to our demise several times. The Moors and Berbers were always trying to break down the garrison walls and regain control of Tangier for their leaders. We saw several soldiers' heads displayed on those walls after they were beheaded by the native warriors. I worry about Roger trying to get the last of the English Regiment out of there before they are killed or something worse at the hand of their enemy or by Moulay, their leader. The living conditions at the garrison were adequate, but the natives are very poor and wage war with neighboring tribes most of the time. The Berber children play in the streets and have very little to eat. Morocco is a beautiful place to visit, and I miss the days there in a way. The scenery is like a mask that hides the suffering and sickness. I lost two husbands there which I dearly loved and found George, the love of my life. However, I am glad to be back home in merry ole England with my family and beautiful daughter. "

Margaret, speaking of the past, said," After you and father left for the garrison, many people in our neighborhood died of the dreadful Black Death. The officials said that the plague was caused by the fleas on the rats carrying the disease from household to household. This is hard to believe because so many people died so quickly. I don't think the rats could be that bad. It is almost like it was being carried in the air in a black fog. All the sneezing and coughing didn't help, either. Mrs. Cooper, Mr. Rowland, Mr. Terrell, and Mrs. Ferguson all from the neighborhood had horrible deaths. All were buried in the church cemetery at St. Olave down on Hart Street."

Katherine, "They were all good people. That is too bad. "

Margaret, continued, "Then there was the Great Fire of London which burned down our neighborhood. We will have to go down their sometime. You will not recognize the old neighborhood. Many homes in the inner circle of the city within the old Roman wall were burned to the ground and laid for a long time in ashes and rubble. These neighborhoods were eventually rebuilt. Uncle William's home down by the Thames where I was living was spared by the Lord. He never wanted to tell you about this in a letter, because he did not want you to worry about this since you were so far away in Africa."

Katherine, sadly, " I regret that I did not get to go to my brother's funeral several years ago. But it was so dangerous to travel here, and I wanted to remember him like he was when we were children. "

George had been paying close attention, "Sounds like your Uncle William took great care of you."

Margaret, proudly, "Yes he did , and he introduced me to many great privileges and successful people. It is certainly exciting to be together again. Maybe we can see more of each other now that you are back in England and in Deal. We don't get there very much. Richard travels mostly to other countries. He will tell you all about it when he gets back home. It is time for dinner, now. "

They all sat down to dinner and enjoyed the meal and continued to get reacquainted again. Margaret had described her work for the Jennings family and explained that their daughter, Sarah was one of her best friends. She said that Sarah had married a military man named John Churchill who had also been in Tangier with her father, George Elliott and Alexanders father, Robert Spotswood. Sarah had recently been appointed to the bedchamber of Princess Ann of York, the daughter of James, brother to King Charles II of England. Margaret went on to explain that John Churchill was always loyal to the throne and was one of the country's most accomplished military leaders.

George Mercer said, "That is true. I remember John Churchill from the garrison in Tangier. "Looking at Alexander, "Maybe you will fight with him in England's future wars. God knows that we will be fighting somewhere against the Spanish and the French."

Alexander nodded and was in deep thought about all the history of his family that he was learning. Margaret was not only physically beautiful like their mother, but she was also ambitious and proud. He knew inside that she meant what she said about being a big sister and helping him in life.

Margaret noticed Alexander staring into the glowing hot fire of the fireplace in the central parlor. Alexander seemed to be comforted by the fire as it took the chill off the room.

Margaret, "Are you thinking about Morocco? Do you wish to be there under the warm tropical sun and the feel warm breezes off the Mediterranean Sea instead of dreary, cold London?" The glow of her beauty and her attractiveness were indisputable.

Alexander, sounding very mature, "I think it is better in England. A lot of the people in Morocco are very poor and have very little except the clothes on their back, their farm animals, and their religion. The land is beautiful in North Africa with forests of pine and juniper, mountain tops covered with snow, and fast running , flowing rivers headed for the sea. I am grateful for the experiences of seeing it all and living it all. One time , Roger and I took an expedition to Mt. Toubkal, the tallest peak in northwest Africa. The people along the way were friendly to us because there was no military opposition on our part. We were dressed in Islamic djellabahs so that we did not draw attention. The natives were a curious bunch like anyone seeing strangers for the first time. There is nothing like climbing a mountain or anything that compares with the view at the peak."

Margaret, "It seems so intriguing, Alexander, you know a lot about the world for such a young man."

Katherine agreed, "He always has spent time reading and meeting people. He is very curious about everything. He studies Latin, astronomy, military history, business, religion, and philosophy. He has been spending a lot of times at the guild halls and with the lords of the manors, houses, and estates and how they manage. He has this quest to see how things work and how people feel about their lives. He tries to understand about social status and patriotism. He has told us more than one good story about his findings."

Margaret" I can still remember some of the good stories you told us in your letters before you all left for Tangier."

Katherine, explain the story, said, "Ever since a pirate at sea named, Redbeard put a curse on him and Roger, he has learned as much as one can about real life and real curses. The pirate curse was that they would be rich, famous, and handsome. "

Margaret noticed that Alexander was looking a little embarrassed and dropped his head to look away as if he had been shamed. "I would not pay much attention to what an ole pirate would say. There is nothing wrong about being rich, famous, and handsome. Although what comes with it could come more responsibility for living wisely and the fear of losing your looks or wealth. You and Roger are already handsome, and you can't change that unless by some witches spell." Margaret started to chuckle at her own remarks.

George, who had been listening, chimed in, "Many of the lords tell Alexander for him to be successful, he should prepare himself to head for the New Colonies in America. They have told them that a lot of their families have made a fortune, there. They say that the climate is moderate and have a long growing season. That the resources in America is inexhaustible, and the trees are in abundance, and their enough animals for food from one coast to the far coast. The English in general have done very well in the colonies with their tobacco plantations in the colony of Virginia and the rice and cotton plantations outside of Savannah and Charleston in the Carolinas. Also, in small meadows once plowed can yield bumper crops of wheat, barley, and corn in the virgin sod. The natives that lived there introduced the potatoes to England and all Europe, and the traders made big money buying and selling potatoes. The turkeys that the rich take for granted here in London were brought here from the Americas. "

Margaret" How interesting. I see you have helped young Alexander in his interest in schooling, also."

Alexander, "Do you want to go to America when you get older? "

Alexander pondering for a moment, " I think that if I will go there, it will be after I finish my formal schooling and military training. It would be another great adventure. England is getting very crowded and most of the resources are vanishing. Maybe this is where I will fulfill or end the pirates curse. "

Margaret said, "Maybe, so. May the Lord reveal your destiny to you that the lords have described and if this land is where you will make your living. "

Alexander, liking her interest in his future, said, "I will pray. The lords told me that America is a vast continent with millions and millions of acres of land with very little native population living there. The native people are mostly hunters, gatherers, and farmers. There are some kings in the various tribes, and there are some warriors and slaves. There are no major armies like the French or Spanish Armada. In fact, there is very little resistance to the English settlers, and the weapons are primitives like bows and arrows and knives. The only source of real resistance is from the pesky French in Louisiana and the greedy Spaniards in a place called California. Not all of America has been explored or even surveyed. It is a vast frontier with much game to hunt and many meadows to plow and harrow. Many of the colonists have become rich in their tobacco crops in Virginia. On the way to London from Deal, we saw Lord Culpepper's estate, and he is now governor for the king in that colony. He has millions of acres there to grant to new English settlers. Like London, the new colony has much death and disease like the bubonic plague but for the most part, these diseases are rear there. We can credit the Spanish for introducing farm animals and horses. America, once a land of buffalo and deer in abundance, now is a land that contains thousands of horses, sheep, cattle, and goats. The Spanish mustang is also in abundance and the natives, called Indians, tame these horses and ride them all over the meadows and grasslands and use them in their game hunting. Unlike England where we only hunt for sport, all people their hunt game for survival. "

Margaret seemed fascinated with the story, said, " Please go on."

Alexander obliged by continuing his story, " In the new world, there are no large cities and not many stone or brick roads. Only buffalo, deer, and Indian trails lead the settlers back into the frontier. Then there is frontier that no Spanish, French, or English settler has ever seen. One thing is that there is an abundance of trees, one right after another. One settler said one squirrel could jump from tree to tree for a thousand miles and never have to touch the ground, and there would still be trees." All in the room found this amusing.

Katherine made remarks directed to Alexander. "You are spending a lot of time in the guild halls listening to those dreamers. "

Alexander, a little surprised by his mother's seemingly disapproval, said, "Mother, all I am saying is that wood is used to build cities, galleon ships, furniture , castles, fences, and many buildings. Wood is used for keeping fires going at night and building huts and cottages, and the trees in England are becoming scarce. In America there is an inexhaustible supply of wood which could be shipped to England and someone could make a good living doing this."

Margaret, showing an interest, concluded, "It sounds like they would become rich without very little effort or work. Maybe the pirate was right and that you are cursed to be rich. "

Alexander half listening to his sister, was trying to make the point, " There are trees and animals in North and South America that we have never seen in Morocco or England. We have not even seen their names in Hebrew, Greek, or Latin. The English have been in the New World for about 70 years and are settling much of the land. The settlers have taken barley, wheat, and rye to be grown in the large fields. The colonists have planted fruit trees and started vineyards which has been adopted from the English. "

Margaret asked sincerely, "Do you want to be rich by being a woodsman cutting wood or rich being a farmer?"

Alexander, " I don't think so. I would rather be a land speculator or planter." One of the lords at the guild hall said that even a cow farmer, pig farmer, or shepherd could get rich raising stock when there is so much land. The farm animals eat a lot of corn, and if you understand the corn business you can control the Indians. If there were no planting of corn in America, there would be no culture. The Indians have not offered much resistance to the English colonists so far. The Indians use stones on sticks to dig up the ground and plant the seed. A planter could use metal tools and raise better crops. America is a Garden of Eden with plenty of food for everyone. The colonists have large plantations and have servants and slaves to help their production. Many a slave have been shipped to America for working the crops. Another good thing besides plenty of land, wood, and game, there are plenty of fish in the rivers. Even the lakes are full of fish. One company pulled 750 million pounds of fish out of just one river called the Potomac which is close to Lord Culpepper's land. They not only have plenty to eat but have plenty of fish to sell. I am told that there is not much gold or silver there, but just vast domains of land with virgin sod and timber. "

Margaret said, "Sounds like a place that I could move to also. "

Katherine proudly looking at her son, said, "I told you that Alexander listens to all kinds of people and has a good head on his shoulders. He is such a good student at the garrison school."

Margaret said, "You mentioned a place called the Carolinas, I believe this is a place named Charleston that my husband, Richard mentioned he wants to start a rice export business, there. Maybe Alexander can help him there someday."

George, proudly, "I believe Alexander can do anything he sets his mind to. He is very resourceful and can talk on a myriad of subjects. He is constantly reading and writing. I know we are very fond and proud of him. "

Margaret exclaimed, "I find all the talk on Africa and the New World fascinating. It is like the success of the past and the hope of the future. We can talk more later. And after breakfast tomorrow, I will tell you about our life and my friends in England." Looking at Katherine, " Mother some of your friends are still living down on Hart Street. We will have to introduce Alexander to some of my friends so the curse will continue." She slightly chuckled. "I am also proud of you, Alexander."

Margaret showed the Mercer family and Alexander to their guest rooms. Alexander said his prayers and was thankful to have Margaret for a sister. She was not only attractive but was pleasant and smiled all the time.

After a good night's sleep, they had a breakfast of fresh ham, hash brown potatoes, and eggs. Alexander commented, "This is better than the foods at the navy barracks."

Margaret, smiling, "Eat up little brother. You have some more growing up and more learning before you plan your future." Alexander laughed.

Margaret, keeping her promise, said, "I said last night I would tell you about my friend Sarah Churchill. I was a servant in the household of her father, Richard Jennings, who was a very successful businessman with interests in building, banking, and trading. Sarah Jennings always had money and through powerful and rich family and friends, she was introduced to John Churchill, who is a general in the Kings Army and was very popular with King Charles II, and was a major factor in the success of the Civil Wars and Spanish Wars. They were married and have four children. John introduced Sarah to Princess Ann, niece of the King and daughter of James, Duke of York, the King's brother. Not always being rich, famous, and powerful is as good as it seems. Princess Ann has a beautiful sister, Mary who married William III, the Prince of Orange and he was also her Dutch cousin. Anne and Mary can never get along. Anne could not even attend the wedding of William and Mary because she had smallpox at the time. Anne and Mary fought over friends, status, over religion, over finances, over rank, and I could go on and on with it. It got so bad between them that their father sent Anne to France to live with an aunt so the two sisters would not see each other so much. William and Mary have had no children, and Anne recently married George of Hanover and has had many miscarriages. All the money and the power in the world could not make these two women happy. They have had a lot of anxiety and disappointment in their life. Sarah tells me a lot about the princess's unhappy life because since July, Sarah has been one of her maids in Anne's bedchamber, and this is a very coveted and distinguished honor. The other ladies in attending Anne is Anne Spencer, Countess of Sunderland, Anne Villiers, and Baroness Abigail Moshen. Ann's father gave her some rooms at Whitehall Palace, where the kings and queens conduct the royal business and the palace contains about 1500 rooms and most are empty. It is just down the street from St. James Park, where the kings bird hunt for pleasure and sport. Anne has many servants and Sarah has met a lot of Anne's powerful friends. "

Looking at Alexander, Margaret continued, "Once you are old enough, we will find you a suitable wife. Maybe you or Roger can take over the command of the Queen's regiments when John Churchill retires. I am sure that the kings and queens will reward you all handsomely if you continue to win the English Wars."

The conversation went on for hours until it was late in the morning and teatime. There were discussions on the kings, the soldiers, Whitehall Palace, schools, and Sara Churchill. Around noon, the conversations were interrupted by a knock on the door . It was a messenger delivering a letter. Alexander noticed Margaret demeanor had changed from cheeriness to a look of worry and concern.
Margaret started reading the letter and was frowning. "It is Richard."

Katherine asked, "My dear child, Is Richard all right?"

Margaret answered," Richard will not be home for Christmas. His business took longer to conclude than it normally does, and the weather is worse than normal this time of year in Norway and Scotland. He said that the winds and the currents on the oceans are disturbing and frightening. He states in his note that he will probably not be back until April. "

Katherine empathizing, " My dear child, I am so sorry."

Margaret said, "Many people have said because the summer has been so hot , that this winter will be extremely cold and one of the coldest ever. The creeks and rivers are already frozen over. "

Katherine, trying to make Margaret feel better, said, "Don't worry. Margaret. I know you will miss him, but he is safer being where there is food and shelter. When he is traveling on freezing ocean water many dangers seen and unseen can cause havoc. Alexander's aunt , Bethia, stays with us in Deal . She always said that her father , Robert Spotswood, was gone for many months and sometimes years in Europe, when he did services for King Charles I. This made it hard on the wife and children, but they learned to life with it. Somehow, they managed the day to day living with the Lord's help and grace."

Margaret started smiling again. Looking at Alexander, " Weather permitting, we will go for a stroll tomorrow to Westminster Abbey and Whitehall Palace."

Alexander, looking happy, said, "I think that is splendid!"

The next day after breakfast, Margaret took her mother and George, and Alexander for a short walk to Westminster Abbey. Along the way they saw many tall old buildings, castles, and palaces. Inside one of the crypts in the Abbey known as God's Acre , Alexander saw a memorial chamber which contained, kings, queens, and notable people of England. One of the graves was of great interest to Alexander. It contained the grave and a large monument that was of his great-great grandfather, John Spotswood, who had been an Archbishop of St. Andrews and had served Scotland and England with distinction. He had been mentioned in the letters given to him by his late father. Alexander felt like he knew who he was. John Spotswood's well-preserved tombstone had in-scripted; "He lived 1565 to 1639. Historian of Scotland, former member of the Privy Council. Put crown on King Charles I, 1625." He was buried next to the memorials of the Archbishops of Canterbury.

"I know you are proud of your ancestor, Alexander." Margaret said. "We still use the Prayer Book he helped write in the Anglican Church. "

Alexander proudly said, "I am very proud. I also saw the grave of the father of George Kirke, father of Col. Kirke from Tangier and the grave of Richard Elliott which is your grandfather."

Margaret asked, "Yes, but how do you know?"

Alexander answered," Roger told me about his burial inside of Westminster Abbey."

Alexander continued to look around and was impressed by the size and carvings of the monuments in the indoor cemetery and crypts of St. Benedictine's Chapel and St. Margaret's Chapel. He saw the tombstones for Geoffrey Chaucer, Ann Hyde, Oliver Cromwell, King Edward I. King Edward III , King Edward V., Edward VI and John Milton. and many others.

Margaret, "Very good, we can walk back to my house because the air is chilly, and you don't want to be sick for Christmas."

Alexander replied, "Yes. "

The next day was Christmas and after chatting about the family, they sent down to dinner. They prayed and thanked God for the birth of Jesus. They were a small family but learning how to get along with each other. One of the threads that bonded them together as a family was their Christian faith. Alexander must have been thinking that it was good to have Margaret for a sister. She knew a lot and was very respectful of Alexander's losing his father early in his life as she had lost her father early in her life and their mother being the other common thread that bonded the family together. Their mother's husband, George Mercer was a good man and loved everybody.

The next day Margaret was eager to show off her big city to Alexander and show her mother the things that changed while she had lived in Morocco. She would get one of the servants to obtain the harness and gear to hitch the calash to two of the Cleveland Bay horses that the Andrews owned. They would travel on the main roads of central London and show the sights around the neighborhood where Margaret and her husband lived. The air was tolerable, but a little chilly and two layers of wool cloaks seemed enough to challenge the chilly air and keep the family warm enough to enjoy the best views of London. The heavy dry snow that had fallen to the ground before Christmas had almost disappeared as quickly as it had come. There was still a white thin layer on the city, but it was quickly melting in the bright sunshine. The snow would not interfere with the outing that Margaret had planned for the Mercers.

Margaret told the coachmen to drive the Cleveland Bay horses down to the park nearest to their home. Margaret told the family that Richard and she enjoyed walking the gardens and admiring the flowers that were so beautiful.
As they drew near, Margaret said that this park was part of the land next to Burlington House. Isaac Newton would come out to this park and look at the stars and planets. She went on to say that John Denham, a previous owner, had the house designed like a Palladian mansion but was very large and ornate for a private residence on a country lane. The mansion was planned in the form of a double pile, some 80 feet wide and 50 feet deep, fronting north and south and flanked by transverse wings, each a single pile of some 24 feet by 75 feet where the raised terrace extended between them. The principal rooms were contained in two stores, the first story

being 12 feet high and raised about 4 feet above ground level. The second story having rooms 15 feet tall that were covered with beautiful tapestries and large paintings.

Margaret explained that Denham had sold the property to Richard Boyle, 1st Earl of Burlington. Alexander must have thought the Denham House was one of the best houses he had seen. It was a two-story red brick home dressed in wood and stone in a simple but in grand style. The great house had a row of columns in the front but the columns in the middle of the house were recessed to give a curved line in the front. The estate had very large gates in the courtyard and had a Gothic look about them. You could see the large gardens in the back through an open gate in the red brick garden wall. The lawns were divided into four distinct gardens by great walks and cross walks. There were statutes in each of the four sections of the three-acre garden. The Mercers and Alexander saw the grounds surrounding the house. Burlington Park was now located on the north side of Picadilly Street. Apparently, Burlington House once stood on the south side of Picadilly Street. The street was once called Portugal Street. The name of the street was changed because of a famous tailor named Baker that lived on Portugal Street use to sell shirt collars called piccadilles. Baker's shirts were popular with the gentry and when the street's course was changed, the new name of Picadilly Street was created. Margaret ordered the coachmen to take them to Hyde Park. Margaret explained that this was an 800-acre park, once used by King Henry VIII for deer hunting. King James I let some of his gentry friends hunt there and finally Charles I opened the park to the public. There was a little creek called the Little Westbourne where the royals could leisurely run small boats on the Creek. The family got back into the carriage, and the horses took the carriage on south of Hyde Park to Knightsbridge and galloped on the bridge built over River Westbourne towards Chelsea. Chelsea, a small village, was noted by Margaret as a nice attraction to see for a couple of reasons. King Edward I introduced his wife, Matilda De Brabant to the English citizenry at this place, and there had been a large happy crowd that stood there long ago by the River and wished the King and his bride good cheer. Chelsea was known for a hospital where wounded soldiers and retired citizens go to get well. It had been designed by a famous, London architect, Christopher Wrenn. He had also helped the Earl of Nottingham develop the south side of his palace, simply known as Kensington Palace that had been designed close by to Hyde Park. King James I wanted to set up a college in Chelsea to study the different religions, but he never got that accomplished. Also, Chelsea had a lot of marshes next to the river and the cattle didn't seem to have problems there, but many a person had drowned in the marshes not paying attention to where they were walking. Margaret pointed out a lot of the ditches the Elliott children use to play in when they were young. The landowners around Chelsea had small gardens and would take their fruits and vegetables down to the city markets .There used to be a horse ferry that would take the travelers across the river. The Mercers and Alexander could tell that Margaret was having a good time showing off the attractions.

Margaret had the coachmen stopped and she began to explain the following Westminster countryside. "If one would take this road called The Old Kings Road out into the country, you can get to Kensington Village. Also, over there is the Earl of Neate's Palace. He has cooks that cook doves and pigeons in special ways that could fill the emptiest bellied soldier. The King has had his cook come up to Neate's and train the Kings cooks from St. James Palace. The Neate's Gardens covers over two hundred acres of land. The Earl did a great job on designing this old castle. Over to the right are the five gardens of Mary Davies. She owned five gardens when she married a Grosvenor .The Grosvenor family owned thousands of acres in Chelsea, Kensington, and Knightsbridge. They built many elegant 4 story homes in the Belgravia Village. These houses were unique and elegant in appearance and stood out proudly above the others because they were all painted in a magnolia color. One of the five gardens was named Grosvenor Gardens named after him. At first, they were owned by the Freeholders of Ebury but they were eventually bought by many different owners until they were handed down to Mary Davies . One of the gardens was named Belgrave, and one of the gardens were bought by a man name Pimlico. He was wealthy based on selling tea and selling a brown type of ale which people came from Westminster to purchase, so this road is called Pimlico Path and it goes back to my home. We will go back to Westminster to see The Queen's garden and all the blackberries at the St. James Garden and crosses over Vauxhall Bridge Road. There are many find gardens in Neat and Pimlico. The palace of the Earl of Neate was a large one with many marble columns in the front portico. Once you get into Westminster, we will see Lord Goring's Garden and the gardens that are there and the mulberry trees that are in front of Nottingham Palace. These mulberry trees were planted by King James. There is not much to see except beautiful woods and flowers at the parks."

The carriage came upon Tothill Fields Bridewell which was in the village of Westminster. Margaret described this as a pauper's prison for able body people who were indolent and could not pay their debts. She mentioned that there was a lady who had been jailed there for not paying her debts. The guards found 10 pounds on her when she was taken into custody, and she told the guards to use it to pay the minister when she dies so that he will say a nice eulogy about her life. The name Bridewell was adopted from the name of King Henry VIII's home named Bridewell but was later turned into an orphanage by Henry's son, King Edward VI. They got back in the carriage and came upon the Jewel Tower, Westminster Hall and Palace, and The Edward Tower on the Old Palace grounds. The towers were close to a big wall that separated Westminster Abbey from Westminster Hall. There were moats around the towers, and they were blended into the gardens within the walls. Margaret explained that King Edward III had built these towers to be part of the government and to store all the government records and official correspondence. It had been a source of government records ever since the time of King William the Conqueror, when he established a palace which used to be called Thorny Island. The Edward was a 4-ton bell used to keep time. It was rung every hour so the people at the court would know the time of day. The towers rose high above the palace walls and were made of Kentish rag-stone to blend in with the rest of the Palace. Westminster Palace had at least 1000 rooms. Alexander must have thought this was the biggest building so far that he had ever seen covering some 3 acres of land. Margaret explained there were thousands upon thousands of documents stored inside in the rooms and had all the records of the kings since 1497 and all the journals of the House of Commons and Parliament. Some of the more read documents were the Bill of Rights of England and the official order to execute King Charles I. She said the three-story jewel tower on the Westminster Palace grounds was mistaken sometimes for the jewel house. The jewel house was a separate building further down to central London next to the London Tower where all the crown jewels were stored along with coronation regalia, the Crowns of the King, and any jewels and any gold and silver that belonged to the Crown. This jewel house was always guarded by the Coldstream guards. Westminster was a formidable place but was quiet today because of the chilly weather and not many citizens stirring around after the holiday of Christmas. One of the first houses they saw was Arlington House lived in by 1st Earl of Arlington. He was one of the important committee members on Tangier when he had served as Secretary of State. He was given administrative duties and orders to keep Tangier as a thriving British colony. He was also postmaster general for 18 years and improved the mail service. More importantly he had been deemed a Baron for the last 20 years, so he was very well to do. The house was about 80 feet by 80 feet and had many gardens and courtyards. Alexander must have thought that this was a coincidence seeing one of the Tangier Committee members' homes of the committee that had helped send his father to Tangier and having been in charge of the letter carrying system which was extremely important for communication with family from far away.

The carriage soon arrived at St. James Palace. It was a building built by Henry VIII and two of his children died there. It used to be a hospital but had been abandoned over 100 years ago. Alexander could see the gatehouse on the south side facing St. James Park. It was a six-story brick Tudor building with adjacent polygonal turrets with mock bombardments. Queen Elizabeth would spend the night here when the Spanish Armada would come up the Thames. Charles I slept here the night before his execution. Charles II had really improved the appearance of the park. Lot of the kings would go hunting in the park for sport. Margaret was smiling as she spoke to her mother, step-father and half-brother, "Princess Anne lives here, and my friend Sarah Churchill serves in her bedchamber. The street we are going down Pall Mall which goes out to Charing Cross. Pall Mall undoubtedly must be named after the mallet and ball game."

The coach and horse stopped at the Cross Statute of Charles I which had been only been built a few years. King Charles II ,the son of King Charles I, had decided to honor his father in this way. The tall statute in central London must have been very impressive to Alexander. Margaret explained that this statute had originally been a cross called the Eleanor Cross built some four hundred years earlier by King Edward I in honor of his wife, Eleanor of Castile. It had been standing there in that same spot until about 30 years ago during the English Civil War when it was torn down. About 100 years before, a gentleman named Sir Thomas Wyatt lead a rebellion against Queen Mary because of her pro-Catholic views on the Roman Catholic Church and wanted her replaced by Lady Jane Grey. A thousand defenders of the court put down this Wyatt's rebellion. Conspirators were either hung or drawn and quartered. Wyatt surrendered and he and his followers were punished. Margaret explained the Charing Cross Inn which the center of travelers was coming and going from all outlying areas of the English Island. In front of the inn were numerous inns and taverns where Londoners would come and watch the public beatings of malefactors at a place called the Pillory that was close to the statute of Charles I. This seemed to be social gathering and entertainment center. Margaret pointed to an old house to her right and said, " To the right of Charing Cross is the great Northumberland house which has two huge gardens on either side. "

Margaret explained that in the original layout of this part of London and especially after the Great Fire that most houses and palaces were built on 4 to 10 acres sights along the River Thames along a street called the Strand. On the river side of the houses lots was a big quay that went along the River Thames all the way up to the Tower a couple of miles further in towards the city. Most of the homeowners had stairways or steps from their homes and palaces down to the river usually as a part of a garden or a well-kept meadow.

Then Margaret pointed to the left of Charing Cross at The Royal Mews and said, "These are the royal stables where all the king's and queen's horses and carriages are kept."

Margaret asked the coachman to go on up to Northumberland House. She was using architectural terms that made Alexander curious. The entire family was seeing beautiful scenery and getting a history lesson and all of them seemed to enjoy the family outing. Margaret began describing the Northumberland house. It was one of the grandest homes that Alexander probably had ever seen. It was 162 feet wide facing the street with a turret on each end. The Earl of Northumberland had built this house about 100 years ago out of brick and stone. It had been built by the Percy family, one of the wealthiest and most powerful families in England. Most of the heads of the families had served as either barons or knights. At the top of the central facade was a large golden statute of a lion that was the symbol of the Percy's strength. The most impressive part of the building was the large courtyard in front and door leading into a Jacobean style of apartments for the individual family members. Also, there was a 4-story gatehouse made from carved stone. The house was just as deep as it was long and its garden in the back went further back towards the Thames. Alexander must have been thinking this was the largest and most magnificent home he had ever seen.

The horses seem to like nibbling on the partially snow-covered grass as the carriage stopped. The next house they would stop at was York House, given to the Archbishops of York and used by the Bishops of Norwich.

Margaret explained, " King Henry VIII bought it some three hundred years later and now is owned by George Villiers, 2nd Duke of Buckingham. He has kept the place it immaculate condition from the Italian style gate house to the steps from the garden to the Thames." Margaret went on to say that inside the house, there was a very valuable art collection and over fifty Roman statutes of Caesars, gods, and goddesses. For the first time, Margaret asked the family to look across the river unto the marshes of Southwark. There had been a bend in the river at Charing Cross and the family could now see more of Southwark. It referred to as a borough and part of Surrey County. There were many famous writers including Shakespeare and Chaucer that wrote about happenings at Southwark. Margaret said that there was a great fair held there every year near the Church of St. George, the Martyr. Margaret said she wanted to take the family there sometime.

Margaret said, " Lets walk for a while and stretch our legs."

Margaret looking at Alexander, "Do you like the tour?"

Alexander, smiling, "Yes, indeed. This is a large town with spacious buildings and yards. These people have to be very rich to run these homes and keep them up."

Margaret, "Yes, they are very rich. Some people which disobey the king are usually hung or punished. Those who help the king are rewarded in some way."

She continued, "For example, this next house, The Durham House was once lived in by Sir Walter Raleigh, the writer, scholar, sailor, and statesman. He accomplished many great things by trying to discover the Virginia Colony and his colony got lost at Roanoke Island, but it made it known that gaining control of the New World for settlement was possible. He later went on to be the favorite of Queen Elizabeth, and he was given this house. He was one of the most famous people that London has ever seen. He introduced tobacco as a luxury product from the Americas and had a pipe that was two feet long. He did much to make the British empire rich with the gold he got from the Azores. He did much of his writings from this house overlooking the Thames. He had several sons, but I believed they all died. He soon lost favor with the king, because a friend said he was plotting evil against James I. He was later executed in the Tower, and all he could leave besides his estate was a note saying that tobacco was one of his best friends during his misery."

Alexander was appearing to enjoy this tour very much. It seemed as there were more than just building and architecture but lessons of life, of loyalty, of punishment and reward.

On the way up the Strand, Margaret directed their attention to the left, "This is Drury Street named after Robert Drury, 1st Earl of Essex. There is a Royal theater there that is called Drury theater and has been playing plays there for a long time. This was once interrupted by the Puritan takeover by Oliver Cromwell in the 1650's when they took control of the English government after the Puritan War or the English Civil War. The royalists led by Charles I was opposed by the Puritans called Roundheads, because they had short hair. The Puritans rebelled against many of the established Church of England's policies and they were opposed to other religious groups that did not use the Bible in the strictest sense. The name Puritan means having no pleasure. The Puritans are serious about everything,   about hard work, original sin, and Bible reading. They thought all operas, plays, songs, and art should be abolished so the Drury Theater was closed for several years while the Puritans were in control of the government. When Charles II came back to power, the Church of England became the established church again, and the theater opened with more plays than ever. The audience sat in a semi-circle facing the stage in different heights depending on the individuals highest ranking. The props were on wings and shutters so they could be moved easily, and the benches were covered by a rich blaze. Many of the Puritans were banned and went to the New World in Massachusetts and were better known as Pilgrims. Others went to Virginia and others fled to Holland and then to America. Anyway, we will have to go to plays and productions at Drury Theater."

"This is the Russell house which is a beautiful house, but I dare not talk about it that there is rumor or allegations that the owner has been involved in a plot against Charles II, so we will just drive on by this house and enjoys its majestic beauty," Margaret explained.

They finally got to the Savoy House. Margaret commented, "This was the former residence of John of Gaunt, the fourth son of Edward III, King of England. He has built the finest home in Westminster as he was the richest man of the time because of his marriage to the heiress of The House of Lancaster. It is said that he owned vast amounts of land in every county in England. In fact, he was married several times and had many children. He was also a brilliant knight and fought many wars against the Spanish and the French. Shakespeare gave these words to John of Gaunt's character in the 2nd Act of his play, *The Tragedy of Richard II* which we had to learn in finishing school. It goes like this.

This royal throne of kings, this sceptered isle, and the hand of war,

This earth of majesty, this seat of Mars,

The other Eden, demi-paradise,

The fortress of nature built for herself.

Against infection and the hand of war,

This happy breed of men, this little world,

The precious stone set in the silver sea,

Which serves it in the office of a wall,

Or as a moat defensive to a house,

Against the envy of less happier lands,

This blessed plot, the earth, this realm, this England.

Katherine applauded her recitation by clapping her hands and Alexander said. "What a beautiful part of the play. How do you remember all that?"

Margaret, blushing, " I barely remember it. There is a story that John unintentionally insulted the Bishop of London about some church matter, and the church goers became very unhappy. They came down the streets with fiery oily rags and sticks and were going to burn the palace down. They started by getting some of the elaborate furniture out on the terrace on one of the quadrangles and started a fire. They saw there was a wine cellar there full of wine. John and his family escaped out of the palace and summoned the guards for protection. The rebels from the church started drinking the wine and forgot about the fire and somehow got trapped in the fire and burned to death."

Katherine, sadly, "That is horrible, and I guess the palace was not spared. It must have been beautiful."

Margaret said, "It had many elegant pieces of furniture and many paintings, tapestries, and ornaments from all over the world inside the grand hall which is supported by 12 marble pillars that are 20 feet high. It stood deserted and charred for almost 100 years until the shell was rebuilt and one of John's descendants, King Henry VII turned parts of it into a hospital. The rest has been repaired and restored at great expense. "

Margaret" continued, "We will be arriving at the Somerset House next. It has been lived in by many of the Royals. The present queen, Catherine of Braganza stays here. She practices the Catholic faith in the chapel by the waterfalls, a fountain, and in the gardens. The building has three or four different kinds of architecture which is interesting. You see a chapel, livery stable, garden, and many outbuildings. This was also the palace for James I's wife, and she practiced Catholicism, too, in the chapel. After the Duke of Somerset died, the place has been used mainly for storage or for visiting royals from other countries. Even the army and navy use some of the rooms as barracks for the soldiers."

Margaret said to Alexander, "Please do not drink wine to excess because it will affect your judgment Sometimes great caring comes out of great sharing. Henry made good use of an old building rather than destroying it completely."

Alexander must have thought that his sister cared about him and his future. Alexander could see that they were getting close to the end of the Strand and Margaret said that they were now arriving at the Essex or Leicester House. Tall stone walls surrounded the premises. Essex was a 42 room mansion with galleries, banqueting hall, and a chapel on the grounds. It was named for a Devereaux, Earl of Essex. The great structure was used as a meeting place of the Knight Templar's. This place was well fortified with gates and archers and was protecting something of value. The people inside were trusting in the walls and the gates.

Margaret began her tour, "Alexander. You must trust in the Lord for your life's direction. You see that during this tour many noble men have died for some cause or for someone they were loyal too. Your own grandfather was killed because he sided with Charles I. We might be killed if we stand with Charles II. The only real battle is how we accept our Lord's grace. Bishops used to stay here when they visited the royal courts. The original builder of this home was not liked because he sided with King Edward II. So, he is buried under the foundation of this house. There is a field named Devereaux in his honor. There is a fine garden, stable, and blacksmith shop. There is a deep sloping lane that goes by the house on the way down to the river, and it is called Milford Lane. No one knows how that name was derived. At the blacksmith shop, the owners would collect their quick rents from the business from the previous owners in horseshoes because they were always plentiful and always lucky, worth their weight in gold, and would insure good payments. Towards the north side of the strand was a theater called the Globe and a field where prize fighters came to fight each other for money and sport. Again, they have a sporting event that allows the dogs to bite at the feet of poor oxen. I don't see much sport in that. The crowd gets a little loud and obnoxious especially if they drink a little too heavily. I prefer good old cup of tea, myself."

Alexander for the last several miles you have seen the fine palaces and homes of some of the most powerful and richest people in England and the British Empire. They moved up here so they would not be downwind of the dirty, smelly part of London where they do not smell the smoke from the factories and upstream from the spread of fire. It is a beautiful setting. You have seen that the rich don't always have it so good. There will always be people who do not see things the way you see. You must believe in yourself and work for the good of the country. You are descended from these people but unfortunately you will not receive any of their wealth. You will have to earn wealth on your own. Maybe what these ancestors gave you is the desire and talents for acquiring wealth."

Alexander seemed to be taking in all of the sights and sounds of Westminster Area and greater London, said, " I like looking at all the big houses and castles, but I don't know if I am ready to manage a large household and control vast amounts of land."

Margaret chuckled, "Indeed, maybe someday you will. You are very schooled and mannered for 9 years of age, and I will help you anyway I can, because, you are my little brother, and I love you." Katherine and George smiled because the newly found brother and sister relationship was seeming to go well.

Margaret, "We will go up to see the Monument and The Tower and the Tower Bridge. We will not have time today to go into St. Paul's Cathedral and All Hallows Cathedral, the oldest cathedral in London. "

On the way up to the Tower, they talked about the British museum that had artifacts from all over the world, but they would have to see that at another time, too. This was the museum that Roger had wrote home about in his letter from London when he had stayed with Margaret a few years earlier. They soon drove through a remnant of the Roman Wall where the City of London begins and the royal district of Westminster ends. The road was a well-traveled road but not too many people were about today.

The coach would take them up to Fleet Street and then to Ludgate hill by the church and the prison. They would be headed up to Pudding Lane where the great fire of London had started. Unlike Westminster where the homes were made of brick, Kentish rag-stone and limestone, and materials that were not as capable of catching or spreading fire, the homes in the capital city of London was made from timber and pitch. They were close together and the streets were narrow making everything seem more vulnerable for a fire. They soon got past Newgate Hill area and was at the 200-foot-tall Roman iconic tower called the Monument. It was the tallest structure that Alexander had ever seen. It was in memory of the great Fire that started in the king's baker shop over 20 years ago in 1666. Margaret explained that a baker and his family were awakened in the middle of the night by a neighbor that his house was on fire. The family got out, but a maid refused to leave and therefore perished in the fire. The fire quickly spread. Because it was windy, and the houses were built so close together that the fire easily jumped from roof to roof and from street to street. The bucket brigade began to bring buckets of water from the Thames to dowse the flames but to no avail. The dry summer had made almost everything in sight dry and combustible including hay, tallow, hemp ropes, coal, and timber storage, and the dry trees and grass.

Margaret continued, "King Charles II came down from Westminster quickly and tried to save as many lives as he could and ordered the people to flee for their lives. The fire men tried to use gunpowder to blow up the houses in front of the fire as a firebreak so the fire would stop but it kept going for three days. Fortunately, the fire did not spread over London Bridge or through the gates of the city's Roman wall that surrounded the city but the damage was devastating. St. Paul's Cathedral situated a few blocks away was burned completely down and the fire became so hot that it melted all the lead supports and rooves and towers and spines. There were about 13,000 houses reduced to ashes. Also, 84 churches and 12 great halls perished. There were reports of 100,000 homeless and only 4 deaths. It took a few years, but houses and churches started rebuilding within London's Roman Walls and the economy became better. Charles II who has always been popular and especially with the ladies had almost got blackened and dirty and almost burned to death trying to save everyone else. This monument salutes the hard work of many people of London and surrounding area for overcoming a great tragedy . The church of St. Margaret's on Fish Hill up the road got burned bad, too. It is told that the wives of the fisherman would bring their husbands daily catch up to the Fish Hill Market to see fresh fish every day, but talked so vulgar, that when they went back by the church, the priests had to close the windows and doors so the worshipers would not hear the vulgar language. The saying was stared that the fish are always fresh, but the language is always foul."

They soon had got on the road to the Tower. Around the tower was a smelly moat. It drained into the River Thames which was running swiftly by the Tower. The tower was an infamous prison that was tall enough to be seen in most of London. It had been reported by many people in London as having been full of ghosts and ravens flying around the Tower. They appeared to be more than ravens and were unidentified spiritual messengers. Alexander had remembered the story about the Ravens and wished that Roger was with him now. Alexander saw the seven ravens, but he did not see any ghosts. The Tower was not only the home of the crown jewels but had been the home of Henry III and Edward I. The tower they had lived in was called White Tower but was lighter in color than the present tower. The Tower was designed by King William the Conqueror, who thought the white tower would look more formidable. The prison tower is said to have only executed a few prisoners inside and most of the hundreds of executions over the years were on Tower Hill behind the Tower Castle. The 7 ravens would hardly fly because their wings had been clipped but managed to form a 7 shaped pattern to the curiosity of young Alexander. There were huge cannon barrels hanging over the castle walls and the tower was well fortified.

Margaret said, "Well this is the good, bad, and the ugly which I showed you today."

Katherine and George had been quietly conversing in the coach as Margaret was showing off the sights of her beloved London. Alexander liked her style and confidence and the way she showed pride in her city. He sensed that she would be successful. He was very grateful to her for planting a lot of ideas in his head and for her encouragement. The horses and carriage started back to Silver Street which was a few miles away. They would arrive at Margret's home way before dusk. They were feeling the warmth of the winter sun, but it would not be in the sky much longer as it was setting west of Westminster where they had started earlier on their adventure this day. On the way back, Alexander asked Margaret a lot of questions about London, her friends, and how she obtained her knowledge about history. She had explained to him that it was all the reading that had been required in school. She also admitted that a lot of it was what her friends had told her. Alexander told her that he appreciated the journey around town, and he would read more about the history of London.

George also told Margaret he was grateful about the tour of Westminster and that Alexander had access to the libraries in the garrison school in Deal. George mentioned the fact that Alexander's father wrote books on plants, his grandfather wrote books on law ,and his great-grandfather wrote many books on history and religion.

George went on to say, " Maybe , Alexander will also be a great writer and storyteller. "

Katherine said, " I am so proud of you, Margaret. I knew you would be successful, and I know you will help Alexander."

"Yes, Mother." Margaret chipped in.

Alexander was deep in thought and knew that the trip by St. Benedict's Chapel in Westminster Abbey to see his great-grandfather grave was no accident. He sensed the importance of his ancestors' importance to England and Scotland. He had heard George quote a British writer who said ,"if we do not respect the noble achievements of unknown ancestors, we will probably do nothing to be remembered by remote descendants. "

After a few days stay in London, the Mercers and Alexander were anxious to get back to Deal. They took the same route back through Maidstone, past Leeds Castle and down the narrow road through the beautiful Kent County countryside and arrived in a few days at their home in the garrison. The family had spent one wintry night in a charming country inn along the way as to keep warm from the wind's persistent chill. Bethia, like always, cheerfully, welcomed them home from their family outing and wanted to know all about Margaret and all the sights they had seen. After they all took off their outer layers of coats and cloaks, they settled by the warmly glowing fire and enjoyed tea and each other's company.

Bethia, " I have had the awfullest cough and can't get rid of it. The doctor at the navy hospital can't seem to help me. "

Katherine replied, "I am so sorry. Maybe eat some soup and bread and you will feel better. We may have to get out some of the Scottish herbal medicines to cure you." she said half-jokingly.

Bethia, "I hear it is going to be an extremely cold winter."

George in agreement, " It seems to already be colder earlier in the year than I remember in previous years in England. We did truly have nice winters in Morocco. "

Katherine nodded, "Yes, yes."

Alexander was oblivious to all the conversation and was buried in books in George's library learning as much as
.81

he could about Scottish and English history. Alexander had a better understanding of his destiny and his journey was now just beginning. His dying father's words were now more meaningful in that he wanted Alexander to be the Spotswood that would bring that name into prominence again in history and make it honorable and respected. He must have felt that he was making steps in the right direction by getting a good learning foundation and by meeting Margaret and knew that he could learn a lot from her. He sensed that Roger and Margaret might be two of the keys to his success.

A few months went by after the trip to London. It was in 1684 in March of the year of our Lord and Savior . It was the coldest winter on record that anyone could remember. The North Sea was frozen in most areas outside of Deal. The River Thames was frozen to a depth of 12 inches. Most people were scared to get outside in fear of getting frostbite or freezing to death. On sunny days, the brave souls would get out on the ice and try to find something fun to do to counter the dismal stays indoors. The Mercers had received a letter from Margaret talking about the winter activities in London. She stated that there were frost fairs in which the skaters and children would ride their sleds on the ice. Others would play pall mall, cricket, ten pens, or ball games out on the ice .There were circuses and food booths on the ice. One of the families named Chipenwell started showing animals like horses and elephants doing tricks on the ice having no fear that the ice might break. Some vendors would bring the bulls, goats, and sheep out on the ice, and the crowd would watch the bull baiting with the dogs biting on the bull's legs for amusement. The ice was frozen for 2 months. King Charles II even took a walk across the frozen Thames from his palace to Southwark and bought a souvenir card which said, "you have received a card from the Frozen Thames." Along with all the merriment in the streets and on the frozen rivers, lakes, and seas , there also was the day to day risks of survival. All the fireplaces and stoves were burning wood and coal, and the smoke was billowing out of the chimneys so thick that it was hard to breath and even see the skies above. Animals had trouble finding food and water under all the frozen ice and snow and many starved to death. Shipping of goods and food, sugar, tea, and tobacco from the colonies were delayed and there was a scarcity of some items. Katherine, George, Alexander and Bethia had it pretty good in Deal and was able to keep warm and fed at the navy garrison. In Margaret's letter she wrote that Richard had been delayed another two months in Norway from the ice storm. The Mercers also received a letter from Roger that had been sent in December that they finally received in April saying that he was almost finish evacuating the final group of soldiers out of Morocco . Roger and the men tore down the mole and the harbor. He wrote that it did not take long for Moulay and his warriors to take control and regain Tangier for the Berbers. Roger had been reassigned to Flanders with his regiment. This would be a good country for him to serve in and it was closer to England.

Bethia, who was a great aunt and always a faithful servant to the family kept growing weaker and wearer and her cough was worsening. The cold weather took its toll on her and she succumbed to the sickness. All the doctors in Deal said that there was nothing much they could do and Bethia died in late spring. Alexander and the family were devastated. Bethia was a quiet one and never interfered in the raising of Alexander but told him about the Spotswoods and their home in Scotland. He felt as if it had not been for her, he would had very little connection to the Spotswood family. When the weather got better, her remains were transported to Darsie Castle, the one sacred place where the Spotswoods considered their ancestral home. Alexander must have felt that he had lost a faithful companion as she would spend hours with him reading and writing and helping him with his homework in the garrisons in Tangier and Deal. He would certainly never forget his aunt.

George Mercer kept his word and assisted Alexander with his studies. He promised Alexander that he would learn everything to be successful.

George, looking at Alexander, "You will have enough knowledge that you can be a doctor, lawyer, president of a college or king of a country. "

Alexander, " I would like that. I find history very interesting. I must be able to read complicated manuscripts and write meaningful letters to be successful. The prayer book written by my great grandfather is very impressive. "

Alexander read book after book on science, astronomy, history, law, medicine, poetry, and military strategy. He found reading books on leadership and war to be fascinating. He studied many subjects from the books in the library. George taught him how to write messages and how his letters could convey clear statements to the readers and recipients. George would always say that the world is full of halfway written letters and inefficient dialogues. The listeners only listen halfway which makes for confusion between speakers. Sometimes it sounds like people who do not put the right kind of emotion or time into their letter writing are just writing and speaking to hear their head rattle. George would teach Alexander to write a letter which would entail fact, feeling, and reasoning to get response. Alexander would then say he could get facts, but it was harder to express opinions because of his lack of experience.

George to Alexander, " Put the known facts in your letters and tell people how you feel about the facts. Then ask the readers how they feel about the facts. This will cause them to act. This is an important lesson that you can practice now and for the rest of your life. Alexander, you will be able to get people to take some course of action when needed. "

Alexander, "Thanks for this training."

News traveled across England that King Charles II, the merry Monarch had died. It was a shock to George ad Katherine Mercer. The king was only 54 years of age, and he supposedly had a mysterious bout of apoplexy.

George said affectionately, "Charles II had been a good sovereign and lead a noble fight against bubonic plague, the Great Fire of London, and successes in domestic and foreign policies. "

Charles II would be succeeded by his brother, James II, a Roman Catholic.

George, "Parliament will suspect James II, the successor, of being pro -Catholic and pro-French. I think he will want religious liberty for all."

Alexander, "I think it would be a great thing for someone to worship as they pleased. And not forced to do so a certain way ordered by the king."

George, "I see you are learning the facts and expressing your feelings. This is good. We have practiced mainly the Church of England faith and it will always be there."

In a few months, Katherine received a letter from her daughter, Margaret in London. She wrote about all the family matters but at the end of the letter stated that James II was not the most popular king, but he had given some rooms to his daughter Anne at Whitehall Palace and her friend Sarah, would continue to be one of the ladies assigned to Anne's bed chamber. Along with Ms. Mashon, Ms. Spencer , and Ms. Venables.

In the letter, Margaret wrote that Roger was appointed to the Queen's Dowager of Foot, under John Granville, 1st Earl of Bath. He would mostly likely join in a rebellion against James II with James Scott, the Duke of Monmouth, the illegitimate son of Charles II who thinks he should be king. Roger will be fighting with Sarah's husband, John Churchill, who had been known to the Mercers since the early days at Tangier. Parliament is in favor of getting William of Orange and husband of Mary, the daughter of James II, to be the king. Nothing is coming of this yet, but it is perilous times, and we must be careful of our allegiances. Margaret stated that Parliament may be waiting to see if Monmouth succeeds.

George after hearing the news, " It is interesting how this will all develop."

In a few months John Churchill's forces defeated Monmouth. James II retained his crown but was getting more
.83

disfavor from his family and the public every day. James II's daughter, Mary seem to think her husband, William of Orange would make a suitable King of England. William was gaining more favor in his Dutch Republic and very popular with the English citizenry. In a few years, unbeknownst to Roger, he would be called on to attempt to get William of Orange , leader of the Dutch Republic elected during the Glorious Revolution. William now was referred to as King William III of the Dutch republic wrote a declaration at Hague which would establish the laws and customs of England which he felt James II had altered, ignored, and annulled in favor of laws and customs favoring Catholicism. The declaration would maintain all the laws and customs and above establish the laws and religion of the worship of God as Protestants. William saw that his father-in-law was not making any concessions to the Protestants and began to gather an army to take over England which he felt his wife, Mary had a legitimate claim to. Williams naval fleet consisted of 40,000 fighting soldiers, 500 navy ships, and 11,000 war horses. They had 28 cannons on the ships, plenty of supply boats, and fishing boats.

The day would come when William decided to lead the charge and take his fleet to the English coastline. He decided to chance the stormy weather in the North Sea and fight the turbulent waves to bring his war ships to the English Channel through the straits of Dover. He had decided not to invade at Plymouth because it would be hard to navigate the ships in the waters and the strength of the English Navy was headquartered there.
Alexander had received a new letter from Margaret saying that James II did not know what to do about the upcoming invasion. And that he somehow thought the winds of God would soon blow the overthrow of the government away, and the whole threat would somehow blow over. On hearing that the army at Deal had been put on hold and high alert, and while James II was making decisions on how to handle the overthrow, Alexander went on to the highest white cliff at Dover to see if he could see the navy of King William III coming down the straits of Dover.

By this time even the French government was helping to finance William's invasion of England. His stakes were getting higher, and the war more inevitable.

Alexander on the cliffs of Dover saw the fleet coming down the channel. It was an impressive sight.
He saw 25 rows of 25 warships symmetrically across from each other letting the wind and sun move them freely in the blue turbulent waters. It made for a beautiful formation. For miles and miles and hours and hours the ships were headed for an engagement in England. The Dutch soldiers were saluting the coastline as they were sailing. There were bands playing music and marches and the soldiers were in a festive mood. Occasionally, they would fire volleys and salute their King William III for his leadership. They seemed to know that their goal was to liberate the Island of England from Catholicism, and that William would return England to the once familiar laws and customs of the Church of England.

Alexander must have worried that Roger would have to fight against these men and might even lose his life. William III must have thought his army strong enough and large enough to defeat the strong English Army.

King James II showed his reluctance even more about preparing for war by appointing Earl of Feversham as Chief Commander of the English forces and declared that King James II's newborn son would take over the throne if something happened to James II's kingship.

Margaret had sent another message to the Mercer family that Anne had decided to side with William III, her brother-in-law instead of her father, because she didn't like the selection of her baby brother as the next king of England. General John Churchill had switched allegiance to William III because of his being oversighted as the Commander in Chief. Sarah Churchill had informed Margaret of all the changes in allegiances. Margaret went on to say that Roger was in good health and spirits and had been promoted in the Bath Regiment. She also mentioned that there was a rumor that James II had already arranged to exile to France.

William III on schedule invaded at Wincanton and Torbury and was marching directly to the Castles at

Westminster and London. He found little opposition and mostly deserters. It seemed like England would have a new King and Queen without much resistance. Lord Winchester and Parliament prepared for the transfer of power from James II to William and Mary. The new rulers would move to Westminster to live and would be close to Anne and her rooms. Margaret stated that she would write more later. Later when it became official of the new rulers' ascension to the throne, they would move to England.

King William III and Mary did not want to live at Whitehall Palace as it was too close to the river and William thought the moisture in the air adversely affect his asthma. They moved into Kensington Palace but went to administer the royals' business at Whitehall.

 The other countries and some of the opposition parties would challenge King William III and would sometimes challenge England militarily, but William would prove successful in his battles. He won the battles of Derry , Bantrey Bay, and the Battle of Boyne. William personally led the charge against James II and the French at the Battle of Brabant and Battle of Killenkrankie. William worked on a New Bill of Rights when he wasn't defending the English against his distractors.

Alexander and the Mercers would be positively affected by the new leaders. They had always enjoyed the barracks life and going to the Anglican Church on Sunday and learning and reading. Everything they had heard about the new regime would not change that. Alexander would read books by John Locke, John Milton, and Jonathan Swift to occupy the time. He occasionally would go the he guild halls to keep up to date on farming produce and trading.

Margaret stated in her letters that Queen Mary had upset her sister Anne, by having their own uncle, Henry Hyde, a very honorable man, indeed, and Sarah's husband , John Churchill were arrested on suspicion of treason. It had been rumored that they had tried to stir some public support for the return of James II to the throne. This was not true, and the court dismissed the charges against him. In John's case they kept him in the Tower for a while. The court of public opinion was so much in favor of John and so much against Queen Mary that John was released from the tower prison. This pleased the citizenry because they knew he handled many successful campaigns on the Battlefield. Queen Mary recognized this and gave him an earldom.
Alexander must have been thinking that for a monarch to be successful, he must get the facts and listen to the wishes of the populace.

Margaret went on into her letter that Queen Mary wanted to establish a college in the new World in the colony of Virginia so the wealthy planters could have a place for their children to learn basic reading and writing and the history of England.

Queen Mary got sick with a fever and missed church Sunday for the first time in 12 years. She was normally fit as a fiddle and walked the long distance from Kensington Palace every day to Whitehall. In fact, she was so sick she could not visit her sister Anne, who was also sick with a miscarriage. When they finally got together, they got in argument over power, finances, Sarah, and vowed never to speak to each other again. Apparently, Mary thought that Sarah Churchill to be a gossip and tried to influence Anne too much. Alexander always liked hearing about the events in London via Margaret. The letter he read made him really think.

Margaret had written another letter and stated Queen Mary has died of smallpox. She said Roger had come by briefly one day, and that Percy Kirke had just died also. He had been one of the Governors at Tangier. Roger also said that Redbeard, the Pirate, had died at Sea and his ashes were spread over every sea in the world. Alexander must have thought this good news about Redbeard, but he somehow felt that the curse he had put on him many years ago did not die with Redbeard. Roger also had told Margaret to say that when he was in France fighting under Churchill with the Grand Alliance of the Dutch, they went into cities that people had died from the famine in biblical proportions. There were not many crops because of the war, and then there were the droughts. What food they had; they gave to the soldiers first. He said that the truth will never be known but about two million people have died in France from hunger. Also, there were similar famines in Russia and Finland. Roger reminded us to get a cellar full of food, so we will not perish if famine comes to England.

In the spring of 1695, in the year of our Lord and Savior, George Mercer died suddenly of a fever. He was 65 years of age and had lived a good life. He left a very nice inherited estate and money enough for Katherine and Alexander to live off and moved to London to be closer to Margaret, the only other family that Alexander knew in London. Margaret helped them find a nice place at the Golden Square between James Street and St. Johns Street in Westminster close to the area and Bleak Street where Margaret and Richard lived. George's memorial service was in the Anglican Church Cemetery in Deal. He was later buried in his home church's cemetery in Ireland. He had taught at the garrison school for 10 years and had spent that many years and more teaching Alexander every subject one could imagine.

Alexander mourned the death of his stepfather for a long time. His father, Robert Spotswood had been a kind and loving father also although he barely remembered what he looked like. George had given precious and unselfish time to Roger and Alexander. George had taught them about living, about life, about purpose of life, and about the love of God. Alexander would cry about this secretly and must have felt that he had lost part of his own life. He once had told Roger that he knew that George had unconditional love for them.

Katherine and her son arrived to begin the next chapter in their lives in summer of 1695. They moved into a house on Golden Square. This house had been selected by Margaret as one of her favorites, and it would be nearby her house on Bleak Street. Golden Square was a well-known square of three-story houses that surrounded a courtyard in Westminster that was formed around St. John's Street and St. James Street. The houses were three stories high and three windows wide. Katherine and Alexander's house was built of three stories and brick and had a raised band between the two lower stories. It had a modillion ease corniced below the steeply pitched roof. It had flash framed sashes with plain openings and flat gauged arches. The door case had a beautiful scrolled ornamentation around the frame. The roof had three casement dormers. There had been oil lamps on tall posts by the street so the homeowners could see the front yard. Many of their neighbors would come out in the evening in the lighted yards and tell stories or play musical instruments. Behind the house was large fields owned by a Mr. Burlington. He had no interest in selling his land for the rapidly growing population. Alexander would come out late at night and look up into the nighttime sky and look for Sothis his personal star. No matter where Alexander went, the star seemed to follow. Alexander had heard from the neighbors that a Mr. Flamsted had discovered Uranus , a planet, after several years of study. The neighbors encouraged Alexander to keep studying the stars because of their beauty and mystery. They also told Katherine and Alexander that the houses were well built some 30 years earlier by a Mr. Crosby and Mr. Tyler and that many types of families had come and gone out of the neighborhood since then. There had been tailors, soldiers, actors, hay traders, salesmen at the stores on the Strand, sea captains, ship builders, and many of the workers at Whitehall Palace and St. James Palace. There were a mixture of the gentry and well to do people. Presently, there was a widowed duchess, a painter, army officers, a writer, a singer at the local opera house, a widowed peeress, a baronet, a knight, and a Mrs. Brown who worked with Margaret's friend, Sarah for Princess Anne.

Alexander liked this place as he got to ask his neighbors lots of questions and learn their opinions. In the summertime there would be large gathering of the neighbors in the square arguing about the affairs of the Whigs and Tories. It would sometimes be drowned by the musicians who would play their trumpets and other musical instruments in the gardens and in the courtyard square. Amongst the residents at the Golden Square was a painter who used his talents by painting the landscapes around the beautiful neighborhood. The scenery was very pretty, and the painter sold a lot of his paintings of the Golden Square and this made the square even more well known.

It would be during the next few months, Alexander Spotswood, now a young man of 19 would soon have to make a living for himself and make an honorable name for his family. He felt his mother was doing better. For a while it seemed she would just drift off and stare into space , grieving over the passing of her husband. As the days passed, his mother, Katherine Mercer seemed not to daydream as much now. She seemed happier now that Margaret lived close by and they were getting closer by sharing more family time together.

Alexander decided that he would follow the footsteps of his father and grandfather and become a soldier in the English Army. He must have thought his half-brother, Roger Elliott would be proud of this decision. He could receive the best of training in London and be able to study at night. Alexander enlisted in the army and became a well-trained soldier in the Queen's Dowager regiment under John Granville, 1st Earl of Bath. For the next few years he would get the best military training in the most powerful army in the world. He could practice working out the fields used by other platoons near his house at Golden Square. Alexander worked hard at his training and became one of the best cadets in his brigade. He learned several foreign languages including Latin , French, and Spanish. He also took courses in military administration, accounting, and letter writing. He delved into all the subjects and was determined to master them. There seem to be some unknown spirit driving him. His grades were good. When he was not in training, Alexander and his mother would go the Church of England up on Silver Street. He would ask the priests to say the liturgy in Latin and he would practice speaking Latin and then try to explain what the verses meant. Alexander liked serving in the army in London, the military and commercial center of the empire. He would have a much better life here than he would have in Tangier or Deal, England. He would have more choices in food, shelter, and employment in a large city. He could attend more sporting activities and theaters and see various performers in every field of entertainment. On one occasion, Alexander got to visit the British Museum which his brother, Roger had told him about. There were all kinds of artifacts and art in the museum from almost every country in the world. There were special collections of cloth, decor, and sculptures from Europe, Asia, Africa, China, and the Colonies. There was also artifacts and tools, Indian items from East Indies, Canada, and the Americas. Each item told a story of its origin and importance in history.

Other times, Alexander would go into the theaters. He especially favored the shows on Drury Street and Lincoln's Square. He particularly like the plays, "Loves Last Strife", "The Bachelor", and a "Way with Words" by John VanBrugge. He liked the play "The Way of The World" at the Queens Theater in Dorset. He particularly liked the "Fairy Queen" by Henry Percival, and Shakespeare's, "Hamlet". Alexander also like the ease of aces to the libraries and there was no limit to how much literature, poetry, and prose from all over the world. He must have thought that London is a fantastic learning environment for a curious young student. He was building the foundation to become a well-educated, cultured, and successful man.

Margaret was very busy with her job with Sarah Churchill and her own household duties, but she could now visit Alexander and her mother more often. She just lived a few streets away. Her husband, Richard was seldom there, and she had no children to raise and occupy her time.

Alexander speaking to Margaret, "I will be getting my commission soon in John Churchill's army."

Margaret replied, " You sure are working hard to get your commission."

Alexander remarked, "Anything that is worth anything is worth working hard to get."

Katherine said, "We are proud of you and Roger. "

Margaret smiling at Alexander, "Since you are a smart and handsome young man, I can introduce you to some eligible ladies and one of them will want to marry a career army man. "

Alexander politely, " When I go wife hunting, I may seek your advice. Until that day, I will get busy in my career and then pick one of the beauties myself."

Margaret couldn't help but find that amusing and chuckled respectfully for Alexander. When she contained her composure, Margaret said to Alexander, "There are not too many women like our mother who loved and stayed faithfully by three different navy husbands. "

Alexander, "Yes, I would like someday in the far future a wife like my mother. Right now, I feel my duty is to take care of my mother. "

Margaret said, " It does not hurt to look at pretty fashionable ladies. Don't tell me that with your handsome looks, Westminster girls do not flirt with you. "

Alexander smiling, "I do see them, and occasionally I flirt back, but I don't want to lead them on. Everything is open and up front with these women. I want to be truthful with them, and this will make for a better life for them and me."

Margaret responded, " With your religious upbringing I know you will do the right thing."

Alexander added, "I have to get my military career started and my job started before I can marry and be able financially to provide for a wife. "

Margaret being agreeable, said, "You are practical. I thought a pirate said you would be cursed and rich. I would remind you that you might put love somewhere in that plan and love your wife. It would be better if she also loved you, too.

Alexander retorting, "Why of course! The pirate curse is always in the back of my thoughts, but I haven't felt the curse of being rich yet." Margaret chuckled.

One evening, shouting could be heard on the street on St. James. Alexander rushed out of the house. Whitehall Palace was on fire just down the street and they could see the tower of fire rising in the air from their vantage point. There were some crowds of people in the street that remembered the scary Great Fire of London of 1666. Alexander, Margaret, and Katherine ran down the street to Whitehall to see if they could help in any way. The smoke above Whitehall was billowing up in the nighttime sky. The fire department which had been formed a few years before could see the large task ahead of them as this was a gigantic building with over 1000 rooms. The fireman and their limited equipment were no match for the out of control fire. The people started a bucket brigade to carry water in buckets from the Thames, but it was too late. All the residents and employees of the palace made it out of the burning building safely. Everything in the palace was destroyed including all the art and sculptures. One painting of noticeable loss was a valuable Michelangelo painting.

Margaret was remembering this is where Charles I slept before he was hung, and Charles II died of a stroke. All the busks of the kings and queens that had aligned up in the great hallway were destroyed. The Chapel that belonged to the palace grounds and was located adjacent to the palace was also destroyed. It had been built only 10 years earlier after having been designed by the well-known and well like architect, Christopher Wrenn. Margaret must have been thinking that this must be a Protestant curse. Others might think that it must be a Catholic curse.

Katherine reflecting, "All we can do is to pray that God's will be done. We don't always know or understand why things happen the way they do. "

The only thing that survived was the banqueting hall that was across the courtyard and the wine cellar on Downing Street. The White Hall fire caused a physical loss and emotional loss for the country. Alexander, Katherine, and Margaret sadly returned to their home knowing they had not been able to do much. The burning of the King's palace would be a well-remembered event in the history of England. The building could be restored but the enormous loss of papers, paintings, and sculptures were immeasurable.

Alexander and his mother continued to live and enjoy the best of London. In 1702, the sad news came that King William III had died, suddenly, and there undoubtedly must be a succession plan that would be made known to the English citizens. This would be a chance for Princess Anne to become Queen. One thing in her favor was that she was a Protestant, and the Bill of Rights spelled out that she was the most likely successor to the throne of England.

On hearing the news, Alexander said, "How did King William die?"

Katherine answering, "He had a bad fall from his horse on the way back from Chelsea. His horse spooked at a sudden noise in the bushes. The king, usually, a very good rider fell off the horse onto the ground and broke his collarbone. He then got pneumonia while healing and died. You know how he always said he could not live close to the river because of his breathing problems. "

William had been preoccupied in his last days about preventing a potential famine in England. Already in Finland a third of the people had died because there was no food. He also wanted to bring a patent to the Parliament from the Royal Society. The patent was a steam pump that was designed by Thomas Morley that would make it easier to get water out of the coal mines. This would help the 700,000 coal miners get water out of the mines and would increase the production of coal which was already 80 per cent of the coal mined in the world. This would greatly affect the economy of England and make for better working conditions for the miners."

Alexander responded, "That is too bad. He will always be popular because he wanted people to worship as they pleased and for his military successes at Boone and Droghelda. He made the English and the Dutch proud. Isn't it ironic that he was William III of Orange and William III of England? He will always be respectfully remembered as Good King Billy."

Margaret came over one morning at teatime and wanted to discuss the change in administration. Margaret said, proudly and excitely, "Mother, Sarah Churchill is inviting us to the coronation in a few weeks. Are you happy for us?"
Katherine gasped, "Forevermore! She really doesn't know us that well. Are you sure you want us there?"

Margaret smiling, "Why, yes, Mother. It will be so glamorous and regal and fun. You will see the most distinguished people in England and ambassadors from the other royal courts in Europe."

Katherine pondering in her thoughts, said, "My biggest issue is that I don't know what to wear or have anything to wear."

Margaret excitedly, "I will take care of that! Oh! mother, are you excited?"

Katherine responding, "Yes!" She started daydreaming about what was about to happen.

Alexander had been listening very intently. Margaret looked at him and he said," I don't know what to say."

Margaret, you can start by saying, "Thank you Margaret for thinking of us."

Alexander blushing, "Forgive me, dearest sister. I am thankful for the opportunity."

Margaret said," Alexander, please wear your best military uniform to impress the new Queen and the pretty
.89

ladies that will be attending. You might find your future wife there. You will probably be the most handsome man there. This is a special night for the Churchills and Sarah will be planning it to be the best coronation that England has ever seen. I did enjoy teatime and I must be running again. I will see you later. Love you both." Margaret then kissed her mother as she left the house.

One day in March of 1702, the Coronation of Queen Ann would make a large difference in England and little did Alexander know she would indirectly help him later in his military career and business. It was a sunny but chilly day. The ceremony that had been planned by John Churchill and Sidney Godolph of Parliament was about to begin. Alexander, Katherine, and Margaret had just arrived at Westminster Abbey and were taking their seats with the gentry and the nobles and royal family members. Outside of the Abbey, there was a large crowd of London citizenry that wanted to be a part of the historical day or maybe had come for curiosity sake. The crowd was peaceful, and most people believed that the policies that William had started or believed in would not be reversed or changed by Queen Anne. After the ceremony, General John Churchill would go the Royal Court in the Netherlands, England's long-time ally against the French, to confirm that nothing had changed at the court except the name of the new leader and the Dutch could count on England as always.

Queen Anne was coming out of Kensington Palace where she had lived temporarily during the few weeks while there was the transition from princess to queen. Some of the time she had stayed in her long-time home at St. James Palace. Her rheumatism was so bad she could hardly walk so she summoned her aides to get her some yeoman to carry her to Westminster Abbey. Her husband George was walking by her side as she was being carried. She had a ruddy face, was short, and stout built. The beautiful and demanding Sarah Churchill was behind Princess Anne giving instructions to those in the company. It appeared to on lookers that Sarah oversaw the coronation instead of her husband and Parliament.

Anne had already saw to it that John had received a Dukedom which some in the crowd might say was because of Sarah's constant influence on Anne. Anne was dressed in a crimson cloak which was adorned with jewels and precious stones of all kinds. It had lace of real gold and silver and she had rows of diamonds in her brown hair. Alexander must have been thinking he had never beheld such a sight.

The coronation soon began when she had the yeoman drop her down to the ground so she could walk into the ceremony, out of sight of the crowd just outside the great hall where the guests were waiting for the ceremony to begin. She hobbled in and smiled at everyone and raised her hand in a triumphant and welcoming way. After she sit down at the queens table and throne, Thomas Tenison, Archbishop of Canterbury crowned her with a gold imperial crown covered with hundreds of sparkling diamonds which sparkled brightly under the candlelight in the Abbey. This crown would signify her absolute authority over every English subject in her empire. She also had golden armill bracelets wrapped around each arm. Her coronation mantle was made from ermine. She had been wearing the golden ring over her white gloves to signify her marriage and complete devotion to her country. She was wearing a dalmatic linen styled tunic and a colbium sindonis, a sleeveless white linen shift worn during the coronation ceremony. She had the scepter of the cross in her left hand and the scepter of the dove in her right hand. There were five guards behind her, each one carrying a coronation sword. One of the jeweled swords was of justice, and one was of mercy. Another guard was carrying a golden orb that had been used by her uncle, Charles II, in his coronation. The orb had a round golden sphere on one end signifying Jesus's dominion over the world and the Queen as defender of the faith. At the head coronation table were beautiful golden tankards with ladles, cruets, glasses, patens, chalices, and platters. One of the patens was used to hold the Eucharist bread. One of the silver platters had an engraved scene of the Lord's last supper. On the altar, there was an ampule, a holy flask of anointing oil, and a maundy plate to hold holy water as part of the service. On the mantlepiece in the great hall room were golden garniture vases used in decorations. All around the table were altar plates of gold and silver.

 The coronation service soon began. A prayer was then given by John Sharpe, Archbishop of York, and then he gave a dedication sermon based on his reading of King James version of the Holy Bible in Isaiah 49:23." And Kings will be thy nursing fathers, and their queens thy nursing mothers, they shall bow down to thee with their face toward the earth and lick up the dust of thy feet, and that shall know that I am the Lord, for they will not be ashamed that wait for me." Then George, Anne's husband, and also her first cousin, paid her homage and said he would be a faithful husband and a loyal subject. Alexander waited patiently as the closing prayer and blessing on the food in the dining hall had been blessed. There would now be a feast to celebrate the dedication of the new Queen of England.

Alexander would be a little nervous about meeting the queen as she looked very sober and sickly. Alexander, however, could not take his eyes off Sarah Churchill who had to be one of the most beautiful and elegant ladies at the coronation. She had very fine and pretty brown hair of anyone he had ever seen. She seemed to be very charming but very talkative and outspoken with everyone.

Margaret said, "Let's meet my friend, Sarah."

Alexander, with a very slight smile, "With delight."

Approaching Sarah and the Queen, Margaret smiled and said, "Greetings, my honorable Queen. I would like to introduce you to my family. " The queen nodded and was polite and said, "Greetings" but seemed under the weather or overwhelmed by the large crowd and noise in the room.

Margaret smiling, said proudly, "I present Lady Sarah Churchill, the Duchess of Marlboro, looking at Sarah and the Queen, "This is my mother, Katherine Mercer and my brother, Alexander Spotswood. They have recently moved from the garrison at Deal to Golden Square here at London and Alexander is in the Queens Army."

They nodded and shook hands with one another. Wearing his best uniform, Alexander awkwardly bowed before the Queen and Sarah and said, "I am pleased to meet you, your majesty and Mrs. Churchill."

Sarah looking at Alexander, "Margaret has told me about your father serving as a chirosurgeon in the British Navy in Tangier. She didn't tell me that you were one of the most handsome men in England. "

Blushing and slightly embarrassed, Alexander said," You are very kind and charming, and I am glad you are good friends with Margaret. Thanks for the invitation on behalf of our family."

Sarah being very flirtatious, "I see you wear the Queens uniform proudly. Do you like serving?"

Alexander respectfully answered, "Yes, and I like the training I have received."

The beautiful and outspoken Sarah said directly," Undoubtedly, you have heard or met my husband, General John Churchill," She was glancing at John from a distance as he was speaking to some of his friends in Parliament. Sarah continuing, "John told me that Tangier was a beautiful but dangerous place to live when the English were there." "
"Yes, it was." Katherine said as if not to be left out of what seemed to be just a conversation between Sarah and Alexander. Margaret and Katherine looked bewildered at each other over Sarah's infatuation with Alexander. Sarah couldn't keep her eyes off Alexander. Even the Queen started to notice the lack of Sarah's attention toward her and Sarah's focusing on Alexander instead, as if Sarah was under a spell.

 Alexander answered her question, "Yes, I know your husband. General Churchill. I like serving under him."

Sarah looked back at Alexander, "You are very handsome and polite. I will tell my husband that he needs to take
.91

care of you and use your survivor skills for my friend, Margaret's sake. "

Alexander politely, "Thank you, Mrs. Churchill. I will appreciate any assistance. I do realize that I do have to earn my own right to advance in the army and life in general. "

Sarah speaking more officially, said, " I'm sure he will appreciate all your hard work and the willing acceptance of your responsibilities and for your loyal service to England. I am trying to persuade my friend, Queen Anne to promote John to Captain General."

The Queen was politely listening but seemed to be thinking about something other than Sarah's conversation. Margaret picking up the hint that the Queen wanted to move on or go back to St. James Palace politely interrupted Sarah. Margaret said, "Thank you, Sarah. We have taken up a lot of your time. We have enjoyed the coronation ceremony and banquet. You have other guests that you will want to meet. We will see you later."

Sarah said looking at Alexander, "I hope so." And she couldn't take her eyes off Alexander and he couldn't take his eyes off her.

After they left, Margaret as usual smiling said, " Good thing younger brother that she is a married woman, or you might have found yourself a wife."

Alexander sheepishly, "I enjoyed her company, but she is too old for me." Margaret and Katherine laughed. Alexander was glad he had met Sarah and would think about her many times, but he did not want to interfere with Margaret's fondness for her.

Margaret reminded Alexander. "Seriously, you made a great impression on Sarah, but don't get any outlandish intentions about her."

Alexander, "I will admit I enjoyed her beauty and her self-confidence, but I wanted to make a good impression on the Queen."

Katherine, "I think you did because Sarah will not let the queen forget you." They all three laughed and left the banquet hall.

On the walk home and after thinking about the events that occurred there that evening, Margaret said, "Sarah is beautiful and famous and probably the second wealthiest lady in England. The wealthiest lady is her boss, Queen Anne. Sarah just inherited the wealthy manor of Wimbledon. She is happily married to the most able military leader in the country, and she works for the most powerful queen in the world. Sarah will help you if she says she will. She could also cause you trouble, Alexander, and get you sent to the Tower and beheaded."

Alexander quickly replied, "I don't want to go there!"

Katherine to Margaret, "I see why you like working for her. She is charming, smart, and ambitious."

Margaret, Katherine, and Alexander walked on to Golden Square . Alexander must have been thinking that this was a new chapter in his life. He had enjoyed the socializing with the finest people of London. He knew that this would not be the last time he would see Sarah Churchill, and he knew although she meant what she said about her assisting him, he would need to concern himself with his books and training and set his sights on being the best military man in John Churchill's army.

A few months later, Alexander found himself entrenched in army life and was sent to the battlefield in Flanders.

His company was known for their bravery and perseverance. They would practice military maneuvers with the Dutch Army led by Count Eugene and his military leaders.

Alexander got word that John Churchill was promoted to a Captain General. Furthermore, John had ordered that Alexander would be promoted to Quartermaster General. John believed that his success will be determined how well his troops were supplied and by his consummate ability to get a highly organized person like Alexander Spotswood to administer that vital supply line.

During the next few months Alexander became busy supplying the troops with everything they would need to be ready to win the inevitable war with France and Spain. The beauty of Flanders and living outdoors in the tents reminded him of the modest conditions he had known from his boyhood in Tangier. Now he was building his career and where these steps led might be unknown, but he was excited about the future. Once in a while he must have thought that Sarah Churchill had in some way had got involved with his becoming a quartermaster . And he was grateful, if she did get involved, because he liked helping and leading his fellow soldiers.

Soldiers Field in Flanders

Brave the soldiers on Flanders field,
With determined hearts they showed zeal.
For victory comes from brave souls,
At high cost as Death takes tolls.

The flowers now grow where soldiers fell,
Plowshares now turn earth where war was Hell.
Crosses on graves line the bloody way,
Where drumbeats of war had their say.

Off the stage and into the ground,
The dead soldiers hear no sound.
Waiting their turn for judgment day,
Their lives too short, their bones to stay,

Lonely the soldiers on Flanders field,
With thankful hearts we must yield.
Our tears of joy for victory they won,
The soldiers were brave before they were done.

Robert Taylor

Above poem inspired by Flanders Fields and Other Poems written by Lieutenant Colonel John McCrae of Ontario, Canadian Expeditionary Forces. Poem written in 1915. Lt. Col. McCrae had thoughts like most people do about the struggle of life and death.

In Flanders fields the poppies blow

Between the crosses, row on row,

That mark our place; and in the sky
The larks, still bravely singing, fly

Scarcely heard amid the guns below.

We are the Dead. Short days ago

We lived, felt dawn, saw sunset glow,

Loved and were loved, and now we lie

In Flanders fields.

Take up the quarrel with the foe:

To you from failing hands we throw

The torch; be yours to hold it high.

If ye beak faith with us who die

We shall not sleep, though poppies grow

In Flanders fields.

While Alexander was in Flanders, he received letters from Katherine, Margaret, and Roger. Roger was a career army man and was busy fighting in the battles of the Spanish succession wherever they were and whenever they started. He was a skilled soldier and without question proud of Alexander for having been promoted from lieutenant colonel to quartermaster. Undoubtedly Roger and his brother dreamed about the boyhood days in Tangier and living the good life in London. Margaret would write about what was going on in the royal court with Sarah and Queen Anne in her letters. Katherine would mention her daily routine, the neighbors, and her adventures traveling to the great sights in London. The letters seemed to always cheer Alexander when he was in the field .

One night at the campsite, Alexander was sitting out by the campfire and staring into the flickering light. A soldier which Alexander thought he had never seen before came out of the darkness as if to come out of nowhere and startled Alexander.

The newly arrived soldier said, " I mean no harm. I saw the light and just want to get a little warmth by the fire from the chilly night air. "

Alexander said, "Help yourself. I was just resting and praying that tomorrow will bring another splendid day."

Strange soldier said, "It will be a great day tomorrow. In fact, it will be a great month and year here in Flanders.

It is very peaceful and quiet here tonight. It was not always that way. If you have some time, I will tell you a tale that few people know about firsthand. "

Alexander seeing that the soldier was sincere, "Sure, I always like to hear a good story. Go right ahead. Here is some hot tea to warm your stomach. "

Strange soldier, "Thank you very much. The story goes like this. Once upon a time there were many small towns situated in the valleys of Flanders and in the foothills of the great mountains near a big lake. They were anything but peaceful, but growing, thriving, loud, and noisy. There was one town in particular that had a dog with a loud bark that kept barking and barking. The townsfolk started to get annoyed by the constant barking and told the owner he must do something to quieten the dog or the townsfolk would take the situation into their own hands and would silence the dog. The owner was puzzled as to why the dog kept on barking for hours on end. He went up to the dog and said., " Stop the barking as loud as he could. " The owner yelled and yelled at the dog. It seemed that the dog was trying to tell the people something as if they had to get into their fishing boats, quickly. The dog started running up one of the hills and then he would run down the same hill. He would run back up the hill and then would run back down the hill. The owner said he must want me to stay on top of the hill as the dog got quiet when the owner went up to the top. When the owner came down the hill, the dog started barking again. He kept on barking for several more hours. One of the annoyed townsfolk was a fisherman by trade said, "we have heard enough. We will catch the dog and take him to the top of the hill." Suddenly a wall of water 30-foot-tall was coming down the valley floor. The fisherman jumped into his boat and carried by the water to higher ground. He got out of his boat onto solid ground and realized that his life had been spared. His fellow townsfolk were not so lucky, and they had perished, except for one baby girl. The baby girl was carried out of her room in her cradle through a large window of the house when the water started rising. And while the baby was sleeping, the dog seeing the floating cradle, jumped into the waters and drug the cradle and baby to safety to dry ground on a hillside by the waters. The baby survived the ordeal. Two hunters were standing on the hillside and witnessed the entire incident and found the baby in the cradle. They looked around and thought they were lost, because there was no city where they thought it had been. They wondered where this lake had come from. They saw no other people in the vicinity. On seeing no one, they carried the baby and cradle to a nearby cottage. The family in the cottage said they had never been on the other side of the hillside and didn't know any of their neighbors. Eventually, one of the hunters said that he and his wife could take care of the baby until its parents were found. The hunters would occasionally go back to the hillside and lake where the baby was found. Through the years, no parents came forward saying they had a missing baby girl. The hunter and his wife raised the girl as their own, and she became the prettiest girl in all the land of Flanders. Later when the girl got older, she married a Prince of Flanders, and they would go to the pretty lake. She was always happy when she was by the lake or on the lake. They would visit her parents at the cottage, and they never ever told her that they were not her real parents. On the day of the flooding, the old fisherman had been spared by the rising flood waters and had rowed back to what d to be the town and had seen the dog pulling the baby girl to safety and taking her back to their cottages. The fisherman said the dog disappeared trying to find his owner or find the parents of the baby. He figured the dog might have ran away scared or just disappeared into thin air never to be heard from again. The fisherman told those that would listen, that the town was cursed and had been covered up by a lake because the townsfolk were so stingy and mean. When the fisherman told the tale about a lake covering the entire city, they thought he was just telling a story or just too old about remembering the facts. Some of the folks thought he might be a little drunk from beer made by the nearby hop fields. Nobody could believe that a whole town had disappeared. Years later the Prince was fishing on the Lake and thought he had caught a very large fish. He pulled up a solid gold jewelry box. He is thinking that there might be gold coins or jewelry in the box and took his knife and pried open the lock. Inside was no gold except for a cross that had the inscription "our baby, our life." And a nicely written letter with the words, "we pray that we will be saved from the rising water and if we cannot, dear Lord, will you save our precious little baby girl and give her a happy life. She is all we have to give to you. Thank you for the gift of life." The Prince did not know what to make of this letter or relate it anyway to his wife. The royal couple did have a good life together and raised happy and generous children.

Alexander, " Am I gullible or is that a true story?"

The strange soldier looked him straight in the eye and said, "Yes, it did happen, if you believe the old fishermen." The strange soldier went on to say that there are many lakes in Flanders that cover once flourishing towns and cemeteries.

The strange soldier said, "No one can ever explain where the walls of water come from. Maybe they come from the wind and the seas. They seem to be isolated occurrences . There are a few things that are always consistent with any story about the lakes and towns. There is always a barking dog which is never found after the event. There is always cursed townspeople. An older person later tries to tell the story, but no one believes. There is always a floating baby in a cradle. The town has no churches. And years later there is something floating in the lake water that gives a small clue about the past."

Alexander fascinated by the story, "That is some story! There has to be some lesson in all this."

The storyteller looked at the watch in his soldier's uniform. Looking at Alexander, " If you believe in only what you can see, you will limit yourself. You must also believe in things you cannot see, if it comes from the Lord. Trust in the Lord no matter what you are led to believe."

Alexander looked down at the campfire and it needed more wood for light and warmth from the chilly night air. The soldier was no longer sitting by him at the campfire. Alexander must have thought to himself, "Did the soldier storyteller disappear in thin air. Are my eyes and ears playing tricks on me because I am tired? Was it just a dream?"
Alexander looking at his watch and saw that it was time to go to bed and rest. He looked up into the starry nighttime sky and saw old faithful Sothis, his bright star watching over him. Feeling that all was well, he prayed that all the talk about lake covered villages was not in vain.

Alexander would keep busy in Flanders for the next several months perfecting his military skills in the English Army. He was getting the duties of a lieutenant colonel perfected and learning the skills of a quartermaster general. His fellow comrades noticed his tenacity and attention to detail. His ability to listen and motivate people were better than most of his fellow soldiers. His inquisitive nature about how things work, and his observation of cause and effect would suit him well in the years to follow. Part of his training had included a month-long study at the Board of Ordnance at the Tower in London. This was the part of the War department that was responsible for supplying the lands, forts, and military posts with supplies in the defense of the British realm. He learned all about cannons, battle axes, swords, maces, scepters, shields, breast plates, and other weapons, and the military uniforms for the army and the navy. England was entering a time of colony grabbing and settling as well as defense of its homeland against the French and Spanish. Alexander could apply his knowledge and practice his dealing with many facts and details would be useful to John Churchill in the War of the Grand Alliance with the Dutch.

While Alexander was at the Tower, he met Isaac Newton, who was in charge of The Royal Coins and the mintage of coins. Roger Elliott had always told his little brother about Newton's interests in physics and astronomy. They had a good chat about the stars and constellations while they had lunch together. Alexander did not tell him about Sothis, but Isaac Newton did tell him if he was interested in the stars, he should talk to John Flamsted, the royal astronomer that had been years earlier by King Charles II. Flamsted was now at Greenwich observing the stars. Isaac had remarked that Flamsted had catalogued almost 3000 stars in the past 40 years and had predicted with accuracy, two solar eclipses, and spotted a planet, Uranus in the skies. Alexander was impressed by Newton as he had been the head of the Royal Society and along with Edmund Haley received a copy of

Flamsted's sky atlas. After the meeting with the Board of Ordnance and a visit to the Royal Mint with Isaac Newton, Alexander went on home while on a leave from the army.

Alexander wrote to his brother, Roger Elliott, to tell him of his promotion to Quartermaster General. He told Roger about his visit to the Tower as a visitor and not as a prisoner. Roger wrote a reply that he was very proud of his brother. Roger wrote a return letter and asked Alexander to make sure he put in a requisition for a new body for Roger because of all the battlefield wounds he had taken in battle. A letter came from Margaret and Katherine asking him about his army life in the tents and on the march. Sometimes it would be many months before the letters would be received. Alexander must have thought if he ever got out of the army, he would like to work on improving the mail delivery service. He enjoyed the letters from his family and would read them over and over again.

One day his superior, Col. Salamander Cutts called him into his office in the officer's tent and reviewed with Alexander what the official duties would be as Quartermaster -General in his division. Salamander had been the soldier in Tangier that had almost got in a duel with Roger. Salamander wrote poetry and books when he wasn't actively engaged in leading troops. He was a baron in his own right from Ireland and had been instrumental in some of the small battles of the War of Spanish Succession for England.

On entering Salamander Cutts' office, Alexander did the customary salute and standing at attention.

Salamander said, "Your title effective this day will be Quartermaster General. You will be responsible for the supplies of and the discipline of troops. You will be in charge of supplies. You will be the warrant officer for 5000 men. Are you ready for the task?"

Alexander without hesitation and a strong voice, " Yes sir, it would be an honor to serve."

Salamander continued with the commission, " You will be like the Colonel in Chief. What it takes some men to do in 8 years of service, you have been able to do in 2 years. You have impressed the senior officers and are on the right journey to becoming successful. Lead your men with honor and distinction. Do not let this fall on deaf ears."

Alexander carefully listening to the last cautionary remark saluted and said, "No sir, I will not sir."

Alexander took his job seriously and none of the men in his regiment ever questioned why he was chosen over them even when they had more experience than him. They felt as though he earned it though a few of the men said that he was friends of people in high places. They soon stopped their grumbling when they saw how tenacious Alexander was in completing his assignments and providing them with enough supplies. It seemed that destiny had pulled Alexander out of the trenches and place him on solid high ground and a prominent position. Alexander must have sensed this and known down deep in his soul that he must perform all his duties faithfully and diligently and proficiently lead his men and supply the supplies for his regiment whether it be food, shelter, artillery, or with more reinforcements. He knew he would be making critical military decisions when the future wars came about. With his rank and this job, he would be in the inner circles with the senior commanders planning battle strategy. He would be prepared to go into the heat of battle in the heart of the war.

In 1704, Alexander and his regiment would be the key players in the Battle of Blenheim for England. His athleticism in playing games with Roger in their boyhood, his mountain climbing experience, his having been exposed to extreme heat in the great Sahara desert , and his exposure and learning how to defend himself from the consistent bombardment of the garrison in Tangier would prove beneficial in his role as a quartermaster. Certainly, the enemy, The French and the army of the Holy Roman Empire couldn't be any more formidable than the savagery of the attacks he had seen on the garrison by the Moors, Berbers, and Turks. The difference now would be that Alexander would see to it that the Army would be better supplied. The English army would not be confined to a garrison or fort and would not be on an isolated African beach a thousand miles from England without reinforcements in close proximity as Fort Tangier had been. Alexander knew that his regiment must keep the Allied troops of the French from controlling England and dominating Europe. Alexander had been told that up to this point in history the commanders of the troops would order all the supplies for the fighting army, and it was not uncommon for wars to be lost because that particular side did not have enough food or bullets for the troops. There were many droughts and famines and weather conditions that could also adversely affect a supply line. Alexander must have thought than John Churchill was showing a brilliant battle strategy by delegating the ordering of supplies to many of his men and by doing so he could focus on his troop strength and the battle lines. The troop strength at Blenheim for the British would be very impressive. Churchill would lead nearly 50,000 men divided into 78 battalions and 127 squadrons of Calvary and 90 cannons. The French and the Allied troops would have 66,000 men divided into 66 battalions and 181 squadrons with 66 guns.

Queen Anne had come to power in England just a few years earlier and had now proven herself to be a world leader that all would respect for her power and word . She ruled one of the most powerful countries in the world, and she did not want anything to change that course. She was determined to help keep France from dominating Europe. She wanted to keep the support of the Dutch Army in Flanders under Prince Eugene of Savoy. The strength of the Dutch and English Army would be unsurpassed, and she was impressed with John Churchill as commander. The army would consist of well-trained guards and dragoons armed with the best short flintlock muskets available. The regiments of horse soldiers would be given trumpets for signaling and field maneuvers. The scouts and the dragoons would be equipped with a drum for signals out in the field. The foot gunners would have the best muskets and swords. The cannons would be pulled by the best horses in England and Scotland. Queen Ann was making bold decisions and seeking advice from John Churchill. These were even bolder than some made during the Reformation in 1685 . They had to keep the French Army out of Flanders even though the Dutch was reluctant to do battle. The French had a well-tuned war machine and was in peak condition and had won most outings in Europe and proving themselves with winning battle strategies. The French would be led by Marshall Tallard, Marshall Marson, and the Bavarian King under the direction of the French King, also known as the Sun King, the incomparable King Louis 14.th The queen pulled out all stops and ordered that All the Queens and Kings Horse Guards, Royal Dragoons, and the Royal Welsh Fusiliers would help Churchill. She called on friendly courts around Europe for their troop support. She wanted to beat the French on the Battlefield at Blenheim. She knew that all the diverse fighting groups for the English would respect the title of Duke which Churchill possessed rather that plotting a strategy with a committee of the Captains and Generals from around English Isles and the friendly allies in remote headquarters in some remote location. She had made up her mind on Duke Churchill to be the final authority on all battle plans at Blenheim. He would be the single person that could lead a mixed army to victory. He would be able to gain his men's respect and admiration and loyalty.

Alexander took his role seriously and had supplied the troops with everything they needed. For over a year, his regiments had prepared for the upcoming conflict and battle with France. In May 1704, Alexander wrote a letter from Flanders that was addressed to the Golden Square in London to his mother, Katherine and sister Margaret.

Dear Mother and Margaret,

I regret that I haven't sent more correspondence to you during the last year and half, for I have been at camp in southern Flanders. I have been restricted somewhat by the secrecy and security of the location and the nature of our mission and our whereabouts are unknown. We have survived the great windstorm in Flanders that almost destroyed Flanders and England. I pray that you were spared any discomfort and suffering. From our military reports, the most wind damage was to the English Navy at Plymouth and Deal. I heard that the Eddystone Lighthouse in the harbor and hundreds of ships were torn to pieces by the uncanny wind. We lost several ships off the coast of Flanders as well. The French lost some ships. Our troops will be meeting somewhere in Europe joining the full English and Dutch Army to meet and defeat the French Army of Louis 14th. You or I cannot not discuss these plans with others nor can I disclose the location where we will fire the first shot and lead the charge. John Churchill says that Roger will be joining us in battle which you may already know. Please pray for our safety and the Lord's will to be done.

Next Tuesday, I will be riding in the horse Calvary on a journey of several hundred miles. We will travel over farmlands, meadows, woodlands, hills, and mountains. The most disturbing part of the journey is crossing the many rivers, marshes, and creeks with our foot soldiers. The Dutch Army will face the most resistance. For now, we have plenty of food and companionship. Many of the soldiers tell great stories to keep their mind off the ensuing battle.

I trust that London life is keeping you amused, and you are getting plenty of rest.

Margaret, I am keeping a watchful eye on our beloved commander, the Duke and making sure that he has plenty of men and military supplies.

Do not worry as I am in the service of the Queen and in God's hands. I do not know the outcome of all this or when I will see you next. You know that I love you all very much. Sincerely and Affectionately,
Alexander Spotswood.

After Katherine read the letter, she looked at Margaret. "Alexander has always been a good son and a thoughtful man; I hope nothing happens to him and Roger. "

Margaret comforting her mother, "It is a good letter. I think there is nothing to worry about. They will make it through the battle. If they can survive in Tangier, they can survive anywhere."

On Tuesday as he had promised, Alexander started down the path to southern Germany with the main force of Duke Churchill's army and the army of the Grand Alliance. They would march through the rugged mountainous terrain for 250 miles from the camp in Flanders. They received a message from Prince Eugene with the Dutch army and some of the English regiments. They had traveled through the Black Forest and were already asking for reinforcements. He would need them to keep the French troops from entering Bavaria in southern Germany. Prince Eugene had reported that he had a small skirmish with the French in Schellenburg and that he would meet and join up with Churchill and the main army close to the Kessell River, a small tributary river on the Danube River. The French would be sure to cross here because it was a well-traveled crossing and only 5 miles from the Danube River. Part of the Frenchmen in Tallards's army had already set up camp and set up the French position north of the village of Blenheim, Germany on the Danube. Tallard was betting that Churchill would not attack because of having what appeared to be a smaller army than his, and he figured it would be difficult to get enough supplies to his forces on the Danube. The other part of the French Army was positioned at two small villages also close to Blenheim at Lutzinger and Oberglaus. Whichever army could capture Blenheim and control the river crossing would have an advantage in battle. The French not having many infantries and the army being split made them more vulnerable.

The night before the battle, a company that included John Churchill, the Duke of Marlboro, leader of the British Army and Allies, Prince Eugene, leader of the Dutch Army, Alexander Spotswood, and Charles Churchill, brother to John Churchill and leader of one of the hardest fighting regiments; all climbed to the top of one of the tallest church steeples on one of the rolling hills surrounding Blenheim and looked down at the upcoming battlefield. They basically saw two opposing armies, the British primarily in blue uniform and the French Army primarily in green. They were very close to each other and both camps were stretched up and down the Danube and sleeping in hurriedly set up tents. Night was falling and the soldiers of both armies would most likely be called to prepare for battle when the rooster crowed, or the sunlight would start peaking over the eastern horizon.

John Churchill said, " If I were a betting man, I would bet that there are 100,000 troops in Blenheim area tonight". Looking at Alexander, he went on to say, " Are we ready for battle, Quartermaster?"

Alexander saluting and proudly responding, " Yes! Sir!"

Churchill, "Good, the French are thinking that we will not strike at the two camps until we have been fully supplied and they will want to attack us first. We are already fully supplied. "

Salamander Cutts, " And we can make it difficult for them to get field signals from one part of the French army to the other part of the French Army." Cutts continued confidently, " I think that we are strong enough to drive them back and occupy the town. "

John Churchill looking at a map, "The French and Bavarians are camped on the ground behind the groves of trees on the Nebel River between Blenheim and Lutzinger north of Blenheim and like Commander Cutts says; they will try to encircle us and cut off our supplies and break our lines."

Prince Eugene pointing to the map, "I can attack the smaller portion of the army here, which is about 2 and l/2 miles away, because there is a road that goes by my troops to Blenheim which you cannot see from here because of the hilly terrain. There is only one problem that we must cross that Nebel River by foot and horse without a bridge because it has been destroyed. It would take too much time to get all our troops and guns across the river unless we build a temporary bridge to cross the river."

John Churchill calculating that idea, "Then, that is what we will do. We will build a temporary bridge that is strong enough to get all the troops, horses, and guns across. We must do this quickly and out of sight of the French Army and quietly enough not to give away our plan. When we get all the troops across the river, we attack the Bavarian portion of the French Army in southern Blenheim, and they will be the ones trapped by the Danube. Our main Army will attack Tallard's main army in the north and we will eventually have two battlefields and the two French armies will not be able to encircle us or trap us."

Alexander was awed by seeing history being made in front of his eyes.

Salamander confidently, " I will get several battalions of foot soldiers into Blenheim led by Charles Churchill to help build the bridge and then support Prince Eugene into the village of Blenheim even though it looks fortified, to quickly defeat them, and then we will put all our strength into the heart of the French Army between Blenheim and Lutzinger capitalizing on my belief that Tallard believes we will not strike first or he would have set up his lines already. "

John Churchill, " We will meet at 6 am in the morning and our main army will meet the French Army at Lutzinger for a surprise.
Alexander spoke up. "I will personally and secretly deliver these orders to all the captains and field officers to coordinate the attack. We will be ready for engagement."

"Well spoken, Alexander! Well Spoken, Quartermaster!" said John Churchill.

The English Army started working on their pre-battle plans, orders, and maps. Everyone would do their part. Charles Churchill got the bridge built across the Nebel and the lower ford of the Danube. It took several hundred men and axes to build a rudimentary bridge across the rivers . In a few hours at dusk, thousands of English soldiers would cross the bridge and fight the French. Alexander kept busy that night making copies of the orders and maps and helped the commanders explain the plans to the troops. By midnight, every captain and officer in the English army knew where and when they would engage the French. Alexander lay down on the ground and said a prayer and said, "Let me mentally be prepared for the ensuing battle." He knew that Roger was close by somewhere and he wish they could have met and talked before morning to console each other.

The next morning 6 o'clock came and the plans were followed religiously. John Churchill took the main road to Blenheim from his headquarters and the camp of his men . They passed through the beautiful field of grass and flowers and crops on the way to Blenheim. They soon crossed the shallow Kessel River. There were little farms and villages and cottages on the way and by the roadside. He knew that soon thousands of musket balls would soon be flying and interrupting the tranquility of the otherwise majestic picturesque setting of southern rural Germany. The anxious Calvary had to show patience so as to let the foot soldiers go first and set up the lines. Once the lines got set, they would be ready to bring up support from the rear. Prince Eugene broke off his battalions and headed for Blenheim to attack the Bavarian part of the French Army. After having crossed the quickly made bridge further downstream, the foot soldiers still had trouble marching to Blenheim in the wet and muddy marshes along the Danube on the way to Blenheim. Tallard and the French Army still did not look for Churchill to strike because it looked like he was headed farther north to get more supplies for his army and horses. In fact, he was so convinced that he sent most of his troops out to get hay and forage from the nearby farms for their horses. However, the silence was soon broken. The drumbeats of the dragoons started signally the orders the English had prepared. The trumpeters signaled the troops . The battle had begun as a surprise for Tallard. He quickly tried to muster his troops and get them back from the hay fields on the farms and reorganize his troops to defend themselves against Churchill. Tallard had said something under his breath as if to say, "If the English want a fight today, we will give it to them."

Salamander Cutts kept his promise and lead his battalions up to the Nebel River and help reinforce the temporary built bridge and get all the troops across so they could support Prince Eugene in the fortified village of Blenheim against the Bavarians. They soon got the guns poised to strike at the French and Bavarian troops, and the French in Blenheim started to return fire. They also had been startled by the early morning attack but were more organized than Tallard and his army north of the village. In fact, the army was in such a disarray that Churchill make a quick decision and took the army across the Nebel's makeshift bridge and support Cutts. He must have thought he could capture Blenheim and then the entire English Army would then be able to overwhelm Tallard forces when they got reassembled. John gave the order for Cutts to make a charge on Blenheim. Cutts soon took his men right up close to the fortified walls of the Blenheim. Churchill's men soon outnumbered the French army in Blenheim, and they started encircling the village.

The first round of fire had killed many of the French troops. The second round of fire from Cutts's men were more strategic against the French cannons. They took a few enemy cannons out of commission. Alexander was riding up in the regiment with Cutts. Alexander was in the heat of battle riding up to the gates of Blenheim seeing how the supplies were holding up. Bullets were flying over his head. He saw the smoke and heard a big blast from the French cannon fire. He got hit hard in his right side by a small cannon ball and was knocked off his horse. It knocked him completely out of his saddle of his brave military horse, and he fell to the ground. He cried out because of the unbearable pain and fainted at seeing the blood from his body and from the pain. He lay there for a while and when he regained his senses, he was unaware what was happening around him. The French was able for a while to keep up heavy fire, but this part of their army was losing ground.

The French Army and the British Army exchanged fire for several hours. Many soldiers on both sides were either killed or wounded. In even got so that the fire between the two armies were getting scarcer, so each army started fighting hand to hand in the streets of Blenheim. Neither side could make any progress. Prince Eugene held his own but could not solidly defeat the Bavarian army. The Duke of Marlboro, John Churchill , seeing that the English might take control of Blenheim decided to lead an assault on Tallard in the fields north of Blenheim and Klutziness as originally planned. His men were loyal to their leader and was used to him making necessary changes on battle strategy in the field and could easily follow the signals with the drumbeats and trumpet calls. They soon overwhelmed the remnants of Tallard's Army as they still had not got into complete military battle configuration even after several hours. Tallard started to get his men to retreat and disperse. He was captured by one of Churchill's Captains as he was fleeing and some of the men were jumping into the fast-moving Danube River, hoping they would not be captured. The Bavarians in Blenheim soon surrendered to Cutts and Prince Eugene who had persistently launched assaults on the village. Some of the French Army burned their colors on their flags and uniforms rather than giving them to the English Army which the French soldiers despised. The French and Bavarian Army were soon defeated at Blenheim. The modified plan in battle created out of necessity worked better than the original battle plan, but victory for the English was all that mattered. It had been a solid victory for the English and the Grand Alliance under the leadership of the Duke of Marlboro. His quick thinking and good judgment had resulted in a win of this battle this day.

Alexander had laid unconscious and asleep on the battlefield in front of the Blenheim battlefield for several hours. When he awoke, he knew he had been wounded, and he could see the Union Jack flag flying in Blenheim which mean they had won this battle. He looked up straight to the sky. He was in field with wounded and dead soldiers. Some of the wounded were moaning and blood was everywhere. He saw ravens circling above him. He survived the battle. He was weak and soon passed out again. The next time he awoke it was evening and the sky was very dark. The ravens were gone. His vision was blurred, and he was weak. He saw some faces looking down at him. Roger Elliott was holding a lantern and shining it in his face.

Roger asking Alexander in a worried tone, "Are you alive little brother?"

Alexander mumbled, "Roger, Is that you?"

Roger answered, "Yes, it is. It has been a while, and I hope you would recognize me. I am so proud of you and knew that you would show no fear. We beat the army of the Sun King. We have had many challenges in life, together. Save your strength. You will need it to get well. You have taken quite a big hit from this three-pound cannonball in your side." Roger was holding a bloody cannonball in his hand. Roger continued, " This ball would have killed a lesser man. Remember the curse put on us long ago, that we will be rich and famous. You are not rich but are becoming famous. You will live to fight another day. But you must heal first. I thank God that you will be going home alive and not be buried here with these other brave soldiers."

Alexander was very weak and groggy and trying to speak coherently, " Thank you Roger. I hurt so bad, but I don't remember much. I thank God you are alive, too."

A familiar looking man named George Hamilton was standing next to Roger. He said, "Alexander, I don't know if you know me, but I am one of the Commanders here too, and I was impressed last evening how you delivered the orders, maps, and instructions for the Duke. You helped us defeat the French by making sure we had plenty of bullets and food and tents, and other items. I wish you well, brother. If you hadn't helped to prepare the troops, we might all be dead by now." |

John Churchill walking through the battlefield and spotted Alexander, "You now see why you were chosen for Quartermaster. If we don't have the supplies to fight, we cannot do anything but lose wars. We are not about losing. You proved today that you have real courage and strength. You have proven yourself today in a way that will honor your family and your country. You will be of great value to England when you get well."

George Hamilton and John Churchill soon left to take care of the dead and for the others that had been wounded.

Roger, "Speaking of family, I will send a letter to Mother saying that you will most likely live and be coming back to stay in the army hospital at Chelsea to recover from your injury for a while. Here is the cannonball that hit you. You can keep it for a souvenir."

Roger put the ball in Alexander's coat pocket. The wound had left a big hole in Alexander's side, but it wasn't bleeding anymore. He knew he had been spared. Today was his day . Something had been watching over him. He remembered to look at the starry night sky and he and Roger found Sothis. Alexander believed that his star followed him everywhere at all times even when he couldn't see it.

Alexander said , "Thank you Lord for sparing my life." He felt at ease now. He was reunited with Roger and Sothis was still faithful in the sky, and God had been gracious and loving enough to spare him. Why? That would now be the question that Alexander Spotswood would have to answer for himself.

On the Battlefield at Blenheim on that August day, around 40,000 French and Bavarian soldiers lay dead and 11,000 were captured by the English and the Grand Alliance. The bodies were piled high and, in the marshes, the fields, the roads, the streets of Blenheim, in the River Danube, and all through the villages. The English and their allies lost 12,000 men. Over a hundred colors flew over the shallow graves that were dug in the nearby fields. The war had been brutal but was won by Churchill's outsmarting the French on making them guess whether he would engage them in Alsace or Moselle. He used his march from Bebburg near Colgne to come down the Danube at Blenheim to keep them guessing. The Calvary was more successful for the British even though they had been outnumbered by the French. The horses used by the French were sickly and did not get the supplies like the British counterparts. Alexander had made certain that anything the Calvary and infantry needed; he would get for them. Now he lay in a near death bed situation and would be transported to the Army Hospital at Chelsea. This would take him on the battle stage and let him think about his future while he lay in recovery. He was so glad that Roger had been there to encourage him.

In late August of 1704, Alexander lay in a hospital bed in Chelsea. It was not that far of a distance from the Golden Square in Westminster. Alexander's mother and sister would visit him quite often. Ironically, it was the same hospital that Margaret had pointed out to her family ten years earlier when Margaret and Alexander had met at Christmas for the first time. Alexander would read his books and occasionally daydream about returning to the army life. John Churchill, because of a strategic and decisive victory over the French had made himself very popular with the English. He would go on to fight more wars in the Spanish Aggression. His quick and strategic thinking made him one of the best military generals in English history. Queen Anne liked Sarah Churchill for being one of her ladies of the bed chamber. Queen Anne respected Sarah's advice and ordered that a Palace be built for Sarah and her husband, John Churchill, and they would call it Blenheim. Salamander Cutts, had fought under King Charles II and his career in the military was outstanding. He also had a love for writing poetry, and he had published books on his works when he wasn't on the battlefield. Charles Churchill who had led the Calvary and a few battalions of foot soldiers would retire to his brother's palace. George Hamilton, one of the commanders became promoted to the rank of Lieutenant General. It was generally accepted by all citizens in England that John Churchill had earned all his rewards.

Alexander, now 25 years of age, had always been a bundle of energy and had a tremendous quest for knowledge. He had gained experience as a military leader and as a supply officer who had a knack for budgeting. Now he lay almost helpless on the hospital bed. He would spend hours looking out the windows in the beautiful hospital designed by Christopher Wrenn. He liked and admired the architecture and began drawing pictures of the hospital to occupy his time. He found drawing and architecture to be very interesting and wondered if this was a profession he should go into. It would require some studying in art and design, and he thought he would learn as much about designing buildings while he waited for his good health to return.

One day, one of the nurses came in to cheer Alexander as he was feeling helpless and useless to his country and commander while lying there waiting for his wounds to heal. Alexander would be the first to strike up a conversation.

Alexander asking, "Am I done for, nurse?"

Barbara smiling, "You may call me Barbara. My name is Barbara Villiers. We are not that much different in age. You do not have to call me Lady or Mrs. Villiers. "

Alexander fishing for an answer, "Will I get well, again?"

Smiling and looking at Alexander with her sparkling blue eyes, Barbara said, "You will most likely heal. You had a big hole in your side and was unconscious for a long time. If you follow the doctors and nurses' orders and my orders you will heal nicely. One good thing is that you did not lose any limbs." And then she giggled like a schoolgirl would over some boy's good looks.

Alexander, blushing at the nurse, "Thank you for wanting to help me."

Barbara continuing to stare at Alexander, "You are very welcomed." Alexander couldn't help but notice her blue eyes and beautiful black hair, second only to Sarah Churchill for having fine thick hair.

Alexander said, "My family has come here to visit several times."

Barbara replying , " I know. They know my sister-in- law, Anne Villiers who is in Queen Anne's court. My husband was killed last year in the Battle of Flanders right after we were married. I volunteer at the hospital to help the soldiers mend and help the families of veterans get through the grief when the soldiers in their families die."

Alexander in an empathetic tone, " I am sorry for your loss."

Barbara staring directly at Alexander with a smile that seemed liked she was appreciative of his empathy for her, asked , "Alexander, would you like me to read you some books?"

Alexander said, "Yes, I would like that."

Barbara read him some lines from "Life Worth Living." She also had in her possession one of Lord Cutts poems.

Alexander on seeing the poem and the name of the author said, "I served with him at Schellenberg and Blenheim in the battles of the Spanish Succession. He is a career soldier and a very capable and accomplished leader. We called him "Salamander." He is from a well to do Essex family."

Barbara brought the poetry book close to Alexander's bed stand. He had never been that close to such a beautiful woman except his mother and sister. He was fascinated by Barbara. She began to read "Song" by Lord Cutts.

Only tell her that I love,
Leave the rest to her and fate,
some kind of planet from above,
May perhaps her pity move.
Lovers on the stars must wait,
Only tell her that I love.

Why, O Why should I despair,
Mercy's pictured in her eye.
If she on a vouchsafe to hear,
Welcome hope and farewell fear.
She's too good to let me die,
Why, O why should I despair.
(Written by Lord Cutts)

Barbara placed the book on the nightstand next to Alexander and kissed Alexander on the forehead and said, "Wasn't that a beautiful verse. I would read more, but you must get your rest." Barbara was a little surprised at what she had done but was pleased with his response. He had smiled and was blushing.

Alexander," I didn't know Salamander could write so well. It is beautiful."

Barbara curiously, "I would say that he is quite talented. What about you, Alexander? Are you in love with anyone?"

Alexander surprised by her questioning, "Why no. I have no one special. I have been spending my time with books and working on my military career."

Barbara continuing with more questions, "You are quite handsome; don't you think?"

Alexander answered, "I never really have thought about that. Once I was told that being handsome would be a curse for me ."

Barbara chuckling, " It is not a curse at all. The young nurses set outside your room and giggle and talk about how glad they would be if they could be your wife."

Alexander, " I am flattered, but marriage for me will have to wait. I have to get settled in my career first, and I can't see my wife living in a garrison like I did in my youth."

Barbara smiling, "I must be going but I will come again if you like my reading, and I would like to chat with you. I will not let you die ." She wickedly laughed and said, " Pleasant dreams. "She reached over the bed and kissed him one more time on the forehead as his mother use to do when he said his prayers every night when they were back in Tangier.

Alexander must have thought what all this means. Only tell her that I love, leave the rest to her and fate. He soon fell asleep and he knew in his heart, mind, and soul that this would not be the last time he would see Barbara Villiers.

The months went by and Barbara would come by frequently and would help him with his exercises so he could walk uprightly again. She would stay for a while and read him books and tell him about the plays going on at the Drury Theater and at Lincoln's Inn. Every time she would leave Alexander, she would say, "I will never let you die." Then she would laugh.

Margaret and Katherine visited quite often, too. They would keep Alexander informed about the events in London, the coming and goings of Sara Churchill, and Queen Anne. They would brief him on Roger and all the news about the wars . He enjoyed their company, and he felt close to his family. On Christmas Eve, he thought it was so good to have family. And was hoping to get out of the hospital soon. The doctor told him he would be able to walk again and use his arms, but he would not be able to be a soldier, again. If he continued with the exercises and training, he might be able to get back to his regular strength before he got wounded at Blenheim.

Alexander would often stare at the cannonball, an unwanted gift from an unknown Frenchman at Blenheim. He was so proud to have been in the British Army and liked to be called Colonel. His father would have smiled and said, this is your fate. On much reflection while staying in the hospital, he knew he had the learning and talent to pursue interest in business or shipping. He had an interest in farming from the days in Deal but wouldn't have the resources or strength to handle farm commodities. He wondered what his father would have thought about his situation. His life was flashing before him and he knew that the good Lord would not leave him, and his family would support his decision about his future.

When Barbara visited, she most always said what Alexander wanted to hear. She would say, "Believe me, you have what it takes to be a well-known success. Stop your moaning about the past years and have some wine and face your fears. It is time to celebrate the rest of the days of your life."

Alexander sipped the wine, and said, "It has a good taste."

Barbara was acting a little silly, said, "It is very expensive right out of my very special cellar. We'll feel fine when we down this wine."

The way that Barbara was saying this poetry made Alexander amused. He had never seen her so relaxed before. Alexander started thinking about the military life again.

Barbara offering encouragement, "You will soon get back to a normal life. She pulled out a second bottle of wine from her long cloak. This is a red wine from my vineyards on my manor."

Alexander explaining his preferences, " I prefer red wine which gives me more energy, less heart problems, makes me calmer, and gives me a deeper sleep."

Barbara laughing, "You expect a lot from a bottle of wine."

Alexander smiling as he listened to her kind voice, said, "This wine also has a nice flavor."

Barbara went ahead and finished the white wine and said, "It will keep me healthy and make me loose some pounds. " Barbara pulled off her cloak and she had a beautiful figure.

Alexander admiring her beauty, "You do not need to do anything about your weight. You are perfect in every way."

Barbara smiling, "Oh my! Is that the wine talking? That is the first compliment you have ever given me, Col. Spotswood. That will be your Christmas present to me. You know, I really like the name Spotswood. It sounds so mysterious and authoritative."

Alexander chuckling, "I like the name Spotswood, too. I am happy when you visit! You always make me feel hopeful and that everything will turn out as planned, and there will always be a satisfactory outcome."

Barbara said sincerely, "Here! Here! This toast is "Thanks to the Lord for sending his Son. And his birthday. And for saving us from our sins."
Alexander and Barbara toasted each other, then the Queen, Chelsea, London, and then toasted all the soldiers on the battlefields."

They toasted when the wine bottle was empty, and Barbara said, "Here is to love. Leave the rest to her and fate. I will not let you die."

Barbara came closer and closer to Alexander and was laying on top of him. He was quiet and allowed her to snuggle up to him on the bed. His eyes were starting to drift, and he looked like he was falling to sleep.

 She thought she would wait till he woke up so she could say goodbye, but she came drowsier, too. She soon fell asleep on the other half of the hospital cot snuggled against Alexander. Alexander, whether he knew it or not, had one of the most beautiful women in England next to him in bed. Whether Barbara, knew it or not, she had put herself in a very vulnerable position with one of the most handsome men in England. No one will ever know what really happened in that Chelsea hospital room that Christmas Eve.

It was Christmas morning and Margaret and Katherine decided to come to Chelsea hospital to visit Alexander. They had Christmas breakfast and got in the carriage by stepping on the carriage stone, so they could more easily step into the carriage. They rode the ten-mile journey to the hospital and soon entered the familiar hallway to his room. Some of the nurses out in the hallway started giggling and Katherine and Margaret looked at each other as if to say why are they giggling. The two ladies opened the door and walked into Alexander's room. They were fully surprised to see Barbara and Alexander fully dressed but still sleeping in bed. The opening of the squeaky door caused the two sleepers to awaken.

Katherine face was blushing red and she said, "Good Morning in a loud voice. I now understand why the nurses were giggling in the hallway. "

 These loud words made the couple set up in bed, and Alexander embarrassed and said, "We got talking and both fell asleep. I assure you that nothing happened."

Katherine in a stern voice, "What is the meaning of this?"

Barbara, looking a little embarrassed, quickly got out of the bed and said, "Good morning, Mrs. Mercer and Margaret. I had come over last evening to bring Alexander some gifts and to cheer him. We got talking and fell asleep. It is quite innocent!"

Margaret kept quiet and just looked at the wine bottles on the nightstand.

Katherine also looking at the wine bottles, "A little cheer? Did you enjoy your company and cheer?"

Alexander still sleepy eyed, "Yes, mother."

Margaret chuckled.

Katherine, "I don't find that remark amusing. Why if Anne Villers finds about this, she will tell Sarah about it and then all England will know about this."

Margaret, "I think you are making a bigger deal about this than it really is. Nobody is going to say anything about a Christmas visit or Christmas gift from a nurse."

Barbara left the room as quickly as she could.
Katherine, looking at Alexander, "Are you in love with that woman? Although she is very beautiful, she is 20 years older than you are. Should you not be keeping company with someone your own age."

Alexander, " She is not that much older than I am. Yes ,I should be in the company of younger women. Yes, one day I will find a suitable wife, and it will be a long way off in the future. "

Margaret chuckled again, "Looks like a curse! Beautiful men seem to attract beautiful women."

Alexander soon got will enough to leave the hospital and went back to his home at Golden Square. Barbara did not come back to visit him ever again, and he must have been thinking what this all means. He missed her companionship. He didn't know if it was truly love between them or not, or that he was just fond of her, or just admired her for her beauty. Barbara was a caring person and had many generous qualities. She was well learned and had good manners. He knew he was glad to have made her acquaintance. Never again did Margaret or Katherine question Alexander about Barbara Villers again.

In the summer of 1705, Alexander was again living at The Golden Square with his mother. Margaret was still living on Silver Street but by herself. Her husband Richard Andrews had died of a tropical fever while traveling on business in the West Indies. Margaret had been alone a lot of her married life as her husband, Richard Andrews was always traveling.

Katherine and Alexander had just received a letter from Roger from Gibraltar.

Dear Mother, Margaret, and Alexander

I received the letter which stated that Richard had died in The West Indies. I am sorry for the family's loss. I never got to be with him much, but he was always charming and pleasant to me.
I have been assigned to Gibraltar to help defend the country from Spanish invaders. For accepting this call, I have been promoted to Brigadier General in the English Army. John Churchill is still leading troops in the battles of the War of Spanish Succession. I will form my own regiment and coordinate the troops. I am eagerly awaiting my appointment as Governor of Gibraltar.
The one benefit on leaving home in London is adapting to the more comfortable climate of Gibraltar. It is warm year around and cool breeze blow across the straits like it did long ago when we lived in Tangier. The starry nights are cool and clear. I am hoping I get to see that comet that Sir Edmund Halley is talking about. It seems like the sky shows the planet and stars in a better light in this part of the world. Before I left London, I heard that Queen Anne kept her promise and that she would build a large estate called Blenheim for Sir John Churchill and construction was just starting on building the Palace. I also heard that Queen Anne bestowed knighthood for Sir Isaac Newton, for his studies in gravity and physics.
I trust that Alexander has had enough time to fully recover. I will inform you that I never really recovered from my battle scar from Steenjkirke.
Mother, Gibraltar will be a good place to live. Write often.

With deepest regard for your health and with love always, Roger

---

"I know that I will be proud of Roger know matter what he does," said Alexander after he read Roger's letter." I hope he will be proud of me when I go into business. I will need to put all my thinking into my business and use all the knowledge I have accumulated to make a name for myself."

Katherine said, "I know you will be a great businessman. "Alexander had met some of the business partners of Richard Andrews, Margaret's husband. These partners were successful in importing and exporting all kinds of commodities. He knew that he would have to use most of his savings as venture capital for his new business. Alexander agreed to meet Richard's partners and then start a business with Mr. Starke and Mr. Richard Brayne.

They were seasoned business agents in importing and exporting of goods from all over the world. London was the financial capital of the world and a strong English military power over the French and Spanish would keep it that way. They would contact every mule and camel caravan and any cargo shipping company that left the docks in Plymouth and they would become potential associates. Alexander rented a business office space close to the Golden Square down on the Strand. It had large windows that gave a beautiful view of London and the River Thames.

Mr. Brayne was recommended by Margaret. He was a tall slim man with brownish hair. He was polite and had a good sense of humor to work with. Mr. Stark was a red-faced blondish man around 50 who was short and stout and more businesslike and showed less charm. Both Stark and Brayne seem excited about the new business adventure that Alexander was proposing. Both men had much experience in financial dealing and banking. The banks had just started up in London and their knowledge would be valuable to Alexander. Both men were also in stages of life to use their business experience to continue to be successful but didn't want the responsibility of dealing with all the financial correspondence and necessary paperwork. These men had several business contacts which would help the business get launched quickly and successfully. The business was called simply, Spotswood Trading Worldwide. They would engage in buying and selling goods from any country where an English merchant ship could load goods at a dock. They all agreed that they did not want to get involved in slave trading or transporting of slaves. They would speculate on silver, gold, and diamonds out of Africa. It was profitable although there was always the risk of pirates robbing them on the open sea. Over the course of the next few years, they enjoyed each other company and often talked business over lunch. They would sometimes go to dinner and then see a new play at the Drury theater or the Royal Theater. The business partners were making a lot of money. It seemed like every business decision they made was the right one at the time and everything they ventured into turned to gold.

One day, Alexander was sitting at his elegant walnut office desk, shuffling through some papers and letters when a young lady came in through the front door. She was a beautiful blonde-haired girl with turquoise or greenish colored eyes and was very petite. Alexander had a shocked look on his face because of her unbelievable beauty.

She smiled and began the conversation, " Are you Mr. Spotswood?"

Alexander said, "You can call me Alexander or Colonel, if you wish."

The young lady continued smiling and said, " Have you seen my father? Forgive me, sir. My name is Butler Brayne and my father is your agent, Richard Brayne. "

Alexander got out of his seat to address Butler, "Why yes, I see the resemblance. Your father told me had four daughters, but he didn't say how lovely they are. Your father went down to the Dockyards this morning. He should be coming back to the office any minute now. "

Seeing how pretty she was , he continued his remarks. "Won't you take a seat and wait here a minute if you would like."

Seeing how handsome Alexander was, she politely said, "Yes, I believe I will, if I won't be a bother to your business schedule."

Alexander, "With your permission, we could talk awhile. "She nodded her head as if she agreed.

Alexander, "Richard has always said he was proud of his daughters, but he has never talked about their beauty."

Butler, blushing, " He said you were a very hardworking businessman and said you were an integral part of the military campaign at Blenheim."

Alexander," Well I can't talk much about that ancient history, but I can show you a present I got from the French during the battle. He pulled a cannonball from a corner cabinet which had curious initials on it."

Butler asked, "Is that the cabinet that Sarah Churchill gave you with the big S engraved in wood on the front door?"

Alexander wondered how she knew so much, said, "Yes, it is, and this lead ball is the only valuable thing I store in it. The only thing that the ball is good for is sending me to the hospital for several months. "

Butler listening intently, "You are very fortunate to still be alive."

Alexander, "Yes ,and I am feeling better now." He couldn't help but keep his eyes focused on her beautiful face and eyes. He continued, "Is Butler a family name?"

Butler, "At school, I am called Anne, but I prefer to be called, Butler. I am named in honor of my godfather, James Butler, 3rd Earl of Ormonde." It seemed she could not keep her eyes off Alexander, also.

Alexander, "Then, I will call you Butler."

Butler," I like the girl's school I attend at Marleybone. I love to read about history, poetry, and romance."

Alexander's face turned red as he started to blush. "I learn to read by accessing the Bible. My father and mother taught me in a garrison school when we were stationed in Tangier, Africa with the Royal Navy. We will have to take the time to talk about history and poetry if your mother and father agree."

Butler acting a little grown up for her age, "They will let me make my own decision now that as I am 16 years old. I have heard my father say that you are very polite and have good manners."

Alexander curiously, "What else does he say?"

Butler answered, "That you will be successful in life and become famous."

Alexander said, " In some ways I hope that is true, but I would be happy if I were in love with the right lady."

Butler speaking authoritatively, "You will probably know that when the time comes when you find the right lady for yourself. "

Alexander, "You are very knowledgeable about life."

Butler added, "I like reading the Bible, too."

Alexander confessing, "I should read it more often. I miss going to the services at the church."

Butler thinking about how to help Alexander, said, "You can go to St. Mary's this Sunday. Will you go with our family?"
Alexander, "I would love to go but what will your parents think as I am twice your age. And what about the parishioners? Won't they think the worst?"

.110

Butler, "We are just worshiping. They barely know each other. They may think you are a family member or friend of the family. My parents know what you are really like."

Alexander laughed, "You are very clever."

Butler being considerate, "I will have father give you the directions."

Alexander and Butler talked for a long time. He forgot all about his business, and she forgot why she was waiting for her father. Richard Butler walked into the office, finally, and was surprised to see his daughter there.

Richard Butler, " Why are you here? Is there something wrong with your mother or the house?"

Butler, "Not really , father. Alexander and I have been talking."

Richard looking to Alexander, " Forgive me, sir."

Alexander making Richard at ease, "It is quite alright. It is harmless. We have discussed and solved many of life's problems. "

Butler said, "You said, Father, that I should take a more active interest in your business and learn the value of a pound sterling."

Richard embarrassed and Alexander smiling said, "Yes we do learn the value of hard work and an honest day wage around here. "

Butler, " There are other ways to get large amounts of money such as inheriting it."

Alexander chuckled even harder than before.

Richard Bryan, "Please , Butler, Mr. Spotswood does not want to hear that."

Alexander said, "Butler, I can't think of any source where I will inherit large sums of money. I will have to earn it."

Butler giving an example, "In the case of my godfather, James Butler, is a very successful soldier, inherited the Earldom of Ormond. He is a general, Knight of the Garter, and a Knight of the Thistle. He fought in Monmouth's Rebellion, the Williamite Wars, and in the Wars of Spanish Succession. With all this service, Queen Anne might give him a Palace like she did General Churchill."

Richard a little more serious and in a sterner tone. Said, " Butler, Please, Mr. Spotswood does not want to hear about our family history. You will remind Mr. Spotswood why he cannot finish his military career. He fought bravely with Churchill at Blenheim."

Butler dropped he head down as if embarrassed and became quiet. Her excitement seemed to turn instantly to sadness.

Alexander, "On the contrary, I think It is fascinating to listen to. "

Richard looking at Butler, " You have almost talked my partner to death. "
.111

Alexander said, " It has been refreshing to see the innocence in her voice and the confidence she has in people. "

Butler looking at Alexander, " Mr. Spotswood, would you escort me to church on Sunday with my father and mother."

Richard looking sternly at Butler and said, " That is quite enough. You are too bold and high spirited today."

Alexander looking charmingly at Butler, " I would be delighted to attend church with your mother's and father's consent. Which church do you attend?"

Butler, "The Anglican Church in Marleybone named St. Mary's. It is a church for saints and sinners and suitable for kings and queens."

Richard looking dumbfounded, " You have my consent to go with Butler and our family. We will meet you outside the front entrance of the church at 10 am. "

Butler on leaving the office said, "Goodbye for now."

Alexander looking happy with the events of the day, said, " I will see you Sunday."

Sunday soon came and Alexander was at St. Mary's at 10 am. It was a tall stone church with iconic columns and a tall steeple with a bell that had graced the London skies since King Edward I. After, Butler introduced her mother, Ann Brayne and Butler's sisters, to Alexander, they stepped inside. The Church had a beautiful stairway to the balcony and a large congregation had almost filled every pew in the church. It was obvious that Richard Brayne was known by all and he shook hands and greeted the other attendees. Richard introduced Alexander to Samuel Wesley, the pastor. The pastor was leading two young boys to their seats in front. Mr. Wesley introduced them as his sons, Charles Wesley and John Wesley. The pastor said to Alexander, "I am nervous to preach today, and I am not sure what the Lord has placed on my heart. I am also nervous about my sons misbehaving."

Alexander said, "They look like fine young lads." Looking at the boys, Alexander said, "Do not misbehave for your father's sake. "

The older boy Charles spoke up and said, " You have my word and have my honor on it."

Alexander, " I believe you."

Butler and her sisters, Anne and Dianne and Mr. and Mrs. Brayne, and Alexander sat on a pew close to the front. The sermon would be about strangers in a foreign land. They all listened intensely to the sermon, "God, the father is always with you." The sermon particularly had a special message to Alexander . The main lesson of the message was that no matter where you travel in the world, God is always with you. Even, if your biological father is in Heaven, your Heavenly Father is with you. Even if no one in the World knows your name when in other lands, the Father of Abraham, Isaac, and Jacob knows your name.

The sermon was based on bible verses in Deuteronomy chapters 1 and 8. Observe the commandments of the Lord, your God and walk in his ways and revere Him. For the Lord your God is bringing you into a good land, a land with streams and pools, and water flowing in the valley. A land with wheat and barley, vines and fig trees, pomegranates, olive oil and honey, a land where land will not be scarce, and you will lack nothing. The land where there are rocks and iron and you can dig copper out of the hills. When you have eaten and are satisfied .

Praise the Lord for the good land. Thank Him for what he has given you. Be careful not to forget the Lord your God. At the end of the sermon there was closing prayer, invitation to join the church, and benediction and closing hymn. The pastor came to Alexander's pew and asked him and the Braynes to stay for lunch and to come back again the next Sunday. He said that the Braynes are God fearing people that he had known for a long time. The Brayne family and Alexander seemed to like the sermon.

Alexander said, "I would like to stay if it is pleasing to the Braynes. "

Richard and Ann Brayne said that it would be fine. On the way to the tables in the garden outdoor, they passed along some beautiful flowers growing next to the church's cemetery. The table was full of food and drink and all the parishioners that stayed for lunch enjoyed the fellowship with one another. Alexander asked Butler if she want to take a stroll in Regents Park which was across the street from the church provided it suited her parents.

"Butler asking for permission, "Why yes, mother, you and father don't care if we take a stroll in Regents Park."

Richard said, "Why, no. We will wait and mingle with our friends here at church." Butler and Alexander left the church to go outside to the park.

Ann Brayne to her husband Richard, "Don't you worry about Alexanders intentions with our daughter?"

Richard Brayne, " Why no, dear Anne, he is one of the most handsome men in London and the girls and ladies giggle and flirt with him all the time when he is on the street, in the pubs, or in the theater. Yet, he does not flirt with them or encourage them in any way. He is respectable to everyone and will probably someday be rich and famous."

Anne, "It is not Alexander, that I am worried about. It is Butler, I know her. She is hoping he will court her. Our daughter is in love with a handsome colonel and businessman."

Richard, "I think it is infatuation for now with her. They are surely pleased with each other's company."

Anne, "Think what you will. We might do better and then we could do worse."

When Alexander and Butler began their walk in the park, they chatted about the scenery, the lake, the flowers, and the wildlife. Pretty soon they were having thoughts about the morning's sermon.

Alexander, "You know, Butler, I think God is good for giving land to his people for obedience to him." Butler, can you imagine a place where there are plenty of streams, where families can live in peace, and be blessed by the Lord? "

Butler, " My uncle, James, said if he had not been a general in the Queens Regiment, he may not have been given an Earldom, but he had always asked God for a blessing and he eventually got one."

Alexander sharing his knowledge, "I have only heard talk about one land that has these qualities and that is The Americas."

Butler corrected him politely, "The Bible is talking about Israel. They are being given the Promised Land."

Alexander, "They may be all that, but the people at the guild hall in Deal said, The Americas have enough land that even a shepherd can be filthy rich."

Butler, "There is more to life than being rich. It is sometimes a curse. What is important is how you treat each other and how you reverence God."'

Alexander telling some secrets of his past, "A pirate told me that I was under a curse and he stole my sword. The curse would be that I would be rich among other things."

Butler, "Don't trust the pirate. The love of money can be a curse. Trust in the Lord and he will help you get to Heaven. It is harder for a rich man to get to Heaven than it is for a camel to get through the eye of a needle."

Alexander looking enlightened, "I could forget about the pirates curse, but I don't want to forget that truth you have just spoken."

.

It had been a good start in the two young people's lives. This would not be the last time they would have deep discussions. For this day, Alexander had learned more about his destiny and learned more about Butler. She was a remarkable young lady and much wiser than her years. They would see each other over the next few years occasionally, but she was busy in school and there was such a difference in age, but he seemed to like her company. They would go to The Drury theater to see plays or go to the observatory and look at the telescope to see the moon, stars, and Sothis. He would not tell Butler about his fascination about the star and how that particular star was always with him when he looked for it. He could tell she was interested in him as a friendly companion, but he knew they were not ready for marriage because of her schooling and his taking care of his mother. He was fond of her and thought of her often.

Alexander was busy at the office and had additional family duties now. Alexander lived at the Golden Square taking care of his ailing mother, Katherine. He would keep busy at work building his business and take care of Katherine when he got home at night. He and Margaret would take her out in the courtyard where people always gathered to gossip, listen to the music, and listen to story tellers spin their yarns. Katherine seemed to like the crowd and they were good neighbors. Katherine was getting weak and weaker and would have unexplained stomach pain. Alexander and Margaret had her see a doctor at the hospital in Chelsea.

The doctor came out of the room Katherine had been admitted and broke the long-awaited news to Margaret and Alexander. He said that her symptoms were the sign of a very serious disease and recommended they take her to a specialist in Ireland. Margaret said that she would arrange to get a boat to take them across the waters to Ireland. Margaret would get an appointment with the specialist. In a few days they took Katherine to Doctor Wright who would examine her. Katherine could verily walk at this point and would need nursing care around the clock. He took Katherine into an examination room and Margaret and Alexander waited patiently outside the door. The minutes seemed like hours to the two of them. Alexander said that he had written a letter to Roger notifying him of their mother's health but didn't know how long it would take the letter to get to Gibraltar.

Alexander said, "If I could only speed up the mail service and be able to help my mother more."

The doctor said, "I sincerely wish I had good news to tell you, but regrettably, I don't. I think your mother knows that she does not have much longer to live. She has an extra ordinary amount of peace about her and said she knows about her destiny and will soon meet her three husbands in Heaven. I do not think you should move her back to England as the trip will surely make her condition worse."

Margaret broke down and cried. Alexander looked sad and looked down at the floor. His mother had always been there when he needed someone to talk to or listen to a good story.

When Margaret and Alexander entered the hospital room where their mother lay, Katherine said softly and weakly, "I will be alright to stay here in Ireland. I do not feel like making the trip back to London. I would like to see Roger, soon, if he could come."

Alexander, "Mother, I have sent a letter to him, but I will send another and explain your wishes to him. He will want to come. He is so far away, and letters travel so slowly."

"I know he will come, "and Katherine nodded off to sleep.

Alexander told Doctor Wright that they would have to go back to get their business and personal affairs in order so they could come back to stay with their mother.

As soon as Margaret left the room, she started crying and after a few minutes regained her composure, said, " I have only known my mother for the past 15 years or so, as I grew up in England, but I love her and don't want her to leave us."

Alexander said, "I know, and I don't want to see her go this way. I will write another letter and notify Roger. " Alexander wrote another letter, to Roger.

_____

My dear brother, Roger Elliott in Gibraltar Nov 1st. 1709
Although we are worlds apart right now in miles, we want you to come home immediately. Our mother health is deteriorating rapidly and is not expected to live much longer. She has asked for you to come home so she can see you once again.
Margaret and I are arranging things so we can stay with her in Ireland as that is her wishes. She is too weak to travel.
I have been thinking of us when we were growing up in Tangier and all the good days we have had together with our mother and fathers.
Will see you soon. Respectfully and affectionately, Alexander and Margaret

_____

Alexander knew that it would take several months before the letter arrived in Gibraltar for Roger to leave his post and come to London.

Alexander returned to London and into the house on Golden Square and seemed empty without his mother. It weighed sorrowfully on him of his being away from his mother. He felt helpless as she was now so deathly sick . Alexander knew that his faith in God would keep him peaceful and knew that he could trust in the Lord to help him get through the coming days. Margaret would go to her home and would get all the legal papers ready.

Doctor Wright greeted them at the door and said, "Come into the chapel."
The Doctor began, by saying, "That I am regretful and that your mother had taken a turn for the worse. She died a few hours ago after I had summoned you to come back to the hospital. I am very sorry. She died in her sleep and peacefully."

They both hugged each other, Alexander, "I don't know that I could bear the thought of seeing my mother pass away. "

Margaret could not even talk as she was crying with all her might.

The doctor said, "I will leave you alone, but she did say in her last words; make sure the Love of God is in your soul. My love for my children is forever, and I hope my children will get married and have their own happy families. " And Margaret sobbed uncontrollably.

They went into see their mother one more time and sensed that their lives would now start on a new journey without her presence.

The funeral service and burial were held at St. Mary's in Marleybone, in London. In the first few days of November of 1709, Katherine Maxwell Elliott Spotswood Mercer died, and it was truly a sad day for friends and family.

Margaret and Alexander would have to tell Roger about the loss of their mother when he arrived from Gibraltar.

At the funeral service they gathered at the Church of St. Mary's. Pastor Wesley began reading scripture from Matthew 5:3-8.

Blessed are the poor in Spirit; for theirs is the kingdom of heaven.

Blessed are they that mourn; for they shall be comforted.

Blessed are the meek ;for they will inherit the earth.

Blessed are they that do hunger and thirst after righteousness, for they shall be filled.

Blessed are the merciful ; for they shall be merciful.

Blessed are the pure in heart; for they shall see God.

The sermon seemed to be appropriate for the faithful and loyal follower of Christ, Katherine Mercer. She had been a minister's daughter and had married three God fearing men who had preceded her in death. The kind words of the pastor resonated with her children even though they were deeply grieving. Alexander and Margaret friends consoled them as best they could. Butler came to the service and hugged Alexander on his departure from the cemetery grounds. She must have sensed he wanted to be alone to handle his grief. He thanked her and her parents for paying their respects.

Margaret's friend, Sarah Churchill came to the funeral service and offered her sympathy to the family. She remarked how well Margaret and Alexander had taken care of her. She even remarked about how successful Alexander had been in his business and how he put his social life aside took care of his mother and that the Queen may have a special assignment for him. Alexander was puzzled by what she meant.

Alexander and Margaret went on to their homes and for the next few weeks and pondered all about the family's memories made in Tangier, London, Deal, and Ireland. They would miss their mother's daily presence, but they would not forget her smiling at them the last time they had seen her. She had smiled as though she was at rest and at peace.

Roger in a couple of months arrived at the docks in London . The children of Katherine Mercer reunited at last and they continued to talk for hours over the good times they all had shared with their Mother. After a few days and a visit to his mother's grave, Roger, bid farewell and said the duties at Gibraltar would need his attention and he wished the best for Alexander and his business. Roger also wished the best for Margaret and hoped that she would remarry and have a happy family as their mother had always wanted.

After a few weeks went by, Sarah Churchill invited Margaret and Alexander over for supper. Sarah's husband, Lt. General John Churchill was between wars and left the war arena of the Spanish Succession for a while. The great warrior, John Churchill had left General Salamander Cutts in charge.

The Churchills sat down at their big dinner table in the formal dining room. Margaret and Alexander sat down at the table and Alexander offered a blessing on the evening meal and they began eating venison and vegetables.

Sarah, " We still have fond memories of your mother, Alexander and Margaret. She surely was able to make you successful and gave you all many good qualities."

Margaret, Yes, "We miss her and thank you for your kind remarks."

Sarah, speaking to Alexander, "You have learned many great qualities as a soldier, a gentleman, and a businessman. You have been very successful running your own company. I envision you as being able to accomplish great things and be able to help the Queen carry out some of her goals."

Alexander politely, "Thank you for the remarks, But I don't know how I could help the Queen."

Sarah remarked," She remarked to me and Margaret once that you are very handsome, and if you were as good in leading your fellow countrymen as you were in your looks, you could change history."

Alexander a little blushed, " I know that you mean well, and I am very humbled and flattered."

John Churchill who had been sitting and eating very quietly, "In other words, we are doing very well in our war with France but General Hamilton who you bravely fought with at Blenheim, has been assigned the position as Colonial Governor of the Colony of Virginia, in the Americas. He is too busy in the war to adequately do the job as a Governor. Sarah and I think you could be the acting Governor of Virginia and live there, too. He would actually have the title, but you would be the Governor in theory and receive one half of the pay. Once you got established you could also continue your business interest in London and America in tobacco, or timber, or land, and continue to be a wealthy man."

Alexander quit eating as he was taking in all the conversation. "There are certainly more qualified men or politicians that could do a more skilled job in running the colony. Would you not agree?"

Sarah speaking truthfully," That is why the Queen likes your honesty. The job is not about the Whigs and Tories but about administration and loyalty to the Crown. "

John Churchill, "The Queen and Hamilton think that your administrative abilities are excellent. Your opposition would be William Byrd and James Blair who are the leaders of the Council of Burgesses in Virginia. They both have different opinions on how the Colony of Virginia should be run. William Byrd is a good man and a wealthy man who will help the land speculators and business growth and believe in keeping control to only a few wealthy individuals like himself. James Blair is the Chaplin we have who will make a concerted effort to improve education, arts, and culture. He   is a capable leader and very religious. He believes in population growth, education, freedom of religion and the power delegated to many individuals. You mostly would relate well to Blair because he is Scottish and well educated in the Church like your Scottish ancestors. He undoubtedly studied about your John Spotswood, the Archbishop who wrote the prayer book. It does not matter, however, if they agree with you or not. You will be doing what the Queen and House of Commons wants to get accomplished in Virginia. You will also at the same time try to keep the million and half Virginia citizens also loyal to the Crown and make them feel they are living in England. The land is beautiful and almost unlimited. The Indians are sometimes a little troubling, but with your military experience you will be able to handle that. With all the trade and ships coming and going from the ports at Jamestown and Yorktown; there is a real and potential threat from the pirates especially around Okracoke Island up to the Chesapeake Bay. Some of the gentry that is already settled in Virginia have lived very well. Others may struggle by trapping, hunting, and gardening and live in very primitive conditions. There are no paved Streets like there are in London. You can be an empire builder and build Virginia to become a better place. It can be yours!"

Margaret excitedly, "It sounds wonderful. Alexander, I know you can do it. Look at Roger. You asked him how he liked running Gibraltar and he loved it. Mother would be so proud. "

Alexander was a little shocked but seemed very interested, "I have always wondered what it would be like to be
.117

in America."

Sarah, " I have heard it is a fantastic opportunity for business. It is a young colony and is not settled by any large army or have many inhabitants. The French or trying to gain control of parts of America and The Spanish have already claimed some of the land for themselves. I imagine that someday it will be only controlled by one country and that country should be England. "

John looking at Alexander, "I have faith in you, Alexander. Will you at least consider going to Virginia?"

Alexander paused, looking around the room. He must have thought that there is something in the mind , soul, and spirit saying yes. He hoped it was not part of a curse speaking for him he thought for a second.

Alexander humbly and confidently said, "If the opportunity arises, I will go to Virginia. "

The Churchills and guests soon finished their meal and talked a little more about America and then Margaret and Alexander left the Churchill home feeling like destiny was calling. They went on home that evening wondering how it all would turn out.

In a few weeks Alexander got called to the Military Office near St. James Palace and met General John Hamilton. Alexander was impressed by the large hall that led to General Hamilton's Office. On the walls were at least a thousand rifles that were mounted uniformly and symmetrically which made a large display of weaponry to show England's military strength. The British after all had the strongest army in the world and this would be an extravagant display of military strength.

After some small chat, General Hamilton got down to business." You have won Queen Anne's approval."
He offered the Lt. Governorship of Virginia to Alexander Spotswood, now about 34 years of age who would become the leader of one of the most successful English colonies. Hamilton explained that Alexander would get a briefing by the Queen, the House of Lords, and the House of Commons. He would meet with all the important committee leaders that would deal in the governorship affairs of Virginia before he left London. This would take a couple of weeks. He would be heading for America in June right before the hurricane season in the tropics, so as not to interfere with the sailing.

Alexander knew that his business partners, Mr. Starke and Mr. Brayne could take of his business. He had Margaret as his only family to worry about, and she said she would be all right living in London and would eventually want to remarry.

Alexander thought that he must tell Butler something, but he didn't know how to go about it or know exactly what to say. He thought that Mr. Brayne might have told her about his new life. After the church service one Sunday, he went and set next to her at service. She was quite beautiful, and Alexander did not want to upset her in any way.

Butler started the conversation, "Father says you will be leaving for Virginia in a few weeks. It sounds like a good opportunity for you ,Alexander."

Alexander, "Yes, it is, but I will miss seeing you at the church and at the theater."

Butler giggled, "Yes, I will miss you, too, but above all I want you to be happy."

Alexander asked, "You will miss me? I think about you a lot now, but I don't know how it will be not seeing you at all."

Butler, "We can write to each other and keep in touch. I know that you always do the right thing. You once told me you had to build your business first before you settled down with a family."

Alexander, "Why yes, I did say that, and I may be only over there a few years maybe and then I can settle down. These last few years I had been taking care of Mother and I wanted to be with you more than I did."

Butler," Alexander, it is alright. I know that you are fond of me, but we are not ready to settle down. I would not be a very good wife for you right now. And there is no other man I would rather be with. If it is meant for us to be together later, it will just happen at the right time. You are destined for something great. You have many special qualities that set you apart from others. I don't know that I could share your attention with all the ladies in Virginia."

Alexander said, "You would certainly be the wisest and most beautiful of all. "

"Thank you , Alexander." She kissed him on his cheek like a sister would, and said," Goodbye for now. Do come visit us before you leave."

Alexander, "Oh yes, I will."

Alexander soon was done with his training with the Queen and Parliament. He had met all the Lords that he would have to correspond with, and he had said goodbye to Margaret, and he promised he would write to her often.
He started to get on the ship, *HMS Deptford*, to sail to America. He turned around and saw Butler Brayne. She was dressed in her finest dress and looked radiant. Her natural beauty at 19 was remarkable. Butler was smiling from ear to ear.

Alexander could see his partner Richard Brayne and his wife waiting in a carriage at the road entrance to London on the mainland across the bridge from The Portsmouth Dockyard where the ship would leave for Virginia. The Braynes had brought Butler down to the spit head at Portsmouth Dockyard. It was at the spit head or deepest channel in the Ocean channel where the man of war, *HMS Deptford*, that would take Alexander to his new home. Alexander waved goodbye to the Braynes, and then cast his eyes on Butler.

Butler smiling and jokingly, "I want to go with you , but I forgot to pack my bags."

Alexander smiling, " Maybe next time. Anyway, you are not dressed for sailing."

Butler," I will not say, goodbye, because we will never be apart in thought and spirit."

Alexander," I will miss you and I will write to you. "

The oarsmen took up the anchor and the sailors set the sails to catch the wind and the oarsmen untied the ropes from the quay . The ship was ready for sailing.

Butler trying to act happy for Alexander, but she was sad about his leaving her behind, "Well, the Lord has given you a pretty day to sail. You are going to miss the boat if you hang around here."

Alexander asked, "You know that I love you?"

Butler answered, "Yes, I know. Don't forget me though. I will be waiting for a letter from you telling me all about

Virginia."

Alexander sincerely speaking, "You are too important to me to forget. I will be waiting for a letter from you to keep me aware of your comings and goings in London. I can't say goodbye, either. I can only say that I will see you again after my assignment in the Colony, but I will be thinking about you every day. "

Alexander couldn't help but kiss her, and then he quickly jumped from the dock to the ship. The boat started out in the water and Alexander and Butler waved to each other as long as they could. Butler turned her back on the ship as soon as Alexander was out of sight. She went quickly to sit on the chairs on the quay and began crying. She was thinking about all the things that she should have said to him such as, "I love you, too, Alexander or I will wait for you here or I pray nothing happens to you in Virginia." She hoped that he knew this already. She then asked to herself. Lord, is he the man for me? She turned around and looked at the ship fading in the horizon. She quickly gained her composure and went to join her parents who had witnessed the farewell and had been waiting patiently nearby. They sensed how important this day April 3, 1710 was for Butler. This might be the last time she would see Alexander Spotswood. The thought of not ever seeing him sunk into her head once more. She hoped that he would keep his word and write to her, and she would anxiously await his letters from Virginia.

The *HMS Deptford* was leaving the navy docks at Portsmouth. It was a fully rigged sailing ship loaded with 50 guns. This man of war was about 30 years old but in good condition and was the standard 125 foot by 35-foot ship. It was part of a convoy sailing beside the *HMS Bedford* which was a bigger 70-gun man of war. In the convoy were six merchant ships that would be taking supplies and products to Jamestown, a colonial fort on Virginia's James River. The Captain of the *Deptford* was a rear admiral in the British navy named Tancred Robinson, who was about 25 years of age and had made trips to Virginia before. The route would take them southerly with the winds to the Canary Islands or further south and then take the trade winds across the North Equatorial channel and just south of the seaweed obstacles that were part of the Sea of Saragossa. They would come into Barbados and then start northerly though West Indies and the Caribbean islands up to the Florida coastline and eventually to the port at Jamestown.

Queen Anne had also provided the new lieutenant governor with 15 personal servants, a secretary, named Robert White, an Oxford graduate who was considered one of the most brilliant students that ever attended there. Also, in the entourage was Alexander's hostess known as Ms. Thornton and Dr. William Cocke, who would be Alexander's personal physician. They would all get a cabin close to the gun deck as there were sailors on the lower decks and the conditions were not as pleasant. There were also about 30 other passengers on the ship. It was smooth sailing and an English Union Jack Flag was blowing on all 8 ships. It was a beautiful day in early summer and sunny. Alexander looked back at England and had a lot of emotion in his head. He was leaving his sister, his business friends, and the one lady who could be his wife and make him happy. The roar of the waves calmed his nerves and he was soon thinking about the long voyage. It would take several weeks to get to Virginia even if the winds were favorable.

Alexander would study his official colonial papers given to him by John Hamilton, the Governor who would stay back in England to bring the war to conclusion. He would discuss the papers with Robert White so they could start working quickly with the Virginia House of Lords and Burgesses when they arrived in Williamsburg, the government headquarters of Virginia in the new world. The voyage seemed routine to Alexander as he and his family had spent so much time on a man of war coming from Tangier to Plymouth, England, 26 years earlier. He still did not like being confined to such a little space and living in a cramped, unclean place even if it was a temporary situation. The food was not good or plentiful, and he remembered having to drink the wine and alcoholic beverages because fresh water was not always readily available. He did sleep well and continued saying his prayers as he always had before he went to bed. Now he thanked the Lord that he had met Butler, and that he would seek God's wisdom on what to say to her and write to her. He had always been told that

.120

those you think about last before you go to sleep at bedtime are the ones you have the most feelings for.

After a few days on the voyage to The Colony of Virginia, one man came out from the lower deck as if to appear out of thin air. Alexander thought to himself that he hadn't remember seeing this man before. If he had been around the ship, he must have been by himself hiding or so quiet that he went unnoticed. Certainly, he had not mingled before with the other passengers. The curiosity was getting to Alexander. He went up to him on the foredeck while the young man was looking at the full moon. One could see his face clearly. He had black hai and was very handsome indeed. He had a modest styled business suit with a striped cravat which made him look professional enough to be a student or young businessman.

Alexander, started a conversation by saying, " How are you this nice evening?"

Young Man replied, "Ahoy,   I am just fine, sir. You look familiar. Do I know you?"

Alexander said, "I am Alexander Spotswood. I have a business in London. I am headed to the Colony of Virginia. I came out here to look at the stars and the moon."

Young man, "I am Edward. I am heading for the Caribbean Islands on business myself. "

Alexander remarked, "I don't think we have met, but I am sure it will be a good voyage."

Edward asked, " Do you think the stars and moon will bring you fortune?"

Alexander replied, " I don't know. I hope so. I just admire them for their beauty and calmness."

Edward prying, "Are you English? You have a distinctive way of talking. You have had excellent tutoring, or you have a gentry background."

Alexander being friendly, "I am mostly English, but exposed to Scottish and some other languages. I have a military background. I was born in a garrison hospital in Tangier, Africa and got some schooling there."

Edward responded, "Alexander is not an African name."

Alexander replied, "True. It is a Biblical name with a Greek origin. In Latin it means " defending mankind."

Edward said, "I should have figured that one. Alexander the Great was a Macedonian and Macedonia is close to Greece . I have been to Tangier when it was ruled by Moulay He was ruthless. My dad was a sea captain of sorts. I traveled with him to almost every port in the known world."

Alexander decided not to tell about his life in Tangier to an unknown stranger, "Is that the business you are in?"

Edward bragging, " Yes, I am carrying on my father's business. Mostly in the Caribbean, Europe, and recently West Indies, and the Americas. As soon as I get my business going, I will find some pretty lady and marry. I have a girl in every port now."

Alexander said, "I had to retire from the military, and then I started a business of my own. I am going to America to start a new life. I have only heard good things about all the opportunities there."

Edward nodding his head in agreement, "You can get rich growing rice, tobacco, corn and wheat. Even the governments will buy food for their citizens in Russia, Finland, and France because of the famines they have had there in recent years. Millions of people have died of starvation. How can some of the great armies of the world feed their soldiers and war horses, but many of their own people die for lack of food. I see it all over the world."

Alexander said, "That is a great idea, but it takes time to grow crops and ship them, unless the owners have the grain in storage already. Won't the famines be over?"

Edward explaining, "Using the same reasoning, it takes time after a drought or bad crop to get the crops and gardens going at full production again, but people need to eat every day. There is money to be made by producing, storing, and selling grains. "

Alexander agreeing, "You have a point. I saw that firsthand on the manors in County Kent, England."

Edward said, "I hate to see people suffer and die. I've seen my share. Since I live on one of the 7000 islands in the Bahamas, I am almost convinced that there are curses put on people and countries. There are so called "voo doo" priests that are free men and are descendants from the first Africans brought over in bondage, who put curses on the people they do not like. The priests are called boheas. You have probably seen them or heard of them because their curses are supposed to have their beginnings in Africa."

Alexander not discussing his curse, " I have heard about curses being put on people, but I have never seen a bohea."

Edward," The voo doo priests believe in a medicine that comes from the bushes on the Bahama Islands. They believe that this bush medicine will cure a lot of ailments and if used correctly can be used to prevent themselves from getting curses, or for getting curses cured that was put on them by witches who practice witchcraft. The Spanish who have waged war against the natives of Bahamas have also waged war against the voo doos and witches so there are few people involved in this and the bush medicine. When you get to the Bahamas, you will see a church on every street, too, and the saints oppose the sale of any bush medicine. Now my men who are expert salesmen take this bush medicine to every port in the world and sell it as a medicine that cures most ailments. The natives now are trading and selling; bananas, rice, tobacco, and vegetables, and fish. The islanders believe in mermaids that appear to them in the blue holes of the ocean that goes to a castle and the mermaids will grant them every wish they desire. There are some limestone stones and blocks of stone that have been sculptured and looked as though they were part of a road or wall of an ancient bridge that was a 1/2 mile from shore near Bemmenee that went to the island of Atlantis. There were two treasures there, one was like a fountain of youth and the other was all the gold that was taken from the Incas and the Florida Indians that they had mined in the New World long ago."

Alexander must have thought if this man was just telling a story, or is this really true? Edward seemed convincing and knowledgeable.

Edward continued, "Atlantis disappeared below the water because of all the weight of the gold on the island and it was sucked down in the ocean by a gigantic blue whirlpool during a storm caused by an angry god. These big holes can suck an entire ship down below the ocean surface, even a ship as big as this one. The islanders who try to take their ships out to find Atlantis and all the gold, die trying to locate the lost island of Atlantis. Now the fountain of youth must have been in the land of the Florida Indians because the natives who live there never look like they are no older than 30 years of age. Legend has that anyone who tries to follow the Florida Indians to the Fountain of Youth usually die or have bad luck, bad health, and always loose anything of value. "

Alexander," Did Atlantis really exist? I've always heard that the waters of the Bahama Islands have hundreds of Spanish Galleons that were full of heavy gold that sunk during violent windstorms and rainstorms. I have heard about an underwater graveyard of ships which it is almost impossible to visit and to bring the gold to the surface because the water is too deep for the swimmers. Did they vanish in some kind of blue hole? "

Edward thinking about that statement, " I guess that is true, too. Now According to Herodotus, a Roman historian from thousands of years ago, believed in Spanish Galleons and wrote about them. The Romans had ships long ago that were so large they could carry 5000 fighting men, and when they crossed though the straits of Gibraltar, they had much difficulty because the ships were so large."

Alexander, "Those boats sound too large and that seems almost unbelievable."

Edward continued, "The Roman's had a merchant ship called the microphoric that could hold 365 tons of barley, wheat, or pepper. Some of the ships had hulls that could hold 150 tons of wine from the Mediterranean vineyards. The ships had 4 large sails as big as 4 blue whales and a complex rigging system to utilize the wind to move the large amount of weight. The Romans took these ships to Egypt to bring ½ million pounds of grain out of Egypt to keep the Romans from starving. The Egyptians became rich and powerful from all the trading. If we could only get enough grain out of the Far East to feed the starving nations of Europe, you could make a fortune just hauling the grain. One time one of the ships landed on the island of Atlantis when they had come a few days out of the straits of Gibraltar. The soldiers on returning to Rome swore to the emperor there were temples and castles built out of pure gold. The emperor scolded them severely when they did not claim the gold for the Roman Empire and bring some of the gold home as a proof of the existence of Atlantis. When the sailors returned to the place where they had sailed into the island before, the island was gone. Atlantis had disappeared. They searched around that part of the Atlantic Ocean for 3 months and sadly went back to Rome empty handed. They told the emperor that they could not find the island. The emperor asked, "how does an entire island disappear?" One of the sailors said, it was an earthquake or some kind of blue hole windstorm.

The emperor said sternly to the returning sailors, "Do you think I am a fool? Maybe you will have me believe that Atlantis was a manmade island like Cleopatra constructed in Egypt with the 250-foot floating island off the coast of Alexandria. Are you leading me to believe that Atlantis floated away to one of our enemies?" The emperors ordered the sailors to leave him or he would flog the sailor rats one more time.

Alexander, "Interesting! Does the Atlantic Ocean get its name from Atlantis?"

 Edward thinking, "Maybe, but Greek mythology would tell you that it was named after Atlas, who the real god punished for choosing the wrong side in the Battle of the Gods. Atlas was forced to hold the sky up high away from the ocean while God finished his 6-day creation and they both rested on the 7th day. The Atlantic means the sea of Atlas and was called that by the Romans, Greek, Persians, Egyptians, and the yellow men of Cathay."

Alexander, now the one to pry, "You are well learned! May I ask you where you went to school?"

Edward, "I have had no formal education. I was born and raised on a sailing vessel headed to the West Indies from Bristol , England. I have listened to many stories from people from all over the seven seas . Most people are eager to tell what they know if you ask them something. In other words, I have taught myself what I need to know. So, Alexander the Great, you are about to build an empire in the New World?"

Alexander chuckling, "No sir, not any empire for now. Let the British do that. I am merely a servant of my country and my Queen."

Alexander, "Does anybody really know about Atlantis or what the people were like?"

 Edward replied, " The Romans had the first maps of their roads and their seas and carved these paths on a stone with all the known roads, seas, and land masses, and known countries. The stone was mounted by a
.123

harbor by the sea. They called this stone, Tabula Roma as if Rome was in the center of the universe. They show a Christian nation at the east end of the Mediterranean Sea called the Israelites where there are Jews and Jesus is their Messiah. Then on the Western entrance to the Mediterranean Sea at the Straits of Gibraltar, the Romans said there were a sea people living on an Island, about a hundred miles further west, called Atlantis. Only a few Romans ever met the sea people, because they stayed to themselves and did not travel in easterly directions. There is an account in one book written by a Roman historian that said there once was a Roman sailor escaped from the Island after being captured there. That Roman sailor told many hard to believe stories about what happened on the Island. Why he was captured or how he got free has never been explained, but the sailor said he had no reason to lie about what he witnessed. He said there were circular canals going around the island. There was a large pyramid in the center made of stone which he thought were like the Inca Mounds in South America, but he never saw anyone worship there. There were warrior guards at the front gates, and there was a big wall around the island and there was only one way in and one way out. The inhabitants wore face guards over there face and you could not tell what they really looked like. Their clothes were of metal and looked kind of like armor. They were excellent swimmers under water and didn't seem to have to come up for air very much. They seemed to be more advanced than any other country in the world. They lived up in tower like structures that were 40-feet tall which had walkways between the towers. There were also storage towers which held grain for food, but no one would tell where the grain would come from. The Atlanteans planted gardens around the towers and always had plenty to eat. They ate mostly fish from the ocean. Their leader named Salta, had a way of turning the ocean saltwater into drinking water. Salta built a fountain of fresh drinking water which was in the middle of a pond of water in which mermaids swam around in the pond. The God of the Universe had created a garden of Eden on the eastern edge of the Mediterranean. The unknown god of Atlantis had many gardens and vineyards at the western boundary of the Mediterranean at Atlantis. It was a one of a kind island with a continual supply of fruits, vegetables, and drinks. Their mere existence was unexplainable to the ancient Romans, Greeks and Alexandrians who were considered the most advanced societies in the ancient world. The Roman sailor who said he had escaped from Atlantis, reported that he witnessed these people for about six months. He said the Atlanteans did not work and did not have schools, hospitals, stores or churches and did not have any children. The men were all the same size and appeared to be about six feet tall and black hair and had blue eyes behind their masked faces. The women were all the same size and appeared to be about 5'8 inches and had long black hair and blue eyes behind their masked faces. The people did not show emotion and did not speak out loud, with their mouths or tongues, but seemed to be content with each other on the island which was like a paradise. In fact, they communicated to him by their eyes and mind and he could somehow understand what they were saying to him. They understood his thoughts. When other nations ended up on Atlantis shores, the Atlanteans were able to understand the travelers no matter what country they were from. They usually would give supplies to the travelers but would not let them enter the island gates. If the travelers came in by force or by an attack, the Alantians would have what appeared to be lightning come out of their hands and destroy the enemy. The enemies would vanish in thin air. Another power that the islanders had were they were able to appear before you in one place and then quickly vanish, then could reappear in another spot in front of you. They did not like mixing with strangers."

Alexander, very curious about the story, " That is amazing! "Do you think the Roman sailor was telling the truth?"

Edward, " He would have no reason to lie. He wasn't sure or could never explain why he was held prisoner or how he was able to escape, or why he was allowed to escape from Atlantis." I guess the Atlantians figured that no one would believe just one person's story and figured he was just a sailor who had drank a little too much or had been in the sun too long on the open seas. Some of his fellow Romans did think that he might have been drugged or tampered with to tell the rest of the world what the Atlanteans wanted the rest of the world to know about them. They were a peaceful people and seem to be interested only in the gold and silver of the Indian tribes in America, especially the Inca Indians and the Florida Indians. They had boats that carried the treasure from the Indians back to their island, but the boats did not have sails or oars. How these boats were powered were unknown. How they got the gold and silver was unknown. But the ships traveled quickly from port to port. They never traveled east from Atlantis to Rome or any other Mediterranean ports. They only traveled west to the Americas unnoticed and were never seen by anyone. They would leave their mark. The mark was a warrior with a spear at a gate with an A on the gate. It would be found carved on the sand on a beach, a bark on the tree, or on a rocky mountain ledge. I would assume the A was for Atlantis because the main gate at the Island had an A carved into the stone gate. Their leader, Salta had tremendous powers. The sailor said he could build gigantic walls and towers destroyed either by an earthquake, by pointing his finger at the spot where he wanted walls, and they would just appear. Where the walls came from was unknown, but they were as hard and heavy that 20 men could not lift even one of the stones."

Alexander, "That is unbelievable."

Edward responding, "The sailor kept saying when pressed that he swore it was the truth. He said that Salta spelled backwards is Atlas, but he says that he did not believe the leader was the real Atlas."

Alexander asked, "What do you think happened to Atlantis?"

Edward, " It was probably destroyed by an earthquake because of all the weight of the island and the gold or it could have been destroyed in a blue hole by a violent storm which would put the island itself on the ocean floor which the depth of which cannot be measured. I guess it is possible Salta and all of Atlantis could have decided to disappear in thin air, one day, long ago."

 Alexander exclaimed, "It would be interesting to know what really happened to the people."

Edward said, "We will be passing by the area where Atlantis was located in a few hours. There will be nothing to see. If you could fly like an eagle you could fly to the east and soon be back in Tangier."

Alexander, "Tangier is a beautiful place but too dangerous for me now. I had better get to bed."

Edward, "Good night, Matey."

Alexander went on to his bunk and took one last look at Sothis, the other stars, and the moon. Everything was going well as planned. The seas were calm, and Alexander would dream about the Island Paradise, but it all seemed so far away and mind bending. He would say his prayers to the Lord and pray for the safety of the ship and for the safety of Roger, Margaret, and Butler. He didn't really get to know Edward but thought him to be a good storyteller.

The convoy was headed south carried by the currents and winds in a southerly direction. The *Deptford* and *Bedford* and the merchant ships would be in the western African port of Dakar soon. Dakar was a western Africa seaport, frequently used as a port by all British merchant ships traveling to the Americas and Indies. It was located close to the British Fort of Saint James and the Goree Islands and very close to the mouth of the Gambia River that came out to the turquoise colored sea and tree lined coast. In fact, the first thing that the passengers would see were the baobab trees that were at the dock area. They were as wide as they were tall shooting up from the savannah like wooden monuments into the bluish African skies. These trees looked like a welcoming giant in the tawny grass that dotted the savannah around Dakar. In fact, these trees looked like they were uprooted and then placed upside down. There bare limbs looked like a tangled mass of tree roots barren of fruit and leaves. They looked lifeless but were being used at the port for markers and for their unique natural beauty. In fact, one of the baobabs tree trunk had a big chunk of wood cut out of it and replaced with bars to be used as a holding cell for prisoners. Another had been made into an outdoor chapel so people could come in from the desert sun and rest and pray inside the baobabs tree trunk. The other trees had large carvings on them. One

.125

had a large lion carved on the trunk held on by a hemp rope and another baobab had a map of Africa on it showing the major trade routes jotting out from Dakar.

Alexander and his entourage soon came off the *Deptford* and went to the English's dining hall to eat while the ship was being loaded for the long voyage to Barbados. He set down to modest and well received food from the natives. The ladies from along the Gambia River had brought up some oyster stew they had made from oysters they had gathered from the river. They also had some fresh fruit and bread made from cornmeal. The ladies seemed to be very polite and modest. Alexanders hostess, Miss Thornton told him that he should not get to friendly with the women because some of the sailors had been talking about some of the women who would sell their bodies and services to them for the men's pleasure. Alexander had too much on his mind about finishing the voyage to Williamsburg, Virginia and running the colony once he got there. He was not going to let anything be said about his character and especially any gossip of his taking advantage of a servant at a remote port. The ladies giggled around Alexander because of his good looks and his prosperous looking attire. He was also polite and told them thanks for bringing up the good tasting oyster soup.

Soon they would be on board the ship again and headed west for a 3000-mile voyage to Barbados. The Captain Robinson had disembarked here and would be replaced by a Captain Morris, a navy sailor from nearby St. James Fort. Captain Morris was a skilled and a technically savvy sailor which had made the trip across the North Atlantic Equatorial trade winds and currents many times before.

The sea seemed to have more swells than normal when they first started out and you could see the anxiety on most of the passengers faces. They wondered if the sailor was too young or too inexperienced to get them safely to Barbados or on to Williamsburg. After a few days, the seas calmed down and the boat seemed to be going faster towards the destination. Alexander went up to see how the Captain was doing and to see if he wanted any company, but Alexander saw that he was extremely sick. Alexander called for the coxswain to take over the steering of the *Deptford* and his personal doctor, Dr. Cocke to see if he could make a diagnosis. The doctor soon appeared with his medical bag and looked at Captain Morris who had been removed to his quarters. The doctor saw the nosebleed and vomit that had just been exhumed out of his bloody and saw that it was black in color. Dr. Cocke said the Captain was suffering from black vomit, a disease that was not uncommon at sea, but he couldn't tell how serious it was. It was usually the manifestation of a more serious stomach disease which caused red blood to turn blackish because the stomach was unsettled. I think the best thing for him to wait it out and see if it is temporary or something more serious."

Alexander asked, " What can we do for Captain Morris? We are a long way from land in either direction."

Dr. Cocke answered, "Prayer is the only thing now."

Captain Morris moaning in pain, "My stomach has been hurting ever since we left Dakar. I first thought it was something I ate, but I am not feeling well. If I die at sea, I have no next of kin. Please throw me overboard."

Dr. Cocke trying to reassure his patient, "We will do everything in our power to get you well."

Captain Morris still moaning, "The chief petty officer or coxswain can float this boat for a while. But we will have to see if there a is anybody on any of the ships that can get us to Barbados."

The passenger Edward appeared at the scene and surprised Alexander because he had not been seen Edward for a while.

Edward said, " As a gentleman and a sea captain myself, I can get the *Deptford* to Barbados or as far as Martinique. The British Navy will see no difference in the quality of sailing. For payment, I will request a free voyage one day back to England. "

Alexander overjoyed at the offer, "He is a sea captain, and his father was a sea captain. "

The chief petty officer said, "That will work for me, and, by the time we get approval from the Department of Admiralty ,we will either be at Martinique or we will be at the bottom of the ocean." Edward got up to the steering gear to study the course that had been charted from Dakar to Barbados.

Alexander confidently, "I have faith in you."

Edward, appreciating the vote of confidence, " I hope so sir, because we don't have many choices, do we?"

Alexander, "You are correct, Edward."

Edward explaining his reasoning, "The last thing I would do is to end my own life while sailing, so I have a selfish motive."

After observing Edward adjust the sails and steering, Alexander said, "You make it look easy."

Edward hoping for the best, " It will be all right. It will be all right. One has to be fearless in this life."

The next morning , Captain Morris died, and as he requested, his lifeless body was lowered overboard in a dignified ceremony and Edward was introduced as the new captain.

Edward told all the passengers and crew, "We will get to Barbados on schedule, baring no conflicts with pirates or storms."

Everything seem to be going great and after a few weeks, The *Deptford* and the *Bedford* and the other six merchant ships were getting closer to Barbados.

One day on the journey ,Alexander asked Edward, "Have you ever been to Barbados?"

Edward answered, "I have been there many times. It is a good place to get resupplied and take on new water. It is an English colony. It goes back to a time when the English and Oliver Cromwell brought over settlers from Ireland and Scotland to harvest the tobacco and cotton crops and trade the goods to bring in money to the English coffers. They soon could not compete with the tobacco being exported from the Colony of Virginia, so they started converting to the raising of sugar cane to make sugar. Sugar is now their main cash crop and produces more sugar than any country in the world. It is one of the best seaports in the new World, one being Port Royal in Jamaica and the other being Jamestown in America. The white settlers of Barbados are very poor and are called Redlegs. They probably are doing better in Barbados than they would have in Ireland or Scotland. They have imported many African tribesmen to help harvest the crops. I would say that the country is about half Redlegs and one-half African descendants. Of course, you have the plantation class and owners who live better than the Queen of England. It is an island paradise. We will be there in a few days, and then I will leave you at Martinique."

When Edward and the *Deptford* sailed into port, the passengers had spent the last few weeks on the choppy seas. They were glad to be on solid land. There were combination of palm trees and water oaks and ficus trees on the island. The ficus had roots that looked like beards so therefore the name Barbados meaning bearded was used to name the island. After the Deptford, Bedford and the six merchant ships got resupplied, they started sailing northernly to San Salvador Island, Abaca, and Martinique.

.127

The boat was well equipped to sail the turquoise seas in the Caribbean. One day, Alexander, went up to check with Edward.

Edward on seeing Alexander," Ahoy, Matey!"

Alexander returning the greeting, "Ahoy. Where are we headed seeing that Edward was looking at the map and had a sextant and compass on the table?"

Edward answering, "We are headed to Martinique. When we get there, I will depart from the ship and meet my friends and be on my way to a business deal."

Alexander said, "All the passengers owe you a great deal of gratitude."

Edward said, "I was glad to do some sailing again. Indeed, I needed to get to Martinique quickly and it would have taken too much time to get another captain, and there were none on the other ships behind us."

Alexander stating his plans, " I know what you mean. I have my work waiting for me in the Colony of Virginia."

Edward sincerely speaking, "I wish you a good life. It will take some getting used to since you are a man of travel and letters."

Alexander agreeing, "Yes. How many days are we from the port at Jamestown, Virginia?"

Edward answered, "About three more weeks I would say. It depends on the sea captain you get at the next port. Sometimes the storms get bad along the Caribbean Islands. You have to sail through the Bermuda Passage Way and stay west of the Saragossa Sea, and hope the pirates are smart enough to stay away from the merchant ships and man of wars."

Alexander asked, "What is the Bermuda Passage Way?"

Edward answered, "It is a triangular area out in the sea out in the Atlantic east of the land of the southern Florida Indians and then to a point traveling down to Puerto Rico Island and then back northeast again to Bermuda Island. There is many a tale told in every pub at any port you can name in the world about ships disappearing into thin air never to be seen again, after sailing into this triangle. Even if the Bermuda sea passage is calm and the skies are clear, the problem is that no one has ever seen a ship disappear and live to tell about it. Even Columbus said his compass acted funny when he went through the passage. The Pirates have no problem going though there because they are not afraid of the sea. They are fearless and would risk death to get through the passage if they get wind of a treasure chest or a ship of worth nearby. I think sailing though here is a matter of the mind. Alexander, tell the Captain to show no fear when you go through here and your ship will be fine. "

Alexander asked, " What is the Saragossa sea?"

Edward answered, "It is east and south of Bermuda. If a captain tries to avoid the Bermuda Passage and goes too far to the east in the Atlantic Ocean, they will get tangled in the seaweed that is thick on top of the sea water. Even sharks and whales do not like to mess with the Saragossa Sea. The seaweed gets on the bottom of the ships and rudders and slows the ship down to a dead iron pace."

Alexander curiously asking, "What is that?"

Edward laughing, "That is no pace at all. It is when the wind is so dead that a ship cannot sail or move. Thus, being stranded and who will come to bail you out? The answer is no one. "

Another thing, ships have sunk if they sail to close to the coast in shallow waters. A good captain can tell when you are into close to shore and could get dead panned? A good captain will get you to Jamestown. I have a friend that owns an Island called Okracoke Island that is on your way. Tell the Captain not to stop on this Island for he despises all Englishmen and will cause harm. For one thing, he may not kill you outright, but he may talk you to death. You had better get some sleep. The stars and moon are bright tonight. I see your favorite star up there."

Alexander, "Yes, the faithful star, Sothis, never lets me down. Good night."`

In a few weeks , Alexander and his ship *Deptford* and all the ships made it up the tropical island paradise named, Martinique. A captain was there to take Edward's place. Edward just got off the boat without any baggage and hurriedly disappeared in the midst of the islanders. He turned around and waved goodbye to Alexander.

Alexander waved back and wondered why there were no farewells given by Edward other than just the wave.

One of the island's dock hands asked, Alexander, "Do you now that guy? Is he a friend of yours?"

Alexander answered and puzzled by the questions, "I just met him on the ship, and he helped the crew and passengers by getting the ship from Barbados area to here when the captain died of black vomit. He is not a friend exactly, but he is a good sailor."

The dock hand laughed. " He ought to be a good sailor. I believe it was Blackbeard the pirate, himself coming back from England. " The dock hand kept on laughing for a while.

Alexander was speechless, " He was nice to us and only said his name was Edward. I didn't get his last name. "

The dock hand, more seriously, " His name is Edward Teach and his father was Redbeard."

Alexander thought to himself. "Was this the little boy all grown up that was with his father that day when Redbeard stopped them on their voyage from Tangier to England? Does he still have my sword or knows what happened to the sword? The curse cannot be broken if the sword is not given back to me.

Alexander was puzzled, said, "He does have black hair, but he doesn't have a beard."

The dock hand, " He shaved it off for the trip, and he is wearing nice clothes instead of pirate haberdashery."

Alexander asked, "Does he live here?"

Dock hand answered, "Oh no, he lives on one of the islands down here in the Bahamas. Most of the time he will come in with sabers, swords, and 3 braces of pistols in hand. He wears little bows in his hair and scares people by shooting off some kind of fireworks in his beard."

Alexander worried about what the other passengers would do if they knew about the pirate, "Please don't tell anyone he was sailing on the ship. He did us a favor by keeping us safe at sea, and I want to see him safe for now."

Dock hand, "You got my word. Just buy me some rum and my memory will fade. I guarantee it." Alexander
.129

handed him some coins to buy several cases of rum. Alexander kept looking to see another glimpse of Edward Teach. He soon saw a ship with the crossbones flag on it leaving the harbor. The pirate ship was in the middle of the horizon on the sea and soon disappeared from sight presumably headed for more swashbuckling action.

Alexander said to himself, "Imagine the tall tale, if it could be told. No one would believe it anyway."

All the eight ships got restocked and again they went through choppy seas northerly towards Jamestown, Virginia. The new captain was not talkative at all, and Alexander talked to his staff about what their plans would be when they departed the ship for the last time in Jamestown. They got through the Bermuda Passage, avoided the Saragossa Sea, and did not stop at Okracoke Island as suggested by Edward Teach, although it looked like a calm place southeast of Roanoke Island where Sir Walter Raleigh had landed many years before. Alexander was thinking that maybe Edward had not wanted him to see any pirates that might be residing on Okracoke Island.

They were soon in Jamestown, gathered their belongings and would take a smaller type river boat up to the York River, and they would spend an evening with Mrs. William Barkeley at her plantation near Williamsburg. On hearing that the colony was getting a new lieutenant governor, she had sent an invitation to Alexander and his entourage in England to come and stay with her before they would arrive in Williamsburg, Virginia; the new home of Lt. Governor Alexander Spotswood. Mrs. Barkeley was a widow in her eighties but was full of life, energy, talk and sharp as a tack. Her husband who had died over twenty years before was one of the most respected men and most popular former colonial governors in Virginia. He had fought the Indians, established tobacco as a leading export crop, and put down Bacon's rebellion while he had been governor. Undoubtedly Mrs. Barkeley would give some good advice to Alexander to help him to get to know the colonists of Virginia.

Once they looked closely around Jamestown, they saw a wooden fort build of wooden staves and very primitive looking buildings. Alexander thought that the fort might keep out a few Indians but was no match for the Spanish or French armies. He was giving introductions to Mr. White, his secretary, Ms. Thornton, his hostess, and Dr. Cocke. Alexander assured his servants they would be safe. He thought if only Butler was here to see this. Again, he thought, maybe she is not ready for this kind of country living. Butler was used to the glamor and amenities of London. It would be many years before these Virginia cities would look like London. Alexander had to be thinking, God has put me here for a reason. I will find what the reason is and make it good.

All of a sudden as an omen to come. There was an unexpected shower of lights in the sky much as fireworks all over the Virginia skies. It looked like comets were going from cloud to cloud and lightning at the same time. At first the newcomers were afraid but soon the light show stopped almost as quickly as it had come.

Alexander exclaiming, " What a welcome that was!"

Ms. Thornton, "A little modesty would do you some good, Col. Spotswood." He laughed at her remarks.

At Williamsburg 30 miles away, William Byrd and James Blair, two of the most powerful leaders in Virginia where having coffee at one of the local pubs and were startled by the unexpected and frightening light show.

William Byrd to the pub's owner," What is going on outside?"

The pub owner said, "We have just got word from a rider, that the new lieutenant governor, Col. Alexander Spotswood has arrived on Virginia soil, and he is ready to make a good impression for Hamilton and Queen Anne. He must have tried to catch everybody's attention with a bright comet show."
William Byrd being facetious and smiling, "I guess we will soon learn what extraordinary powers the good Lieutenant Governor Spotswood has for Virginia.

Part III Journey from Williamsburg to the Blue Ridge Mountains

The frigate, *Deptford*, had made it the voyage from England across the Atlantic Ocean to Virginia arriving at the mouth of the Powhatan River, now renamed the James in honor of the former King. It was late in June of 1710 . After disembarking the larger *Deptford*, they were now comfortable seated on the river boat, *Crowshaw's Cutter*, named after one of the famous Jamestown settlers, Rawleigh Crowshaw. The *Cutter* has it was popularly nicknamed was sailing smoothly up the main channel of the river. Along the banks of the river were some sandy beaches and shrubby brush. Once the Cutter got going up the channel a few miles, the scenery quickly changed to thick forests along both sides of the river. The forests consisted of a mixture of oaks, red cedar, and sweet gum trees.

There was not much evidence of civilization except for an occasional deteriorating cabin and Indians looking at the new arrivals from their vantage point on the banks of the river. The native Indians seemed friendly enough and were probably getting use to the traffic going up and down the river from Jamestown to the Atlantic Ocean. Every once in a while, the new arrivals would see deer and other forest animals running obliviously along in some of the open meadows along the river. The passengers were seeing some of the wild Spanish mustangs the along the beaches were also grazing in the fields. The passengers were seeing the remnants of Kicoughtan along the James River and the wooden fence like staves of a fortress wall of Fort Algernon. This fort was once used as a strategic line of defense against the waring Indians. This fort had proven so successful for the earliest colonists that they had long been abandoned and new forts had been built further away from the coast as the settlers moved further westward and inland. The Indians had also been driven back further inland. Marsh and swamps surrounded Kicoughtan and the land wasn't suitable for growing cash crops and one would have trouble even finding enough space for a garden for food crops. The first colonists had already established some plantations further west of Jamestown that produced the valuable crops they could exchange for gold and silver. Most of the plantations had large gardens to sustain the families, servants, and laborers of the large plantations.

Alexander was beginning a new chapter in his life. He was now 34, quite tall and handsome, very quick to accept responsibility and fully equipped to take the leadership role in Virginia. He was a respected businessman in England, and the knowledge he had learned from his business dealings would serve him well. His curious nature and reserved nature and confidence would serve him well. He was now experienced in military, education, and business affairs. He had no family obligations as his parents were in Heaven and he had no wife. He sometimes thought about Butler, but after arriving, he thought it wise that she finished her education in England. The Colonies were still primitive and only the well to do gentry class had a relaxed way of living in the country on their estates. Alexander and Butler were used to the busy hustle of London with all its amenities. Virginia was a rural paradise with many resources and natural beauty but lacking in social events and entertaining plays and theaters. The earliest colonists had tried to duplicate their way of life in Virginia from the easy way they had lived in England, but they often lacked the resources to do the same things they were accustomed to doing in merry ole England.

Alexander and his entourage soon disembarked from *Crowshaw's Cutter*. The other passengers besides the Spotswood troop soon dispersed into the streets of Jamestown and into the wilderness. Alexander's secretary, Robert White, Ms. Thornton, the hostess, and Dr. Cocke were leading the group of servants to a smaller vessel that would sail them up the James River from Jamestown to the banks of the James close to Williamsburg . At the banks they would be met with a welcoming party from Williamsburg which would be a short carriage ride of a few miles to Williamsburg, the center of political and military power of Virginia. Alexander would govern the affairs of this large colony from Williamsburg. He was anxious to get started in his governorship and making a name for himself.

Ms. Thornton asking, "Alexander, this is your colony. Are you ready to take charge?"

Alexander, "Yes I am. I will not make a quick judgment about Virginia by what I have seen at Jamestown. It is a lot more undeveloped and smaller than I imagined it to be. We really are out in the countryside, now. I am glad to come into office without lots of pomp and circumstance. I do not like all the formality of the English when they change leaders. "

Ms. Thornton, " Well , you have not been disappointed then. In a few hours after traveling up to Bacon's point, we will be greeted by a small group of Williamsburg citizens. They will take you up to Cold Springs Plantation, the home place of a previous Governor, William Barkeley. He died some twenty years ago, but his widow will keep us in her guest house, and I am sure you will get a briefing on what the job of being a governor of the colony is like. She is very outspoken much like Sarah Churchill is in England. It will serve you well if you listen to her advice."

Alexander, "I know it is good to hear about the past so you can see how things will probably be headed in the future, but all the governor's decisions must be mine, and I will accept the accountability that comes along."

Ms. Thornton, "Well said, Alexander. Virginia is your new home. For how long remains unknown. You may take up roots here and marry some planter's pretty daughter and get a plantation of your own."

Alexander chuckled, " I have no desire for that right now. I just want to be a well-respected governor and have no plans for marriage."

Ms. Thornton, "With your good looks , you may not have a choice . Love may bite you and after all you are in the land of Virginia, a land for lovers and for lovers of land."

Alexander still chuckling, "We'll see to that!" As if there was no chance for him to be smitten. He briefly thought of Butler again but briefly as he was busy looking at all the new and majestic scenery. The entourage quickly got on the smaller sailing vessel and was gliding over the smoother river waters and arrived safely at Bacon's Point landing. The traveling party was graciously greeted by a handful of citizens waiting to greet the new governors and his party. After introductions were made, and a brief welcoming speech by a Mr. Lewis Burwell, some salutes were made by some militia and musket balls were shot in the air. This was a nice tribute honoring Alexander in his new post. Alexander soon got in the carriage for Cold Springs.

Ms. Thornton coaching her employer, "Once we get to Cold Springs Plantation, we will have dinner with Mrs. Barkeley. Her husband who died many years ago was one of the most popular colonial governors in Virginia in the past. She will undoubtedly show you her gardens and house, so please look interested. If she takes you out to the Cold Spring from whence the name came, please be careful drinking the water. If you gulp the water, it will make you sick because it is so cold. Sip the water and let it warm up a bit if you can. You do not want to offend her by not drinking the water. Some of the other governors and burgesses has visited her and have drunk the water and they lived to tell the story."

Alexander laughing. "I will take your advice. I just remembered a story that my mother told me once about a well in Scotland that had special powers. The waters in that Scottish well could heal the sick and make blind people able to see. I will not get sick. I don't want to upset anyone that wants to help me in my office."

Ms. Thornton, "Good! Mrs. Barkeley is well respected and could have ran the colony herself based on her marriage to the former marriage. She has a lot of friends in the colony that would support her and will also support you."

Alexander said, "I will need support and cooperation amongst the citizens to be effective."

Ms. Thornton said, "You're not only good looking but you are wise for your age." Alexander laughed.

The entourage left from the landing at Bacon's Point down a dirt road path to Cold Spring Plantation. It was a large beautiful stone and brick home, much like the ones on the Strand in London that Alexander was familiar with. There were several outbuildings. Some were for the farm animals, some were for the servants, some buildings were a granary for storing wheat and corn. There was a tobacco curing barn. There was a woodshed, an outdoor summer kitchen, a smokehouse for curing ham, a garden shed, a chicken coup, and a well shed This was all interesting to Alexander. It reminded him of the days when he used to talk to the feudal lords at the guild halls in Deal.

Alexander looking at all the land and buildings, "Now this looks more like what I thought I would see in Virginia."

Ms. Thornton looking around the plantation, "It looks like a prosperous working plantation. It had been maintained well by Governor Barkeley. He had some of the best attended socials and dances. He had only to defend it once during Bacon's rebellion. His militia kept him and his family safe when Nathaniel Bacon and his soldiers tried to overthrow the established government. Nathaniel Bacon's estate is further up the road on the way to Yorktown."

Alexander looking worried, "I guess I had better prepare for a rebellion, too."

Ms. Thornton speculating about the future, "Hopefully, you will only have to deal with the Indians, the pirates, and the burgesses and maybe some well-meaning ladies who are looking for a well to do husband."

Alexander said, " I was thinking more along the lines about how I would deal with the Queen, Parliament, the French, and the Spanish."

Ms. Thornton speaking, "You will have your hands full. Mrs. Barkeley is outspoken, but she is well respected and is very political. I trust you will use her advice wisely."

Alexander listening carefully, "Yes, I will."

The entourage soon got out of the carriages and was walking up towards the entrance to the house which were behind the big portico on the front veranda. Mrs. Barkeley came out to greet her guests and gave orders to her servants to take care of the guests' personal belongings. She was directing the servants to take the guests to their quarters.

Mrs. Barkley, a well-groomed and dainty lady in her eighties with long white hair, still looked young and spry and smiling, said, "Hello, Mr. Spotswood. I am pleased to meet you. Welcome to Virginia and I will see that you have a pleasant beginning in your new homeland. " Looking at the others, in the entourage, she said," Welcome to all of you."

They nodded politely and said almost in unison, "Thank you."
Alexander, "Thank you, Mrs. Barkeley, I am pleased to be here and looking forward to talking with you, and we do feel welcomed. I have liked the beautiful scenery of the Virginia countryside and what I have seen since I have come up the River from Kicoughtan and Hampton Roads."

Mrs. Barkeley understanding Alexander's trip, "I know you were glad to get off the man of war after being abroad for several weeks."

Alexander, "Yes, it was a long journey from England, but I am anxious to make a fresh start in the New World."

Ms. Barkley, blushing and smiling, "My husband and I use to make those trips . It was always good to come home to Virginia. You will do just fine in the Colony. No one told me that you were such a handsome man."

Alexander smiling, "Thank you , Ms. Barkeley. I don't look at myself that way, but you are very kind."

Ms. Barkeley, "I will introduce you to my granddaughters when we get inside."

Ms. Thornton couldn't help but smile as she knew that Alexander would be the most eligible bachelor in Virginia. After all the introductions and getting acquainted, the party went inside the old mansion. Once inside, the parlor was surrounded by a winding stairwell to the upper rooms. Ms. Barkeley introduced Alexander to her granddaughters, Catherine, Mary, and Martha. They were in their early twenties and as beautiful as their grandmother. They were dressed in their best gowns and were smiling showing their natural beauty. They arose out of their chairs and curtsied before Alexander.

Alexander said, "Good afternoon ladies, you don't have to be so formal around me. Looking at the three sisters, he said, "You are very beautiful, and I see the resemblance to your grandmother. "

Mrs. Barkeley chuckled, and the girls blushed and giggled. Ms. Thornton was smiling because , Alexander had made a very good first impression.

 Pretty soon after a volley of chit chat with the Barkeleys, they all took their seats at an elegant walnut table in the spacious dining room. They had supper of venison and vegetables and some wine from the cellar that had come from the vineyards just beyond the orchard. After supper, Ms. Barkeley, the granddaughters, Alexander, and Ms. Thornton all retired to the den for getting acquainted and for more conversation.

Mrs. Barkeley, "Do you think you will like, Virginia?"

Alexander honestly answered, "From what I see personally and from what I have been told by Mr. Hamilton and others, I will like it very well."

Mrs. Barkeley, "I hear that you are well read, went to schools in London and Tangier, and have a great curiosity about many subjects including history, the Church, and Scotland. I heard that you got hit by a cannon ball in the Battle of Blenheim and was spared by the good Lord. He wanted you to live so you could work for him in other ways."

Alexander politely, "That is correct. I am guilty as charged."
.135

Mrs. Barkley and the very quiet but attentive granddaughters smiled, " My husband was like that. He wanted to be learned on ever subject and wanted the best for the citizens of Virginia. It took its toll on him. He often would take a walk along the road next to the tobacco fields and be in deep thought and walk along the orchards and would study the silkworms to see how they could help him with the cotton crop. He was always thinking about how to improve the colony and please England."

Alexander, "I would be pleased and honored if I could do such an admirable job at being a lieutenant governor. "

Mrs. Barkeley," You were put in charge because of your talent and your willingness to serve. I want you to succeed because , this is a pivotal point in time. Virginia needs to expand because of the influx of planters, colonists, and immigrants coming from all the countries in the world. There have been many famines especially in France and Russo and the people have nowhere to go that will help them. England , Germany, and Flanders are crowded and have very little to offer. Virginia is the one colony that is filling up fast with settlers but there are millions of acres of beautiful farmland west of the Blue Ridge Mountains about a two-week journey west of here. This land could be claimed by Virginia and England and allow Virginia to have a western defense from the French and Spanish. The French has claimed land northwest of here near the Great Lakes country and land along a river the Indians call Mississippi. The Spanish have stayed further South near the Florida Indians. They have also come up some of the rivers in the Carolinas but have been busy in Africa and in the Land of the Incas to be a threat in this part of the New World."

Alexander listening intently, "Yes, I have heard this, Ms. Barkeley. I think it would be good to build a string of forts for defense along the Blue Ridge to protect us from the French and the Indians. I think the safety of the frontiersman in the western part of the colony is extremely important. I believe we need to strengthen the militia. I want to confine the Indians to the lands far beyond the Blue Ridge Mountains to serve as a buffer between us and the French especially in the Miami Valley region."

Ms. Barkeley liking what she was hearing, "Oh, yes, the Indians. I can show you the arrows still sticking in our log foundation when they attacked here years ago. They are somewhat peaceful now but still will need to be negotiated with to keep the peace with the settlers."

Alexander seeing that Ms. Barkeley is all about business at hand, replied. "I want to expand the use of land for the settlers by reducing or eliminating the quit rents that the settlers are burdened with. I want to encourage the sale of small parcels of land of manageable 5000-acre estates rather than promoting the sale of large tracts of land exploited by land speculators."

Mrs. Barkley, " I think you are on the right path, but the second most powerful person in Virginia already owns 180,000 acres of land and some of King Charles II friends received millions of acres. You will have a fight there, but it can be won."

Alexander, "You must be referring to Mr. Byrd, but he may say that he is working the land and is not interested in making profit by selling and buying land."

Mrs. Barkeley, "Mr. William Byrd has an advantage that he comes from a wealthy family and is spokesman of the Tidewater planters. He will oppose you at every step of the way. He is still trying to figure out why they chose you instead of him to run the colony of Virginia. Your understanding of how the settlers and their families live will give you the advantage with the majority of the new settlers and they will follow you. "

Alexander, humbly, " I have wondered that myself" The granddaughters were just smiling away listening to the
.136

weighty discussions.

Mrs. Barkeley, " I hear that Parliament wants the trading policies with the Indians upgraded to reduce the risk of war. Undoubtedly, you will get involved in a pow wow with the Indian Nations. They have a government, too. You will need to respect their concerns. A lot has changed since the days of Pocahontas and the Powhatan Nation. The Tuscaroras have a settlement south of us about 10,000 people and a strong army in the Carolinas just a few days horseback ride away. They are along the Pimlico Sound and what would prevent them from coming up to Williamsburg by land or sea. When my husband was governor, he had to deal with Chief Oppechancanough and then make a new peace with remaining Indians and this peace went unviolated for many years."

Alexander, " I definitely have to build up the militia and maybe get forts south of us also"

She empathized with Alexander and did not continue to smile as he described the horror of living in hostile surroundings in Africa and feeling somewhat safe in a fortified garrison.

Alexander, " I have seen the beheading results of English soldiers when you are outnumbered by the rebel natives in Tangiers. It was a frightening sight. I do not want anyone to have to experience that barbaric cruelty." The girls looked frightened. They seemed to admire his toughness and courage he must have attained from being a former soldier as Alexander spoke with authority.

Mrs. Barkeley, " You talk about safety , and another concern is the pirates off the coasts. They wreak havoc with the shipping of supplies and intimidate travelers from England to Virginia. The colonial governors of the other colonies have either ignored or have not wanted to deal with the pirates interfering with the food supplies. How can we build a country if we don't have adequate supplies?"

Alexander, " That is a good point. I know I have seen the English take action against William Kidd, who was a notorious pirate who wreaked havoc against the English and the people of Long Island Colony. His dead body hung for many years from a gibbet at Tidbury Point in London to make an example for all to see that piracy is not a good occupation."

Mrs. Barkeley, "And while you are at it, you will have to deal with James Blair. He would say that he is the most important person in Virginia. He is in control of the Church and the founder of the College in Williamsburg, which needs much repair by the way. In 1705, the main buildings for the students burned down and has been rebuilt partially by funds given by Queen Anne. She asked the architect, Christopher Wrenn to design a new building, and it will be beautiful and practical when finished. James Blair will fight you on every matter in the Anglican Church. It will not matter to him that your ancestors help write the Prayer Book and was an Archbishop at St. Andrews. He will take charge of the religious influence on Virginia his way. He has already been the undoing of two colonial governors."

Alexander surprised and impressed that Mrs. Barkeley knew about his family history, said, "Thanks for the advice. I have a faith in God and know that He will lead me to do the right thing. Many people who sit in churches do not know the Lord the way they should. God knows I have come short of his expectations, but I want to be in His will. I have no religious or political agenda against Mr. Blair. We will be cautious and do things that would bring honor to our Lord and Savior. As far as Mr. Wrenn is concerned, he has designed many of the famous buildings, palaces, and cathedrals of London. As I laid in a hospital in Chelsea after the war of Blenheim, I study some of his architectural designs. I hope to meet him some day. I am not so anxious to meet, Mr. Blair. "

Mrs. Barkeley. "Amen, Alexander, I believe you will hold your own. Mr. Blair will let you worship as you please so long as it is his religious beliefs. One thing I will say in favor of James Blair is that he helped represent the colonist planters and Virginians well before King William and Queen Mary and got them to endow 300 pounds to establish that respectable college at Middle Plantation or what is now known as Williamsburg. The king and queen wanted three things taught to the students of the gentry class in Virginia, those things being language, divinity, and natural philosophy. The wealthy planters would rather keep their children at home for college rather than sending them to Oxford or Cambridge. One thing that Blair and Neal, a former governor could not get started was a postal system so mail could get between towns and villages in reasonable fashion. As far as some of the former governors were concerned; many tried to start a profitable linen manufacturing society for making cloth for all purposes. There was also the push for products made out of fur and leather from all the hides that the hunters and trappers were accumulating."

Alexander making notes of the issues, "I want to work on all those issues, and I want to also work on the tobacco issues and want tobacco graded and use it as legal tender. I want to introduce habeas corpus issues in the colony and will see to it the courts respects habeas corpus for its citizens. We will be a colony of laws and fairness. "

Mrs. Barkley," I see that you are not only the most handsome governor in the colony, but you are well versed and will be the most able one."

The granddaughters tried to hold their giggles. Ms. Thornton could see they were infatuated with the new lieutenant governor.

Mrs. Barkeley again continuing to smile at Alexander, "You seem to know a lot about the issues already. "

Alexander, "I feel like I have learned a lot about the issues from my own experiences in war and businesses and by studying history. I have bought a library of books with me so I can entertain myself on lonely nights. "
Again, the pretty granddaughters giggled as if they would like to be a part of his busy life.

Alexander blushed, " I would like to meet Robert Beverly whose writings I find fascinating on the history of Virginia. I find his firsthand experiences helpful."

Mrs. Barkeley responded, "I will see if I can introduce him to you. I will tell you now for you may not know that he married Ursula Byrd, one of Mr. William Byrd's sisters. He, however, is a gifted man that has his own beliefs. You must remain careful about the politics you choose to talk to Beverly about. I don't believe that William Byrd and Robert Beverly or that close now, since Ursula died about 12 years ago. Robert Beverly grieved for a long time and got busy writing his history book to keep busy. In fact, you would be wise if you find a place for him and his brother, Peter, in your administration because their father was so popular and well respected with the people. Their father was head of the Assembly in the Colony and used great judgment on complex concerns. Robert is not only an author of history but owns about 3000 acres up at the mouth of the Mattaponi River. He would help you with treaties with the Indians because he has written much about their superstitions and their beliefs. He has a real fascination for the Indians. He is quite the master of grapes from his vineyards and known for his wines which have a very unique taste."

The granddaughters did not speak but did seem very interested in the conversation. The oldest granddaughter, Mary poured some tea for Alexander, Ms. Thornton, and her grandmother. Mary did say flirtatiously, "I hope you like your tea hot, Mr. Spotswood."

Alexander blushing managed to say, "Yes, but please call me Alexander or Colonel."

Mary said quickly, " Yes, Alexander. " Alexander although immersed in his thoughts on leadership, he noticed Mary's beauty and her politeness. He must have thought he would have to be careful as not to encourage or discourage a relationship. The last thing he needed was to upset Mary's grandmother, the most powerful and political lady in the colony . In fact, he must have thought that Mrs. Barkeley was a lot like Sarah Churchill in England. They both were always on the know of all the issues of the populace.

They soon retired to their guest rooms in the big mansions.

When Ms. Thornton saw that there was no one listening, she said, "Should I ask for a militia guard at your door so no one will disturb you tonight?" Ms. Thornton was chuckling at Alexander's situation.

Alexander with a very businesslike tone, " Very amusing! I don't think that is necessary."

Ms. Thornton smiling, "The only problem I see for you in Virginia is that all the single ladies will be fighting over you."

Alexander, looking a little annoyed, "It has been a very busy day. I want a little sleep and being alone will be fine."

Ms. Thornton, acting in a coy manner, " My, my, we are a little grouchy aren't we. For what it's worth, you did a fine job out there tonight."

Alexander, yawning as he closed the guest bedroom door, "Thank you and that will be all for now. Goodnight." and he went into the guest bedroom and closed the door behind him to get some much-needed sleep, some quiet, and some peace.

Ms. Thornton looked at him as he was closing the door, "Good night and pleasant dreams."

Ms. Thornton stood outside the bedroom door in the large upstairs hallway. She paid little attention to the elegant paintings and sculptures that adorned the walls. Ms. Thornton, who was a beautiful black haired, blue eyed beauty was in deep thought. She might have been wondering what it would be like to be romantically involved with Alexander. All the past weeks on the journey, Alexander had been polite to her, but he had kept a respectable distance between them. He was after all charming, handsome, and eligible. On the voyage she had the opportunity to observe and fantasize about him. She would watch him, and he always used good manners and talked easily with everyone. She started to think that Alexander might want her as a lover or wife and might just be shy. She had watched other women stare at him and flirt. She was more beautiful and talented than they were. She started to think that she wanted him as a lover and also as a boss. She asked herself if she should go quietly into his bedroom and throw herself at him. Then she thought she had better not cause a scene in Mrs. Barkeley's house. Alexander might just get upset and end the relationship before it started. She kept asking herself, should I go in his bedroom and see if he wants to make love to me. She paced the hallway for a few minutes alone in her thoughts as the Barkeleys had already retired. She must have thought that all he can do is say that he doesn't want me now, but we can court properly as the gentry are accustomed to doing. She then said to herself. It would be wonderful if we found out we were destined to be together. She opened the bedroom door and looked around the room. Alexander had read from a prayer book and left it on the bed and was already fast asleep because he was weary from the day's activities. Ms. Thornton said to herself, "There will be other times for me to get close to Alexander' and I will wait until he seems interested. Indeed, he might think that I am too forward or that I would sleep with any man. I will be ready when the time is right for both of us. We do not need to be lonely. Ms. Thornton went into her guest bedroom and must have thought that her life in Virginia would be better and maybe Alexander would not take her for granted.

The only lady that Alexander wanted to dream about was Butler Bryan. He had already been exposed to some of the most beautiful women in Virginia, but they could not compare to his Butler. He felt more and more that he wanted her to be with him, but she was not able to come to Virginia just yet. He had to get settled and get some of the work done before he would have the time to devote to a wife and family.

The next morning , they all awoke to a very heart breakfast of eggs and ham and fresh milk . They managed to have some coffee which was sometimes hard to get in the colonies. After breakfast, Mrs. Barkeley and Mary showed Alexander around the plantation. Mary took him to the orchard and cellar area where they grew and stored the fruits and vegetables in the gardens, orchards, and meadows. Mrs. Barkeley, beaming with pride, showed the new lieutenant governor the mulberry and cherry trees, the raspberries, damsons, gooseberry bushes, and blackberry bushes. She also showed him acres of hazelnut, walnut, and pecan trees. She told him how every plantation had to be self-sufficient to take care of the family, servants, and laborers. Unlike England, where there was every kind of store, here you live by what you grow, buy, and sell. The colonists were not used to hunting for meat but grew their own farm animals for food, milk, and eggs. Eventually after touring the gardens and orchards, they came upon the famous cold spring that the plantation was named after.

Alexander asked, "Can I have the honor of drinking from this spring?"

Mary said, "Please do and make a secret wish and it will come true."

Ms. Barkeley said, "Go ahead." Alexander made the wish that Butler would come to Virginia soon and be happy in a new home. Of course, if he said it aloud, then the wish would certainly not come true, and he might upset the Barkeleys.

He sipped the water and said, "This is the coldest water, I have ever tasted. In fact, it is colder than the frozen ice we used to touch on the River Thames in the wintertime when I was a young lad."

They then went back up to the main house where the carriages were loaded, and the rest of the entourage was ready to continue the journey just a few miles away. Alexander took his place in the carriage.

Mrs. Barkeley said, "May God Bless you on your new position. May God Bless your new country and your new home."

Alexander was happy about his visit at Cold Spring and said, "Thank you very much for the hospitality and please come visit me in Williamsburg anytime you want."

Ms. Barkeley smiling, "We will, Alexander. I know you will be successful. You remind me of my husband and his honesty about things. Farewell for now!" And they went back inside as the horses and carriages continued the journey for Williamsburg. Mary stayed out on the porch a little longer than the rest waving to Alexander and the rest of the party.

Ms. Thornton to Alexander in the carriage so no one else could hear, " If you do not call on that lady in two weeks, she will be calling upon you. I would want to be called on also if I were that lady and you were my man." Alexander did not comment but just smiled. Ms. Thornton smiled also knowing that he didn't get angry when she brought up the subject of courtship. Only the Lord was knowing what was going on in all their thoughts as they went down a dirt road to their new home.

Soon, the caravan of carriages started down the lane towards Williamsburg. Alexander and Ms. Thornton rode in the first carriage. Robert White, the secretary, and Doctor Cocke were in the second carriage, and the fifteen servants were in the next 4 carriages. Then there were also 4 more carriages carrying their household items and personal belongings. Alexander was smiling as best he could, because he felt as though he had not been in Virginia long, he was already familiar with some of the people and situations he would face.

Mrs. Thornton, " Colonel, you seemed to handle yourself pretty well with the Barkeleys."

Alexander smiling, "So you think so? Mrs. Barkeley is a grand lady and very knowledgeable. She was very informative and courteous in trying to assist me."

Ms. Thornton, " And the granddaughters seemed to be interested in your success. One of them would be a fine catch for you!"
Alexander, "I have no plans to meet or marry anyone right now. I just want to govern the colony admirably and follow the lead of my half-brother, Roger Elliott. He is now Governor of Gibraltar close to Spain and Africa where we grew up. I have received several letters from him explaining what he is dealing with and advising me on how I should organize the priorities of the colony, and how to earn the respect of the people. So far he has never married and said he would not want to put a wife through that kind of daily stress."

Ms. Thornton, "There are lots of men who have been effective colonial governors that are married and do just fine. A wife can support her husband through all kinds of trials. Give them a chance. Besides, Alexander, you may not have a choice. The single ladies in London and Virginia find you irresistible."

Alexander replied, "The future Mrs. Spotswood may have to wait until I get out of office, build up my business, and save some money."

Ms. Thornton, "You don't sound too romantic, but most men aren't. Sometimes men need love from a woman. Give one of us a chance." Alexander laughed as if in agreement with Ms. Thornton on that .

The carriage caravan soon arrived in Williamsburg, and a few people had gathered by to meet by the governor's mansion so they could meet and talk to their new lieutenant governor. Alexander got out of the carriage, stood straight and tall, with his strong chin and pleasant face and greeted the crowd. He waved to the people and the crowd seemed to be pleased with his appearance and demeanor. He looked round and noticed the beautiful Governor's Mansion, but it appeared unfinished. Outside the mansion, Alexander saw that there were not any pretty gardens, flowers, or bushes as he was accustomed to seeing in the palaces in London. The yards looked abandoned and seemed more like pastures for cattle grazing. The streets around Williamsburg were not laid out in straight lines, as if they had not been surveyed. The church named Bruton was rundown and the cemetery needed care. The College called William and Mary also had significant fire damage and needed refurbishing. There were several merchants who had set up shops. The shoppers seem to like the assortment of goods because they were busy and there were many wagons loaded with supplies to take back to the plantations.

Alexander met some of the people, and they asked him how he liked Williamsburg. He was very careful and said, "Though I feel definitely that I am out of the Country of England, I feel glad and proud to be in the country of villages and plantations. With your help, we can make this country the most respected colony of England. "
The audience seemed to like his remarks and cheered. The crowd soon disbursed, and some came by and shook Alexander's hand and said they wished him well.

When the crowd was out of earshot, Ms. Thornton, "My God, Alexander! You certainly have your work cut out right here just in Williamsburg!"

Alexander said, "I like this town. It is a charming village and has certain obvious needs that I can address immediately. I have heard that there is no mayor and no constable. I will see that we appoint some interested parties and elect some town folks to make and enforce the laws that they want to see enforced in their town. I will give them definite plans on how to make this city more beautiful and more attractive to businesses and visitors."

.141

Alexander, addressing Mr. White, "Please make a note that we want to set up a town council and have certain plans for attracting business to the most important governing center in Virginia."

Ms. Thornton, "Well done, Alexander. You are a man of action."

Ms. Thornton, Alexander and the secretary, Mr. White soon crossed the streets to some small clapboard houses with cedar rooves to settle in their new home. Williamsburg seemed to be a picturesque town nestled in the middle of a dense forest under a cloudless blue sky. Williamsburg had taken over Jamestown as the financial and governmental center of Virginia in 1698. In the last few years, the town had grown quickly in number of people and businesses. It was the most prosperous town in the colony. The town had growing manufacturing and mercantile businesses. There were jobs for everyone coming from England or from the other colonies. There were bankers, post riders, bricklayers, wheelwrights, blacksmiths and farriers, tanners, coopers, coach makers, cabinet makers, tailors, jewelers, weavers, surveyors, preachers, servants, hatters, soap makers, candle makers, and carpenters. There were apothecaries, ship wrights, cutters, farmers, surgeons, dentists, and teachers. Alexander was glad to see the shops on main street bustling with shoppers. Most of the goods were from England, but some were made from other colonies. One store was called Blair's store and Alexander asked if that belonged to Rev. James Blair, and he was told that it was mainly owned by Archibald, the brother of James, but James had a small ownership in it. One of the stores was called Burwell's store. Alexander asked if the store belonged to the Burwell Family, which had so many burgesses in the family and also owned so many thousands of acres in the colony. He was told, yes and that the Burwells owned many houses and much property in the colony. Alexander saw that the rich stores were fully stocked with all kinds of provisions as if they were in a store in London. They had many goods including much food stuffs and liquors.

After supper, feeling unnoticed and unknown, Alexander took a leisurely stroll through the residential neighborhood close to the Palace as the new Governors Headquarters would be called. He saw that the houses were mostly built of brick, but many were built of local timber and preserved with oil and lead paint, much as if he were in London. He noticed that the citizens he met on the streets were friendly and generally spoke. They were dressed in the same neat and orderly manner as the gentry would dress as if they were in England and had a relaxed air of confidence about themselves. Most of the people had some kind of coach, berlin, chaise and chariot by their house indicating they could afford to travel in a comfortable manner to visit others in their social class. Most of the owners of the houses had servants which were from all kindreds, races, and tongues, but were mostly English, Irish, or Scotch.

He was thinking that he must write Margaret, Roger, and Butler about his first day in Virginia, and how proud he was to be the leader of such a prosperous country. On his way back he looked at the Bruton Church and surrounding cemetery that looked as if were overflowing with tombstones. He must have thought that the church had many families as members and thinking he would probably attend services there. In his study later that evening , Alexander had hurriedly unpacked his personal belongings and found his favorite scroll pen and ink and scribbled a letter to Roger and a letter to Margaret. He put more thought into his letter to Butler.

My most beautiful, Butler,

I have thought of you often since I left England. The voyage was long, but pleasant enough. I will want to share with you the next time we meet about some of the acquaintances I met on the voyage as they were very interesting characters indeed. Listing them, now might be boring for you. I did arrive in Jamestown harbor safely a few days ago and started my journey to Williamsburg, my new home. It is a very delightful, charming, and prosperous village. It compares in no way to London except in the mannerisms of the people who remind you of the English gentry. They are happy, healthful, and thriving and live comfortably and peacefully. I want to work on improving the appearance of the city to visitors and potential newcomers to the village. The Palace where my living quarters will be is simply not ready or finished yet, so I am living in a nearby house. I have plenty of supplies, foodstuffs, and books to read in my spare time. The church is a little worn from much good use and I will praise the Lord for giving me such a charming countryside and manors to oversee for the Queen. In summary of Virginia, it is my best retreat from England and a welcoming haven for any true Englishman and church going man.

I am looking forward to meeting Mr. Byrd and Mr. Blair who are in the Council and some of the burgesses, tomorrow. I will be giving them my plans for Virginia and of course, they will be telling me of their achievements and brief me on their beliefs.

Within a few minutes after touching Virginia soil, there was a spectacular light show, darkness, then light show and a double rainbow that came overhead. I take this as a good omen and trust that the Lord will watch over me here as well as he did in London.

I miss you, and I miss our conversations and wish you were here to celebrate the start of the new chapter in my life. I cannot describe how beautiful, the rivers, the trees, the meadows, and scenery is.

There are still lots of danger here, also with Indians, pirates, and greedy landowners.

I met a widow Barkeley, whose late husband was a governor and she is very gracious and informative. I trust you would like her. Her advice seems sincere and genuine.

I am hoping all is well for you and your family . Now is the time for you to enjoy the time of your youth and schooling. I want to hear from you about your adventures and outings. The time will go by quickly and we will see each other again.

Affectionately, Alexander

Alexander took the letter to be sent to England to the local Post Office Building. Mr. Custis, also a patron coming into the mail room, commented to Alexander, "I hope our mail is not lost. Sometimes it sits here or there in England for weeks before it is delivered to the recipient."

Alexander said, "I hope this will get their soon. Maybe as the new lieutenant governor of the colony, I can look into the mail system and improve it."

Alexander would later meet his staff, his lovely hostess, Ms. Thornton, and Mr. White, his secretary at the Palace . On his way, he came into a small tavern conveniently located on London Street, one of the main streets close to the Palace. Inside, was a, handsome, middle age man, reading some printed material. He looked fit, well groomed, and well dressed, and very well built. He took his eyes off his reading long enough to notice Alexander entering the tavern. He quickly spoke.

The man at the table asked, "Would you like coffee or tea, Col. Spotswood?"

Alexander asked, "Tea would be fine. "How do you know who I am?"

"I am William Byrd. It is my business to know who you are. You match the description that was given to me by a fellow Burgess who met you yesterday. I regret that I was not able to meet you as I had planned, but business came up that needed my immediate attention. After tea , we can walk up to the Palace if you wish, so we can share ideas together. You do have an agenda for the colony do you not?"

Alexander kind of taken back by his directness, replied, "Most assuredly. It will make us even a more respected colony to England."

William Byrd smiling, "I have lived here many years, and, believe me; that will take a lot of skill and luck."

Alexander confidently, " I have a lot of whatever it takes."

William Byrd, "I like your enthusiasm , but you will find a lot of opposition."

Alexander rebutting, "Maybe from the powerful clans in the assembly, but not from the citizens of the colony."

William Byrd, smiling, "I will give you that one. The Burgess es are stubborn and fixed in their thinking. They will do what is best for them. "

Alexander speaking his beliefs, "I propose that there be a better selection process for the Burgesses, so we are not having the same families ruling Virginia generation after generation."

William Byrd, " I see that you have been doing your homework. I hope you do not get discouraged easily, because the burgesses are reluctant to change especially coming from Britain. They have brought a lot of money into England's coiffures from the sale of commodities from their plantations and the unpopular payment of their taxes."

Alexander making his point, "They also have made a fortune and spent a fortune to send their children to England for learning and have not prepared for the defense of the colony from enemies or looking to expand the colony to the west. I propose we have a strong military, tobacco-based economy, more good universities built in the colonies, and looking for growth opportunities on the western frontier."

William Byrd looking for opportunity, " That means more land for the planters to invest in?"

Alexander responding, "Not necessarily. I am talking about smaller land grants for the masses of English, Irish, Scottish and other folks settling here. I propose they will be small family farms, settlers building homesteads, plenty of jobs in factories, importing, exporting, and making it a safe place for families to grow gardens and provide for themselves. I foresee more smaller villages and hamlets and not more large plantations just for the success of only a few people. We have to build more roads and bridges into the back country. I will do everything in my power to discourage land speculation just for profiteering."

William Byrd showing disgust on his face, "Again, I hope you do not get discouraged easily. Many former governors have had their own good ideas, but have been stopped by the burgesses, the people, or by the King and Queen.   Have some more tea. For example, my friend Blair has been trying to get The English to refurbish the Bruton Church across the street, but like true Englishmen they would spend 500 pounds on this tavern and only 50 pounds on a church. I oppose the buying and selling of slaves, but do you think that the English would eliminate slavery in this colony?"

Alexander, "I understand what you are saying. I am looking forward to working with you. I do not plan on establishing political enemies in Williamsburg. I will entertain all discussions on any issue. My work will speak for itself."

William Byrd laughing, "I see neither one of is short on confidence. I too, listen to reason and rationality."

Alexander, "Truly spoken. That is one thing we can agree on."

While drinking tea, they personally chatted about family, Williamsburg, and Virginia. Alexander must have thought it best to understand what makes William Byrd do the things he does. Alexander could see that he was haughty, shrewd, cunning in business and personal affairs and a very learned man.

Alexander asking, "Tell me what makes you think the way you do?"

Byrd, "Are you jealous or just curious by asking? "

Alexander answered, "Curious." as they began walking to the Palace.

Byrd, "As you see, I am not bashful nor modest. I am extravagant in everything. I turned 23,000 acres into an estate of almost 200,000 acres. I have founded Richmond and Petersburg with God's help who I pray to daily. If I forget, I ask for forgiveness at confession. I occasionally sleep on the hard ground with blankets in close proximity to my plantation house, so my body remains tough. I walk over my gardens, vineyards, and estates to keep my legs strong. I take a swim twice weekly in the James River below the falls near Indian town to keep my body strong. I mean I do this year-round whether there is ice or snow in the river or not. I feel at ease with all kinds of people especially the ladies. I hire fiddlers to play at the tavern, so I can dance and flirt with the other burgesses' wives. I am unpredictable and I am scared to have malice toward my fellow man. I have been known to do a few insane things to get attention or make people laugh. I will cheat at cards, read books from my 3000-book library all night in Latin, Spanish, or Italian if I find the subject fascinating. I never feel threatened or stressed. I have too many talents at my disposal to be a failure at anything. I will let you in on a secret; when my first wife died of smallpox, I felt helpless, but not useless. I figured I could make our children's lives easier and happier some way. Another secret, I trust you, Alexander, although I will probably not agree with you in politics, but I will respect you and probably include you in my diary several times. You will see that I have this special power which I see in the stars that you have a connection to the stars ,and the stars speak of your success as a governor of Virginia. For myself, my turn as Head of the Council will not come soon and will not come about until you are long gone and out of office."
Alexander must have thought, how does he know about Sothis, my personal star.

Alexander, "Quite interesting, Mr. Byrd."

William Byrd continued, " I will tell you now that you will accomplish much, but eventually be defeated by Blair and his friends in England. You will not marry until you are out of office. Your wife will be truly of English blood and will be the most charming and most beautiful woman in Virginia. I envision her in a great palace with forest animals which seems odd to me. You are a capable military leader and will show force when you need to. You are a deeply religious man and may do better as a clergyman than anyone else could in Virginia. Even though you say you do not want to have vast amounts of land, you will have vast amounts of land. The pirates will curse you; the Indians will love you, and the Germans you try to help will not understand your good intentions. You are perplexed by a pirate's curse which you do not understand and your brother who knows about the curse will not be there to explain the curse if it is broken. Yes, you will be loved by the people of Virginia and your family and, yes, your name will go down just like mine as being one of the most famous and respected names in history. In fact, I will write the real history of Virginia, someday when I have nothing else to do, and I will see that we get treated fairly. I knew the day when you stepped on Virginia Soil with your boots, the Lord put his stamp of approval on the landing because there was a light show in the stars and skies that has not been seen in the history of mankind."

Alexander, "Amazing. I hope you are correct. God is in control, however!" Alexander must have been thinking this was an unusual welcome or is Byrd just trying to intimidate me so I will go back to London.

Byrd explaining his relationship to God, "Yes. He is! Things you can always count on are God, the sun, moon, and the stars. You can always count on me to be unpredictable and brutally honest. After the Court of Sessions today and after he Assembly Meeting with the Burgesses of Virginia, I will introduce you to James Blair, a very powerful Virginian and a man of the cloth who you have to walk carefully with. He has already seen to it that two former governors have been disposed of before their term ended. He will leave you alone if you leave him and his Church alone."

Alexander, "You know that I can make no such promise. It is what the Queen wants and what the citizens want. If he stands in the way, he may be moved."

Byrd, "You legally have the power to do this, but you will not get backing from England. In fact, England told Blair once when he asked for money to build a Church school for the colonists because the colonists souls need to be saved as much as the English Church's patrons' souls, the English government did not back him. They said to him, "Damn the souls in Virginia, send us your tobacco money to finance our wars. He did just that. They will back him because of all the money he has collected for them in Virginia."

Soon Alexander Spotswood and William Byrd entered the Assembly Room of the Burgesses representing all the counties in Virginia. A hush replaced the earlier loud chatter of the men as they took their seats at the tables and chairs in the Assembly Room. The Burgesses must have perceived it a good omen to see the new leader of the colony with the well-respected and efficient Byrd who they knew to be very political and savvy with all friends and foes.

Alexander looked very polished and confident, standing tall and straight with his firm square jaw and curious smile. William Byrd took his seat at the Council table and previously decided by Blair that Byrd would introduce the newly appointed lieutenant governor. Byrd banged the gavel on his oak table to call the Assembly to order. Ms. Thornton and Mr. White was also present.

Byrd, " Before God and all Present, Honorable Men of Virginia, I want to introduce you to our Lieutenant Governor Alexander Spotswood, who has been sent by Queen Anne, in place of our Governor, George Hamilton, 1st Earl of Orkney, as leader and authority over the governmental affairs of the Colony of Virginia and will have authority to enforce all laws and doctrines addressed to the Colony by the House of Commons and the Queen of England. May God give him the grace and wisdom to administer these laws fairly and appropriately and to lead the defense of our colony from all enemies from within and without the colony.
Colonel Alexander Spotswood, a descendant of the ancient and noble Scottish Spotswood family was born in Tangier, Africa where his father served in the Royal Navy with distinction. His grandfather was Lord Justiciar of Scotland. His great-grandfather was the Bishop at St. Andrews Parish and the person who put the king's crown on the head of King James I of England at his coronation and the king for whom Jamestown was named. Col. Spotswood served as a quartermaster General in the English Army and showed his bravery at all battles in the Wars of the Spanish Succession especially riding with Hamilton and Major General John Churchill at the battle of Blenheim where he was severely wounded and could not return to service. He has owned his own successful business in London. We wish you Godspeed, Mr. Spotswood."

Byrd went on to say at the outset, "Rev. Commissary James Blair will say the Opening Prayer and then Col. Alexander Spotswood will make his remarks."

Byrd set down in his chair and Alexander must have wondered how William Byrd knew so much about his family. He glanced down at Ms. Thornton who was smiling and trying to look innocent of any collaboration with Mr. Byrd. She had apparently talked to Byrd ahead of time and now Alexander knew what he meant when he said he like to talk to pretty ladies. Alexander was very humble about his past and his family's accomplishment and had wanted to keep them more private. He didn't want to look like he was boastful or landed his job by being someone's favorite. Soon, the respected gentlemen of about 45 years, Reverend James Blair, got up to speak. He was an attractive man with distinctive brown hair and blue eyes which seem to be piercing at times.

Blair began, "Let us pray. Our father, we recognize you alone as our supreme leader. Help us as humble servants of Queen and country to follow your leadership and that all Virginians will have the souls saved from the fiery furnace of Hell. May your words from the Psalmist and prophets guide us in our praise of you and that all men present will follow your leadership. We pray for the growth and security of our colony. We pray for the safety of our citizens. Please hear our pleas for mercies from our sins. We asked this in the Lord's name. Bless this meeting and your humble servants gathered here today. Amen"

The crowd in attendance and Alexander said Amen in unison.

Alexander, " Good morning, Ladies and Gentlemen, Thank you, Mr. Byrd, and Mr. Blair,
I see great things that have been accomplished by the distinguished gentlemen before me. Surely, the Lord has blessed the Colony of Virginia. We can disagree on many things in this room , but one thing we should all agree on, that the Lord God Almighty is in Charge of Virginia and its future promise to England as a growing nation."
The Burgess applauded this statement at the outset, and Mr. Blair gave a wry smile.

Alexander continued, "It is a tumultuous time in the history of our colony which has experienced its birth in 1607 and continual growth since that time. It has been a time of Indian Wars, land speculation, piracy on the ocean, the unchecked delivery of Spanish fleets of treasure from the Americas, and the balance of European power between the continuing war between England and France. I am almost certain that they will want to bring this war to our shores . I believe me must act responsibly as a governing body for the Crown and protect of those things we believe in." He received a little applause.

Alexander, continued. Many of you have families in England and Scotland and have made the long journey from there with the hopes of making yourself successful in your endeavors and to help make this the most respected colony in English control. On the long voyage here, I had time to reflect about my country, my personal history, and my assignment. I do not take it lightly and do not assume I know more than anyone else. I do need your strong opinions in order to make a strong colony."
Again, more applause.

Alexander continued, " I realize that I may not be popular, but that is not what I am about. Many of you are related to each other by blood or marriage and that has not seemed to be an issue with the government of England, but I would encourage you to vote and believe on issues as your heart and mind dictate without the influence of those around you. Because events happen that alter history, we may not be able to support an issue because previous generations have believed that for generations and generations. Think about issues that affect your family but also how it affects your neighbors' family or someone's family that have different circumstances than you."
The people did not applaud because Blair had two sons in the assembly, the Byrds, Burwells, Carters, Lees and other families had dominated the assembly for many years.

Alexander continued, " I want to adopt the policy of habeas corpus in Virginia which will give citizens the right to a fair and prompt hearing. The Burgesses applauded loudly. "I want to reduce or eliminate the land tax and quick rents so to encourage more settlers to come to Virginia. I want to reduce the amount of land used for speculation and the land used more for homesteading." Byrd 's jaw actually dropped open as he was not prepared to hear this.
"I want to free our seas of the nuisance of pirates and the free the land of hostile Indians. I propose to do this by allowing the Indians to attend our Christian schools at William and Mary College. I want to encourage trade with the Indians and talk to them at our Council Meetings. There has been enough talk about eliminating them at our Council Meetings. I want to keep our Tobacco export trade strong by grading tobacco that is sold and use tobacco as a legal tender in Virginia. This will allow farmers with smaller acreage of land to invest in land and

buy parcels of land as Virginia expands to the West. As we expand to the West, we will need to build forts south of Richmond, Mr. Byrd's City to protect us from the Spanish and the Tuscarora Indians. I propose we build a road to the falls on the Rapid Ann River west of here on the way to the Blue Ridge Mountains. I want us to explore the lands that is west of the Blue Ridge that has only been explored by the explorer, Lederer and a few other explorers. We may need to build a line of forts in defense against the French, between this Colony and the Great Lakes, Miami county, and the City of Chante De Louis on the Mississippi. Our focus has been to develop the plantation system from our founding at Jamestown a little over 100 years ago. The early planters, colonists, families, and your ancestors have accomplished much, but we have to be able to protect what they have worked for. We do not want it taken by the French, Spanish, or the Indians. I want to expand the manufacturing businesses, especially mining, and timber business. There is a shortage of coal, iron ore, and timber in England. We need to trade for money, gold, silver, and other goods for our homeland. I propose we build a better trade relations and relationship with the Colony of New York and the Colony of North Carolina. We have much to offer them. They have much to give us."

The Assembly men stood up and applauded and shouted. "That is right. That is correct."

Alexander continued, "I will help build the universities, the towns, the roads, the bridges, the manufacturing, the timber business, the plantation system so we will be the example of the way an English colony should be. I believe in using money wisely. One of the immediate things we should agree on is to improve Williamsburg as our center of government. I want to see the Palace completed so visitors have a place to come for official business. Not just as a personal residence for myself because my accommodations are satisfactory. I would like to see gardens, streets, and the grounds taken care of by gardeners and servants. I would like to see the main building of William and Mary to become a brick structure and become the best-looking university in the world. I would also like Bruton Church to have a steeple and be refurbished and be the best kept building in Williamsburg as it reflects the honor and glory of God. And the peoples said ...."

And the men in the Assembly said, "Amen" Rev. Blair stood up and applauded on that remark.

Alexander making his closing remarks, said, "I will not be the most experienced lieutenant governor that you have met, but I will be the hardest working. I am here to serve, God, my Queen, my Governor, the people. God Bless Virginia and Bless us all."

The members of the assembly applauded out of respect and agreement on some of the proposals.

Mr. Byrd stood up and administered the oath.

Mr. Byrd, "Mr. Alexander Spotswood, Do you swear before Almighty God that you will uphold the laws of Parliament of Great Britain and be loyal to the crown and this body, the representative of the people of the Colony of Virginia with unswerving loyalty and personal discipline?"

Alexander firmly, "I do."

Byrd, "Will you serve the people as a gentleman with the right conduct and personal etiquette?"

Alexander, "I will."

Byrd, "Will you use your knowledge and wisdom for the betterment of the colony with personal scruples and not attempting to attain a personal fortune?"

Alexander, "I will."

Byrd, "Will you stand up as a leader regardless of circumstance bravely using your personal abilities and talents?"

Alexander, "Yes, Sir, I will."

Byrd, "Do you believe in God as the sole God in the Empire and colony and that the citizens may be able to worship Him in the manner they choose?"

Alexander, " Yes, I do believe."

Byrd, "Col. Spotswood has answered all the questions correctly, and I need to hear your confirmation by saying; Yay, if you agree; Nay, if you disagree."

All the Assembly and Council Members said Yay in agreement and they applauded for Alexander one more time.

Things were changing in Virginia. The old society and social class would still be important but would be modified by a more liberal view on how to collect money and spend money for England. Alexander would be a fighter for all current and future Virginians in spite of birth or social rank. He would be a friend to the Indian and farmer, an architect of buildings, a town planner, a military man settling for only a strong militia and strong fort system. He would become a Virginian in spirit if not by birth. He would elevate the church to a new level of respect. He would promote land ownership, expanding the frontier, and promote mining opportunities. He would promote learning, education, and culture. He was 34 years of age, full of energy, happy in life, strong in historical perspective, and an eligible bachelor. Would he marry a lady from the ruling class, or would he wait as Bryd predicted? Only time would tell.

The assembly would conclude the rest of its business by noon. Byrd did what he said he would do. He introduced Commissary Blair to Alexander.

James Blair, " As one Scot to another, " You dazzled the crowd. They seem to like your speech."

Alexander, "Now I have to put action into words."

Blair, "My advice is not to move too fast. You may leave them behind, or they may leave you behind. I like the fact you want to get the Church refurbished. As I am the rector, I have had trouble convincing England that this must be done. Maybe you will be more blessed."

Alexander, "I will see to it . I have some other ideas on how to improve the Church that I can discuss with you later. I feel as governor I have the obligation to see that all the church has governor selected rectors in them. I do not see anything wrong right now about your remaining the rector at Bruton for now. We have to see that all the churches that have vacancies in the pulpit will soon have rectors and ministers. "

Blair, " That has been my job as commissary to fill the vacancies. I believe that a clergyman who has studied for the divinity would be more qualified to see if a person has been called to preach."

Alexander, "That is not the issue. It is a duty of the royal governors. We can work together on this, but for now, we need to find more rectors that are from England than from Scotland. "

Blair walked off shaking his head.

Byrd, "I know you feel the need to hold your ground on this. I would let him cool down and approach him again later. You can see what the burgesses think of this."

Alexander, "I don't want him to be an enemy right away or at all for that manner."

Byrd, "He takes pride in the fact he got the capital moved from Jamestown to Williamsburg in the first place. He was about to talk the people and King William in to establishing William and Mary University. He has been the only rector at Bruton as long as most people remember. He has been a well-respected champion for shaping the demeanor of the colony and making it a Christian entity. He has married one of the wealthy daughters of a Tidewater planter. He has two daughters which were married to two of the men on the assembly this morning. He is moody for a religious fellow and gets into these petty quarrels, and it gets more attention that it deserves. He will fight face to face, toe to toe, and will not compromise. He is very political, and his thinking gets confused with all the quarreling. I must be going, See you in the morning. I have to find some fiddlers and then some women to dance with."

Alexander shaking Mr. Byrd's hand, "Thank you and I will see you tomorrow."

Alexander turned around and Ms. Thornton was there, and she said, " You handled yourself very well, Alexander. Mr. White wrote down all the proposals and speech. He has a list of the Assembly members and the counties they represent."

Alexander, "Thank you.   Are you ready to go with me up to see the Palace? I want to get started on getting this project finished but I have to have a good idea of what the Palace still needs."

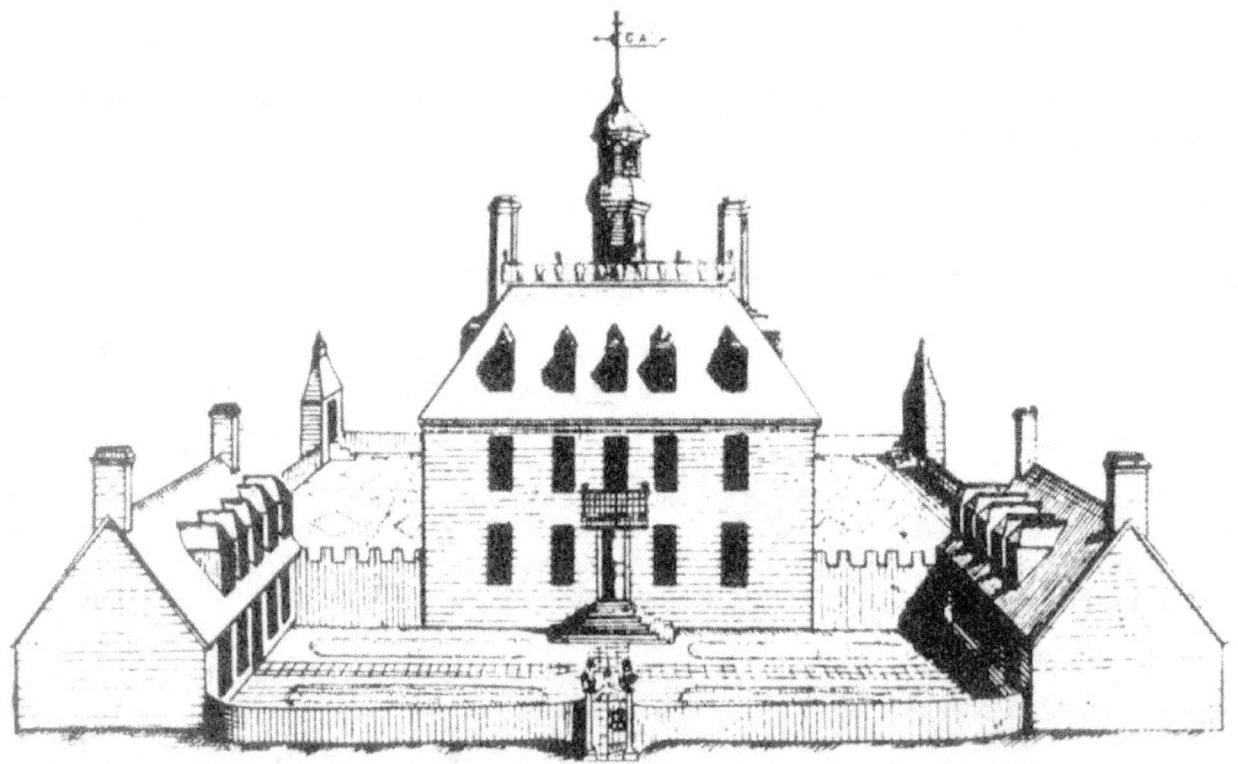

Alexander, " I guess you really gave me a big endorsement when you helped Mr. Byrd write the in introduction for me ."

Ms. Thornton flirtatiously, " I guess you can thank me for that. And by the way, that is all I gave him. "

Alexander ignoring all of her remarks, said, "Thank you, Ms. Thornton. You really did like the speech? "

Ms. Thornton was irritated because Alexander would not flirt back and seemed to miss the point that Byrd would flirt with her, but Alexander seemed to ignore her and was already wrapped up in his work.

Ms. Thornton, "I would really do anything for you. Just ask. I want you to ask......" She stopped as Alexander wasn't apparently listening anyway.

Alexander was preoccupied in his thoughts and was formulating a plan on what his next move as governor would be and half listening said. "Yes, Ms. Thornton." He kept on working on his plan oblivious to anything else.

 Alexander and Ms. Thornton soon arrived at the Palace a fairly large building consisting of about 2600 square feet. The building was about 54 feet wide and 48 feet deep on a 63-acre lot. The palace house was divided by a large wall between three sections, the kitchen on the west side, main room containing the state rooms and Alexander's future apartments, and the stables were on the east side of the complex. The front lawn consisted of about three acres lined with big oak and walnut trees. As one walked into the main room in the front, there was a large hall with a parlor room in front right and the dining room in the back right of the main building. There was a powder room and spacious closets on the left side. On the front left side of the great hall on the first floor was a pantry. As one waked to the back of the door there was a passage that led into the ballroom which would hold about two hundred people and further back was the supper room which could hold about 30 guests. By the passage to the ballroom was a stairwell that led to the 2nd floor of the palace. The rooms upstairs included the governor's bed chamber closet, study, a library with about 1000 books with a guest bedroom on the back side and a great room which was directly above the big hall and front parlor below. There was a passage to the garret floor or the third floor. Here were four storage rooms and also some small rooms for the servants' quarters. There were large fireplaces on the extreme east side and west side of the house. One warming the front parlor and the middle room upstairs. The one on the left was warming the pantry and governor's bedchambers in the wintertime. The house was designed to be as warm as possible in the winter and cool as possible in the summer by hits drought system. In the stables were also poultry, gardening tools, coaches, horses, and plows for the gardens.

The Palace also had two wine cellars, a vault , a slate roof, and constructed out of brick with slash windows. It had a deeply pitched roof with dormers and a tall cupola in the center that was easily observed from the outskirts of town. The kitchen and stables were only one story but had the same pitched roof with dormers and a shorter cupola on each building. There was a small courtyard in front surrounded with a rock fence that blended in with the English styled main house. This Palace when finished would be the cultural, educational, and governmental center of Virginia. James Blair said that it would be the most expensive and best looking home in the New World. It was being prepared to be the home of Alexander Spotswood, Lieutenant Governor.

Alexander looking carefully at the architecture, said, "It is not the largest building I have seen, but the most beautiful. It looks like a miniature model of Castle Howard in London, the ancestral home of The Howard Family. This family married into the royal families of England. I will get this building finished and add some personal embellishments to it. People will be talking about this house everywhere in the New World. The gentry class will want to model their courthouses and Anglican Churches after this Palladian style. I will propose in the next assembly to leave the great room on the second floor wide without walls to give a statelier appearance. I wish it could be painted a light blue which is the color of peace and healing. I will plan for a garden like the ones in London which will be about 250 feet by 150 feet. I will enclose the garden with a four-foot-high brick wall with gates, ditches, and canals so there will be plenty of water access to the gardens for plants and flowers. I want to include a small orchard of fruit and nut trees within the garden. It will put some of the royal parks in London to shame."

Ms. Thornton asking, "You plan this all in your head, don't you?"

Alexander answering, "Yes, I guess I do. I will have to draw it into a formal plan to present to the Assembly. I want it in writing so that it does not become a headache for the builders. I remember my sister Margaret telling me about Sarah Churchill always getting into arguments with the builders and it took more years to complete their mansion, Blenheim Palace. I want to get the project done here before I get elected out of office. I think there should be little offices attached to the kitchen and stables to be used for storage , and offices for you, Ms. Thornton and for Mr. White. There can be a pipe to bring in heat or a small coal or wood stove for warmth in the winter. The weather doesn't usually get that cold here in the winter, I am told. Also, the butlers and chambermaids can also have small attached rooms to the kitchen and stables. I guess, I will need 30 such dependencies attached to the kitchen and stables because that is how many servants and staff members I have. That is also allowing three guest rooms for traveling dignitaries."

Ms. Thornton, "Sounds like you are trying to keep women out of your house. "

Alexander," No that is not it at all. I have a country to run, not a woman to chase."

Ms. Thornton, "I guess. I am not wanted around here anyway. However, if you change your mind and want a woman's advice, please come to my room."
Alexander, although 34 and a young successful man was blushing like a schoolboy. He just pretended not to hear that and went on talking about the diplomats. Alexander looked at Mr. White who was still taking notes and the new lieutenant governor continued" I will have the 12 Councilors or Secretary of the Council coming over from time to time. I will have lawyers come for legal and judicial business, and clergymen coming over for career prospects. There will be petitioners wanting favors, sea captains needing passes, British officials inspecting the colony, Indian agents, people applying for American citizenship. I want to have a portrait of Queen Anne hanging in the hallway for all to see. I forgot to mention that some visitors will be military leaders needing orders for action and supplies. In fact, I want to put a gun collection of muskets and swords and the cannon ball that almost killed me on display in the Great Hallway so that all who will visit will be impressed by our potential military might. I would have displayed my father's sword, but a pirate stole it long ago. This is the way the British display arms in the Admiralty Office in London, and that is what I want in Virginia. I want to show our loyalty to the crown of Queen Anne and the military strength of our colony. I also, want to designate one room as a chapel. This is where I want to put the desk that Sarah Churchill gave me and where I will place the Spotswood Bible. I will have to give appropriate authority to the butler to take care of the buying and handling of food and make sure he is able to feed the servants every meal. He will be given specific instructions on how to decant the wine, clean the middle rooms , store the china collection after every use, and have adequate supplies of food in the pantry so it will not waste or ruin. I will put him in charge of the laundry maids and insist they change the linens and draperies at the changing seasons of the year. I cannot get that involved in running the household."

Ms. Thornton who had stepped out for a few moments had come back into the room, because she was curious about the plans of the Palace .said, "Another reason you might get yourself a wife is that she could run the household for you. " :

Alexander, "Then there would be children and more details that would take me away from my business and then there would be the need for nurses and midwives etc. and etc." Ms. Thornton showed her disapproval by smirking.

They walked to the stables and saw three handsome carriages.

Ms. Thornton, "This is the finest coach I have ever seen."

Alexander, "It looks like the one my sister had in London. I would be just as happy riding in this day to day delivery cart that the butler uses to get supplies for the household."

Ms. Thornton "You will need to ask for a gardener if you are getting a big garden and the stable boys can also work in the garden. You will need a blacksmith and farrier to put horseshoes on the horses. They will need saddles, bridles, furnaces, blacksmith tools and farrier tools to keep in the stable."

Alexander, "Good idea. You are now sounding like a hostess and business partner."

As they went upstairs, Alexander hat noticed Mr. White sitting on a chair in the study just writing his notes quickly and neatly.

Alexander to Mr. White, "What are you doing."

Mr. White, "As your secretary, I am preparing your address about your needs here for the Palace and I think I have every word of everything you have said about the needs."

Alexander, "Thank you Mr. White. I am glad for I don't know if I could repeat all of it."

Mr. White, "I will stay out of your way, be close by, and just take notes and perform your other requests."

Alexander beaming with pride, " It is all starting to fall into place."

Ms. Thornton, " Except for the Mrs. Spotswood part."

Alexander again ignored Ms. Thornton's flirting and looked off to the study and was noticing some of the books of the former, Governor Nicholson. One of the books had been written by Alexander's father, about the plants in Tangier and how they needed care just as the plants in England would need great care.

Alexander, " This is a proud moment. My father's book has undoubtedly been on the same three continents that I have been to. You know that Nicholson designed the brick arrangement of the stars, moon, and Jupiter and placed it on the House of Commons building which he designed into the letter H. He did a very impressive job not to have any formal education in architecture. We just have to finish it all. "

Ms. Thornton, "You will need to get violins, cellos, pianos, and other musical instruments for the ball room. You will want to have social affairs for the young gentry of the colony . I think it would not hurt if we practiced the minuets sometime so you will be ready to entertain your guests."

Alexander said, " I will say you are thoughtful, and I don't want to appear to be a spoiler, but they will have to entertain themselves."

Alexander was deep in thought about all the work that needed to be done to beautify the city of Williamsburg and his Palace.

Alexander planning some additions, "I will ask for a consultant to see how much it will cost to refurbish William and Mary College and the Bruton Church. I don't think it too much to ask for a steeple for a church. After all, the church should be the most used and best looking and best maintained building in the village."

Alexander and his entourage all went to supper at an inn on the Duke of Gloucester Street. After supper they all

.153

retired to their respective rooms. Before Alexander went to sleep , he looked up into the night sky and saw Sothis. Alexander prayed to himself in the darkness of the room, "I guess you must be approving of this, Lord God. Thank you for my new home and for my new challenge. I pray that Roger, Margaret, and Butler are in good health and spirits. I pray for my colleagues; Mr. Byrd and Mr. Blair. They are wealthy and sensible men. Surely, they will want Williamsburg to be a center for beauty and strength. Amen."

The next day, Alexander and Mr. White presented the needs to finish the Palace, get money for the Church , and get money for the college. The proposal also included a request for a mayor , alderman, constable, jail, and a budget for a Palace guard. The Assembly surprisingly and unanimously voted yes to almost every request.

 Mr. Lewis Burwell, one of the burgesses, said, "We need to have the best-looking town in the Colonies and show our wealth and strength to the nation. We need to be proud of our capitol city We now have a lieutenant governor with the backbone to lead the efforts. We also now have a man, Mr. John Tyler that is willing to take on the project from where Mr. Carey stopped his work."

Alexander must have thought that there had been some prior discussion that he had missed about Mr. Tyler, but he was elated the Burgesses had voted in his favor and had appointed a Contractor. It would take a few years for all the projects to get finished and the central government in Williamsburg was flourishing, growing, and being noticed. With each project completion, Alexander was getting a good reputation for design, town planning, and understanding people's sense of pride. Alexander agreed with teaching Indians religion at the College if that would help Williamsburg get money for streets and buildings.

The weeks started passing and Alexander was generally accepted by the Burgesses because of his energy and determination to improve the quality of life in Virginia. Work would soon start on the Palace, Bruton Church, and William and Mary College, and the workers were encouraged by Alexanders attention to detail. The town was taking shape and the business were thriving. Besides Blair's Mercantile, there was also a Greenhowe's Store which listed their products for sale in the Williamsburg Gazette newspaper. People seem to be curious and pleased with all the new buildings and additions to their capitol city.

Alexander would write a letter to Christopher Wrenn, the famous architect from London, to look at his plans for the colonial buildings at the Palace, college, and church. He would also ask Queen Anne to approve the appointment of his personal physician, Dr. William Cocke to be the Secretary of the Council to replace Edmund Jennings. The Board of Trade quickly approved of this suggestion as he had gone to school with William Byrd at Queens College at Cambridge University and was well respected in the Colony.

The next year, Alexander received a letter from Margaret his sister and saying that Mrs. Sarah Churchill was worried about Queen Anne's sudden distrust of her and her husband. John Churchill had been questioned for his loyalty to the Crown. Margaret stated that the quarreling between the Queen and Sarah was getting worse, but she hoped Anne would not bring Sarah's husband into question. Margaret was hoping that John would be acquitted and resume his commission in the British Army. Margaret wrote in her letter that because John was not leading the troops in the war and in the field of battle, English would be bogged down for a few more years in Flanders fighting the French, a place Alexander remembered well.

Alexander must have thought , if the Queen has been persuaded by some enemies of the Churchill, that they have been treacherous, then who can you trust. Alexander said to himself, "I believe that it is a sinister plot because John Churchill is an honorable man. Somebody cruelly has stabbed him in the back. I wish I was in England to help him."

As time went by, Alexander learned that John was cleared of treason. This encouraged him that fairness still existed in the government.

Alexander also received a letter from his brother, Roger in Gibraltar. Roger stated that he was enjoying his job as governor of Gibraltar. He also had written that he recently had married a distant cousin who had inherited property in Barnes, England. He had not seen the property yet but hoped to visit there soon. He mentioned that his wife was with child. Roger also wrote that he felt more like a leader of an army than a leader of the people and that he was constantly in battle with the Spanish, Moors, and pirates off the Barbary Coast. They were causing him much stress and many personal health issues. Alexander was happy that Roger had been promoted and that now and that he would be now be an uncle.

Alexander also received mail from Spotswood Trading Worldwide which was written by Mr. Sparks and Mr. Brayne that business was flourishing and that Alexander's cousin, John Spotswood had come by to audit the records and everything was proper. In the letter there was no mention of Butler Brayne and this disappointed Alexander. Periodically he would get letters from his family and business partners. He soon realized he was a long way from them and wanted to go back for a visit and see Butler. He missed their lively conversations and romantic moments together. He thought about her beauty and kindness, but he was not ready for a relationship.

In the fall of 1711 , Alexander was called on by the Governor of North Carolina Colony to help him with the trouble they were having with the Tuscarora Indians. A large number of French Huguenot German and Swiss families under the leadership of Baron Degraffenreid, had been sent from England to settle land near the land between the Pamlico Sound and Neuse River and The Indians did not want the settlers there. The French had been refugees from the wars and famines in France and found the Indians just as inhospitable. Some of the settlers had been killed and their homes had been burned, and there were no peace talks between the settlers and the Indians. Alexander sent part of the Frontier militia to the aid of the North Carolina settlers. He must have believed that if the Indians could not live peacefully with the new colonists in the colony further south, they would probably head north to Virginia as Byrd had earlier predicted. The war was finally stopped after two years of strife and battles. This war had taken its toll on the settlers and their families. Alexander knew what it was like to be confined to a fort or garrison or home to be safe from the enemy. In Tangier, there were times when he would stay within the confines of the garrison to reduce getting personally attacked by the waring Moors and native tribesmen. The Tuscaroras had brutally killed many innocent colonists in the last few years. While the militia was fighting the Indians in the Pamlico area, Alexander had met with some of the peaceful Indians in Virginia. He met with representatives from the Sapponi, Mattaponi, Pamunkey, Chickahominy, Rappanhannock, Occowaneachee, Nansemond, Cherenbuka, Nottaway, and Powhatan tribes. He received some information from the Indians and some promises. Alexander also made promises to the Indians that would keep the Indians peaceful in settlements in New York and further west of the Blue Ridge Mountains. The forts that Alexander got authorized by the Assembly be built on the Rapidan River and at Christianna (named in honoring Christ and Queen Anne) and located south of Williamsburg as a buffer between Virginia and the Carolinas to monitor Indian activity. These forts were welcomed by the settlers in Virginia and Alexander went there often to offer his support and increase his popularity with the new settlers. As governor, he increased the trade between the Indians and the Virginians, and this made for more peaceful relations. Alexander took some of the Indians children to the Indian School that was part of the agreement with William and Mary College so the school could get larger endowments from private citizens and the English government. He ran out of money to send all the Indian children to school, so he asked for private donations from the Anglican church and he donated a lot of money himself. The problems with the Indians would cease for now. It was learned that the French, however, was trying to stir them up in the Great Lakes region far away northwest of Virginia.

Alexander received praises from the Assembly for keeping peace with the Indians and enhanced his reputation for being a friend of the Indians.

In turn, the leader of the settlers in North Carolina, named DeGraffenreid was so pleased with the outcome with the Indians, he asked Alexander if they would allow more German and French families to settle in Virginia at the new fort on the Rapidan River. DeGraffenreid told Alexander that some of the settlers were farmers and some were miners. Alexander said that their potential settlement in Virginia would be great for the colony. Out of his own money, Alexander funded the settlement. Degraffenreid, under the agreement and patronage of Queen Anne bought some of the best, skilled, and hardiest families from Siegen, Germany to settle near the horseshoe bend in the Rapidan River. The German settlers soon arrived in Williamsburg and made the 40-mile trip to the Fort by cattle drawn and ox drawn wagons and the roads had to be cleared as they made the trip. Alexander met the 9 families and showed them the two-mile square are around the horseshoe bend. These pioneers knew why they left Germany because of their religious persecution and also knew what they were getting into in Virginia. This was the first known German settlement in the Virginia Colony. Alexander showed them the crudely made fort that the militia would use for scouting and as a wilderness home. He told them they should make the fort larger and bigger and they later drew up and built a five-sided palisade fort that would be ample room to protect them from any Indian attack. Alexander got to know each one of these mining families in person and helped them finance the iron ore mining. They would call the fort, Fort Germanna after their homeland and the members of The Assembly mentioned their settlement in a resolution in 1714 when they offered to build a road to Germanna. To the west of the Rapidan river lay some of the richest pastureland in Virginia with large fields, meadows, and rolling hills. Alexander must have thought how sturdy and hardy these families were. They built their 9 houses all in a straight row with 9 sheds where their chickens, hogs, and cows would stay. They cut down every one of the trees around the fort and converted logs into timber suitable for housing and storage. The Germans were all good gardeners and knew how to hunt and prepare game for food. The families met together daily to pray and sing and met for worship twice on Sunday. Alexander told them they could worship as they pleased and so they did. The English would have preferred they would have been Anglicans instead. The settlement was surrounded with a fence made out of wood poles around the nine houses and lots in a five-sided pentagon shaped palisade. This must have looked like a star from the top of the trees. Alexander said they would have to pay no levy or county taxes if they lived there for seven years and help defend the Virginians against the Indians. Alexander told them he would seek iron furnaces and iron making equipment to help in production of iron . He encouraged them to also mine for silver and gold dust which had been reported being discovered in the nearby creeks and caverns. The families were told that the Sapponi Indians could bring their furs to Fort Germanna in exchange for English or Virginia made goods, but the Indians never really came around that much. Much of the game had dwindled in numbers and the better game hunting was west of the Blue Ridge and in central North Carolina, and the Sapponis would go where the game was abundant.

Alexander seeing that North Carolina was being settled quickly by Irish, Scotch, and English immigrants had a fear that there would be another Tuscarora outbreak or Indian attacks on these new settlers. He formed what he called the Virginia Indian Trading Company which was a public company where the owners could trade with Indians to promote peace and after two years would assume control of Fort Christianna. The Sapponi Indian Confederation which also consisted of Enos, Occawanachee and Tutello tribes took advantage of the Trading Agreement and the 300 or more Sapponis became skilled farmers and peaceful traders throughout Virginia and North Carolina. This was acceptable at first to the Assembly and to the Parliament in England. Again, a diplomatic and business solution proved best for the moment.

When Alexander got back to the Palace, one day in 1714, there was a letter from J. Spotswood, from London laying on his desk. He feared the worst because he only heard from him when there were significant changes going on in the family. Alexander quickly opened the letter reading.

Alexander, I regret to inform you that Roger died peacefully in London and will be buried in Barnes. He has been ill for a long time and never really recovered from a wound from the war in Flanders. He leaves a wife, Catherine and two small children. They will be well taken care of. You probably have heard this already, but Queen Anne has died. Most likely a Hanoverian, George I, will become King. God, help us all.
Your business in London is thriving and your partners says that it is well.

Sorry for the loss of your brother and cousin, Roger. I wish I could have told you in person, Affectionately, John Spotswood.

Alexander set back in his chair. He took this hard. His older half-brother had meant the world to him. He remembered all the walks along the beach in Tangiers the garrison school, the meetings in London, and the mountain hike to Mt. Toubkal in the Atlas Mountains. He remembered his comforting words on the battlefield at Blenheim when Alexander thought that he was dying. Alexander would need a few days off to recover from the overwhelming grief. The time passed quickly but the loss of Roger would never be forgotten. Alexander would send a long letter of sympathy to his sister, Margaret.

The year was now 1715 in the year of our Lord and Savior. Alexander was approaching 40 years of age. He went one day to check on the settlement at Germanna. He observed the nine German families. They all seemed to be doing well in their new home. They had made much progress. Alexander had attended one of their prayer meetings and couldn't help but notice the love and respect they showed to each other. One of the younger couples had been blessed by a baby and the mother had it wrapped tightly in her arms admiring it with great devotion. He left the stone storage building where they worshiped and told his two guards that he wanted to go up to the banks of thee Rapidan River at the horseshoe bend and just stare at the sky. They took charge of Alexanders horse and he walked towards the five-sided fort and garrison that was attached nearby.

Alexander looked up to the starry sky and he could see a full moon and Sothis staring back at him. He looked at them if he was looking for a message or signal. "I must be lonely. I have people around me all the time, but I feel lonely. I think about Butler a lot but haven't heard from her in a couple of years. I wonder if she finished school. Maybe she got married. I miss her. What would I say to her if she was here? Would she want to live around here? What does she think of me? I have to find out. I would go to London if I could, but my job is keeping me here. I have Assembly issues with Byrd. I have to be here to fight for the passage of the Tobacco Stamp Act. Byrd is the Councilman that has shown the greatest opposition to this much needed act and his constant negative debate is disconcerting. I have to fight Blair to appoint clergy to the vacancies in the pulpits of the churches. I will write Butler, a letter and tell her how I feel about her. I know what ever she says she will be honest with me. Alexander was torturing himself with his thoughts about the future he had in store. Would he be unhappy like the pirate curse said he would be? Would he be famous, rich, and handsome, but be unhappy?

A shooting star shot upward across and the plains of Essex across the river. The sky was bright, and one could see many shooting stars going up and down the moonlit sky. This light show appeared random and lasted for a few minutes. It was not scary and seemed to be prophetic.

Alexander started talking to himself again. He was missing Butler and wondered what she was doing. "Maybe this is where I must be with Butler. Maybe I need to settle down here and raise a family. I feel better that I have seen the sky respond than to be in darkness wondering what to do next. Is God answering my prayer? Please show me Lord, what it is I must do. " The sky settled back to normal. Once again, one could hear the rushing water of the river below and see the nighttime outlines of the trees, plains, and mountains to the west.

Later that evening, Alexander asked the guards if they had seen something unusual.

One of the guards named Mr. Booth said that he had seen only a bunch of ravens staring at him from a boulder which was located in the middle of a field just south of the five-sided fort. At first, he thought it was Indians staring at him.

Alexander, "I hear that it is an old Algonquin burial site. You saw nothing in the sky?"

Guard, "Nothing in the skies."

Alexander, "That is odd!"

Guard, "I guess so, but there is a full moon which causes craziness."

Alexander, "I guess" He must have wondered if the light show was meant just for him by the Lord.

When the guards and Alexander got back to Williamsburg, he wrote a letter to Butler telling her he wanted her to come to Virginia and stay with Ms. Thornton. He expressed his love for her and that he hoped she felt the same way about him. He told her to pray about the matter if she was not sure and let her parents know of his intentions. Alexander rushed the letter down to the printer's office where the mail service was located to mail the letter.
In a few months Alexander received the following letter from Butler.

My dearest Alexander,

I was elated to get your letter and wish the miles were not so far apart between us. I believe I could say that I pray for your safety and well-being every day. I have recently finished school and a trip to Ireland and Scotland to visit family there. I was honored that I got to see your mother's grave in Ireland and reminded me how much you loved her. I recently heard that your brother, Roger also laid away to rest in Barnes and you know that you have my deepest sympathy. Your cousin, John keeps father posted on your whereabouts and I feel as if I can dream about your Palace and your colony. I cannot move to Virginia right now and accept your wonderful invitation. I have not met any man with your knowledge, sincerity, and passion for success. I would be proud to help you in your daily life and be with you in courtship, but I believe it is for our best that you finish your assignment in Virginia first , Are you sure this is where you want to spend the rest of your life with a family of your own.? My father and mother have always adored you. They may want you to be more successful than you do. I want you to be happy. I know I could be happy with you. I remember the day when you first took me to church at St. Mary's and a walk in Regents Park afterward. I believe this to be the best day in my life. Please write me often. I will continue to pray for your safety and wellbeing. I want you to reach your full destiny and fulfill all your goals. Affectionately, Butler

Alexander started analyzing the words which he was prone to do with all his letters. I believe she is not ready for a commitment. I believe she does love me. I think she is wanting me to finish my work first so that we could devote the rest of our lives together, when I have a more regular position. I believe her to have excellent qualities. I need to write her more frequently and thank her for her prayers and interest in our success. Let the Lord make the next move in our relationship. Alexander letter to Butler and her reply would be one in the many letters they would write each over in the next few years.

Alexander believed when the stars shot across the skies over the Rapidan River, that was a sign to explore the area and see what lies further west. Alexander was seeing boat load after boat load of new settlers coming from the war torn and famine ridden countries of Europe. They would need more land to settler as the planter aristocracy and the tobacco barons were not going to give up any of their land. At one of the Assembly meetings, 1st of January 1716, Alexander brought forth a proposal for exploration and the claiming of land for King George I west of the Blue Ridge Mountains. Alexander read from his proposal, "I propose, that I lead the exploratory party from Ft. Germanna and follow the Rapidan to its source in the Western Mountains and cross over the Blue Ridge to claim land for England as an extension of Virginia to the Mississippi River. The Sapponi Indians call this land, Shenandoah, when translated means daughter of the Stars. We have Indian reports and maps that have been submitted to Parliament and the Crown will support a party of 50 which would include officers of the colony, members of the gentry class, planters, and Indian guides. There will be servants to prepare the meals and blacksmiths to take care of the horses and farriers to take care of the horseshoes. From my experiences in Africa riding a horse toward the summit of the mountain, good horseshoes on sturdy horses are essential. We will be armed for protection against the Indians and to hunt game as we go along. The process should take about two weeks only to be slowed down by having to prepare a horse trail and wagon trail as we head towards the mountains. A friend of mine, John Fontaine, will go along to make a historical record of the event. Mr. Beverly who also could write the history of the journey will be asked to come along because of his expertise in soils, mining, and business opportunities. We will also have surveyors that will be able to map out the new lands. This should be a good opportunity for Virginia and its citizens. Militia men will also accompany the party and lead us if we are attacked by any foe of the Crown. I ask for the Assembly's approval."

Mr. Byrd, " I agree with Col. Spotswood on this. I would like to pick up another 100,000 acres are so." The Assembly laughed at this statement.

Mr. Blair looking at the burgesses, "Col. Spotswood who I have bitterly disagreed with on the appointment of clergy is on the right tract with this. There will be more settlers coming and the land is unlimited as God's power is unlimited. He has been the only governor that has done anything in his human power to expand Virginia westerly. There has to be good farmland in the Shenandoah and further west. Colonel Taylor, Colonel Smith, Mr. Crowder, Mr. Todd, and Mr. William Robinson will be the leaders that will organize the money, the horses, the wagons, the food, the wine and spirits, and equipment to make this journey successful. We are doing this for our Lord and for King George . By our journey, let us open the door to the West. The worse thing that could happen is that we run into the French and then we could defeat them.

The Assembly said, " Aye, Aye! "The men in the room seemed excited about the adventure of the Blue Ridge Journey.

Alexander left the Assembly and felt good about how well the proposed Journey over the Blue Ridge Mountains seem to go over. The landed gentry from previous generation probably saw this an opportunity to increase their land speculating, but they knew that Alexander Spotswood would counteract this. They would buy smaller tracts of land and lease this land to the immigrants coming to Virginia.

Alexander, happy with his upcoming journey, went to Ms. Thornton's office and said, "We need to invite the citizens of the city and gentry to a ball in the Ball Room on Feb 14th. We will have musicians, dance, and rich food. I will pay the bill myself. This ball will be called, Journey to the Stars. This is your chance to be the best hostess in the history of the colony of Virginia."

Ms. Thornton looking puzzled by the new development, "Alexander, you are serious? You have not lost your mind?"

Alexander shaking his head up and down in confirmation," "No. We have much to celebrate here in Virginia. I will tell the citizens about a journey to expand the western boundary of Virginia which is a little ambiguous right now. How does one take care of a property if you do not know where the boundaries are."

Ms. Thornton, "You are making a little more sense now. But if I knew better, I would say you are in love."

Alexander thinking about the future celebration, "You could say, that I am in love with Virginia or that Virginia is in love with me. "

Ms. Thornton, " I will plan the event and see if it meets with your approval and with your budget. Only one thing, you must promise me the first dance. If you want to practice, we can arrange that, too. "

Alexander, "I am so happy I will dance with you and you had better be fast on your feet. I do not need practice."

Ms. Thornton," I will hold you to that, Colonel Spotswood. By the way, a Mr. Livingston is waiting for you in the study. He wants to start a theater on the Palace Grounds to promote a cultural alternative to the library and the musicians who play in the ball room." Alexander went into the study and greeted a blond haired thin young man. Mr. Livingston, "Hello, Governor Spotswood. I want to start a theater as a business on the Palace grounds. The mayor and alderman have signed in agreement, but we need your approval."

Alexander," Permission granted, have the Council look it over for legalities."

Mr. Livingston, "Don't you want to hear the costs and benefits of a theater?"

Alexander, "I know the benefits. It is about time there is a theater with English actors staring in the New World. I have probably been to more plays in London, than you have, Mr. Livingstone. I used to take my dear Mother and sister to the plays at the theaters in London. I also use to take this special girl friend of mind. I would rather go to a play than read 10 good books. Good Luck and I will see you there. "

Mr. Livingstone, "I am glad you are so romantic!"

Alexander, "I like you're getting quickly down to business."

Ms. Thornton, laughing and looking at Mr. Livingstone. "If you only knew how Alexander Spotswood, the most eligible bachelor in Virginia really is. He doesn't even pay attention to the most beautiful and richest ladies in the land. He is always busy running the colony. He is romantic all right."

Mr. Livingston chuckled and left the room to begin his business venture.

Alexander looked at the beautiful and tempting Ms. Thornton. She had a beautiful figure and a great personality but seemed too bold in Alexander's way of thinking. He knew of no man that seemed to flirt with her or express any interest in courting her. He thought that this was very odd because she was so beautiful with her black hair and blue eyes. Alexander sensed she liked him, and she desired more than a working relationship, but he better not get involved with her until he figured out Butler's plans. He did not want to lead Ms. Thornton on or upset her in anyway. She had been a loyal associate. He said a farewell to Ms. Thornton and went to his room.

On February 14th, the ball was held in the Blue Room at the Governor's Palace in Williamsburg. Musicians played as the social class of the Virginia Colony arrived inside the ball room. Most of the burgesses had come to the Palace. They were with their wives and many introductions were made. It looked as though everyone was happy at the social event of the year. Much of the discussion involved the upcoming event of the journey to the valley beyond the Blue Ridge Mountains. There were plenty of drinks and food and music. Ms. Thornton had performed an outstanding job in arranging the events of the social. Alexander kept his promise and honored Ms. Thornton with the first dance of the evening. He was graceful dancer. Mr. Byrd and Mr. Blair were also in attendance. They had observed every move that Alexander was making with Ms. Thornton.

Byrd said to Blair, "Besides my wife and I, I think they are the most beautiful couple here tonight."

Blair, " Maybe they should get married as they seem to enjoy each other's company. "

Byrd, " I don't think that there is any chance of that. I believe the Colonel is a confirmed bachelor. Even with all my charm, I could not work that closely around Ms. Thornton as I would get distracted by her beauty and never get anything accomplished."

Blair, " Seems like Alexander is focused on business all the time."

Byrd, " Yes, but I believe he is in love with a lady from London. Why he doesn't bring her to Virginia is beyond me. The stars say that he will marry late in life and now it is late in life."

Ms. Thornton did not get any of the other men to dance with her as their wives seem extremely jealous of her. Alexander did not ask any of the other ladies to dance as he did not want to offend any of the burgesses. Overall, the gentry seemed to be enjoying the social and visited with their friends and neighbors. Soon the social was over and all the guests said farewell and said that they had enjoyed their evening at the Palace. It had been a great evening for Alexander as he got to mingle with everyone.

While lying in bed one evening, Alexander was thinking that there was some way he could get Butler to come to Virginia. If there was something he could do, he would do it, but she would have to come willingly on her own terms.

Through the spring, he would check on the miners at Germanna and he would prepare himself physically by walking around Williamsburg greeting the citizens and looking at the assortment of goods in the stores. One Sunday, Ms. Thornton , Mr. White, and Alexander attended church at Bruton Church. Reverend Blair would have a stirring sermon about the heathens burning in Hell and the contrast of going to Heaven. He also preached that Jesus is coming back again like a thief in the night. We must repent of our sins and be saved from our sins by accepting Jesus. Blair was not meek behind the pulpit but had an appealing cadence and speaking voice to deliver the Lord's sermons. The three guests and the church goers left the church grounds after the benediction renewed in their faith and revived in their spirit.

The Church had been refurbished and now had a beautiful steeple on top. It now was the prettiest and well-kept building in the village. Alexander had written a letter to Christopher Wrenn, the architect to help look at his design of the new belfry and the main building at William and Mary College. Wrenn liked the design and made only minor changes in one of the college's auditoriums.

 Alexander would think to himself, what do the parishioners at Bruton think about Ms. Thornton. She is a rare beauty with cold black hair and blue eyes, petite enough and dresses in a similar manner as the gentry class. However, it was puzzling to him why the planters' sons seemed to shy away from her. Maybe they want a less outspoken lady for courtship. Maybe they think they could not make her happy or keep her at home. Maybe it is because she does not have wealthy parents and have a big dowry. Maybe time will answer this question.
Alexander had prayed at Bruton Church for a successful journey in August when they explored the Blue Ridge Mountains and beyond. He wanted to be the first governor to explore, conquer, and settle the lands to the unknown western territory. Could he convince King George, the new leader of the English that it was a worthwhile opportunity for the growth and future of the English Empire. Undoubtedly there were millions of acres of rich soil, thick large forests for timber needs, coal, iron ore, silver and gold in the mountains, mines and caverns west of the mountains to be claimed by the Virginia Colony. Alexander must have thought that the journey to the mountains and the lands beyond would be the most important accomplishment in his governorship.

He would pay faithfully to the Christ,
and seek the pardon of sins in the past,
Righteous men's prayers are sure to be heard,
and answered by the Lord and his Holy Word

He says he will take care of me by a plan,
.161

Only things that will be good and kind,
No disasters will come my way,
When I trust only Him every day.

Amen

Over the next few months, he would gain the support of the English government and the Colonial Assembly for support. Much to his surprise, King George said that he would finance the trip to the mountains and beyond for the Glory of God and the good of the Virginia Colony. Alexander began to plan his supply needs and get a troop for the exploration from a list of honorable, dedicated men consisting of cocked hat gentry and their servants to make the arduous and challenging physical journey to the summit. Reverend Blair had already mentioned a few names in the Assembly the day that the proposal was made to the members of the Council and Assembly There were no reliable maps of the area and very few Indian trails to follow. There were plenty of old folk legends telling about the mystery of the Blue Ridge and only a few English men had explored or even seen the mountains. No horses or wagons had ever traveled over the mountains for no passes had been discovered and mapped.

Alexander made a pledge to the English government that he would see what lies over the mountains and claim it for England. Alexander must be thinking that when he succeeded to the top of the mountain this would be the crowning achievement of his legacy. He prayed daily for a successful journey and for his beloved Butler.

Journey from Germanna

Alexander asked Ms. Thornton to take on the task of getting Robert Beverly to come to Williamsburg so that Alexander good get his advice about the Blue Ridge Journey, now referred by the citizens as "The Journey" . He knew that Robert Beverly was an honorable man because of his recommendation from the conversation with Mrs. Barkeley six years earlier. Alexander had met Beverly at the Assembly and had talked to him at several occasions at the balls that had been held at the Ball Room at the Palace. Robert knew a lot about the unsettled countryside and the Indians that they would encounter on the Journey. Robert would also be instrumental and invaluable in getting the right balance of men, horses, supplies, maps, and an agenda for such an undertaking. Robert Beverly was a smart and deliberate fellow and liked adventure. Not knowing exactly what was on the other side of the mountain was a real question, and the challenge would be something to meet head on. It was a good thing for a man now in his fifties to explore a wilderness when few men had gone on a similar journey and lived long enough to tell the rest of the world about it. Most Virginians, when talking about the area west of the Blue Ridge thought this area was probably kept secret by the Indians because it might be rich in soil and very rich in minerals for gardening and suitable for grazing cattle or for farming. There might me mines of iron ore, coal, silver, and gold in caverns in the mountains. Beyond the mountains, Virginians feared they would run onto other tribes of Indians such as the Miamis which lived on the flat plains before you get to the Great Lakes Region controlled by the French.

Robert Beverly came one sunny afternoon in April to visit Alexander at the Palace. When spring was in its most beautiful state, Alexander was glad to receive him and offered him a cushioned chair for comfort and some tea to refresh himself.

Alexander began the conversation, "Mr. Beverly, I have always respected your writings and politics and how you have built up a big plantation and have been successful in business. I need your support in getting rewards for people taking these risks on ab journey to the Blue Ridge Mountains. It will be a great time for the gentry, a band of men in brotherhood, that will traverse over the Blue Ridge Mountains and claim more land for England. It will be very risky. I expect success but there are lots of unknowns past the mountains, and we need to find some passes to get to the other sides so families can settle that vast acreage. There should be some great rewards for those who take the risks on this journey. I would equate it in the same way when we set up a garrison in Tangiers, or when we had a band of people settle Jamestown, and Plymouth Rock. Will you go? And what do you think?"

Robert Beverly, " You know, Ms. Thornton was eager to tell me about your great plans. You probably didn't want her telling everything she knew. " Alexander laughed as he knew this was probably the case. Beverly continued," I have been thinking about this for a long time and that exploring the mountains and the land beyond is the right thing to do. I would be honored to go, and I know some men who are surveyors that would like to measure and acquire more land."

Alexander expressing his opinion, "You know the owing of vast amount of land for land speculation, I disagree with in principle. However, this cause of expanding the frontier westward should appeal to every Virginian and every English citizen. We are building a new country and increasing the size of the empire so future generations will be able to have lots of land to choose from , a place to settle down, and rear a family. Therefore, the cause is great, and the gentry should be rewarded for building roads to the west. " Mr. Robert Beverly nodded in agreement.

Alexander, "Who are some of the men you can get to go with us on the journey? I prefer we get people who own some land, but not large amounts. That would leave out most of the burgesses, their families, and the oligarchies of would be power hungry. We need to give this job to those who are skilled in business, knowledgeable in Indian warfare, good at hunting, and those who have good survival skills.

Robert Beverly, smiling, because he knew that including himself most of the gentry already had large land masses. He said, "I will name you the ten most influential families of Virginia who will fill the bill and would be glad to make history with you. I, Robert Beverly, will be glad to assist you in this monumental and historical task. My brother, Peter, who is a preacher but also has experience in the Council of Virginia can run my little place at the mouth of the Mattaponi River while I am gone. One gentleman I would recommend is Robert Brooke, from Essex County. He is a surveyor and his family own Toddsbury plantation. The Todd family is a strong family and they would like to see more land made available to Virginians out west of the mountains. You may have heard of Jeremiah Crowder. He has land in various places in Virginia and likes adventure. He can represent King and Queen County. A fourth gentleman coming along could be James Taylor, Jr. from Caroline County. He lives at "Hare Forest and manages a 60,000-acre estate and is an excellent surveyor and has a good reputation. Number five on my list is Captain Christopher Smith, a surveyor from New Kent County. He can use a transit or musket equally well. There is also Augustine Smith, who has a plantation where we could spend the day before the journey because this big plantation is at the beginning of the trail. He will advise us on the Indian trails going up to the mountains. He has a blacksmith shop which he will generously allow us to shoe our horses to help the horses' hooves from splitting. It may be appropriate to ride horses along the coast in the sand and loose marshy soil, but we will be on rocky riverbeds and creek beds, stony mountains paths, and brushy stubble so we will need horses shod with good horseshoes. "

Alexander smiling as he liked the suggestions, "The horseshoes will bring us good luck, too, according to the Irish, Scottish, and English folk."

Robert Beverly, "We will need more than luck to get us back safely. We will need the favor and grace of God."

Alexander, looking more seriously. " Yes, we will. Who else do you have in mind?"

Robert Beverly continued, "There is Christopher Robinson from Middlesex County. His brother, John is one of the most influential assembly members in Virginia. He will promote the journey to officials in England and could run the Council while you are away from Williamsburg. Indeed, Christopher married the widow of my brother, William, when he died a few years ago. Christopher's cousin named, John Robinson will also come along as he is a good hunter and trapper. Another gentleman who can ride well is George Mason the Third from Stafford County who is an excellent military leader. I know his family from way back and they are good, loyal people. Then there is your clerk of the Council, Col. William Robertson. He will be invaluable in getting supplies, guns, food stocks, liquors, horses, and keeping the servants organized. That is the list of gentlemen: Beverly, Brooke, Crowder, Todd, Taylor, A. Smith, C. Smith, Robinson, Mason, and Robertson."

Alexander, "And Mr. Beverly, with due respect, you think they will bring honor to Virginia, the King, and God?"

Robert Beverly, "Yes, your excellency. They are all honorable men with no expectations except to make a little bit of history, a small fortune, and bring more favorable light to the Virginia Colony."

Robert Beverly finished his one cup of imported West Indies tea, and Alexander quickly poured him some more tea from a pewter pitcher.

Alexander, "Then I agree. Have them gather at Augustine Smith's plantation on August 27th. We will shoe the horses, rest for the journey, and have a big feast and celebration before we start so we can get to know each other and be able to ride together as an army would against France or Knights would ride as if we were Crusaders."

Robert Beverly, "By the way, I met a young gentleman from England. He wants to write a journal of the journey to the Blue Ridge. His name is John Fontaine, and he eventually wants to settle in Virginia, and he is a gifted writer, explorer, and soldier. He is fluent in French, Latin, and Irish. His family has a rich and colorful history in France, Ireland, and England. He served in the War of Spanish Succession brought on by King William and Queen Anne. He said he has traveled to many places looking for a suitable plantation in Virginia, and he has talked with many Virginians. He stated that he has sat around many a campfire on breezy, cool nights and talked with planters in front of their fireplaces and even has grabbed some stools and set out in the gardens at dusk watching fireflies with the citizenry. He stated that the subject of what lies beyond the Blue Ridge Mountains always came up for discussion in these meetings. This Journey is the subject of many fireside chats and discussions everywhere he has traveled in the colony. Virginia citizens for the most part have seen four generations come and go since the Jamestown landing and what lies wet of the Blue Ridge Mountains is still an unanswered question. Fontaine thinks that taking control of this land is the most important thing England could do for its future prosperity."

Alexander," Please arrange for me to meet Mr. Fontaine here in Williamsburg."

Robert Beverly , "I will be glad to do so. He came up to visit me on the Mattaponi and is scheduled next month to come again. He is bringing a botanist friend to study my grapes. Mr. Fontaine was fascinated by my three-acre grape orchard as it produced four hundred gallons of wine. I have a combination of grape plants brought over from England and France. The botanist wants to see the soil and see what plants we have compared to that in England."

Alexander responding, "That is fascinating. As far as the map goes, I have ordered that several rangers from the Militia will go out to the mountains in June and do a sketch of the trail to see if they can find a pass. Only a few men have ever been to the mountain range and described the mountains. They say there are buffalo trails, mammoth trails, and Indian trails going by the side of the mountains for hundreds of miles, but no passes that go directly to the other side. We have to look hard and find a pass. It will take too long to go around the mountain range, and this will interfere with the other colonies and possible contempt from Spain and France. Some of the rangers will go along with us on the journey."

Robert Beverly confidently, "We will find the pass, Col. Spotswood." After more casual conversation and after finishing his tea, Robert Beverly left smiling; knowing that they were about to make one of the greatest historical discoveries in the young colony.

One day in May 1716, Alexander was sitting in his office. He called for Ms. Thornton to come in and talk. She had on a pretty new dress she had bought at Burwell's Clothing Store, and it went with her black way hair and beautiful blue eyes. Alexander smiling," Ms. Thornton, I want to express my thanks to you for getting Mr. Beverly to help me with my journey to the Mountain."

Ms. Thornton, "It is nothing, Alexander. You just owe me a coffee or a glass of wine from Liddendales."

Alexander, "Indeed! I do."

Ms. Thornton, "Besides Col. Spotswood, He is probably the only man in The Assembly that sees things your way."

Alexander, smiling, " I am not very popular with the Assembly, am I."

Ms. Thornton, rolling her eyes and smiling. "I will tell you the truth. The only people you are popular with are the planters' young daughters because of your good looks and the perceived wealth you have. The men in the Assembly know you are very intelligent, but they think you are too stubborn. They think you are too friendly to the Indians and the pirates and to the small farmers and miners. They would respect you more if you married one of their lovely daughters and give each one of them 20,000 acres in the land beyond the mountains. Blair believes you are a Christian man, but also have a futile desire to be the Bishop of Virginia. Mr. Byrd, although handsome himself, wonders why you ignore the beautiful ladies and won't marry. Byrd also wonders why you stress so much over doing what is right for the colonists which sometimes is not what the Board of Trade nor what the English Government wants."

Alexander standing up and facing the fireplace and gazing into the fire and not directly looking at Ms. Thornton, he asked, " Ms. Thornton, what do you think about me and this governorship?"

Ms. Thornton, " Col. Spotswood, "You know how I feel. I think you are doing a fine job. You are just what this colony needs. You are not just for the rich gentry, but you care about people in all walks of life. For Virginia to grow there has to be other businesses here besides tobacco, timber, and plantations. These other politicians are set in their affluent ways in acquiring money to keep their way of life going and ignoring the real needs of the average citizen."

Alexander smiling, "I get one vote for being retained as lieutenant governor."

Ms. Thornton, "You probably would get many votes of confidence especially from the ladies."

Alexander showing a little disgust, "There you go again with me being married or women wanting me for marriage.
Someday, I will be married. I just don't want to put a wife through so much strife. "

Ms. Thornton moving closer to the Colonel, "Alexander, you know how I feel about you. I have been fascinated about you since the first day I met you. You can have your way with me any time you want. I think I am a fair looking lady, but I do not have money. I can sense that you are lonely. So am I. You are miserable, I can tell. "

Alexander trying to not be red faced or say something of encouragement. "Ms. Thornton, I know that, I am very fond of you. You are one of the most beautiful ladies in Virginia, and I see the men trying to get the courage to talk with you. I think I could have not found a better Office Manager than you in all the colonies. Most men would welcome the opportunity to meet you, court you, and marry you. God knows it has been difficult for me to act only professionally around you, I admire you and respect you."

Ms. Thornton cutting his sentence short, " But you do not love me. "

Alexander, "Not in the way you want me too. "

Ms. Thornton," But I see you looking at me sometimes as if you love me but then there are times you seem so unhappy. "

Alexander, "You see, Ms. Thornton, I just became 40 years of age a few weeks ago. Not a happy day. I tried to keep it quiet so no one would celebrate a good time when I felt so miserable. It has made me realize that my life has been going along according to plan. "

Ms. Thornton, "No one can know how their life will actually go. We are supposed to trust and obey God."

Alexander, "Well yes I do, and God has carried me most of the time through all my difficulties, but I have to tell you a secret. You seem to be honest in your opinions, and I have always found you loyal. Can you keep a secret? No one else must ever know or I will never get any respect from anyone. Promise me you will not tell Byrd or Blair. "

Ms. Thornton, "This sound pretty serious. You may owe another cup of coffee on this one. Alexander, I love you, I would not tell" Ms. Thornton throws her arms around Alexander and she says, "I promise, Alexander, if it will help you." She then backed up and looked directly into his eyes.

Alexander, "You really promise and swear to me as God is our witness."

Ms. Thornton, "Yes, Alexander."

Alexander, "You see, that when I was a young boy, our family was evacuating from Tangier on our way to England, A pirate ship stopped us, and we feared for our lives. My older half-brother Roger, a soldier in the Royal Navy and my stepfather, George Mercer, and mother were on board. Roger had strong words for the pirate, and I drew my sword on him. His name was Redbeard. He did not hurt us, but he stole my family's sword and said that he was putting a curse on us. He said that the curse would be that we would be handsome, rich, and famous. At first my brother and I and most people would probably say that this is not a curse but a blessing. Well it has been a curse to our family. My stepfather and mother died at a younger age than most people, and my mother was in a lot of pain when she died. My half-brother was very handsome, but he got injured in the War of the Spanish Succession and had a bout of pain on and off in life and died two years ago when he returned to England after being Governor in Gibraltar. He was wounded several times by Moors and Barbary pirates but was never killed. I have always been told I was handsome, and I have made a great deal of money, but I am very unhappy. I saw at least 100 British soldiers' heads, beheaded by the barbaric enemy, Moulay, hanging on the palisade posts sounding the garrison in Tangier. This was horrific. I was almost killed in the Battle of Blenheim and that cannon ball almost destroyed my right arm and breast plate and I was in a hospital in Chelsea for almost six months trying to heal. For a few years , I had a lot of pain and nightmares about the battle scar and seeing all the thousands of dead soldiers in the wars I fought. The sword that was stolen by Redbeard belonged to my grandfather, who was Justicier of Scotland., but he got beheaded for siding with the Crown during the Civil Wars of England. At one time, I even thought the sword itself was cursed. When I turned 40, I felt friendless, fatherless, mother less, homeless with little hope for a happy life. I think I can function like a governor and use my experiences to help others, but it is difficult to be a leader, if I cannot motivate myself or have lifelong goals."

Ms. Thornton in a sympathetic tone, " Alexander, I am so sorry. Don't do this to yourself. Talking about it is good, but you are a Christian and you need to let The Lord deal with all this thinking. It sounds like it is from the devil. Please turn it over to the Lord in prayer."

Alexander, " That is what my sister, Margaret said, also. I have shared some of this this story with her."

Ms. Thornton, "You really are hurting. I can help you get through this. I want to hug you and prove my love for you. We can go up to my bedroom and talk some more if that would help."

Alexander declining her advances, said, "You can help me my keeping this quiet. The only way the curse could be broken if the pirate loses the sword, and it is returned to me. That will never happen, as Redbeard as I understand died many years ago, and no one really knows what happened to the ship; not even his son, Blackbeard."

Ms. Thornton curiously asked, "How do you know that?"

Alexander, "I had met some people on my voyage to Virginia that were natives from the Caribbean that told me about Blackbeard." He dared not to tell her the whole truth and that he had met Blackbeard on his trip to Virginia."

Miss Thornton," I know that the pirate, Blackbeard is feared all along the coasts of the Carolinas up to the Chesapeake Bay and all over the rest of the trade routes to Africa and England. I will not tell anyone but pray that you get peace about all this. You can come to me anytime. My door is always open to you. You make me very happy to be around. I love you and I wish you loved me the same way. I trust you feel better that you got this off your chest." She came on up to Alexander and she hugged him and then looked at him and said, "I have heard you talk a lot about Butler and get letters from Butler Brayne. Is he your friend? Maybe you can get some advice from him."
Alexander, "Butler is a lady and is a close friend. She is a daughter of my business partner. I have always liked to be with her, and we are friends."

Ms. Thornton, "Is she pretty and does he know about the pirates curse?"

Alexander, "she is very pretty, and she knows about it, but she would keep it to herself. She respects me and believes in me. She says I need to believe more in God and less in pirates' games."

Ms. Thornton asking directly in a coy manner, "She sounds like a smart lady. Why haven't you brought her to Virginia? Is she the future, Mrs. Spotswood?"

Alexander worrying about where this conversation was headed, said, "She has a very happy and comfortable life in London. I do not believe she would be happy being a Governor's wife and making a home in Virginia just yet. I have not seen her for six years and a lot may have changed. "

Ms. Thornton, "Alexander, if she still writes, she cares for you. Why don't you let her tell you what would make her happy? She might like Virginia just fine. By the way, my offer still stands. A little competition does not bother me. You owe me a third cup of coffee for keeping my mouth shut about the curse. If it makes you feel better, I believe in you, and I believe what you are telling me. We had better get back to work. The gossip mongers think we are having an affair anyway."

Alexander, "How do you know?"

Ms. Thornton, " Trust me, I make it my business to find out these things. Good day, Alexander." Alexander watched her curiously as she walked away back to her office, and he felt better explaining his situation to her. He was hoping he could trust her. It was hard to ignore her beauty, but she made him think differently about Butler. He was even more anxious to see the lady he would dream about every night.

The time finally came when the diarist, John Fontaine came to Williamsburg to meet Alexander Spotswood. John was handsomely dressed in the stylish clothes of the English gentry when he walked into the office of the Lt. Governor.

Fontaine, "Good Morning, your excellency."

Alexander," Good morning, Mr. Fontaine. Mr. Beverly has told me of your interest on a trip to see what lies over the Blue Ridge. I personally think this area contains millions of acres of rich soil and timber, hostile Indians, and iron ore, gold, and silver in the mountains. I've been told that it is a few days ride to the great Lakes and the Mississippi River. All this can be part of the Colony of Virginia, if we map it out and keep could records of our findings. It may be a risk personally for all who go because of the unknown but we cannot fear the unknown."

Fontaine, " I would be honored to come along, but meaning no disrespect, I have heard that it is more than a few days ride to the Great Lakes and Mississippi River. It is more like a few months travel to the great French settlements on the River. However, I do not know where the Blue Ridge Mountains are located."

Alexander, smiling at his honesty and curiosity. " You just head west towed the sitting sun and you cannot miss the mountain range. Our party will consist of 10 gentlemen and each will have 5 servants and there will two rangers. All the military men have either military skills are excellent hunting skills. There will be pack horses with supplies and hunting dogs. We will make it a joyous adventure."

Fontaine, "Yes sir you can count on me. Mr. Beverly told me that you had the Germans make a trail to the Rapidan and that is where you want to start."

Alexander, "When I first got to Virginia in order to appease the Iroquois Indian troubles in North Carolina, I told them that they could settle at Germanna to have their own land and be a buffer between us and the hostile Indian tribes that lived beyond the Blue Ridge. The Tuscaroras never really came up and took possession of the land. I did hear about some Germans who wanted to escape persecution in Germany. I told them they could settle this land and help guard the western frontier. A few years ago, nine German families under the direction of Baron Van Degraffenreid built a road from Hobs Hill which some people call Fredericksburg 30 miles west to Germanna and built a fort and five-sided palisaded wall around the fort. The nine families all built houses in a row and have their hogs , cattle and chickens, behind the houses. They have built a meeting house where they go to church two times a day. They are extra ordinary citizens. They are hardworking and God fearing. You will get to meet them in Germanna in August when we begin the trip. We will meet on August 27th at the plantation of Augustine Smith to get our horses shod and rest before the journey. He has a large plantation at the Falls of the Rapidan not far from the starting point of the trip. He is well blessed and wealthy and will provide a welcoming meal. The band of jolly gentlemen of the journey will dine with wine and get to know each other. At Smith's, we will organize our supplies and tents. We will take along tents but only use them if the weather gets cold or we experience rain. We will build a campfire every night at dusk that will continue all night long for our comfort and to discourage the wild animals in the forests from attacking us. The Indians will know we are there anyway so will not try to hide from them. They will not be our enemy unless they attack first. We will treat them as friends when we see them. Our mission is to claim land for the King of England and Parliament. It is not to start an Indian uprising. "

Fontaine admiring the gun and saber display on the Palace wall, " I guess I will see you in August then. I will keep good records of our findings. By the way, I admire your gun collection on the wall. It is impressive with all the guns and sabers displayed in a circle. There are probably more guns mounted there than all the Indian nations have combined."

Alexander laughing. "Let's hope you are right on that issue. It was put there deliberately to symbolize the great military strength of our military might of our militia. However, my friend, the Indians can kill you or scalp you with their knives and hatchets. I always expect the worst and hope for the best."

Fontaine, "It will be a successful journey, and I will document it well." He paused, "For the Colonel of Virginia and For the King of England, I bid you farewell. "

Alexander must have thought this journey might be the defining point and the turning point of his career. This is one initiative I can take that will help expand Virginia in every way. I alone chose to do this. I wish Butler was here so I could share this one moment of happiness with her. I will write her and see what she thinks about this. After bidding farewell to the diarist John Fontaine, he walked back to his desk and began writing a letter.

May 24th, 1716,

My dearest Butler,

I hope you are as happy as can be. I wanted to share with you about my latest plan with the colony. A band of around 65 man will carve a wilderness road to the Blue Ridge Mountains where only a handful of English men have dared to go and claim the territory beyond the mountains for England and King George. This will be a large party with many dangers, but I believe the Almighty one will lay his hand on us and bless this undertaking and journey. Many of the details of the journey have already been worked out in a manner to achieve success.

Butler, I wish you were here to see me lead the men to the mountains and to be there when we return. Each of the 10 gentlemen accompanying the group will be rewarded handsomely and will most likely be sent to England for a victory celebration when they complete the feat.

Please say hello to your family and I wish you the best. I have kept every letter you have written and put them in that old desk that Sarah Churchill gave me. When I think of you, I go to that desk and re-read the letters a hundred times. I wish Roger was here so he could help me in my plans. I miss my dear brother. When the father dies that gave you life, it seems you still have the Heavenly Father to pray to and be with, but when a brother dies it robs your joy. I still think about the good times Roger and I had on the beach at Tangiers and how we made the big journey and climbed Mt. Toubkal, the tallest mountain in western Africa. Yes, I was much more fit then but now that I am 40 , I have learned a few things. My doctor, William Cocke said I was in fair , physical health but could probably handle the rigors of mountain climbing. I am so lonely and unhappy. I feel that the pirates curse put on me when I was a boy is taking its toll. I am looking forward to telling you in person about this historical trip if we make it back alive. The Assembly is making it miserable for me about petty things. King George and Parliament are putting pressure on me. They want to keep the colonists loyal and want more taxes and money from them. I am at wit's end. My political enemies want to embarrass and humiliate me in person, on the streets, and in my own Palace. I am under stress 18 hours a day. The pirates are winning at the seas and confiscating our supplies. The Indians are peaceful for now but are planning a five-nation meeting next spring. I feel that it my workload is getting harder by the day. I have written hundreds of letters to parliament, my business partners, my cousin, to the Assembly, to the governors of the colony trying to get a handle on how to improve the Virginia Colony. I apologize to you for not writing more letters to you, but I do not want you to be burdened down. I would not want to have to involve anyone with my concerns in my position. I long for the day when the pirate's curse is taken from me but have the fear that it may never come to pass. Please pray for me that God's will can come to be known in our lives. I sometimes think that we will someday be together if the Lord wills it. I miss you but I want your happiness more than anything. With fondness and love, Alexander'

He finished the letter and put in on the desk of his secretary, Robert White so Robert could mail it at the printer's shop. Coincidentally, on Robert's desk was a letter addressed to Governor Alexander Spotswood from Butler Brayne. Alexander quickly opened the letter, hoping that everything was in order and it would be good news from Butler. It read as follows:

Dear Alexander,

I know you are completely consumed by the duties, but please correspond with me more frequently. Although we have written back and forth many times , I want to see you in London again. It has been many years since we have been together at Regents Park or at St. Mary at church. I long for those times again, Alexander. I miss the times we went to the plays at the Globe or Lincoln's square and the times you came to our family dinners.
Father and mother are well, and I guess have ceased hoping that one of their four daughters will be happily married in the near future and will live happily ever after. They said that they would be thankful for having 4 old maids for daughters. However, Sister, Dorothy has met you cousin, Mr. Elliott Beninger who is a lot like father, but he likes to travel. In fact, he talks going to Virginia and start a new life. Anne and Dianna are happy just taking care of mother and father and going to church each week. They don't even discuss marriage . Even your sister ,Margaret who is completely over scheduled and over worked by Mrs. Churchill finds time for her gentlemen friend, Mr. Richard Giles. He is quite a catch. Ever since the courts acquitted John Churchill for treason, Parliament is ordering the work finished on John's palace. Sarah and Margaret are completely engrossed in the finishing the big palace ordered by Queen Anne for John's excellent military skills displayed in the Wars of Spanish Succession and for his victories at Blenheim , Ouderne, and Ramilies. Margaret has told me over and over again about the big Palace which will be called Blenheim.
Your cousin , John Spotswood came by father's office the other day and inquired about you also. It seems like I am not the only one missing you.
I hope your job is getting easier with time. Turn over all your concerns over to the Lord. Trust and obey Him. Please continue to write. With Love, Butler

---

I do miss her, Alexander said under his breath. I pray that I can see her again after the journey to the mountain. I hope she will not think less of me when she receives the letter I just sent. Hopefully the Lord will get us through this test of courage and endurance and this journey is for his honor and glory.

Maids patiently waiting for their wedding day

At the end of June, the Rangers brought back a map for Alexander and the band of merry gentlemen to take on the journey. It looked like a journey of a hundred miles due the west and followed closely to a river than began its course in the Blue Ridge Mountains. The River about twenty miles west of Germanna looked like it forked, and the southern fork was a River named James which was named after King James I and Jamestown. The river that forked to the north looked like a smaller river and was at some points more like a creek was the Rapidan River that came by the banks of the Germanna settlement. To the Rangers knowledge, no one had ever taken the southern route to make sure it was the James River that went into Jamestown. The Rangers had no trouble with Indians and had seen only a few who were more curious and peaceful than anything else. They found a place up at the beginning of the river in the mountains near a tall mountain peak that could have a road built around it that would lead up to a big meadow. This trail was hard to see because of thick brush and thickets. Once the party got to the big meadow behind the tall peak, there was another winding trail also hidden by thick brush that led down to a valley below on the other side of the mountain. All they could see at the top of the mountain from the big meadow beyond was a valley with a river the Indians called Shenandoah. Also, they could see another taller mountain range to the extreme west which the Indians called Appalachia. The valley below the Rangers called the Shenandoah valley because of the River by the same name.

Alexander said, "It will be a challenge, but I think we have a pass we can use. I can hardly wait to get started."

Through July and August of 1716, Alexanders was busy with the Assembly informing them of the changes of laws and courts in Parliament. Alexander could relay the messages from the Crown to the Assembly better than any other person in the Colony. Unlike some of his predecessors, King George did not feel the need to use a strong grip on Parliament. He gave the members of Parliament, whether members were Whig or Tories, freedoms that they had not seem before. King George , many surmised would just be happy collecting the tax, receive the Virginia tobacco, and leave much authority to the Colonists to conduct and manage their own affairs. The veteran assembly men like Byrd and Blair wanted to back to the old days when the oligarchy ruled in the Colony of Virginia and the king or queen in charge really did not care about the day to day activities in the Colony so long as no one was complaining, everyone is making money and there were no wars with any pirates, Indians, Spanish or French. Alexander usually received his news from Parliament through the Board of Trades. He would have the stressful task of reading the decrees to the Council, Burgesses, and the other government officials.

Alexander was also busy with the Mayor of Williamsburg on municipal affairs such as improving the streets, keeping it peaceful ,periodically checking on the rebuilding of the Bruton Parish, and refurbishing some of the buildings of William and Mary College.

When the Council was in session, Byrd and Blair joined together in opposition to Alexander. They would have hours and hours of debate on tax reform, appointment of Church bishops, and trying to eliminate the quit rents. Alexander looked forward to the debates, but he would be selective on his battles. This was tiring and at some point, they would all come to an agreement, and then they would all go home emotionally drained. Alexander would always end the session with a prayer, " Please bless the current state of affairs of the Colony and may only the will of the people and the will of God make Virginia a better place to settle and call home. Let not the sins of the flesh such as greed and pride make us stumble and fall. Bind Satan so he will not interfere with our decision making. We ask your prayers to help the leadership in our colony as you commanded in your Holy Word. Please forgive our sins in the name of our Lord and Savior, Jesus Christ. Amen."

Alexander must have been thinking that the Lord had abandoned him . He said, "I never thought it would be this difficult in following the rules of the Board of Trade and keep the gentry class happy." Alexander said under his breath, "Lord, I turn over all my trials and troubles for you to handle. I feel like I am fighting s a losing battle with this Council and Assembly Please don't abandon me, Lord."

Alexander went on home where his servants had prepared a big meal, He said, " I cannot eat all this food. "

Ms. Thornton, "You won't have to, Alexander. Mr. White and I are inviting you to join us in your house for supper. We have to cheer you. How can you inspire the planters of Virginia if you are not inspired yourself? We know you are going on a big journey. There is no doubt in our minds that you will be successful. "

Alexander, tired of arguing earlier in the day, he did not feel like starting another argument in the evening time.

Alexander, "Since you went to a lot of trouble and I need inspiration, will you , Ms. Thornton, and you, Mr. White join me for dinner. I will take you to the new theater after dinner to see the new play. I was told by the mayor that it is the first theater of its kind in all the colonies of Virginia and it has the quality of the plays I use to enjoy in London. "

Ms. Thornton, "Now that is the spirit. Let the plays take all the troubles off your mind. I will tell you a good story if you promise not to tell anyone. I hear that King George has got wind of your taking on the mighty Blue Ridge

Mountains. He said that he was glad a former military man was leading the party. Especially, someone that was born in Africa. He thought you might be more adapted to the wilderness than most and since you fought great odds at Blenheim, you probably could lead the party through Hell and back. He is so excited about claiming the new land west of the mountains, he will probably build a monument or palace for you."

Alexander laughing, "Where do you hear this gossip?"

Mr. White, "He found out through some of the members of the old Royal Navy who served in Tangier. They told King George about the times when Moulay, the Berber leader cut the heads off the English soldiers from the garrison when you stayed there with your parents. You did see how the Berber took the beheaded heads of their tribal enemies and mount them on top of the palisade poles on the wall that surrounded the garrison. It is probably not the most pleasant thing to see. They told him how they feared for your life when you and your brother, Roger, the former Governor of Gibraltar took off to climb the highest mountain in Africa and came back alive so he has confidence that you can do the same thing in another continent. He wants to call the land Spotsylvania. He thought it sounded more impressive than King George Colony."

Ms. Burton, "Robert, Hush, it is not the most pleasant thing to discuss at dinner when you are trying to eat. "

Robert White, "I am sorry, your excellency for reminding you of bad events in your life. I know you can lead the men and get a pass over the mountains."

After dinner, the threesome went to the play, " The Reluctant Father." It was a comedy about a couple who argued over the best way to discipline their naughty children. It was not that funny to Alexander and it reminded him of marriage and Butler and what is the best way to discipline young children.

On the other hand, Ms. Burton and Robert White laughed so hard they drew attention to themselves from the other members of the audience. For a brief moment however, Alexander was not worried about his future or his job as Lt. Governor. He was soon brought back to reality when he saw William Byrd and his wife. The two opposing groups spoke to each other and Mrs. Byrd was cordial. William only smiled and said, "Alexander, Ms. Thornton, Mr. White, this is my beautiful and lovely wife, Lucy Parke Byrd. Did you like the play?" Mrs. Byrd smiled and curtsied."

Alexander, "Hello, Mr. and Mrs. Byrd, Why yes, I really did like the play".

William Byrd, " You know, I respect your style of argument in the Assembly. I believe you to be genuine and do not take things for granted, nor do you take things lightly. You know; however, you have helped me become richer in silver and land ownership, and I think you have done a great job with improving the landscape and architecture around Williamsburg."

Alexander not believing what he was hearing, said, "Thank you, Mr. Byrd."

Wm. Byrd, "If I wasn't so busy with my large estate and about 20 years younger, I would beg you to take me on the journey . I also have to stay at home to take care of my ailing wife. I have to help manage the household. "
He was obviously looking at Ms. Thornton's beauty as he was talking to the group. Mrs. Byrd tried not to be obvious but was trying to muster a disgusted look at Mr. Byrd without the others taking notice.

Ms. Thornton caught on, and said to Mr. Byrd, "I am willing to talk to you this weekend if you want to come over again. I want to discuss how the Council and Assembly can promote the new lands west of the Mountains to Parliament and also get the new citizens acquainted with the colony."

Mr. Byrd , a handsome man in his own right, smiled and said, "I would like that. I would happy to see how I could help promote the larger Virginia Colony."

Mrs. Thornton looked at Mrs. Byrd and said, "You are also invited to come for tea and accompany your husband."

Mrs. Byrd, "I trust him to do his job, but can I trust you only to talk about the journey and the new land?"

Ms. Thornton, "My , my, Ms. Byrd, my intentions are honorable. I have known your husband for several years. If he was interested in anyone but you, I would know it and would tell you."

Mrs. Byrd had a disgusted look on her face, apparently annoyed with Ms. Thornton's coyness and flirtatious nature After the conversation and after the play, the attendees soon parted company and started to leave to return to their respective homes.

On the way home, Alexander, " Said, Well, Ms. Thornton, I guess you handled yourself pretty well with Mrs. Byrd. She is a beautiful and a remarkable lady. "

Mrs. Thornton, "Why you sound jealous of Mr. Byrd. Lucy is a beautiful lady and always had money. Her father was the Governor of the Leeward Islands and had much wealth. The problem is that he was stingy and never gave her much money but the best of everything else. When she married William, he wanted to manage the household and put her on a tight budget. She would go out and buy expensive linens and household furniture from Europe as she was accustomed, and William would make her sell it even at a much lower price. They fight over money all the time. He is only intimate with her as a man and woman should be and I suppose they both love each other in some odd way, but they both could be happier with someone else."

Alexander asking, "How do you know all these things?"

Ms. Thornton answered, "It is my business to know about all your friends and foes."

Alexander, Ms. Thornton, and Mr. White continued walking in the cool night air and soon were at their respective homes.

In a few weeks, William Byrd and Alexander met for coffee at Liddendell's tavern and discussed the journey over the Blue Ridge.

Alexander, "Everything has been approved by King George and Parliament. The Whigs and Tories both agrees that the colony should be expanded for future growth. The more English citizens that are transported to Virginia, the stronger our military and economic presence will be in the New World. This may discourage the French and the Spanish."

Byrd, "The only thing that will discourage the French and the Spanish is a new war, not the acquisition of land."

Alexander," We have also talked to some of the Indian Chiefs west of Germanna, and they appear to be peaceful for the moment. Occasionally we hear of a death of a trapper or a scalping, and we cannot forget they are out there watching every step in our journey. "

Byrd," You will have enough men in your company to repel an attack. If not, send back a messenger and the Council will send the entire militia to drive them all the way to the Mississippi River. "

Alexander," John Robinson will be the acting Governor. Robert Beverly and John Fontaine, an Irishman are going to keep records of the journey. They will also put the plats of land of the surveyors in their notes and letters. We have the best surveyors and gentlemen in the colony in the party. "

Byrd Looking a little melancholy and not so confident as usual, said, "My circumstances have changed. I can come along on the journey if you will have me. I am used to sleeping on the ground to keep my body in shape, and I would love to swim in the rivers you cross. I promise to keep quiet, too. Alexander, you may not have received word or received in the mail since the mail service is unpredictable, but Lucy died last week of smallpox. " William Byrd dropped his head and paused.

Alexander looked as though he had seen a ghost. " No, I have not heard that sad news. I am sorry for your loss. You have my deepest sympathy. It was just a few weeks ago, we saw her at the play. You had mentioned she was ailing." "

William Byrd, " Yes, that's right. She suddenly got sick and weak. The doctor in Richmond said he did not know how she acquired smallpox, but she would not live very long. I now know how King William and Queen Mary felt when Mary found out she had smallpox when the rash developed on her arm. The only real problem I had with Lucy was I wasn't attentive enough to her when she was living, and we argued too much over money. I did not like it when she entered my library because that is my domain. My writings and my books and my library are mine alone. I felt so bad when she died. I really think God was punishing me because I bragged on her beauty and her angelic skills as a mother of our children. My personal life seems so empty. My goals seem so worthless without her. "

Alexander sincerely speaking, " I am so sorry. Is there anything I can do?"

Byrd, "Just let me go on the trip so I can use the beautiful valleys and mountains of Virginia to be my healing therapy while I mourn my loss."

Alexander seeing that he was miserable and in obvious pain said, " Yes, you can go. I am sure it will be a challenge and some risk, but anything worthwhile is worth taking a risk. We will meet at Augustine Smith's place on the Falls of the Piankatank River near the Mattaponi River, not far from Ft. Germanna, on the 27th of August and organize our supplies, shoe the horses, and rest up for the arduous trip."

Byrd, "I will do my part to make it successful. I think I will be good for all of us. I heard that you have experience in mountain climbing in Africa."

Alexander," Undoubtedly, Ms. Thornton told you that. My brother who died a few years ago and was the Governor of Gibraltar and I went to the top of Mt. Toubkal and was a trip of a lifetime. We were young men then. Recently, I had Doctor Cocke check me over and he said I was physically fit for such a new endeavor. Unfortunately, Dr. Cocke is not here to verify this as he will be in England for the next two years. His deputy will be able to collect all the taxes and keep the paperwork caught up for the Secretary of the Colony."

Byrd, "Your physician and my college mate, Dr. Cocke would not lie as he was the most respected student at Cambridge University. As one rich and handsome man to another, why are you putting yourself in danger? Do you think that exploring more land for King George will bring you more fame and fortune? Why don't you marry that pretty Ms. Thornton and live happily ever after? Any fool can see that she worships and adores you. What is driving you to work all the time and not find any pleasure in life. If you get killed out there, Blair and I would not have anyone to fight in the Assembly. Then we would have to fight each other to be Governor. "

Alexander, "I didn't know you all cared for me that much," and he laughed. "I am ready to go, and I think the party is ready. This may be my crowning glory or my laughable folly, but I think we will be well prepared and may make me happy in my ole miserable life."

Byrd seemed to be regaining his usual demeanor again , said, "I am miserable because I just lost my beautiful wife. You are miserable because you do not have large amounts of land to care for. You do not have a pretty wife or children to take care of you when you are really old. All you do is write letters and give speeches. Doesn't that become boring for you?"

Alexander explaining, "Why yes it does. I think that is why this journey is good for me because it will be like the adventure I had when I was eight years old in Africa. I like going into unknown places and climbing the mountains. Once you reach the top, you feel pride and a sense of accomplishment. When I am in the Assembly, I feel as if nothing ever gets settled, and there is something always arising that causes conflict and argument. "

Byrd, " Don't tell me that you are getting to old and tired to fight me and Blair. "

Alexander, "Never too old to fight and win a battle. I just need a change of scenery ever once in a while. "

Byrd," May God Bless you in your journey. I will see that the Assembly gives you everything they need and all the support. Maybe you can get another grant of land of 100,000 acres for me and 100,000 acres for you. Between now and then, try to cheer up and think about Ms. Thornton for your wife."

Alexander wondering if Ms. Thornton had put Mr. Byrd up to recommending her for marriage to him, said," I will cheer up knowing we are well planned for the journey. As far as Ms. Thornton goes, I will not mix work and pleasure. Maybe after I get out of office, I will get married but by that time some young man will have already married Ms. Thornton."

Byrd shaking his head in bewilderment, said, "There is hope for you after all, Colonel. Good day and he finished his coffee and walked back to the Colonial government center. Alexander smiled, as if he had finally gotten some respect and support from the Assembly.

The day of August 27th, 1716 in the year of our Lord and Savior finally came. Alexander, age 40 was fit and handsome riding his black horse into the entrance of Smith's estate, called Shooter's Hill. His aids and servants accompanied him. Augustine Smith had been Speaker of the House of Colonial Virginia in previous years and he was fond of Alexander for the work he had accomplished with William and Mary College. Alexander had allowed the Indian children to go to school there to keep peace with the Indians. Augustine had been an original trustee of the college since its origin about 20 years earlier. Also, Augustine had been a Burgess from Gloucester County. He had also been a surveyor in Essex County. He had grown up at Warner Hall on Mobjack Bay near Yorktown , a coastal village just a few miles east of Williamsburg. Warner Hall had been an old plantation built by Augustine Warner, the first man to get land ownership in Virginia and whom Augustine was named after. He was definitely a member of the gentry class and was also a successful planter.

Augustine Smith had built a three-story brick mansion close to the river with a lead roof. Even though it was very large and stylish, it also seemed to be very cozy and inviting. He had a livery stable at the side of the house with three postillions and a coach-and-six. There was plenty of room there and a blacksmith shop so the horses could be shod. The horseshoes would be checked by the gentlemen on the journey for fit. Augustine had built a large fish tank that took up a large part of the rear courtyard that contained several hundred fish. He told all his guests that I guess you all know what you will have for supper. John Fontaine that had arrived earlier and standing by the tank quickly replied, "Will it be fish?"

There tank was so full of fish that they were have trouble swimming next to each other. Fontaine reached his hand in the tank and it didn't take long for him to pull a bass out of the tank.

Fontaine, "Looks like I am getting my own supper." Some of the gentlemen laughed at Fontaine's humorous antic.

Augustine said, "You can hand me the flapping fish, and I will see that it gets fried and given to one of the servants. We have prepared fish for you, and it will be ready at 6 o'clock tonight. I sometimes feel as someone that was in the crowd that day when Jesus took the fish and bread and fed thousands. We started with a few fish in the tank and there are so many fish now, you could not count them all. "

By suppertime, the gentlemen had all arrived and were admiring the estate. In the Company were James Taylor, Jr. of Hare Forest; Christopher Smith , surveyor of Kent County; Captain William Todd of Toddsberry; Capt. Jeremiah Crowder of St. George Parish; Christopher Robinson of Middlesex; Col. William Robertson of King and Queen County and Clerk of the Virginia Council; Robert Brooke, surveyor of Essex; Robert Beverly, the historian; and Col. George Mason III of Stafford County; and the diarist and soldier, John Fontaine. Fresh corn that had just been harvested in the nearby field was served with the fish.

After supper, Alexander gathered all the men together and voiced a rallying cry for a successful journey. He told men they were the finest gentlemen in Virginia, and he would personally see to it they would be rewarded.

Alexander stated, "You have been chosen by the Council and I because you are some of the finest and most successful men in the Virginia Colony. Your reputations for being successful are well known here and abroad in Parliament in England. The King wishes us the best on this unprecedented journey which will be known as the Spotswood's Journey. He will get a full accounting of what land, rivers, and mountains we explore. I thank you personally that you have made this journey important to yourselves and that you will be rewarded in some way for this expedition. I am proud to be the Lt Governor of this colony and even more proud to be the leader of this distinguished group. We will get to know each other and support one another in this endeavor. You will be able to return to your families and estates in a few weeks. I do not know what dangers wait for us before and beyond the mountains. God willing, we will return safely. The fears we have about the unknown will have to be left at the throne of grace. Only time and history will tell us if the journey is important and significant in the history of this world. I believe it will be a turning point that will be looked at by all Virginians as being necessary and timely. Families are coming over daily from all countries in Europe wanting a new life and wanting something of their own. Some come over to escape from religious persecution such as the nine families that you will see at Germanna at the start of the trip. We will follow a rudimentary map that was given us by a few scouts a couple of weeks ago. We will add to the map and also add new land for Virginia and for England. We will follow the Rapidan River south for a while and when it bends west, we will follow that river due west until we get to its source in the Blue Ridge Mountains. As you know, very few men have ever explored beyond the mountains. In some cases, we will have to make our own trail. At other times we may be able to follow Indian trails or old Buffalo trails. Whatever it takes out of us presently will be made up later for us. I will introduce, John Fontaine, a former Frenchmen who is looking for a home for his family here in Virginia. He will compile a diary and notes. He is also a successful soldier who fought as I did for Queen Anne in the Spanish succession and was based in Ireland. He has traveled extensively and has seen and written much and will take us to the journey's end which is a couple of hundreds of miles away. We will have plenty of food and refreshments along the way. We will have fresh game from rabbits, deer, ducks and geese. We can fish in the rivers and eat nuts, berries, and fruits from the trees along the trail. We will camp each night and build a large campfire. We will have an ample supply of beverages such as ale, ciders, beers, bourbons, wines, coffee and tea. We can toast to King George every night for funding our journey. We can tell stories around the campfire, read the Bible, play music or rest from the day's activities. The history and future of Virginia is in our hands and God's hands, I pray we will all take the responsibility seriously, but we can still laugh and enjoy the moment. God Bless our journey.

Augustine Smith poured glasses of wine for the gentlemen, and they toasted with Col. Spotswood.

Jeremiah Crowder enjoying his drink, "I feel better already. "

Robert Beverly, maybe the only one really knowing the historical importance of the trip, raised up his glass and said, "Here is to history."

Alexander raised his glass of wine for a toast and said, "Here is to King George and his health. We will pray for our safety and his health every night." The men toasted good King George.

After a good night's sleep, on the morning of August 28,[th] the men checked the saddles, bridles, and horseshoes on all the horses and pack horses. The horseshoes were not only good luck but would protect the horses' hooves on the steeper slopes and rockier ground on the upcoming trek. They mounted the horses and got to Germanna area before noon. The traveling party saw the nine little German houses all in a row and the fort that had been recently built. They saw the five-sided palisade wall around the settlement. Since the Germans arrival about two years earlier they had engaged only in farming and gardening. They had been anxious to get back into mining as that is one of the reasons, they had come to Germanna. About 4 miles from the settlement was a mine the nine miners had just started working. They said they were looking for silver but had not came across anything yet. Fontaine observed the iron ore furnace that had been built by the nine German men that lived in Germanna and shook his head. He looked as though he thought the mining adventure would not be successful. As they looked around, the party could see the horseshoe bend in the river and believed it to be a good omen. They soon headed down south of the settlement along the Rapidan river and made camp in Germanna. The men, horses and dogs of the traveling party were tired. The families of the Germanna settlement were hardworking Germans . They were friendly and gave freely of their food to the traveling party. The Germans all introduced themselves and were the first Germans to have their own settlement in Virginia. They introduced themselves as Kemper, Fishback, Holtzclaw, Weaver, Hitt, and several other names.

The Germans had some fresh rabbit stew and corn they had just picked from their garden. It was just enough to feed the 60 or so people in the traveling party and made the travelers feel they were getting a home cooked meal. After supper, while the men were retiring for the evening at their campfire, they could hear the Germans singing church hymns before they went to bed. Even though most of the traveling party found this peaceful, Fontaine had come down with a high fever and a big headache. He tried to take some quinine or Jesuit's bark to help him feel better, and he soon fell asleep also.

On the morning of the ninth of August, Spotswood checked his map one more time and said to the men that they should check their gear one more time . In the process, the men noticed that some of the horseshoes were not put on correctly and it would take time to correct. By the time they ate breakfast and fixed all the horseshoes it was one o'clock in the afternoon. By this time, Fontaine took some more quinine and he was feeling better.

Spotswood rallied the men," This is the first leg of the journey and we will head south and follow the River until it bends and is going due west. The trail is very brushy, and the axe men will have an arduous time cutting the thick brush along the river. It has to be done so that later others can follow the trail to the mountains. Let's go.

The axe men cut the brush and saplings along the river, and the gentry looked for game and spotted a deer which was killed by young Robert Brooke. The servants butchered the deer while the axe men cleared the road ahead. By 5 o'clock they stopped and set up camp by a small river and had traveled only about three miles from Germanna. This river would be named Expedition Run by Alexander in order to name it for the beginning of the expedition they had just began. Alexander was a little discouraged about the few miles they had traveled, but he knew that at times there would be slow traveling. He believed they would make up the time later when they got away from the river forests and would be traveling more in the meadows of the Piedmont Region of Virginia. The servants found downed trees and then cut up enough firewood to keep the campfires burning all night.

After the traveling party got done eating their deer meat, they started a conversation with John Fontaine and asked him why he wanted to settle in Virginia. John Fontaine said that he wanted a land of his own choosing and not forced into anything.

John Fontaine told Alexander and the party the following story, and they all listened intently, "As you know my brother Peter and I were raised in a very devout Christian home of French Huguenots and had to flee to Ireland because of religious persecution. When I got old enough to fight the French, I joined the alliance with England and Flanders to fight the French in the War of the Spanish Succession. I was stationed in Barcelona after the town was turned over to the English and later after my tour of military duty was over, I went to England to begin a business. I read my diary for I kept a journal of every day. I served in the war and several times I almost was left for dead but the Lord always kept me alive and I realize for the first time in my life that it was for this very day and for this very journey. I feel gratitude to be able to keep a diary of this journey and very humbled. I was again grateful and pleased when you said that you prayed that God will bless us on this journey. I believe that we will be blessed and bring honor to Virginia, economic success to England, and make the name of Spotswood Journey an immortal and respectful name in the annals of Colonial Virginia history. Let it bring honor and glory to God.

Gentlemen; Taylor, Brooke, Mason, and Crowder raised their wine glasses and toasted Alexander Spotswood and John Fontaine.

Fontaine continued, " Furthermore, I have personally felt the power of God and witness his saving grace in another way. Almost 2 years ago on Dec 7, 1714 in the name of our Lord and Savior , we set sail for Virginia from Plymouth, England on a ship called *The Dove*. The Captain, John Shapely was an old skipper that had sailed the seven seas and then some. The only thing whiter than the caps on a blue sea was his long white beard. We started sailing off the coast of England and for a few days, things went pretty smooth. The Captain was frail and soon got seasick and could hardly utter directions to his crew. They were all experienced sea men who were not scared of the gates of Hell or anything else. They could scare pirates like witches could cast spells, often and with ease. We were sailing along on Christmas Eve just west of the Azores Islands to lessen our chance of running into a storm, when we got blessed with the hardest and coldest rain you could imagine. And the wind blew and blew. It was a bad, horrendous storm as bad probably as one of the bowl judgments in Revelations will be. The wind was so strong that it almost blew the boat over and the pounding waves hammered the boat, and there were cracking noises on the old boat, and we thought the boat would break apart. We also thought we would be lost, and our whereabouts would be unknown forever. The only one who would know would be the good Lord, and he would be able to find us in Davy Jones locker. Through Christmas Eve night we could not bear to raise sail and the wind was mighty and the rain was torrential. We were still cold and wet from trying to save the sails and rigging from the harsh wind from the day before. We managed to find a dry spot on the boat and celebrated the birth of Jesus Christ and then had our Christmas dinner which consisted of damp biscuits and dried fruits which were both as hard as nails. We praised God for his goodness and asked for our safety. During the day, a miracle happened. One of the sailors spotted two large geese above our boat and managed to shoot them and get them on board and was able to cook them over a fire. We had a delicious and hot meal for Christmas dinner. We feasted and gave praise to God for his blessing. The nourishment to the Captain seemed to bring him to his feet and glory again, and he gave the crew some orders. It continued to rain for several more days, and the wind did not lessen up. We again worried that our sails, though stored under the mizzen, would be damaged or that the bowsprit might get broken. Sure enough, one of the big waves came over the sides of the boat and tore away the bowsprit and came within a foot of the foremast. The people on board screamed and thought they were at the verge of death and thought the ship was about to go down. The loose bowsprit kept banging against the side of the decks. We wondered why God would save us one time and then would destroy us the next time. The only thing however broken on the ship was the bowsprit Two of the best of the sailors decided they had best stop the banging of the bowsprit which might cause more damage by loosening it from its head, so they decided to climb up to the top of the foremast in the driving rain and unforgiving wind. They were holding on to the bowsprit after it was freed by holding on to a rope. In the process, one of the sailors fell from the top of the foremost to the deck of the ship. We feared him to be dead, but he soon started moving about. The other sailor fell into the sea when the bowsprit and sail detached, and we feared that he had drowned. However, he was holding on to a rope that almost had cut off his hand, but he was able to hold on to the rope. We pulled him to safety, and he did not die either. We attended to his hand, and I presume the saltwater from the ocean helped to heal his hand. God had saved the men so they could save us. God preserved us from the raging wind by testing our faith. We who had doubt now had a stronger faith. I now say that we pray. We must pray to the Lord, and we must trust and in Him and Him alone.

Alexander hearing John's request for prayer, said, "Gentlemen, listen round. Mr. Fontaine is to ask the blessing on this journey. Let us pray. "Mr. Fontaine, will you lead us, please?"

John Fontaine praying, "Oh Lord, you have helped all of us in times of great distress and we thank you for this. O strengthen us by your grace. Not only have you saved us from damnation, but we ask for your help to sustain us in this important journey. For this successful outcome, we will give you the honor and the glory. You have kept us all from eminent danger many times so we could gather this day to work together for our king and country. Please take care of these faithful men during the journey and for the rest of their lives. We pray for their families that they will be well provided for while they are away. Let us not forget your continual blessings. Show us how to work together. Help us perform your holy commandments until we die. Forgive us when we fail you. In Jesus name, Amen and Amen."

The group responded, "Amen" The band of 63 men and 74 horses and a few dogs all went to bed as they were physically tired from the day's journey. Alexander looked up at the starry sky and saw Sothis. After hearing the prayer and seeing his old faithful star, he was content and hopeful for a good outcome from the journey.

Alexander Spotswood leading the Knights of The Golden Horseshoes over The Blue Ridge Mountains in 1716, {engraving from 1904) One of the most important journeys In Colonial Virginia's history and one of the many significant accomplishments in the Journey of Alexander Spotswood's life.

The servants took turns sleeping and watching for hostile Indians and wild animals. They also kept the campfire bright and hot all night long.   They would sound the alarm if anything would try to harm their horses or attack the party of men. The hunting dogs that had been brought along to help find game, lay patiently on the grass. They were keeping quiet as if they also needed their rest. The noise of the surrounding forest did not keep them from going to sleep quickly.

Alexander said they would call this campsite, Beverly Camp in honor of Mr. Robert Beverly who was on this journey. We will let him rest now, but at tomorrow's campfire, he will us about the Indians we may encounter, because he has studied them and been around them more than any man in the colony other than John Smith and John Rolfe and his wife, Pocahontas.

The next morning at 7 am, the trumpeter blew some sounds that woke everyone . One of the gentlemen asked him if he was trying to sound like a rooster. Everyone was anxious to start the journey again except Augustine Smith. He had acquired a high fever and was perspiring profusely. Alexander told him that he cared about his health and told him that one of the servants could take him back to Shooters Hill. They all had got out of the bed at sunrise, but it took a few hours to make coffee and fix some cornbread. The also had to put out the campfire, repack the pack horses with the supplies, feed the men and dogs, and let the horses graze on the tall grass in the small fields around the campsite. One of the servants had to check the saddles, bridles, and tightness of the horseshoes each morning. Loose horseshoes had to be fixed right away. Another problem had come upon them during the night. Two of Alexander's horses were missing, and it was not known if they had strayed off or were led away by horse thieves. Alexander ordered two of the servants to locate the horses and bring them back to camp. One of the servants was skilled in following tracks and he determined that they had strayed back to the west towards the river. It took them a few hours to find the missing horses in the thick forest. Alexander went on and told the trail blazers to cut the road ahead and get the pack horses and servants to go ahead and carry the supplies and continue the journey. Alexander told them that he would stay there with the gentlemen until the servants bring back the two horses. It was two o'clock before the servants returned with the stray horses. They all started again on the journey following the trail now cut for them by the earlier party. After three hours they caught up with the first party at a river near a silver mine, so they called the river, Mine Run River. They all crossed the little river with the flowing water was only about knee deep. They all traveled until dusk for about three more miles to a river near a short little mountain. They called the river, Mountain River and the Mountain they named Clark Mountain after one of the coon hounds in the party. It seemed liked the coon hound named Clark was out foxed when he was chasing a rabbit up the mountain and the rabbit disappeared in the brush and got away. The men said that they hoped this was not the normal for the dogs not to catch their prey. The party was dependent on the dogs to help them catch and retrieve game when they were hunting for food. The hunters were able to kill two deer along the trail and the cooks started preparing them as soon as the campfire was built for the evening of the 30th. They would name this camp the Todd camp in honor of William Todd of King and Queen County. He was the quietest and timid of the group of gentlemen. He was clerk of the Court of King and Queen County but wanted to come along on Spotswood Journey to establish a plantation further inland. Fontaine said that the campsite reminded him of William's home which was called Toddsberry which faced the North River on Mobjack Bay near Yorktown. Fontaine had seen Toddsberry on his travels looking for a place to settle. The river they were now on, Mountain run had a large meadow on three sides of the Todd campsite with old oak and walnut trees. The Indians had gone to pick up some of the walnuts to eat as they were ready to be harvested. Toddsberry was a mansion setting on a wooded lot with three sides of large lawns on three sides of the house by the river. On the lawns were majestic old trees with indescribable beauty. There were also gardens with square patches boarded by small boxwood hedges and also many little gardens of flowers. There was an old icehouse in the back with a dairy barn used for milking the cows.

William Todd was a deeply religious man of the Baptist faith and had a daughter, Susan that he talked about frequently. William would say the blessing on the evening meal which consisted of deer meat. After supper, Robert Beverly was telling the party what to expect on the trip if they encountered Indians. Robert tried to calm their fears and that the party would not likely see any Indians because most had either moved farther west of the mountains are simply had become extinct. Beverly said, "The Appamattox Indians, the Wyancoke, the Rappanhannock, and the Port Tobacco Indians are all extinct. The Metomkin, Gingoteague, Occahannock, the Pungoteague, and the Gangocose tribes of Indians have only a few living members, the Meherrins have about 30 warriors, the Nanduye, the Nottaways, the Pamununkey, Chichahominy, and the Nansemond tribes have about 100 families left in their little villages. They have been peaceful. The Iroquois who gave the people in the Carolinas a lot of problems did not settle in the lands given to them at Germanna by the treaties and could cause trouble. They have been upset about the white man's encroachment on them. We have brought along to this party 4 Meherrin Indians from south of Fort Christianna who will interpret for us if we have any Indian problems. They are good about finding trails and foods and surviving in a wilderness. You will see that they are not only tall and slender but strong and fast. They are used to sleeping on the ground and know how to live by the campfire. They have brought along bows and arrows for hunting small game like squirrels, raccoons, deer, minks, otters, and beavers. They are used to taking a six-foot reed or stick no bigger around than your finger to spear the fish and they will fish for herring , perch, shad, and catfish in the creeks. They are used to getting game like pheasants, wild turkeys, doves, partridges, and larks and most small birds. They will eat snakes and small turtles too, but I asked them not to get any of those for us. They will show us where we can get fresh water from springs and brooks, but they prefer drinking only water from ponds that are in the sun when the water is warm. They do not drink any other liquid except a syrup they get from a maple tree or a milk they make from hickory trees they call milk hickory. Please do not give them any liquor, ale, beer, or whiskey or we will have major issues in collecting our fresh food every day."

Mr. Beverly continued, "When we get out of this river basin area more onto the flat lands west of us, we will see big game like deer, moose, and maybe some buffalo or moose. We will probably need to use our rifles to bring the animals down. The Indians have a well proven way of killing large game, but it takes too long and is too dangerous to do on this journey. This tribe of Indian would start a fire with leaves and small brush and build a circle about six miles in diameter of leaves and brush and keep the fire burning in the circle .Any large deer or moose would be trapped in the burning circle. The Indians would eventually be able to track the animals down and kill them with bow and arrow and as the animals would not cross over the fire wall of the circle, they would get enough meet to feed the entire village for a while. They would use the furs and pelts for clothing and bedding. Their houses are huts made out if frames of green saplings that bend to make round huts or oblong houses depending on the size of the family. They then cover the sapling with patches of tree bark tied on with cord of wood type ropes." The gentlemen listened intently and respectfully.

Seeing that the members of the party were listening, Mr. Beverly was encouraged and said, "If we come across an Indian tribe who invites you to a council meeting, we must attend as not to insult the honor of the chief. If he has you sit down on a mat, that is a great honor. He may ask you to smoke a peace pipe which is about 2 feet long. Please smoke it even it is low grade tobacco to honor the chief. If he provides you entertainment such as dancing with wild sounding music, please act like you are pleasantly entertained. He may have you spend the night in a private wigwam. He will provide you with food and water. Please try to eat. He may bring you two virgins to sleep with you. One on one side and one on the other to keep you warm. It is a great dishonor to the chief if you do not sleep with the Indians virgins. The Indian girls are taught to honor their guests and provide them with their every need and to satisfy them in any way. They chief will usually only allow this for men of distinction, and this is there way of pleasing their god. The other Indian girls who are not chosen for this service to the guests are usually jealous of the chosen girls. The chief usually will not allow boys or younger men to stay in such a wigwam. Many an Indian attack has been prevented by the white man showing respect to their customs." After Robert Beverly finished his story, he sat down close to the campfire as it was getting chilly after dusk.

Alexander, "Thank you Mr. Beverly for your words of wisdom. With no disrespect to the Indians customs, but I hope we are not put in that situation with choosing whether we will sleep with the virgins ." Fontaine said that he would rather fight in a war than to have to break God's laws regarding adultery and sexual relations outside of marriage.

Most of the men agreed and said, they agreed with that and did not want any harm to come to their wives or families`

Alexander," Mr. Todd, what are you thinking about? I find the advice about the Indians helpful, but I do not believe they will attack the English without provocation from the French. The Indian tribes of Virginia have always been respectful of the planters and have been good traders with them. The Indians who have been taught English at William and Mary are good examples how we are all God's children, and we should learn to get along. Mr. Todd, it is your turn to tell a story."

William Todd addressing his audience, "I was deep in thought about seeing the silver mine today and Van

Degraffenreid's mine east of Germanna the other day. The miners work in these dark cold mines for years and sometimes get rich if they hit a vein of silver or gold. Who knows what the silver mine is worth? Did you hear about the 12 Spanish galleons that sunk in the Atlantic Ocean near St. Augustine Florida?"

Alexander said, "No, I haven't heard. "

Todd began to tell the following story, "This happened sometime in July of last year. A Spanish Treasure fleet of 12 ships were heading back to Spain. Apparently, the ships had been sent to Veracruz, Mexico with mercury to help the silver miners in getting silver gobs of jewelry from the mines in Mexico and also the ships carried supplies to be traded with the Mexicans. The king of Spain decided he wanted them to bring back the silver and gold that had been minted in Veracruz, Cartagena, and Panama to Spain. The Spanish loaded the 12 ships as about as full of gold and silver as you can haul, and they started for Spain. They started at the beginning of the hurricane season. A hurricane came while the ships were sailing the main stream along the Florida coast that carries ships back to Europe. The ships follow the currents and the currents will eventually head east across the Atlantic north of the Saragossa Sea. On the way to Spain, the ships were caught in the strong winds and were ripped apart and sunk carrying the treasure to the bottom of the ocean along with the wreckage of the ships. Some of the ships were found in shallow water about 30 feet deep. Some of the treasure was not found. The treasure was estimated at 14 million pesos. One of the treasures lost was a gold ornament called a pyx that was worn by high priests of the Catholic Church when they have communion. It was valuable and sacred. The Spanish Crown on hearing of the sinking of the treasure ships ordered salvage boats to come but they only were able to salvage about half of the treasure. When the word got out treasure hunters, curiosity seekers, and pirates came to claim their share of the treasure. There was a Mr. Clapton from England who was able to find 350,000 pesos with very little work and in a short time. He headed for the safety of Jamaica so he could hide away from the pirates. Gold and silver, pieces of eight, and gold cobs started coming ashore on the beaches in Florida, and people were collecting pieces of the treasure which was worth a fortune. Just think, if we had access to all that money, we could buy all the land west of the Blue Ridge or we could build a church in every county in Virginia, and we could live happily ever after. Five or six of the ships have never been found even a year later. I was in deep thought about this and was wondering whether it would still be easy to look for sunken treasure."

Alexander, "Probably not. You might get caught by the Spanish who patrol the waters . You might get just as wealthy by getting a pick and shovel and digging for silver in that silver mine on the Expedition River. "

William Todd, "You are probably right, Colonel, and I do like the story about looking for buried treasure."

Alexander looking happy with the entertaining story, "That it is, and we will toast to all the treasure hunters in the world, whether they be looking for gold, silver, or land. God be with us and King George of England. "

The men all toasted together before the campfire that was keeping them comfortable. Undoubtedly some of them would dream about looking for buried treasure. After the advice from Robert Beverly and the story and tale told by William Todd, the men chatted for a little while amongst themselves. After the story time they went inside their tents to lay on their thin uncomfortable cots and went to sleep.

The next morning of August 31st, the trumpeter sounded the trump and the party of men arose from their cots and started to get ready for their day. The fire was going strong and the coffee and tea were a welcomed delight. John Fontaine was still taking Jesuits root for his headache, and he was drawing a map of the journey and listed the plants and animals that they were seeing along the way. He was a man of prayer and every morning prayed silently for the safety of the party. The sentry kept guard at Alexander's tent so he could sleep peacefully through the night. Alexander was so tired that not even the sounds of the forest at night disturbed his dreaming and sleeping. The Indians took turns keeping guard over the campsite because of their keen sense of smelling and hearing. They could distinguish the smell and sounds of various animals in the woods at night. After breakfast the party started again another day and leg of the journey The men, dogs, and horses traveled about five miles though big oaks, pines, and conifer trees with very little brush or weeds on the forest floor so traveling was a lot easier than previous days. On this part of the expedition, the axe men were not needed as much to clear a path. They crossed a ford in the Rapidan River about five miles into their journey, and Fontaine decided to take Crowder who was a big man and a good hunter with him to hunt for game. They left the party and started for some open fields where they hope to find moose, elk, or deer. They didn't find any of these at first, but they were surprised by running into a black bear, which started to attack them. Crowder shot the bear with his musket right between the eyes avoiding getting killed or mauled to death by the eight-foot-tall bear.

Crowder said, "I will go ahead and skin the bear, while you find some real food. I will stay here and let the bear skin dry in the sun while you hunt"

Fontaine started down a ravine when he saw a deer. He pulled up his musket and shot the deer while standing in his saddle. The horse was spooked by the shot and threw Fontaine off his horse into the ravine, and the horse ran away. Fortunately, Fontaine did not get seriously injured and the fall did not cure or further hurt his headache. He went over to look at the deer. He started after his horse and saw him in a field of strawberry, currants, and gooseberries. He got close to the horse, but the horse was still skittish and ran off again. It was another 30 minutes before Fontaine could get control of his horse. Fontaine followed his tracks back to the berry patches and his tracks back to the deer. He took the rope and found some tree branches and made a makeshift sled to put the deer upon so he could tie the sled to the back of his horse to drag the deer back to camp. He then tried to retrack his steps back to Crowder and the bear and finally came upon Crowder.

Crowder asking curiously when he saw Fontaine pulling a sled, "Did you get lost in the woods?"

Fontaine, "Sort of. My horse threw me when I shot this nice buck, and then the horse ran off, and I finally caught up with him . Throw the bear skin on the deer sled, and we will rejoin our party. It took another two hours for Fontaine and Crowder to find the tracks of the other men on the journey, and they finally caught up with them as they were to cross the river again and get on the south side of the river as the river which had been running north and south was now flowing from the west.

Alexander said to Fontaine, "John , I knew I could count on you for supper and venison it is. Jeremiah, I see you have a nice prize to take home, admiring the beautiful black bear hide. I guess the wolves will have a good supper tonight of bear meat."

Jeremiah Crowder, "I guess they will. What are the Indians doing out there on the river?"

Alexander answering Jeremiah about the fishing techniques of the Meherrin Indians, "They are fishing for our supper. They have taken several logs and have tied them together to build a small raft. In the middle of the raft, they have made themselves a little campfire. The light from the fire cause the fish to come to the raft area and they get in a trance from the fire. The Meherrins then take a spear and catch the fish and collect them and will cook them on the campfire by putting embers and coals on the scales as they do not clean the fish. When they are fried, they pull the scales off the fish. One has to be careful not to eat the bones and entrails, but it is good eating. If we have fish and venison left over, I am sure the dogs will eat it. The Indians also picked some fresh berries and pecan nuts this afternoon."

Jeremiah, "I have never seen or heard anybody fishing like that."

Alexander explaining, "It is an old Indian way of cooking fish."

Fontaine, "Let's give God thanks for the day."

Christopher Robinson, "Hear Ye! Hear Ye! we will now have some punch."

Fontaine, " That must be rum. Isn't that what a pirate would be fond of?"

Robinson laughing, "I think pirates are fond of any drink especially grog."

The band of gentlemen were merry and full of venison, fish, and drink that night. Alexander said, "When you all get up in the morning, I have something special for you to see. Let us toast King George one more time for being a generous King and thank God for being a good God. We will call this Camp Smith for our gentlemen on the journey, Captain Christopher Smith."

Christopher Smith, " I will be honored to have a camp named for me. While we are here at the campfire, I will tell you who I am and what I have been doing. Many of you have asked me if I was kin to Augustine Smith who went home sick yesterday. We probably are related to each other some way, but I do not know. It is true that Augustine Warner Smith is descended from a family at Warner Hall in Mobjack Bay close to Yorktown. He does have a brother Christopher, but he died a few years ago. I am from King William County and recently became a surveyor and Ranger in New Kent County. I am learning the trade. I have felt it necessary to travel to many parts of Virginia and I have been careful in getting to know the planters and the Indians. I was interested in what Mr. Beverly said about the Indians the other evening as I have talked to many Indian tribes in my journeys I had an apprentice who was schooled at William and Mary to be a clergyman and help spread the Anglican religion to the natives. We used to talk around the campfires and had long conversations about surveying, land ownership, and the Indians religious beliefs. I was amazed at what he told me, and he spoke many Indian tongues and near perfect English. He said that the Indians had a certain spiritual belief that they all have heard of and have passed down from generation to generation. It basically says that there was a man they called the Pale Face Prophet that lived about 1600 winters ago that traveled from tribe to tribe. He was a man of peace and carried no weapons. He taught and preached among the tribes and was accepted as a friend. He had white hair and white beard and wore white robes. This prophet could understand over a thousand different Indian languages. He seemed to be able to calm all fears and looked at the Indians with mysterious blue-green eyes. The word traveled from tribe to tribe about the healing powers that the Pale Face Prophet had. There seemed to be no disease or injury that the prophet could not heal. They say this man came to them one day in a small boat from the sea west of a land which the Spanish call Chile or the ends of the earth. That is many miles south of here and is now in Spanish control. He apparently talked to many of the Mapuche and Arconian Indians there. This prophet then traveled north through all this land until they got to this New World and he visited many of the tribes west of the Blue Ridge and East of the Blue Ridge. This man seemed to travel alone and travel quickly. My apprentice stated that he learned at school that the Spanish have verified this by discovering hand drawn Indian paintings in caves and of carved rocks in Indian burial grounds, that show the figure of a long haired man with a long beard teaching and healing the Indians. He further stated that the Indians say that the prophet told the first Indians that there would be white men who would come someday from the sea and live with them, and they all must live in peace. Furthermore, some of the human sacrificing that was in some of the Indians beliefs had to be stopped. The prophet told them when their life stopped, they could have an eternal life if they would believe in him."

Fontaine , a deeply religious man, who had been listening with great interest, said, "This man sounds a lot like Jesus, but the Bible never mentions him being in this part of the world. It would take many years to travel thousands of miles to visit the Indian tribes, and Jesus was crucified when he was about 33 years of age. He did not have white hair or a white beard or at least it is not stated in the Bible. That is a remarkable story!"

Alexander, "We might ask our fiend, Reverend Blair on what he thinks about this Pale Face Prophet and who he might be. Everyone is entitled to their beliefs but there has to be some substance if this story has been passed from one generation to another. When I lived in Tangier, I remember hearing stories of the Egyptians carvings on the worship centers and monuments of the pharaohs which depicted their gods and animals. I guess the Indians could have done the same thing to help them pass the stories down to their children. "

Robert Beverly, "From knowing the Indians around here, they seem to believe in an afterlife, but it has to do with the Earth, Moon, Sky, and Wind. It is an Interesting story. I know that I believe in the Bible and Jesus as being the source of our salvation. We have to be careful in what is in our heart and mind."

All the men agreed with that and they continued telling stories and drinking their nightly punch around the campfire. The men seemed to like each other's company and talked on many subjects such as planting tobacco, mining, pirates, and England were among some of their topics.

The men were soon droopy eyed and sleepy and went to the tents and went to sleep. They must have been thinking what is Alexander Spotswood going to show them in the morning and was the Pale Face Prophet a real person?

The weather was sunny and calm during the day, but it got chilly at night. It was getting daylight when the trumpeter blew the trumpet to awaken the party. He was still having trouble hitting all the notes. Alexander told the men to follow him, and they soon walked up to a hill above the campsite and Alexander said, "Look west, my friends. Isn't that one of the most beautiful views you have ever seen? In front of the men, the view was the peaks of the Blue Ridge Mountains about 100 miles away soaking in the rays of the sunrise from the east. What lay ahead this 1st day of September was the goal of their journey. This majestic view brought smiles to all the observers and was a sense of encouragement to the men. They were now more determined to complete the journey. They knew they had to get their tired bodies moving onward and westward.

Alexander, "We are well on the way. The map I was given by the scouts in May say we should stay close to the river which we shall call the Robinson River in honor of our fellow gentleman Christopher Robinson and for his brother John Robinson who is now the acting governor while I am away from Williamsburg. This river goes up to the base of the mountains, and it will not be an easy task. "

One of the men shouted, "We can do it!"

After eating some dried meats for breakfast and drinking some coffee, the men mounted their horses at around 8 o clock on September 1st and left Smith's camp and headed westerly to where they came to a small creek where the horses were able to drink. When the horses were finished drinking, they all crossed over to the other side as the water was shallow in the river. They decided to call the river Blind Run because it was hard to see in the tall grass along the river. There also were gigantic birches, maples, and oaks that had been there for hundreds of years which were in the flat plains which also hid the creek. Three bears came out of the tall grass and came charging at the men. The bears quickly dropped as the riflemen were skilled marksmen and did not miss their target. Some of the servants stayed behind to skin the bears and add more bear skins to the collection started by Jeremiah Crowder. Undoubtedly there were meat now available for the scavengers. Some of the men said they had eaten bear meat before but rather have some other kind of wild meat. When the men rode their horses though the fields, they were on the lookout for more bears or Indians. Now a little distance from the brush around the river they moved a little more quickly. However, the grass was up to the bellies of the horses and there were bushes and flowers and fields that were attracting bees and hornets. Most of the men got stung by hornets and bees in the field, and the horse got nervous and started moving faster away from the hornets. This diversion passed quickly, and the men soon came up a herd of deer. All the men shot one a piece. It seemed that the game was more plentiful in the fields. The men even soon observed some foxes that were playing in the fields, but the hounds didn't chase them as the men wouldn't turn them loose and kept them harnessed to their horses. The gentlemen were too busy loading the deer on makeshift sleds to carry them to the next campsite.

Alexander said," Let's stop here for about 10 minutes to rest. We have worked hard getting the deer ready for camp tonight. Let's just enjoy the beauty all around us."

The men were glad to hear this because the horses needed to graze a while after their hard morning with the tall grass, and it wouldn't hurt if they rested their weary bones, too.

Alexander said to the men, "I thought I saw some Indians looking through the brush at us, but it looked like they were only women and children. We must increase our watch for warriors and an attack. They are probably just curious, but we cannot assume we will not be attacked."

A loud sounding rifle shot rang out and at first Alexander was startled thinking that they might be getting attacked by some Indians. Col. Mason had killed a snake which appeared to be a copperhead that was moving towards the horses and making them jumpy and snort.

Alexander, "Thank God it was just a snake."

Beverly, "Yes, Colonel Spotswood, but its bite could be as deadly as an Indian arrow through the heart."

Alexander showing gratitude, "Thank God for Col. Mason."

Col William Robertson, "You are blessed, and your nightly prayer must have worked. If we had not stopped, the snake could have spooked the horses and thrown one of the riders."

Alexander, "Yes indeed, Colonel Robertson."

At sundown, the band of explorers and servants once again sent up a camp of the base of a hill, close to another section of the river which Alexander had previously decided to call Blind Run. He said he would name the camp Dr. Robinson's camp as we were close to the source of the river which was also named for him. This had been the best day ever as they traveled 11 miles toward the mountain top.

Christopher Robinson introduced himself to the crowd, " Thank you Col. Spotswood for the honor. As some of you know, I live up on the Rappahannock River in Middlesex County on an estate, I inherited from my uncle John. It is a plantation called "Hewick," and I manage it for him. This was also the name of our home in England and our Hewick in Virginia is most famous for all the political discussion in the study. The gardens are surrounded by a row of weigela bushes with pink flowers . The one reason that they are planted there is because they are deer resistant. I know a little about running a plantation having grown up in one. I have been the sheriff of the county and served in the Colonial Navy and most of you know me as I served as a Burgess from Middlesex. I offer my services to help get us to the mountain top. As the good Colonel has said, my good brother is acting as governor, and I think he is stating his opinions to Reverend Blair and the other members of the Assembly as we speak. My uncle John has only been here a few years in Virginia, but he wanted to see the colony become a success. He loves Hewick but he was called back to London as an ambassador and a bishop in London in the Church of England. I had the great honor of graduating from William and Mary. I am honored and humbled to be one of the Trustees and have the unique circumstance that my step-mother was a widow Beverly and my wife was a widow Beverly and yes I am related to Mr. Robert Beverly by blood and spirit."

John Fontaine, "We will certainly not hold that against you."

The men chuckled as they knew everyone had great respect and admiration for Robert Beverly, Jr.

The men cooked their own deer meat over the campfire that was really getting large, hot, and bright now. It was a full moon and you could see the stars and outline of the mountains to the west.

Christopher Robinson continued, "After supper, I guess you are waiting on a story from me, too, since this is my campsite, If you know me, you know I think that William and Mary College is the best school in the colonies. I would not do anything to discourage teachers and students from coming to this institution but there is so many quirky things that happened there. I have concluded that there are some things that just can't be explained. As you know, the school burned partially down in 1705 and thanks to Gov. Spotswood and Rev. Blair it has become restored, and they had Christopher Wrenn come over from England to help in the restoration. "He is famous for working and designing many prestigious buildings including St. Paul's Cathedral, Chelsea Hospital, and Whitehall Palace. During the fire, there was a student, a pretty Indian girl who had come to study religion and wanted to know why the Indians seem to have different ways of practicing their religion. She disappeared during the fire. One of the teachers tried to find her and searched through the ashes of the fire at the school to see if he could determine her fate. He never found anything but a charred metal cross that had the verse of John 3:16 on it. He took it with him. Years later after Wrenn completed the building, some students would swear on the Bible they saw an Indian princess studying and occasionally looking out of an attic window in Christopher Hall on campus. She appeared as if everything was normal and was oblivious to anyone starring at her. If someone stared too long, she would disappear quickly. One day, some students reported that this same Indian princess was down at Bruton Churchyard walking from grave to grave as if she was searching for a deceased relative or friend. One of the male students started to follow her, and she disappeared in thin air. He went and told his teacher what he had seen or hadn't seen. It was the same teacher that had found the charred cross years earlier. He told the student to go down to the churchyard and he would meet him there in an hour. He went to his house and found the charred cross in a lock box and went on down to the churchyard to meet the student. Show me the last place you saw the Indian Princess. The student went to a spot in the yard where he thought the girl had disappeared. The teacher pulled out the charred cross and immediately it was carried out of his hand mysteriously and the Indian girl appeared before them wearing the cross that was now as gold and shiny as it could be. She smiled and didn't say anything. She began walking towards the river passed an old Indian Village sight, but didn't stop, didn't look back, and kept walking towards the river. The teacher and the student followed at a distance not knowing what they were doing nor why they were following her. When she got to the river, she jumped in without any hesitation or fear. The teacher and student didn't know what to do. They did not see her and feared she had drowned. They watched the water for an hour to see if she would reappear. She never did. The teacher and student said we will keep this quiet and see if she appears again in Christopher Hall or at the churchyard or at the river. No one ever saw her again. The student became a minister, and the teacher on his death bed told the story and that he believed in John 3:16, and he believed he would see the Lord soon. The teacher also stated that he was hoping that he would see the Indian Princess and thank her for sharing the verse with him.

Also, behind Christopher Hall, there was a stream of water in a low place in the yard that was between Christopher Hall and Blair House. Some of the students made a rock bridge that went over the stream, so they did not get their shoes or clothes wet when they crossed over the stream. One student stopped there one day and shouted something to a student up ahead. The sound echoed and echoed and echoed. The student went on by herself and the candles she was studying by in the hall all went out. She was scared of the darkness and prayed that the light would come back. In about ten minutes the light in the candles flickered and the wick lighted itself without any human assistance. This really scared her, so she ran back across the bridge to Blair House. When she got older, she never married and died a spinster. A thought kept coming back to her head.

If you cross the bridge alone, you will always be alone.

If you cross the bridge with a friend, you will always have a friend,

If you cross the bridge with a lover, you will marry and have a home

that will always be happy and never end.

It is said that in a few years that another person couldn't get this thought out of their head;

If you cross the bridge when you are sick, you will never be well,

if you cross the bridge when you are mad, you will always be mad,

If you cross the bridge, without God, you will most likely tell

That bad luck and misery in life is all you had.

John Fontaine, "That is so true, Dr. Robinson, but did you have to tell the story on a night with a full moon?"

The man laughed and agreed that Christopher was a good storyteller at the campfire. They drank some more punch and told some more stories. They again toasted King George, Col. Spotswood, and Christopher Robinson. They soon got tired and went to sleep on beds made out of bear skins and brush and bushes . They were so tired they could have slept well on a cobblestone street.

The trumpeter on the 2nd of September overslept having drunk too much spiked punch. The men had however got up about the same time without all the early morning noise. They were still thinking how many miles they had to go. This was probably going to be one of the hardest days as they were now in the foothills of the taller mountains to the west and they would have to cross many creeks and runs during the day. They were seeing more game and larger wild game and had been fortunate that the Indians were leaving them alone up to this point. The party of explorers had been fortunate that there was a lot of fresh meat given to them daily. They were also seeing large fields with nearby streams and that had good drainage suitable for crops like wheat , corn, beans, maize, and tobacco. This area would me good farmland for settlers coming from England. The gentlemen on the journey equated this living out under the stars every night to being in the army or navy during war time as most of the men had experience in war or had military training. They didn't feel like soldiers but explorers trying to define the maps of a new country ready for growth of people and for business development. They had undoubtedly been on trails that only a few colonists had ever been on. After traveling about 20 miles during the day and crossing creek after creek and riding up and down the foothills, they were ready to camp for the evening. At the very end of the day, a bear came running down a tree near the campsite, but the barking of the hound dogs had scared the bear away and since it was Sunday, they did not shoot any game but used some of the nuts and berries that they had found along the trail. They decided it would be a good night to have a church service, so they retired early. They stopped at a camp at a run called White Oak River. Alexander decided to call this camp Taylor Camp after James Taylor, Jr. of Hare Forest.

Alexander told the gentlemen, "We will all meet at 7 o'clock tonight at the campfire and have a religious service. James Taylor will be our guest speaker."

The nightly campfire was finally built and giving a lot of light and heat, and Col. Taylor asked the men to gather around for a short praise and worship service. Taylor asked John Fontaine if he would give the opening prayer.

.191

John Fontaine nodded, yes.

John prayed, "Father, we thank you for every blessing of life and for life itself. We give thanks for your travel mercies to us. We have not lost any men to death or a terminal sickness. We praise your name, for guiding us these sixty miles towards the mountain top. Sometimes we are closest to you when we are in the valleys as we are here now. Sometimes we are closest to you when we are flat on our back looking up to you needing your forgiveness and mercy. We thank you for all the meals that you have provided for us on this Journey and for our fellowship and companionship of friends. Please allow your will to work in our lives. Be with James Taylor as he talks to us tonight. Forgive us when we fail you. In the name of Jesus, Amen!

James Taylor stood up and began walking to and fro in front of the men. He was well known to most of them as he had recently been a Burgess in King and Queen County. He was also successful in surveying and had received 16000 pounds of payment in tobacco. He grew up in Caroline County and his coat of arms. He was also proud of the family motto; "He conquers that which he seeks."

James Taylor started speaking, "Most of you know me as James Taylor. I am proud to be on this historical and most important journey known as Spotswood Journey. I am a second-generation Virginian as my father came here in 1650 in a ship called the *True Love* from Carlisle, England. I grew up on an estate in Caroline County of 60,000 acres. I have a home called Hare Forest, married a woman whose family was also from Carlisle, named Martha Thompson, and we presently have 7 children, and I am sure there will be more on the way. The Lord has helped me take care of a tract of land that we also own in St. Stephens Parish." The men smiled on that statement. Taylor continued, "I have been blessed to be chosen to come from a large family and also have a large family. We have been well provided for. My ancestors in England helped in establishing the Taylor Merchants Guild of which many fine people have belonged and have been rewarded because of their skilled craftsmanship in the tailoring of clothing. I don't say that to be boastful. We have been blessed. My ancestors worked hard to get what they had. Before the time of the merchant guild in 1555, my Taylor ancestor, Rowland Taylor was a minister in the Church of England under the rule of Queen Mary. She decided that Catholicism would be the religion of England and that all citizens must worship as Catholics. My ancestor, Rowland Taylor refused to do so, and it cost him his life. I am proud to say that he did not die in vain nor did not die without knowing that his family would not forget his sacrifice. His parish was in Hadleigh, England and that is where the bloody Queen had him and others, who believed like him, burned at the stake. I don't say this to bring pity on our family name, but I am proud of what my ancestors believed and how they stood up for their beliefs. The Queen had The Archbishop tell him that he must denounce worshiping in the Anglican Church and his parishioners must worship as Catholics for him to keep his parish. He said he would worship in the only church that believed in Jesus Christ as His Lord and Savior. They Queen ordered his arrest and he was imprisoned. His young son, Thomas saw him being taken to the place of execution. He was put on a stake so that a fire made out of straw and wood would burn him quickly to death on Feb 5, 1555. As he was dying, Rowland Taylor, the Martyr, said for them to forgive the enemies of the one true church to be forgiven. He was struck in the head by Henry Wulf, and his body was burned to death, but his soul was carried to Heaven by the angels. His wife and seven children left behind managed to carry on." The gentlemen listened intently.

James Taylor continued, "We should be able to worship as we please. That is what makes our colony great. I should not be persecuted because I believe a certain way. I know that we will be blessed if we follow the one true God of Abraham, Isaac, and Jacob. The Lord came to die on the cross and forgive our trespasses. I would encourage us to promote Christianity to everyone we meet. It is not this earthly life we have now that we should worry about; rather where we will spend our eternal life after we leave this life's journey. This journey we have taken in the last few days are just a few steps in each one of our earthly journeys. It has been a great time of storytelling, adventure, and making long lasting friendships. We know we are seeking more land for ourselves and for our fellow Virginians. We know that Spotswood Journey is a significant event in English history and the history of this colony. We will be seeing land that has not been seen by too many of our kind. As our colony seeks new land to claim for the King, let us serve God. Respectfully, I ask you to respect my Taylor family motto, which is; "He conquers what he seeks." I believe we will find a land over the mountains that we will claim and conquer for our King. It will the homeland for many English families that can come and live and serve the Lord for generations and generations. Nothing will stop us from claiming this vast domain. Not the French. Not the Spanish. Not the Indians. Not the pirates nor anyone else. Towns and churches will be built. Let us worship the one true God by singing.

The Men said Amen. I would like now to see if the trumpeter could play, Teach me My God, My King by George H. Herbert.

Taylor asked the men reverently, "Let us sing."

Teach me, my God and King,

In all things Thee to see,

And what I do in anything

To do it all for Thee.

A man that looks on glass,

On it may stay his eye;

Or if he pleased, through it pass,

And then the heaven espy.

To scorn the senses' sway,

While still to Thee I tend:

In all I do be Thou the Way,

In all be Thou the End.

All may of Thee partake;

Nothing so small can be

But draws, when acted for Thy sake,

Greatness and worth from Thee.

If done to obey Thy laws,

E'en servile labors shine;

Hallowed is toil, if this the cause,

The meanest work divine.

This is the famous stone

That turneth all to gold;

For that which God doth touch and own

Cannot for less be sold.

The men all sang the hymn in the Virginia Wilderness. These travelers sang in a heartfelt way but never had the song had never been sung so much out of tune. The trumpeter did better than anyone thought he could. The men enjoyed each other's company, and Alexander was pleased with the sermon. He knew that he must attend church at Bruton Parish when he returned to Williamsburg after this journey's completion.

The next morning, the trumpet player showing more confidence, played a faster version of the wakeup call. The men soon finished their coffee, put out the campfire, packed up their mounts, and road their journey weary horses on westward crossing more hills and creeks. It seemed as the trail was getting harder and harder to navigate for the men. They started to go through some brush but soon realized they should have waited for the axe men to cut a wider trail through the thickets. The thorny bushes and briars tore the cargo coverings , their clothes, and even tore up the harnesses on the horses. This was a real test on the horseshoes as it was hard for the horseshoes not to get tangled in the vines and bushes that was densely populated on the trail. Jeremiah Crowder joked and told the other gentlemen that he proposed that James Taylor, the tailor of the merchant's guild would be busy trying to mend his clothes and the other gentlemen's clothes. James Taylor gave a wry smile at Jeremiah's remarks.

They saw that they were at the mouth of a river they thought was the James, but it seemed too far north. One of the surveyors thought this running water must be the beginning of the Robinson River. There had been an old Indian Village near the base of the Blue Ridge Mountain as this must be an excellent place for hunting. A hunter could see buffalo and elk and deer. The men said they wanted to hunt some buffalo, but Alexander suggested they keep eating the fresh deer meat as long as it lasted. If they killed a lot of buffalo, they would not be able to store the meat and most of it would just go to waste. There were old buffalo trails along the side of the mountain, and it looked as if the many previous herds were trying to find passes to go over to the other side of the mountain. This was the same goal as the band of explorers had. They would have to blaze a trail over the mountain if they were to claim new land for King George and England. There were some tall mountain peaks ahead with some trees around the peaks. The men agreed that there must be some trails around these peaks that would get them to the other side of the mountain. At dusk, they again routinely stopped the men and the journey for the evening. The woods were thick along the river, so the axemen cut some firewood quickly, and soon a nice campfire was going again. Alexander decided to call the creek Crowder Creek after Jeremiah Crowder and named the campsite Robertson Camp in honor of Col. William Robertson of Williamsburg, the Clerk of the Council of Virginia, and also in the band of travelers. While the men set up the tents for the night, the four Meherrin Indians set up a trap of fishing nets in the smaller river streams and in a matter of minutes had trapped a hundred fish. Some of the servants quickly built an outdoor stove made out of wood like Indians do to cook their fish whole on a wooden fire pit. The hunters were able to find a flock of wild turkeys so there would be plenty of meat. The cooks that had come along was taking some of the wheat and grinding it against some rocks to make some flat bread. The men would need good meals and lots of rest before they would make the climb up to the mountain top in the next couple of days.

Colonel Robertson was a skilled lawyer and had been in the Council for years. He was also instrumental in helping Alexander improve the buildings and road conditions in Williamsburg. Like Robinson, he was also a trustee of William and Mary College. He was also an experienced vestryman at Bruton Parish. He had come as a favor to Alexander because he liked the way that Alexander had acquired more funding from Queen Anne to add to the size of Bruton Church. He was able to get a belfry and chapel and a fence around the cemetery. Alexander had always said the church must be the best maintained building in the city. Robertson was anxious to make the plea to the rest of the council to get the King to claim land all the way to the Pacific Ocean. He had acquired much land and was anxious to obtain some more. After supper, the men were all setting at the campfire and Col. Robertson said, "I guess you are anxious to hear a story here at the campfire. My story has nothing to do with church, or families, or ghosts, or Indians but one of the most important things of all, and that my gentlemen friends is the weather. Here it is in the beginning of September and we have not had cold weather or cold rain or bad wind. It has been good weather. Mr. Todd talked a little about the hurricane and the loss of the 12 Spanish galleons filled with gold and silver. Mr. Fontaine talked about the bad stormy weather he had when he sailed for Virginia. Weather has been known to alter history and the best made plans of mice and men."

Jeremiah Crowder, "Yes it has been good. I hope it stays good, too! "

Robertson said, "I remember times in the history of the colony and in the recent history of England when that was not always the case. I happen to be in England in London in December of 1703, when an unexpected windstorm hit the southwest coast. It was not a hurricane. It had more force and lasted longer and did more damage than a regular hurricane because I have seen hurricane damage in the Bahamas and Bermuda, and it is devastating. This wind and the rain were so hard that it almost destroyed England and blow it off the map and even blow it off the face of the earth. Alexander, you probably remember this great storm. "

Alexander, "Yes, I believe I was in Flanders preparing for a battle with the pesky French. I did hear of it as my mother wrote me a letter and described the storm and the storm damage. "

William Robertson," Anyway. I was really scared that our inn on the Strand in London was going to collapse or blow away with us in it. The wind was blowing rooves off buildings and chimneys were falling off the rooves. Later I found out that over 2000 homes had either their roof or chimney blown off their house. In fact , Queen Anne was escorted to a secret chamber in the basement of White Hall Palace for her safety. The lead roof had been blown off of Westminster Abbey. Two thousand windmills had been blown over and the blades were spinning so fast that they caused the fans of the wind wheel to catch on fire. Down at the docks and bays in downtown London and south of London Tower Bridge, 700 ships were blown out of the water. They were completely made useless and utterly destroyed after being blown and thrown in one big twisted pile of rubble. Many people were killed in these ships. In some parts of the southwest, the flood waters got so deep it killed thousands of sheep and cattle by drowning deaths. Also, many people in these areas perished also because they could not get out of the way of the storm. It didn't help to have a boat, because the wind would have blown the boats away. Thirty merchant ships loaded with imported goods from all over the world were in the English Channel waiting to get docked into ports in London and Plymouth. The ships and their crews perished in the channel. Altogether, 3000 souls were lost in the channel alone. The port cities were all destroyed, and the wind leveled the brick and timber houses like they were made out of paper. The Eddy Stone lighthouse that guided ships into Plymouth was completely destroyed by the wind and waves and killing the builder, Mr. Stanley and five of his crew. It later was rebuilt, but the toll at the time was high. The British Navy did not fare any better. Twenty battleships and man of wars were utterly destroyed. One of the ships was blown 15 miles inland and turned upside down. All 220 crewmen were killed. The east part of England didn't fare so well either. Four navy ships were destroyed on Goodwin Sands near Deal where Colonel Spotswood used to live. Many of those Navy men that died, Alexander, you might have known. It was a costly storm. I do not think that there was anything like it before, and I hope there is nothing like it ever again. The Navy lost 10,000 sailors because of the storm that day on the 7th of Dec. That was a third of their seamen. This damage and loss would cost a lot to build and replace. You just can't go out and replace 14000 souls." The men looked in awe as Robertson described the damage.

Robertson continued, "I was put in the basement of the inn where I was staying. When I was able to go outside, I saw horrific damage, chimneys missing, factory smokestacks blown away, and many buildings rooves were damaged or missing. It really looked worse down by the docks. I was worried that I would not find a ship that was not damaged that I could take back to Virginia. I finally found one and came on back to Virginia."

Alexander reminiscing, " That was a bad week in England's history. I know my mother said she could not believe the damage."

William Robertson, " Daniel Defoe, a writer said something like, "The Storm, the tempest that destroyed woods and forests all over England. No pen could describe it. Nor thought conceive it unless by one of the extremities of it."

Journalism became more popular and newspapers increased in circulation because of all the reports of storm damage and people searching in the obituary sections of the papers for their lost family members and neighbors who had washed away or died because of the bad storm. The Queen ordered a special day of mourning in January of 1704. A thought that many people had , especially members of the clergy, that the Churches of England and the British Navy were being punished by God Almighty, because of the poor showing of the navy against the predominantly Catholics armies of France and its allies during the first years in the War of Spanish Succession. In fact , the clergy thought that God was punishing England because it was so sinful. The theme of many preacher's sermons for the next several months after the great storm was that sin does not go unpunished.

John Fontaine, "The preachers could also have preached that sin can be forgiven by the blood of Jesus Christ, too."

All the gentlemen said, "Amen!"

William Robertson, "Let's hope that this weather stays tranquil this way for a while. It has been warm and sunny during the day and good sleeping weather at night. "

And all the gentlemen again said in unison, "Amen!"

The gentlemen started to get out the wine, brandy, and rum. They gave the Meherrin Indians some grapefruit juice so they could join the party and not feel left out of the activities. The toast master, Alexander, made sure that everyone had some kind of drink in their hand. With that task finished, Alexander said, " Here is to William Robertson, the finest Clerk of the Assembly in Virginia history."

William Robertson raised his wine glass for a toast and said, " Here is to Alexander Spotswood, a statesman, am explorer, an Army Colonel, and the best Lt. Governor of Virginia at the present time. That was a slip of the tongue. I meant of all times."

Alexander said, "I will drink to that." At that time a brightly scattered meteor shower could be seen in the completely dark frontier sky. "

James Taylor, "Looks like the sky is already greeting us and celebrating our eminent success on the journey."

John Fontaine, " Here is to good food, good friends, and to great mountain climbers and trail-blazers. "

Jeremiah Crowder, "Here! Here! I will drink to that and almost anything else."

Robert Brooke calmly but emphatically, "There is a snake behind you, Jeremiah! By the campfire!"

John Fontaine took the blunderbuss out of his saddle by his bedroll and calmly fired a shot and blew the head off the snake. He walked over to the remains of the snake and said, "It is a rattle snake because of all the beads on its tail. "

George Mason, "It is a rattler all right. They like these rocky ledges and foothills to crawl in."

Alexander, "Mr. Fontaine, your talent never ceases to amaze me. How could you shoot a moving target squarely between the eyes?" "Let us toast, John Fontaine."

All the men said, " Here's to John Fontaine! Drink up!" and they all sipped their drinks.

Robert Beverly, "How are we going to sleep tonight? We are probably in the middle of a nest of rattle snakes."

One of the Meherrin Indians who seemed amused by the comments of the other gentlemen said, "Pardon me for speaking up, but you need much sleep. Do not fear. You might get snake bite, you die. Today is just a good day to die as any."

Robert Brooke, "I am too young to die."

Jeremiah Crowder, "No one knows when they will die. You just have to be ready at all times."

John Fontaine, "I will drink some wine to show my agreement to that. " He raised his wine glass and drank some more red wine.

Alexander spoke as if he had remembered something from his past and said, "We'll be fine when we drink this wine. I will not let you die. Leave the rest to me and fate. "

Robert Beverly, "I've heard that poetry before. I just can't remember where."

Alexander, "It is from some poetical works of Baron and Lord Cutts of the British Navy who served in Tangier and in England. Gentlemen, we better get some sleep as best we can tonight for tomorrow will be another arduous and glorious day. We will have the servants take turns doing watch tonight. Each servant will have a two-hour shift and help keep the campfires going. They will have to warn us of snakes, hostile Indians, panthers, bears, and each other."

The men laughed as they were looking over their shoulders to see if there were any more snakes crawling about.

James Taylor, "That was very well said. Good night, all. We will be climbing up the east side of the mountains

.197

tomorrow. The brush, weeds, and briars will be worse than usual. I don't think any snakes will get inside the tents."

Jeremiah Crowder, "Sounds like good planning to me. "

Alexander rallied his gentlemen, "We will succeed. King George and Parliament are counting on us and knows about each one of you. We are almost there at the end of the journey. History is about to be made. We will conquer these mountains and help settle the land that lies west and beyond the Blue Ridge Mountains. From my personal experience, they are not as treacherous as the ones I have climbed in Africa. Gentlemen, remember these words, "Patior ut Potiar" which when translated from the Latin, means; "I suffer, that I may obtain." I realize that you have suffered some the last few weeks. You don't have your servants waiting on you hand and foot. You have spent valuable time away from your families and plantations , rode though brush, marshes, and weeds and have traveled on rocky and muddy paths. You have waded through muddy creeks and have dealt with insects, drank the flowing waters from unknown creeks, and faced the unknown threat of a wild animal attack or an attack from the Indians. You have slept underneath the stars on hard and cold, damp ground on brush mattresses or bear mats. You also have not had the luxury of knowing what you might eat for your next meal. I again say that we have suffered and sacrificed some. Will it be worth it? Only each of you can answer that in your own way. I believe it will. Some of you will be adding additional land to your large estates. Some of you already possess large tracts of land, exquisite mansions, and have large and loving families. I have none of this. Do not have pity for me for I feel successful even though I suffer so I can obtain. I want you to continue to be successful. This is the time to forget about failing and feeling fear creep in. When you finish the journey tomorrow or the next day, you will become famous in the history of Virginia and the history of England. We have almost obtained our goal. I have enjoyed your company, and this is a very important journey. It defines what we are all about as a colony and as explorers. This is a journey that will affect you for the good for the rest of your lives whether you may think so or not. Patior un Potiar. "

Fontaine, "That deserves a cheer. Hurray for Colonel Spotswood!"

The gentlemen in unison, "Hurray for Colonel Spotswood!" The gentlemen soon retired to their tents. The servants got busy figuring how they would do their watches and keep the camp safe.

The next morning, the faithful sun rose in the east. The faithful and loyal gentlemen rose from a good night's sleep. The trumpeter did not blow the trumpet, but the men were used to rising early anyway. They went about their early morning routine which included packing their supplies and checking the tightness of the saddles, bridles, and most importantly the horseshoes on their horses. This morning, some of the servants reported that some of the men including the trumpeter and become sick during the night and had rashes. Alexander looked at five sick men and saw that they had developed a case of the measles. He knew that these sick men could not continue the journey. He called for the axe men and ordered then to cut down some trees and make some poles out of the trees. He asked them to make a wigwam type structure with the poles and to cover the pole framework with brush, skins, tent material, or any other materials to make a lodge for the sick men. He suggested they use the loblolley pines that were on the ridges as they would be easier to cut and work with than the oaks and hardwoods. He told them to make sure they leave an opening for smoke from the fire that they would need for warmth at night and for cooking during the day. We left them a few servants to look after the sick and some food. The servants would have to get drinking water from the little mountain creeks that were flowing nearby. He told them he would come back and pick them up after the journey was over and when they were on their way back home.

Again, there were some shots fired which broke the silence of the morning. All the men ran out to the horses where they had been tied up to some highlines overnight, so they could get their rest and not wander from the camp. The sixty horses had been tied about 12 feet apart so they would not get hurt or get entangled with other horses. The men had always had the fear from the start of the trail that some warring Indians would try to steal their horses, supplies, and guns. This morning one of the horses had been seem kicking and bucking as it lay on its side as if in excruciating pain. One of the servants showed the men two rattlesnakes he had just shot that had most likely bit the horse and caused its suffering.

Fontaine, "I think the rattlesnakes' bites did poison the horse." He looked at the servant and the servant nodded his head as if in agreement. By this time the servant had reloaded his pistol and musket. Another shot rang out and the horse was put out of its misery. The other horses jittery from the whole ordeal started to break loose from the highline. The ropes held tight and the horses eventually quietened down. The gentlemen started looking around for more snakes as Mr. Beverly had mentioned about camping on a nest of rattlesnakes. After the camp resettled and calmed down, some of the men had eaten some dried fruit and biscuits for breakfast. The smell of coffee permeated the air around the campsite. It took several hours for the axe men to cut the pine trees and build the lodge for their sick companions. When they were finished, the traveling party started heading west again through the foothills of the Blue Ridge Mountains.

By a little after noon they started to see the trail go steeply upward. The axe men who already had a long day were once more called on to cut the brush and clear a path on the eastern side of the mountains. The axe men got enough brush cut that they got about 4 more miles up the trail before dusk. The men looked back and down the trail that they had just came up. They could see much of the countryside that they had left behind during the last few days. It was a refreshing view of the pretty scenery they had just navigated through. They were busy drawing water from a mountain stream, when they saw and killed two more rattlesnakes, a bear, and an elk. The elk they would later prepare for supper, but it would take some time to cook over an open fire. The hound dogs were busy chasing a squirrel that quickly scurried up one of the old oak trees. There were some steep places along the trail where the men had to dismount the horses and lead the horses by the bridle and bit to get the horses further up the mountain. There were some patches of flat meadows along the trail and on the side of the mountains, but the axe men had to cut brush and make a trail so the men could ride the horses through the fields along the way up. They decided to make camp on one of the fields about six miles from the Robertson Camp down below.

Alexander said, "I would call this Rattlesnake Camp but that would be a disservice to Mr. Robert Brooke. We shall call this camp, Brooke Camp. "

They ate supper late as it took time to build the fire and butcher the elk and roast the savory meat on the campfire. The elk meat was enjoyed by the men, and it was a nice change from venison. Some of the men had said they had hoped to find some more deer as they never got tired of deer steaks and cornbread. The men did comment on how dark it was in the woods of the mountains. The moon was not in full moon stage as previous nights and the only light were the innumerable stars above. Th stars were a beautiful sight and Alexander soon spotted his old faithful star, Sothis. As soon as the axe men ate, they went straight to their cots and fell asleep. This day had been one of the longest days of their journey and they needed their rest.

After the meal was over, Alexander asked Robert Brooke, "Mr. Brooke, do you want to tell us about yourself?"

Robert Brooke, "Yes, I would like to. I have listened carefully to all the fascinating stories you gentlemen have shared with us over the last several evenings. I am proud and humbled to be allowed to associate with such outstanding and accomplished gentlemen. I am a surveyor. My father was a surveyor and a famous one. I live in a place called Farm House on the Rappahannock River. I am 16 years of age and have been going on surveying trips with my father since I was 4 years old. My goal is to be the best surveyor in Virginia with no disrespect to Mr. James Taylor of Hare Forest, Mr. Augustine Smith, and Mr. Christopher Robinson. I am willing and able to survey and plot millions of acres of land. I am so thankful I was chosen to come along on the journey. I may be just beginning my profession, but I am learning about leadership, about working together, and knowing that the vast amounts of land to be shared by all. I have no great stories of experience to tell, but I do love my God, my King, and my family. I do remember one story my father told me about these mountains. He said an old Powhatan Indian once told him that these blue mountains have always been under the stars. The Powhatan said that a Great Spirit of the Sky wanted a beautiful place for them to live. God took the stars to help make a sparkle on the nearby river beside the blue mountains . The Indians had lived by a beautiful river that ran through a valley of buffalo, elk, and deer for them to hunt. There was also good soil on the valley floor to raise corn, squash, melons, and many other kinds of fruits and vegetables that the Indian women could prepare for their families. The valley was the most beautiful valley in the land. The Blue Ridge Mountains were in the direction of the rising sun and the Appalachia Mountains covered with oaks, spruces, and pines were in the direction of the sitting sun. The Potomac River being due north and the James River being to the south. Generation and generations of Indians lived in little villages up and down the river for many years in peace. The Indians talked about the beauty of their valley. At one time in their history, an Indian Chief named Shenando led his people and they all wore ornaments and jewelry that was made out of pure gold and pure silver, but he would never tell where the gold and silver had come from. The other Indian tribes that lived in the vicinity of the valley heard about the gold and silver and wanted to have some of it so they could trade for things to make for a better life. One day, this happy life came to an end when some Shawnee Indians on hearing about gold and silver, descended from the northwest in a place called the Great Lakes and came to the peaceful valley to wage war against Shenando and his warriors. The Shawnee wanted the gold and silver and defeated Shenando and destroyed his villages. The families were left scattered and were never seen again. The Shawnees looked up and down the river looking for the source of the gold and silver. They looked in the riverbeds, and they dug holes in the soil, and they looked in the mines and caves of the mountains, but they never found any gold or silver. In fact, they did find some large caverns but many of the Shawnee perished in the caverns during the explorations. During the explorations they found rooms in the caverns that could house 50 to 100 Indian families."

The men seemed to like the story and began drinking more wine, ale, and spiked punch while they listened.

Robert Brooke continued, "The Shawnee lived in the valley for a while until a powerful group of Indians called the Catawbas brought a war party to the valley and drove the Shawnee back to the Great Lakes. The Catawbas settled in the peaceful valley for a while but soon depleted all the game by excessive hunting. They then moved on to bigger and better hunting grounds. They elected not to plant crops in the rich soil or have gardens. In a few years, the buffalo, elk, and deer soon came back to the valley and multiplied again and grew in large numbers. A few small tribes of Indians passing through the valley saw the beauty of the Blue Ridge and was amazed at the soil and the river. They built villages where Shenando had earlier built his villages. They too lived a quiet life like Shenando. These Indians did not pay any attention to the stories about the gold and silver in the valley and said that the mystery surrounding it would never be solved. They believed that the Great Spirit in the Sky had dropped the gold and silver down from the sky to help beautify the land and the earlier Indians saw it and wanted to be beautiful to please God. Later, my father told me before he died 4 years ago that there was an explorer named, John Lederer, that spoke at an Assembly Meeting about 50 years ago when my father was serving as a Justice from Essex County.   Lederer had described this valley and told the Assembly that this valley would make beautiful homes and farms for thousands and thousands of Virginians if they could get to this valley from some kind of pass though these mountains. He further stated that no pass had been found and he did not find a pass yet, but he implored the Assembly to send out a search party to find the pass. Now, we are that party. Furthermore, Mr. Lederer said that even west of the Blue Ridge and Appalachia Mountain ranges was another vast amount of land to the west. Lederer said he saw millions and millions of acres of land from high on a mountain on the west side of the Appalachia Mountains. He told the Assembly that there were as many acres there as there were stars in the universe. He said that the name of Shenando was the only name that was associated with any of the valleys and that is only because of the hope of finding gold and silver. He believed that the name Shenando in Indian language means land between the spruce trees under the stars. The Assembly told Lederer that they would see about exploring the land and would explain all this to King Charles II, but nothing ever came from the discussion and the lands went unexplored. I am excited about seeing first-hand what is beyond the Blue Ridge. I have some of my tools with me, and we can claim the entire millions and millions of acres of land for King George.

Alexander, "That is the kind of enthusiasm we need. Tomorrow, Mr. Brooke, you will get to see what is beyond the Blue Ridge, and we will claim it for King George. We will claim the entire tract of land from the mountain top to the extreme western edge of the tract where it meets the Great Ocean in the direction of the sitting sun. What King George and Parliament does with the land, we will leave it up to them. We will obtain what we seek; the journey's end for now. "

James Taylor, " Consequitor quode unque petit. He accomplishes what he seeks. We are all with you no matter whatever comes our way."

Alexander, " I am proud of every one of you men. We are about our King's business, and I think we learned about each other. We will have one more toast before we retire for the evening. Here is a toast to young Mr. Brooke, who is very learned and wise for his age. "

All the men raised their glasses of wine and said, "Here is to Mr. Brooke!" They then went to their cots and soon fell asleep in their tents and were full of hope for a better day tomorrow.

The next day, the sun rose on schedule. The rays of sun were shining on the green fields and trees below the mountains. The once large looking river below in the east that they had followed from Germanna looked very small from their vantage point on the mountain ridge they had just climbed the day before. It was September 5th, 1716, in the year of our Lord and Savior. It was a life changing day not only for the explorers in Spotswood party but for every Virginian to follow and for every Englishman . Nothing would ever be the same again. Today these explorers and gentlemen would be witnessing land that had only seen by a few Englishmen and only a handful of explorers. The diary that John Fontaine and Robert Beverly were writing would be filled with not only fascinating tales of adventure, but of historical significance that would be shared with the Virginia Council and the Assembly. The diaries would be shared with Parliament, King George, historians, explorers and anyone interested in the land west of the Blue Ridge Mountains. The men on rising seem to have a new spark on life and were very enthusiastic. They seemed to have a new spark in their soul and new energy in their bodies. They arose on schedule even without the trumpet alarm and packed their horses again. They had some grits and coffee and extinguished the campfires. They once again did their morning routine which included checking the horseshoes on their mount and then packed the horses again with supplies and food. This could be a good day for the men as they were close to reaching their goal of claiming the land west of the Blue Ridge for Virginia and the King. They started their climb again in the cool of the morning. The axe men started to clear the brush , shrubs, and trees that was blocking the path on the final leg of their journey. The axe men cut brush for 4 straight hours and then the travelers had come about 4 miles from Camp Brooke. The men kept getting higher and higher from the base of the mountains as they circled around the mountain sides, as they were approaching the top of the summit. There were some Iroquois Indian symbols carved into the bark of some of the trees indicating that Indians had once followed this rudimentary path in the mountains. About one o'clock in the afternoon, the men discovered the beginning of the river down below which was a spring and small stream of water coming out from underneath a boulder. Since this area was part of a big meadow, the horse riders had plenty of room for all to be riding together again. They had been getting use to riding single file on the narrow paths that the axe men had cleared as they were coming up the mountain. The men dismounted and all got a cup from their saddlebag and took a cup of the cold water from the spring. The horses were drinking from the stream of water coming from the spring as it was trickling down to the east side of the mountain to the river that they had followed. They toasted to each other with their cups of water.

Fontaine, "This toast is for Col. Alexander Spotswood who made this all possible."

The men raised their cups and said, "Thank you, Col. Spotswood."

George Mason III, who had been fairly quiet up to this point in the journey said, " Let's say, Alexander the Great, three times!"

They started to chant, "Alexander the Great, Alexander the Great, and Alexander the Great!"

Robert Beverly, "I propose we designate that tall mountain point up ahead as Mt. Alexander."

John Fontaine, "Long live Alexander the Great!" Do all of you know that Alexander is Greek for great warrior and that is what Col. Spotswood is."

Alexander, "Thanks for the great and kind comments but you all are the one who deserves the credit for coming along on this journey. When we get over to that big flat meadow, we will be able to see what is on the other side of the mountain. We will stop again and savor the moment."

At two in the afternoon, the party made the hour-long trip to the meadow which they called Mason's Meadow or Big Meadow. The party stopped a few minutes to rest and Alexander would keep the promise and savor the moment. The climb from down below to where they were now was tiring and exhausting. In front of the men was about a 40-acre meadow with one lonesome white pine tree in the middle of the meadow. Overhead some ravens and some chestnut colored warblers greeted the party. The sky was almost a medium blue and clear and the tall green grass in the meadow was only disturbed by white tail doe and her fawn who was playing in the field. A black bear was running away from the meadow into a thicket in some woods that surrounded the meadow. Water was running across the meadow and going into a waterfall that was falling into one of the mountain lakes on the east side of the meadow and it was so quiet that they could hear the trickling of the water. Alexander sent two of the Indian scouts down to the lake to see if they could gather some mountain brook trout for supper. The mountain had a variety of shrubs mixed in with the bluegrass , spotted with goldenrods, astors, and sunflowers. Along the edge of the meadow there were a variety of trees that lined the meadow. There were mountain pines, mountain maples, hemlocks, and yellow birches mixed together with the spruce trees. Along the meadow a red squirrel was coming down one of the mountain ashes oblivious to any danger. The squirrel did cause the hound dogs to bark but the servants had kept the dogs on tight leashes so they would not get distracted or hurt on the mountain paths. Ever once the men heard an owl that was drowned out by the sounds of the frogs in the mountain lake. As the men started to go out to an overlook of the valley on the west side of the mountain, they heard one of the Indians hollering, "vittadani, vittadani." This was an Indian word that meant deer. The Indians had spotted a deer herd coming out of the thickets toward the Big Meadow as the Indians were catching the trout.

Fontaine, " You know we never get tired of deer meat." The men killed four deer and tied them on a makeshift sled by rope behind the horses as they were going to the top of the mountain. They would celebrate reaching the top and eating deer meat when they made camp later in the day. Right now, they headed for the overlook area and could see the Valley of Shenando below. This valley stretched for miles. It was a beautiful sight. This they could see was only a small part of what lie west of the Blue Ridge. Right now, they were trying to find an easy way to get down the mountain to the west. As Fontaine's horse got to the overlook, his horse spooked, and his rifle fell off the saddle and fell down a steep cliff by the overlook to the bottom below. He may not have secured his musket that well after the deer hunt. Anyway, the majority of the party headed north and west of the overlook and quickly discovered that this path led only to a 500 feet drop from the cliffs below. The party went on to the south side by a smaller ridge of mountains and the axe men soon cleared some trees that led to a path descending the path on the west side of the mountain.

Fontaine, "Even though I will probably never see my musket again, we did find a pass to the other side and west of the land west of the Blue Ridge Mountains. "

All the men got down from their horses and could see that they would descend about three miles to a beautiful sparkling river that must be the river Robert Brook was talking about by the villages of Shenando. It was a clear day, and they could see for hundreds of miles. This is the view they had planned to see for months and had worked hard to get to for the last few weeks. They had reached their goal.

Alexander, I will carve an A on this rock on this mountain and claim this land for King George and all of England." He took some kind of carving tool from his saddlebag and carved the letter A on the big boulder.

Beverly pointing to another mountain, "We will call this mountain, Mount George."

Alexander, "So be it."

The men took turns looking at the scenery from an overlook on the meadow. They could see about 300 buffalo below, about 50 elk, a few moose, and a herd of wild mustangs grazing on the tall green grass. There was a huge winding river that ran parallel to the base of the mountain. There was another mountain range about 100 miles away to the west which they thought must be where the Appalachian Indians had talked about. It was a beautiful sight to watch the animals grazing in peace below and there were no signs of any Indians, French, or Spanish. There were no signs of any hunters, trappers, or explorers anywhere. They savored the moment. They may have underestimated the historical importance of the journey at first, but they now knew they had just uncovered a colonial treasure.

Robert Beverly, "If we did not have the deer to dress, we could eat some big old buffalo meat. Eating the meat will make you a mountain man in a hurry. "

Alexander, "Just as well. The meat would fill us but then what would we do with all the extra meat left over. It might attract some mountain lines or other scavengers. "

George Mason III, "Is it not strange that we have not encountered any Indians? You can tell that these animals are in such great numbers that they have not been hunted to control their quantities."

Alexander, "I don't think there are any Indians around here either. We gave them a chance during the Indian treaties to settle the land west of Fort Germanna to help defend Virginia, if we were attacked from the west by the French who have claimed the Great Lakes. So far, the Indians have not claimed their lands and so far, the French have not attacked. We have been fortunate that they have not come over this mountain to fight us."

Jeremiah Crowder, "Right now it would be hard to get an army over either side of the mountain. And the Indians heard us coming from Germanna because we made so much noise. They probably thought we were a big army and probably ran away."

William Robertson had seen an arrowhead lying on the ground. One of the Meherrin Indians looked at it and said, "It is Injun arrowhead. It looks like Iroquois, but they are not here anymore. This is old. This is from many moons back."

One of the Indians said, "This is also an Indian marking ," as he pointed to a faded carved out arrow pointed to the west on a big boulder. The Indian started southwest on a trail and the axe men followed and they were soon descending down a trail to the base of the mountain on the west side of the Blue Ridge Mountains. There was a mixture of meadows, twists, and turns. The gentlemen kept savoring their moments at the top.

Fontaine, "I guess we had better follow the scouts. We have accomplished a great feat. We have claimed all this land for King George, and we have named one of the tall mountains for him, and we have named the other tall mountain in honor of our leader in Virginia, warrior, and defender. "

Alexander, "Thank you for that honor. It has been a once in a lifetime journey. I certainly will not forget this day. It is not the end of a journey but a beginning of a new era in Virginia history. Do you realize that someday there will be hundreds of thousands of people living in this valley? They will be planting crops and tending gardens. They will be raising hogs, sheep, cattle , horses, and other livestock. What a day! We are blessed! I want to carve another marking on this big boulder and claim all the land as far west as it goes for the King." Again, he pulled a stone cutting chisel out of his saddlebag and make a big A on the rock as they overlooked the big valley below. As soon as he put the chisel away, they all started walking down the mountain path following the Indian and axe men.

It took about two hours to get down the west side of the mountain. It was a lot shorter and not as steep a trail. They entered the fields were grazing and all the noise called the buffalo to stampede and run away. After another two hours, it was dusk

The party made a camp near the river and began to prepare the deer for a late-night supper. Alexander named the River Shenandoah after the Indian chief that had lived here centuries before. The men did what they had done every night for the last several nights. They built a large campfire, fried their deer, and baked some trout the Indians had caught from the mountain lake. They had a new outlook in life. They had just accomplished a task that had never been done before by climbing over the mountain. They again started toasting each other. They would call this camp, Camp Spotswood after their leader.

After supper, Alexander said, " We have not heard from Mr. Mason and Mr. Crowder.

George Mason, "I am George Mason the Third named after my father and grandfather. Our home is Chopawomsic in Stafford County. My father was the first Mason to be born in the Colony of Virginia at Accomeek on the Potomac River. He raised sheep and cattle and had a large estate. He died just a few months ago. Like him, I was a sheriff and once a Burgess from Stafford County. He was a Lieutenant in the Militia and called on several times to repel the warring Indians and their attacks on the Potomac River. My father had a jail built on the Quantico River and I am proud to say I kept it full. I do not want to take away from the celebration tonight for Colonel Spotswood who I do not always agree with in the Assembly. I will say that I congratulate him on his leadership and great accomplishment here today for future generations of Virginians and provided a land that can be settled by countless numbers of English , Scottish, Irish, and Welsh families. I will work hard while I am in the Assembly to get Parliament and King George to recognize this important achievement . I will see to it that the gentlemen here today will receive large land grants for the risks they took here by going on this journey. The map of Virginia is now larger, and our ambition is to settle, survey, and govern this new acquisition, and it has become a new priority. As in the generations of the past, the two main reasons that people come from England to settle is to be able to worship as they please and to become wealthy by owning vast amounts of land. My father was able to obtain land in 4 different counties. There seems to be no limit of land and timber in the expanded colony. If you have heard the news about England lately, these two commodities are in short supply. I salute Col. Spotswood for his leadership and broader vision than most. I feel that the climbing of this mountain behind us was the culmination of all my earthly dreams. I certainly think it has been a great honor to associate myself with this notable band of explorers on this journey. If I have a son, I will name him George the 4th and I hope he will know how important this journey was to me and how much pride he should have for the explorers. Thank you for calling the camp by big meadow, Mason's Camp and the field, Mason's Field. This a great honor and I am humbled by that acknowledgment." He raised his wine glass and said, "Here is to Col. Spotswood."

The gentlemen raised their glasses, "Here is to Col. Spotswood."

George Mason III, "Here is to the Gentlemen of the Journey."

They raised their glasses and said, "Here is to the Gentlemen of the Journey"

Alexander said, "Well said and well done. Thanks, Mr. Mason. Now it is Jeremiah Crowder's turn to speak."

Jeremiah, "I am Jeremiah Crowder from King and Queen County. I am sitting here tonight by the campfire and trying to remember any interesting story from my service in the Militia years ago or some interesting story, but I am speechless for once."

Fontaine chuckling at that remark, said, "Sure we believe that one. "

Jeremiah, "No seriously, no matters what happens to any of us we are all better men for riding with the Colonel. No matter what happens to him, I propose we have a reunion in 20 years. All the men and servants who have made this journey possible will be able to reminisce about the past, and I think we will all have a bright future. Do you agree?"

Beverly nodding yes, "I think it is a great idea to have a reunion planned. I am for it. I propose that we meet at the Palace in 20 years. I understand that it will be finished soon, and I hope that the Colonel will still be the lieutenant governor. The name Spotswood will be in every history book in all the colonies, and he will be well known in England as well. We will meet in Williamsburg at the Palace on September 5th, 1736. That seems like a long way off, but it will be here before you know it. Is that agreeable to the gentlemen of the Journey ? Don't any of you die on me, will you? I will haunt your ghost!"

They were chuckling but all said, "Aye!"

Beverly, "Any opposed?" No one said a word. "Then it is agreed on and we will shake hands on it."

They all huddled together and put their hands together and said, "We agree."

Fontaine, "Now it is Col. Spotswood turn to speak. "

 Alexander said, " This day we have made a great accomplishment for Virginia. I thank you for making this journey successful so far. We still have a way to go in convincing King George that this is also an important day for England. I am thankful that the weather has been fair, and that the Indians have been quiet. I will tell you that I am personally satisfied with this achievement, more so than the one I took with my half-brother years ago in Africa. This journey affects the future generations of people who love Virginia. We will promote the journey and reward your service. Before the journey, I had been reading some books on the Knights and Knighthood in England. You remind me of those knights. I will declare to you gentlemen, that you are now Knights of the Golden Horseshoes. At the start of our journey and each morning thereafter, you faithfully checked the horseshoes on your steeds. This is what a knight would do. He would want to protect his horse or prevent himself from falling if the horseshoes did not fit correctly. As Knights we were protecting our honor by defending ourselves from unknown adversaries. Our prize is more land for England so we will be a stronger empire. A range of mountains was only one challenge, but we conquered it. Four generation of Virginians have come and gone prior to us and were unwilling to challenge this barrier from going westward over the mountains and further west. We have taken away that fear of the unknown. We would potentially be fighting for our country and for our king. I pronounce you all are Knights and I will coronate you later by giving you a pin. This will be a golden horseshoe pin that have real stones and   the words, trancendere de monte which means we have crossed the mountains. The pin will also have a picture of an Irish clover, a picture of the Scottish thistle, and a picture of the English rose. We are a knighthood and a brotherhood that has worked well together, and we have formed a bond between us that will be only understood by us. The pin will be our symbol" The men were smiling and had a proud look on their faces.

Alexander continuing, "I am happy as I have been wanting for a long time to see what is on this side of the Blue Ridge. On our way back home, we will survey some land and mark it for yourselves. I will petition the king and see if he will grant it to you. This will not happen overnight, but I believe it will happen. Alexander took a pen from his pocket and asked John Fontaine for a blank page from his journal and on the piece of paper he wrote "On this 5th day of September 1716, I, Alexander Spotswood, Lt. Governor of the Colony of Virginia claim all the land west of the Blue Ridge for King George of England and this land to be a part of England. He signed it Alexander Spotswood and The Knights of the Golden Horseshoes." He then folded up the paper and stuffed it into one of the wine bottles and put a cork on it and threw the bottle into the newly named Shenandoah River. Alexander was hopeful that the bottle would somehow float back to England. The ancient beautiful river was a symbol of the new life in Virginia. Now many settlers could fulfill all their dreams by settling in the land west of the river.

The men toasted Alexander and applauded.

 Alexander, "Here is a toast to King George and his family, God save the King so he long will reign over us. God, Save the King."

As the men started to walk away and continue their storytelling at the campfire which had become a ritual every night, Alexander stayed behind and asked Beverly and Fontaine if he could talk to them in private. They also stayed behind to see what the colonel had to say.

Alexander, "I hate to tell you this, but I know I should be the happiest one here tonight. I am the saddest one here tonight. My father died when I was four years old. I lived in the fear of getting killed or kidnapped every night because of all the pounding on the garrison walls. As a child, I saw the heads of British soldiers stuck on the barricade's staves after they had been severed from their bodies by a tribal chief named Moulay, He had beheaded thirty thousand of his rival tribesmen. I used to have nightmares for a long time. Our family had to evacuate out of Tangier when I was 8. On the way to England, our shipped was stopped by pirates, and they stole my grandfather's sword. I had a miserable sea voyage to England. Shortly after we arrived in England my stepfather and my aunt died. I had to teach myself a business which has done pretty well over the years. I stayed and took care of my sick mother who had excruciating pain and died a painful death. I enlisted in the Army and was almost killed at Blenheim. A cannonball hit my left shoulder and breastbone, and I lay in a hospital bed for almost six months at Chelsea. The Queen and Lord Hamilton called me to come to Virginia to be a lieutenant governor, instead of being a governor so I don't get but part of the pay I should get. I had a bad voyage to Virginia. The Captain got black vomit and died and only the grace of God saved us. I have argued bitterly and constantly with the leaders of the Council and Assembly ever since I started. I gave some money to fund some German families to come to Virginia and settle Germanna, but I think they misunderstand my intentions and want to leave the settlement. I own no land. I own no house. I have no family here in Virginia. I am a lonely man. You all have mentioned your families, your parents, your children, your wives, and your fortunes. I have none of this and I am lonely. I do not begrudge you of these nice things. I am happy for you, and I am glad you have had great opportunities given to you and some of the things you have worked for. I have written hundreds of letters to the Assembly and Parliament to try to make it a better colony for the citizens. I have worked tirelessly for the citizens, and I am not sure they even know this. I have only the completion of this journey as a sizable contribution to my administration. When you all get home, you will have someone waiting there wanting to hear about your adventures and share this journey I still have a good and honorable name, but when I get home, it will be dreary and lonely and I will not have anyone to share the tales of this great adventure with. I do not want pity for this is the life that has been dealt to me and this is the life that I lead. All this leads up to a point. I have to get over this thought that a curse has been put on my life. I deal with this struggle every day of my life between happiness and unhappiness. I do believe that the good Lord has a plan for each of us and each day we need to ask him if we are in his will. I truly believe that one day I will be truly happy in life."

Fontaine," But you are an accomplished leader and men follow your lead. People respect you. You do have the choice to be happy or unhappy. Enjoy this moment and celebrate with your men. I am only 23 years of age and don't know too much about anything, but I think you are too hard on yourself."

Robert Beverly," Sometimes friends are not enough. Maybe you need to start your own family. If you don't mind me saying so, but Ms. Thornton is a beautiful lady and she adores you."

Alexander, "Yes she is a beautiful and talented lady, but I don't love her. I have a friend in England, but I can't seem to ask for her hand in marriage. I feel like I could not make her happy in the colony because she is accustomed to a big city's amenities, and this is still a pretty hostile and rudimentary place."

Robert Beverly, " This is something you should be talking to her about. Let her tell you what would make her happy. You might get the surprise of your life."

Fontaine, "It sounds to me that you are in love with her. Now you need to find out for certain. You need to know how she feels about you. A family is truly a gift from and a blessing from God. You will be better off in a family. Will you promise me that you will ask her how she feels. You will be miserable until you know otherwise. You are guessing and holding on to something that you may need to free yourself of so you can be happy with someone else. Otherwise you are guessing. It is hard to love someone if they are in love with someone else."

Beverly encouraging Alexander, "Good advice, nothing like a good wife to make a man feel needed and loved. Let's get with the others and celebrate the journey."

Fontaine, "Hear ye. Hear ye!! Have a toast to the end of the journey and a new era for Virginia."

The men raised their glasses and said, "Here is to a new Virginia!"

Fontaine, "Here is to Mt. Alexander and Mt. George ." The men took turns in firing their muskets to celebrate the crossing of the mountains. And the men raised their glasses of drink.

Beverly, "This toast is for Shenandoah and the Blue Ridge Mountains." More musket shots were fired into the air.

Fontaine, "You know that I like the sound of the Knights of the Golden Horseshoes. In France, we called the Knights by the name of Chevaliers and in Spain we called them Caballeros. The horseshoes have always been lucky and that is what we are with Col. Spotswood. Let's toast to The Knights of the Golden Horseshoes. "

The men raised their glasses again and the toasting went on for hours. All the men made sure that ever king and queen that ever had ruled in England received a toast in their honor.

Fontaine, "Let's toast King George and his family and to his health and continued success. Don't forget his son George, who will be most likely named King George II. "

The men all toasted.

Alexander, "Before I say good night, I would like for us to toast our Lord and Savior who makes all things possible."

The men took off their hat and said, "Amen. Thanks to the Lord!"

The men soon went to their cots to sleep and were thankful they could see new lands that only a few men, except for the Indians, had ever seen this part of the frontier. The men slept deeply and peacefully that night. It had been a big adventure. This exuberant feeling they had about seeing new lands might have been similar to the feeling that Christopher Columbus had when he discovered the San Salvador Island and The New World. Columbus may have felt that he did not know where he had just come from nor know exactly where he was headed again. The Knights knew that the world would never be the same after such a notable achievement The next morning the men woke up with great expectations and were ready to mark off their share of the land and retrace their steps back to Germanna and eventually back to their respective homes or Williamsburg. The men noticed that Alexander must have gotten up early and was fishing from the riverbanks of the Shenandoah. He looked like he was in deep thought. He also had captured some grasshoppers that he was using to catch some of the trout or chubb fish from the river. Most of the men took a swim in the Shenandoah River even though it was almost fall, the water and morning sun was still warm enough. Some of the men shot some wild turkeys which the servants soon dressed and cooked on the fire. The men delighted in their breakfast. Jeremiah had spotted the rifle that Fontaine had dropped off the cliff from the mountain above. Although the rifle had fallen 4000 feet to the valley floor, it still worked just fine. Jeremiah used it before he gave it back to Fontaine to kill a 5-foot-long black snake that was crawling through some angelica grass that was at the edge of the campsite. The snake had been making its way through some rhododendrons that were in abundant supply all through the valley. After breakfast, the Knights of the Golden Horseshoes, the war horses, the servants, and the barking dogs started their journey back home. It took a couple of weeks to stop and mark the lands they wanted to claim. Alexander kept his word and picked up the sick men at the makeshift lodge at Hospital Camp. They had become strong enough to ride home but were feeling very weak. After a while they arrived back to Germanna and the German miners greeted the party and were told tall tales from the Journey. After some good German food, the men shook hands with each other and said farewell to each other. They were now on their way back to their plantations. They would all meet together in twenty years. However, some of the men would see each other at their plantations or sometimes see each other in Williamsburg. They had formed a bond of friendship that would never be broken.

Alexander got back to his office on 29th of September in Williamsburg and immediately sent a letter to Parliament along with a copy of Beverly's and Fontaine's record of the map and journey. It described the vast amount of land that the Knights had discovered and claimed west of the Blue Ridge Mountain for the Colony of Virginia.

Alexander stated in the letter that the English could expect resistance from the French in the Great Lakes Region and Spanish opposition along the lands west of the Mississippi River. He stated that he had not encountered any large Indian populations, and the Indians seemed to be quiet for now. In his letter, he also explained he wanted the men on the journey to be knighted by the king as Knights of the Golden Horseshoes. He also sent a petition for the following land grants. He had decided the following acreage to be divided amongst the men.

Alexander Spotswood 80,000 acres

William Byrd 20,000 acres

Augustine Smith 20,000 acres

Christopher Smith 20,000 acres

William Todd 20,000 acres

Jeremiah Crowder 10,000 acres

Christopher Robinson 10,000 acres

John Robinson 10,000 acres

William Robertson 12,000 acres

Robert Brooke 200,000 acres

George Mason 20,000 acres

Robert Beverly 20,000 acres

John Fontaine 20,000 acres.

How the amount of land petitioned for each man was determined was based on what they were able to mark off and claim for themselves. Alexander must have hoped the king would be agreeable to all the requests. He knew that he was excited about such a successful journey. They had not lost any men to death and only one horse died on the entire trip. He had a good feeling about the completion of the journey, but he remembered that he said to Beverly and Fontaine; that when he got home, there would be no one to share the joy of success with. He wanted so much to tell Butler about the successful journey. Would she even care about it? Alexander remembered the advice of Beverly and Fontaine which was to see how Butler felt about him and would she come to Virginia? After a lot of deliberation, Alexander wrote the following letter.

My dearest Butler,

I think you have known for the longest time that I love and adore you. I can't think about anything else but you. I want to ask your father for your hand in marriage, but I must know if you feel the same way. Whatever you think or believe, I will honor and agree with you. We can live quiet comfortably here in Virginia which is growing in popularity and is not as primitive as it used to be. When my official duties end, we could move back to England if that is your desire.

A group of the finest gentlemen in the Colony and I recently made an adventuresome journey to the Blue Ridge Mountains . Our mission was the finding what is on the west side of the mountain range by finding a pass over the mountains. We were very successful and claimed millions of acres of land for King George. It was quite an adventure and a notable contribution to my administration. I hope you heard about it in England. I have petitioned the King for land in Virginia, but it may take a few years to get the petition approved. Once we get the land approved, I will be able to put a very large house on the land.

Whatever you are thinking, feeling, and planning, please let me know.

With love and affection, Alexander Spotswood   Aug 30th, 1716.

Alexander was so excited that he gave the postman the letter directly to be mailed. The postman held on the important letter on the hand. Because he had so many boxes in his hand, the letter did not go into his mail bag as intended and fell underneath a desk unbeknownst to Alexander and the postman. Under the desk, the letter would get hidden and remain there for years. Alexander was so excited about mailing the letter and hoped he would get a prompt response from Butler. Little did he know that he would wait and wait, and the letter never even got mailed and was misplaced.

Alexander did get a letter from Butler in a few months, but it was not a reply to his lost letter. He might have thought it was, due to the timing of the arrival of the letter. It took a few months to get a reply in a letter from England. The letter Butler wrote was as follows

---

Dearest Alexander,

It has been so long since I have heard from you. There is a lot of talk here in London, about you're claiming the entire country west of Virginia for King George. You have many friends and supporters that are wanting to meet you. When are you returning to London? Has all this new popularity made you so busy that you do not have time to come visit me in London?

Father and mother are doing well. They want to hear more about your trip. If you can't come visit me or write frequently , then please write to them. My father has done a lot for your business here and I think you should at least thank him for his service. I hope he can stay well.

Please write again when you are finished with your adventure. Butler

---

After reading the letter above, Alexander tried to think through what she was trying to say, and he felt she did not love him and actually repulsed by some of his actions. He could not leave for London right now as he was leading the largest colony in the New World. He thought she might be patient for a while longer, but he did not want to promise her he was coming for a visit and then something come up that would make it impossible to go to London. This might upset her even more. He knew that down in his heart, he loved Butler, but now he wasn't sure if she loved him in return. He knew he must take Fontaine's advice. And look like he was happy whether he was or not.

Later that year , Alexander received a letter from the postman's old black bag. The postman gave him a letter with an address of Mrs. Richard Giles of London. He tried to recollect who Mrs. Richard Giles was. He quickly opened the letter which read as follows.

Dear Alexander,

I married Richard Giles who is an Anglican minister here in the village of Westminster. We are very happy and plan to have a family someday. I am still working for Sarah Churchill. Her house is so large at Blenheim Palace that we have plenty to do.

I recently read in the magazines that you have trekked over another mountain and your name is well known here in London. I am proud of you for your great accomplishment. It is reported that King George is well pleased with your journey, and he will send some gold horseshoe pins to your Knights of the Golden Horseshoes. The people of England are needing the hope and promised land in the extended colony that your merry band of gentlemen are bringing to pass. King George is ordering Parliament to plan and fund the projects to expand the Colony of Virginia with new roads, schools, churches, new courthouses, new surveys, and new counties. We are proud of your achievements. Virginia seems like such a growing and exciting place and many people are finding success there. I trust you are happy and successful, too. I know that we will not be able to come there and visit for a while. We are building a new house on one of the big lots in Golden Square by St. James Park. It is the same style as King George with ornate carvings. It has dormers and columns in the front and this style is called the Georgian style after King George. I know you will approve of it and be happy for us. Please come and see us. I promise to write you again soon. I just had to get this to you quickly as you never can predict the mail service. I am ending by saying, "Sic jurat transcendere montes" which means he swears to cross the mountains. With love and affectionately, Margaret Giles, St. John Street, Westminster, England.

Alexander was happy for his sister. If he could , indeed, visit London , he might be able to solve many of his personal struggles. There had been no mention of Butler in the letter. He put the letter she wrote in his desk and would head on down to the Assembly Room and would get involved in his work and try not to think about his unhappiness.

In late October 1716, after resting from the journey with the Knights, Knight William Robertson, Clerk of The Assembly, ordered that Alexander be given 3200 acres in the Germanna settlement. Alexander's iron ore business had improved; thanks to the diligent work of the 9 families in the Germanna settlement.

It was a surprise to Alexander as this was his first land patent and now, he was a landowner and potential aristocratic planter. Alexander thought that his friend, Robert Beverly persuaded Robertson to initiate the land patent in the first place. Alexander would get busy with his business acumen and sell some timber off his property to finance the purchase of a mine called Tubal Works near Hob Hill and Leedstown. He would also use some of the money to buy the Massaponnax Plantation and an ironworks factory near the growing city of Richmond in the Colony of Virginia. Alexander again succeeded in his business dealings and would become even more wealthy. Everything he touched seemed to turn to gold.

The Assembly suggested that Alexander live in the Palace, the future home of the Governor even though it was still under construction. It was a brick building 3 stories high with 2900 square feet of living space on each floor. The outside of the building had a large balcony with ornate iron rails around the balcony. It had a dormer and a double door on each side of the building. There was a courtyard on the North side of the Palace which was part of a large park. There was a kitchen, bath house, carriage house, stable, and a laundry room, and a small guest house. This house was one of the largest and most updated governor's palaces in the New World. Inside the Palace, twenty-five servants cared for the governor. There were cooks, groomers, butlers, maids, footmen, gardeners, tailors, and laborers. The buildings had many fireplaces and two large wine cellars. It kept the staff busy keeping the governor and his guests comfortable and well taken care of.

One night chose one of the red cushioned chairs to set in and it was comfortable. He began daydreaming about his new home, the Palace. It was a lot better than the small office he rented across the street to live in and work in. He said to Ms. Thornton, " I know I should be the happiest man in the colony, but I am not sharing my life with anyone but the servants. I will have to entertain here in the grand ball room and start a social life for the gentry class." This may have not been the best person to confide in, because it may be perceived that he was hinting for her to say she would share the palace and her life with him. However, she nodded her head in agreement and never revealed any of her innermost thoughts to him. Alexander went on to have many social events at the Palace. All the single ladies no matter how fine, how rich, nor how pretty could get the handsome governor's attention. After a while he had fewer and fewer balls and he spent less time at each event.

Even with money always jingling in his pocket, it was hard for Alexander to be happy. He was living a lonely life in a big half-filled palace of expensive furniture. To add more fuel to the fire, this furniture seemed to be a source of contention between his political enemy, William Byrd and himself. Byrd thought that Alexander had too expensive taste to be an employee of the government and all the added expense was slowly draining the struggling budget of the colony. It seemed that Byrd thought the entire expense of the house including construction and decorating was out of control and unreasonable. They verbally fought over the expenses, the policy of the tobacco tax, and the other legal issues in the colony. Sometimes there would be bitter debates because they both were stubborn and hard driven men. The one advantage Byrd had was that he came from a large supportive family and this seem to give him peace and purpose. Alexander would go back to the Palace after a long day at work and was worn out completely from the constant bickering in the Assembly.

A new problem was on the horizon. The Iroquois Indians who had lived in peace for many years started an uprising. They destroyed the Sapponi Indian tribe that had been placed at Ft. Christianna on the southern side of Virginia by Alexander. The Sapponis had been placed there by Alexander on the south-central side of the colony to repel the attacks of the Iroquois, hostile Catawba Indians, and other warring tribes. Alexander called on Knight Christopher Robinson of the Knights of the Golden Horseshoes to Albany in the Colony of New York to negotiate a treaty with all five Iroquois nations.

Alexander knew that peace with the Indians at the southern and western boundaries of Virginia was important to the growth and expansion of the Colony. The Indians and Alexander Spotswood came to an acceptable agreement for both sides. The Indians said they would stay peaceful in an area between New York and Northern Virginia if Alexander would give them $5000 worth of money and goods. Alexander made sure they got the money and the Indians remained peaceful and kept their promise.

As Alexander was solving one problem, a new one would emerge. Parliament in England sent Alexander sent a letter to Alexander imploring him to let another 20 German Families settle at Germanna. Alexander knew that the first 9 families that had settled in Germanna had become unhappy and felt exploited in the mining of the iron ore in the mines.

He knew that the first wave could leave the settlement and would cause the new families to be reluctant about coming to the Colony. Alexander ,in order to be in favor with the king, said he would pay for each member of the twenty families way to come to Germanna, but they would have to be indentured servants for 7 years and work in the mines. In order for the Germans to gain trust with the families, he wrote each family a personal letter telling them what a great idea it was to come to the Colonies. They all responded favorably and settled in

Germanna. They did very well and made more money for Alexander. These families did complain about their living and working conditions. Alexander must have thought, "Why does everyone see themselves as right and say that I am always wrong?"

The year 1718 came and still more troubles for Alexander. The pirates who had been wreaking havoc off the Carolinas, Florida, and Virginia coast and unchallenged for some time were getting out of control. The British Royal Navy had been slowing their menacing thievery down somewhat, but the pirates were getting bold and stopping large ships and scaring passengers and crew members to death. One of the leaders were named Blackbeard, the one and the same, that Alexander had sailed with when he was coming to Virginia from England to Martinique. Of course, Alexander did not know who he was, until Blackbeard had sailed away. Blackbeard was now described as a mean looking man with a black braided beard that had jewelry, bones, and ribbon tied on to the beard. He carried three braces of pistols on him. For sport, he would take swords and jab it at his men in the darkness of their rooms or fire pistols into dark ship's cabins to scare his crew halfway out of their wits. He also made the claim that he had 14 wives at different ports up and down the Atlantic Ocean and the Caribbean Sea. He was also now making another claim that he was building some garrison for pirates and building fortifications on Theocracy Island and was starting his own navy. He said his navy would be so strong that they could defend any other navy in the world. He said he was collecting guns and cannons and would have as many weapons as any other fort in the world. Alexander Spotswood said that he thought Blackbeard was a little boastful and just trying to bluff his enemies. Many of the British sailors said that he had not been too busy in the last few years with acts of piracy and his mouth was more braggart than anything else. However, he could scare people by his braided beard, and he could shoot fireworks from underneath his cap. This undoubtedly was some kind of trick by using fireworks to scare innocent people. After all was said and done, he was the fiercest and meanest pirate and best-known pirates of the British Empire and the Colonies of America. A few months earlier he had blocked the ports of Charleston, Carolina and held many of the local citizens as hostages for ransom and took all their money and expensive medicines in the port city. The Governor of the Carolina did not send a militia to stop the blockade, and Blackbeard left of his own accord as he did not want to be on land for too long of period as he might get captured. The governor could not muster enough men to get to Charleston and stop the pirate interference. Some of the wealthy planters in Virginia and the Carolinas wanted Blackbeard to be taken off the seas and wanted protection against acts of piracy for stealing their supplies and commodities. After seeing the petition with the most powerful men's names in the colonies on the petition, Alexander knew he would take action against Blackbeard. Alexander went to the Assembly and at the call of new business.

 Alexander said before the Assembly, "I want approval to capture or kill Blackbeard before he takes over complete control of the seas." He pulled out the petition and Alexander said, "I have a petition signed by some of you here this morning and names of planters in Virginia and the Carolinas that they want Blackbeard and his crew taken off the seas and captured. The Royal Governor of North Carolina refuses to send troops for only reasons known to him, but I will not refuse this petition's request."

Some of the men cheered. William Byrd, who had been carefully watching everyone's reaction stood up and told the Assembly, "Col. Spotswood, you are wrong on most issues that are discussed here, but this time you are doing the right thing. I have too many commodities going and coming from England to be annoyed with this pirate's nonsense. I do not want to pay ransom from my large bank account to this nuisance. I think you should send a request for the navy to attack Blackbeard, but it will take months to get approval from the Admiralty's Office in London. "

Alexander firmly slapped his fist on the podium in the Assembly room, "We cannot wait. We have the preeminent right to defend ourselves and our people."

Byrd, "Yes, you do, but I hope you are not misjudged for overstepping your bounds and taking matters into your own hands without any backing from England."

Alexander, "I will send a letter to Captain Dandridge of the Royal navy to send some man of wars to the Okracoke Island and explain to him that we want to stop Blackbeard from setting up blockades and prevent him from building up his navy and building garrisons and hurting the colonies."

In a few weeks, Alexander received a letter from Col. Dandridge that he was sending one of his fiercest fighting units to Okracoke Island to defeat Blackbeard and his mates. They would try to capture him, or they might kill him in the heat of battle. In a few weeks the navy ship made it to the Okracoke Area in the Atlantic just off the coast of the Carolinas. The navy ship encountered "The Adventurer," one of the pirate ships that belonged to the menacing Blackbeard. Blackbeard's favorite ship, "The Queen Ann's Revenge," a converted French frigate, had recently sank in the waters off Topsail Inlet. This would be to the Navy's advantage because "The Adventurer" was only loaded with a few three-pound cannons, whereas "The Queen Ann's Revenge had 26 six-pound cannons but the cannons were now laying on the bottom of Ocean floor near Bath and were utterly useless to Blackbeard. The pirates on seeing the unexpected navy man of war, started firing at the Navy as soon as the navy got close enough. A battle of gunfire then started. Captain Robert Maynard of the Royal Navy was leading his men in battle against the pirates was stationed on a smaller vessel called "Jane". Maynard was one of

the best fighters in the navy. He jumped off the "Jane" into the cold Atlantic Ocean and swam towards the "Adventurer' where Blackbeard was instructing his men. He soon was able to get on board his enemy's ship and immediately pulled his sword, and he engaged in a sword fight with Blackbeard. Blackbeard's men started to point their muskets at Maynard. By this time, the "Jane" had got closer to Blackbeard and a loud cannon shot rang out and soon the pirates were killed, except for 13 men who quickly surrendered. Maynard and Blackbeard kept on fighting. Maynard would be winning for a while and then Blackbeard would be winning for a while while everyone else watched. The pirate ship turned suddenly in the water as it had been hit by some unknown wind gust by some unknown power. Both fighters were knocked down but Maynard quick regained his balance and drew his sword back and gave one long swift blow towards Blackbeard's head. Maynard severed Blackbeard's head right off his shoulders. The head landed on the ship's deck with blood covering the black beard and ribbons tied to the beard. It was a ghoulish sight looking like something from the depths of Hell. The body of Blackbeard also lay on the ships deck and was covered in blood. Maynard counted 25 stab wounds in Blackbeard's lifeless body. The war with the pirates were over. The navy sailors put chains on their 13 prisoners and transferred the sailors, the swords, the guns, Blackbeard's body, and his head from the "Adventurer" to the "Jane." As the navy ship was sailing away, the Adventurer shifted again. A navy cannonball must have hit a lower deck, and water started to rush inside the ship, and it began sinking. "The Adventurer" quickly sank off the coast of Bath. The navy seaman had mounted Blackbeard's head on the bowsprit of "The Jane" so all the citizens could see their trophy when they got back to the docks at the Navy shipyard in the Chesapeake Bay of Virginia.

Blackbeard , a notorious pirate was killed November 22, 1718 by Lt. Robert Maynard of the British Navy. His severed head was carried on the bowsprit of the "Jane" before it was mounted on a pole near Hampton Roads and remained there for several years to discourage piracy.

In a few weeks after the pirate prisoners were transported to Chesapeake town for trial, an impartial jury found them guilty. This also included Blackbeard's first mate, Israel Hands. They were escorted from the jail to a scaffold in the town square and hung for treason. The 13 bodies and Blackbeard's body were buried on a remote sandy beach near the small village of Chesapeake. Blackbeard's head was taken from the bowsprit and now placed on a tall pole placed by a busy road called Hampton Roads so all the people would see that piracy does not pay well. The life of a pirate is not always fun and romantic . The life of a pirate can be very precarious and dangerous. This group of pirates had not counted on   Alexander Spotswood following the wishes of some of his constituents.

 Alexander Spotswood was the one to put an order into the Assembly to end Blackbeard's successful piracy career. The seamen that carried out the battle against Blackbeard agreed that in 7 years they would get together again and take the skull down and fill it full of rum and each take a sip to celebrate the demise of Blackbeard. Alexander got word that Blackbeard had been killed, and his head was hanging from a pole at Hampton Roads. This was only eight miles from Williamsburg to the port of Chesapeake. Alexander wondered if this was the same man, he had traveled with him on the "*Deptford*" eight years earlier when he had sailed from England to Virginia. But whoever the real Blackbeard had been, he had to be stopped sooner or later. Alexander never went down to satisfy his curiosity and identify the man. He would also keep quiet about what the islander in Martinique had said about the Captain having been Blackbeard using the alias Edward. In any event, Alexander was not going to have his citizens annoyed by pesky pirates. Alexander must have thought even if Edward was really Blackbeard, we sometimes in life have to be rewarded for our good deeds and punished for our bad deeds. After such a brutal death of Blackbeard and hanging of the 13 pirates, piracy seized to be an issue from that day forward on the Atlantic Ocean near Virginia and the Carolinas.

A few weeks later after the burial of the pirates, a navy officer came into the governor's office and the butler identified him as Col. William Dandridge. The officer said," Hello, Colonel Spotswood, I have brought you some gifts. We have heard about your collection of guns and weapons and cannonballs. I see that they are very impressive, " as he looked at the gun display mounted on the wall. "We want to add to your collection on behalf of the Royal Navy."

Alexander smiling said, "Hello, I want to thank you for your leadership in the Blackbeard affair. Thank you for the gift but what is it?"

Col. William Dandridge pulled a pistol and a sword out of a long box that he was carrying, and said, "These were weapons we found on Blackbeard when he was killed. The gun was on his body and the sword had fallen overboard by a shifting in the boat and was falling down towards the ocean floor. One of our sailors named Goss who had also been knocked overboard by the shifting ship, had the sword miraculously show up in his hands."

Alexander slowly and carefully looked at the familiar looking sword. The sword had the letter S engraved on the handle. Alexander then said puzzling and mumbling, "Thank you very much for the gifts. I will add them proudly to my collection. Do you want something to drink?"

Col. Dandridge, "I will take some coffee before I start back."

Alexander admiring the beautiful sword, said to Col. Dandridge," You can be my guest in the guest house tonight on the Palace grounds. "

Col. Dandridge, "I would be honored, Sir, but I must go. It is a long ride back, and I had better get started. Thanks for the coffee!" He then set the ornate cup on the mahogany desk and started to leave. As Col. Dandridge left and Alexander kept looking at the sword with the engraved S, and the pieces all started to come together in his head.

Alexander said to himself, "This was my grandfather's Spotswood's sword. Blackbeard got it from his father, Redbeard. This is the sword that was stolen from me over 30 years ago. This means the sword is returned to the rightful owner and the curse is broken. I have been called handsome and wealthy all my life. I want to live a normal life without a curse and now I believe I can. Alexander looked up and said, "Thank you, Lord! I wish Roger was here, but he died under the curse. I will be free at last, free at last!"

The months started going by quickly and Alexander had a new view of life Even people who argued with him; he would now say that he saw their viewpoint as well, instead of saying they were wrong. He got more accomplished with Blair and Byrd in the Assembly. It didn't matter if he received the 80,000-acre land grant for exploring the Blue Ridge Mountains or not receive it. It did not worry him if someone told him he was losing money from his iron ore business or that his tobacco crop would yield a low grade of tobacco. He didn't even try to stop the German families from abandoning their homes at Germanna and move further west into the Piedmont along the Robinson River. This was the rich farmland that the Knights of the Golden Horseshoes had traveled over three years earlier when they made the now famous Spotswood's Journey. Alexander now more than ever liked to hear Reverend Thompson's sermons. Alexander must be thinking life is good. God is good. He loved the Lord.

Alexander looked at the Bible a different way. He read that it was harder for a rich man to get to Heaven than it was for a camel to get through the eye of a needle. He remembered Butler had told him this long ago. He now favored some verses as they had a new meaning to him, He read, "Do not worry, The Lord knows you and every hair on your body. " The Lord says, "Look at the ravens. The Lord provides for them, and they are supplied with all that they need." He also remembered the ravens he had seen at the Tower of London and the white ravens and the ghosts.

Best of all it was good for citizens to ask him if everything is all right instead of How handsome you are and having people stare at him all day long. He had saved more money than he could ever spend. He prayed now that the Lord would show him His will for his life and keep him healthy. He said to himself, "The dreaded pirates curse that has ruined my life has now gone forever. I can see clearly now. I can see that I need to ask for God's forgiveness my sins and ask that I can be in Heaven someday."

In 1720 , the seven years of indenture ship was up for the 9 German families at Germanna. They had all saved their money and bought 1800 acres of land 15 miles further up the road in Fauquier County. This devastated Alexander because he thought he had been generous to the families and had treated them fairly. The inevitable William Byrd said that Alexander had not treated the families fairly and that Alexander was using some of their money so he could go back to London. Alexander claimed he was not taking any extra money from the families. Alexander told the Assembly that he would plan to stay in Virginia even when his assignment of Lieutenant governor ended. He said that he was doing everything in his power to provide available land for new settlers in the Germanna area and west of the Blue Ridge Mountain. He proposed that the new settlers should not have to pay quit rent taxes for ten years if they would settle in Germanna. This worked and many new settlers came into the Germanna area. Alexander quickly bought 40,000 acres. Alexander started a mercantile store, an inn, a tavern, a church , and a courthouse at Germanna. He started to build himself a large grand house at Germanna. All this infuriated Byrd , incidentally who owned 200,000 acres himself. He asked Alexander why he was changing his position on land purchases. Alexander had argued early on when he first became Lt. Governor that he encouraged small settlers and homes so everyone could have a good life, and the lieutenant governor had campaigned against people buying large tracts of land for speculation instead of for settling. Byrd accused Alexander of land speculation and accused him as being a land grabber at the governments expense. Alexander also would build grist mills on the Rapidan River which would also increase the number of settlers because they would now have a place to grind their grain. Part of Alexanders new home could be used as a courthouse until a new official one could be built. Alexander would insist that part of the public money should be used to build the courthouse in his house. This infuriated Byrd even more. Byrd started gathering information on Alexander's work so he could get Alexander removed from office. Byrd asked Blair to start a list of what Alexander was doing wrong in the affairs of the church. James Blair needed no encouragement as he already assisted in removing two previous governors, and Blair did not like Alexanders tenacity anyway.

 In October of 1720, Alexander saw his personal physician, Dr. William Cocke have an attack of apoplexy and die in the Council Chamber. Cocke's longtime friend and school companion, William Byrd caught the doctor's dying body from falling to the Chamber Floor, and the good doctor and Secretary of the Colony died in Byrd's arms. This sad and untimely incident really shocked all the witnesses and Alexander. The struggling Governor was getting more opposition every day and just lost one of his most ardent supporters. Cocke was one of the most respected men in the colony and had one of the largest attended funerals of any man in Virginia. He would be missed by Alexander because he would most often agree with Alexander when conducting official colonial business. Doctor Cocke's funeral was held in Bruton Parish Church, and he would be laid to rest underneath its foundation.

In 1722, once again. the Iroquois nation threatened war again. So many new settlers were coming into settle the land at Germanna and west of the Blue Ridge in the Shenandoah Valley that these Indians did not like the crowding and all the diminishing of their hunting grounds. This time they asked for a treaty that would keep the Iroquois north of the Potomac and west of the Blue Ridge Mountains. This seemed to work, and the Indians went to new hunting grounds further west and then the entire Shenandoah Valley filled up quickly. There was a wagon road that followed a buffalo path and went way up into the Colony of New York and went all the way down into the Carolinas that went through the heart of the Shenandoah Valley that caused this fast growth. By the time , Alexander got back to his new office in Germanna , he was told that he had been removed from office by William Byrd. He was now a private citizen again. He did find out that King George would honor the land grants given to the Knights of the Golden Horseshoes. He found out that he had received another 40,000 acres that was mostly in Spotsylvania County between Williamsburg and Germanna. The name Spotsylvania would be given to a new county, and it was a named in honor of Alexander for his dedication and service to Virginia. Alexander saw his dismissal as good news. He no longer had to deal with political rivals. He thought that he must have embarrassed Lord Orkney for his constant squabbling with Blair and Byrd, and that is why he must have been dismissed. Now he would be able to take care of his businesses, plantations, mansions, and over 80,000 acres of land. He was now 46 years of age and well to do. One of his friends Hugh Drysdale would take over as Governor. Alexander had worked tirelessly for 12 years to make Virginia stronger in defense and production; better in community services and better roads; and more prosperous. He had been colorful , resolute, and hard driven. He would be proud of his accomplishments of keeping peace with the Indians and settling the new Shenandoah lands, and his Journey to Mt. George and Mt. Alexander on the summit of the Blue Ridge Mountains with the Knights of the Golden Horseshoes. The citizens loved him and new that he fought for them and wanted them to have a good way of life. He had remained wealthy and now had the time to improve his estate and his iron ore business. He would also have the time to improve his business in London. The iron ore was extremely important as the iron ore could be used in making metal tools and guns for the people of Virginia.

He could work now could try growing a better quality of tobacco and live the life of a country gentlemen. He would turn some of his businesses over to a Mr. Tyler of Fredericksburg, an expanding town which had been previously called Hobs Hill. He would live in his mansion in Germanna and be close to his mines and fields along the Rapidan River.

Ms. Thornton knew that when Alexander left the Palace and move to Germanna, she would probably be asked to leave as well and have to find employment elsewhere. She would be hopeful that maybe Alexander might ask her to marry him, and she would live happily ever after. She got busy cleaning and sweeping to keep her mind off Alexander and help in the preparation for leaving the Palace clean for the next governor. She saw a piece of paper underneath the carpet on the desk. She bent over to pick it up and she noticed it was a letter addressed to Butler Brayne on Marleybone Road in London, England. It looked kind of old and dusty. She started to open it, but she didn't think that would be the right thing to do. She started to walk over to the fireplace and thought maybe it best to destroy the letter by burning it in the fire. Again, she didn't want to hurt Alexander and interfere with his wishes. She walked over to the old desk that Alexander had brought over from England and placed the letter in the Spotswood Bible with some of the letters he had received from Butler through the years. She knew he would see it there sooner or later. She would give him the choice to deal with the letter, and that way it would not look like she was trying to interfere with his friends, which might make him upset with her. She continued to clean the desks and sweep the dust around the fireplace. She looked into the flames of the fireplace which seemed to be relaxing and allow her to daydream about the future.

Alexander went into the Palace once more to gather his personal belongings. He knew he must say something to Ms. Thornton who was saddened by the change of regimes. She had been faithful over the last 12 years as his political partner. Mr. White had already moved to Richmond which was an expanding city further south on the James River.

Ms. Thornton who always had been so prim and proper looked at Alexander with her beautiful and sad blue eyes and composed herself enough to say, "Alexander, I dread this day would come. I knew one day that we would leave the office together."

Alexander consoling, " Maybe you can work for Mr. Drysdale."

Ms. Thornton, "After working for you, it would not seem right for me to work for anyone else."

Alexander, "I am thankful for your dedication and for your friendship."

Ms. Thornton, "You know that I want more than that from you, Alexander. Please hug me."

Alexander hugged her and Ms. Thornton started crying, "Hold me, Alexander This is hard for me. I have loved you since I first met you. You were the most handsome, hardworking, kind, and caring man I had ever seen. I know you do not feel the same way about me. I love you, Alexander and I always will. I honestly love you. "

Alexander carefully speaking, "I have always thought that or known that. I will admit there has been times when your beauty has made it hard for me to control myself around you. God knows! You are a beautiful lady, but I have some strong feelings about another lady."

Ms. Thornton, "It is for a lady that you have not seen or heard from in years. Look at me ,Alexander. Look deep into my eyes. Please kiss me. "

Alexander puzzled about what to do, "If I do kiss you, it has to be the first time and the last time. "

Alexander then kissed her as passionately as he could. He did not have a reputation for being the most affectionate man in Virginia. The kiss lasted for several minutes and aroused almost every feeling between a man and a woman that there could possibly be. Alexander managed to pull away from her.

Ms. Thornton, "It is everything and more than I thought it would be. I love you forever and will always be there for you. "She ran outside and was crying her eyes out. No mortal or immortal woman ever loved a man so deeply as this.

Alexander must have thought, "Am I crazy . I have known this woman for 12 years and she is beautiful. We have always enjoyed working together. Yet the lady I love is as pretty and wise as Ms. Thornton, but will she have anything to do with me? Will Butler even marry me? "

As Alexander was walking down the streets of Williamsburg after his farewell with Ms. Thornton, he thought he would step into the courthouse. He wanted to check on the sale of one of his lots in Williamsburg. A young man was ahead of him making a land transaction. The land agent had asked him whether he was old enough to buy land. The boy had said yes and that his mother would be in shortly to sign for the deed and to bring the money.

Land agent, "Sign here, please."

The young man signed the paper.

Land agent, "Is your name, Robert Spotswood? Are you related to the Governor?"

"Not that I know of," the young man stated. Alexander heard all this and wondered who he was. By that time , the young man's mother came in and signed her name and handed the land agent some paperwork. The land agent stated that everything looked proper.

Land agent, "Is your last name, Mitchell?"

Lady Mitchell, "My son has a different last name because his father died, and I remarried. His father stated to me before he died that he wanted his son to come to Virginia and make his fortune here. He is 18 and been working on a farm near Knightsbridge, west of London, and he likes fais strong as an ox. He will be getting work here and staying at this property. I will be going back to London."

Land Agent," I see. I have here what I need. You are free to leave. If I can be of further service, please let me know." Alexander had ease dropped on the conversation. The boy and lady looked familiar. He just couldn't place where he had seen them before. Her voice sounded familiar, too. She had smiled at Alexander and gave him kind of a puzzled look. It might have been because he seemed so interested in the conversation between her and the land agent.

The Spotswood name was not that common. Of course, he never had met some of his Spotswood relatives in Scotland, and maybe the boy's father was a distant relative. When the young man and his mother left, he tipped his hat to the lady and said, " Hello my lady." He looked at the young man and said, "Hello, Sir."

The mother and young man quickly left. The young man started down the street to Liddendale's Tavern, and he hugged his mother goodbye. She got into a carriage and started going towards the direction of the harbor on the York River to catch a vessel headed toward London.

Alexander to the land agent, " I don't want to be nosy, but Spotswood is a rare name in England and Scotland.

.220

Can I look at the contract? " It had been signed by R. Spotswood and B.V. Mitchell. Alexander looked out the window and the lady was looking back at the courthouse. He hoped she had not seen him.

Alexander, "His father has to be distant kin."

Land Agent, "Do you have some business Col. Spotswood?"

Alexander, "No I forgot. I have to be somewhere."

Alexander hurried out of the courthouse and went into Liddendales. The young man was at a table drinking some imported black tea.

Alexander, "Can I sit with you? I noticed you in the courthouse. My name is also Spotswood. In fact, my father's name was the same as yours, Robert Spotswood, "

Robert Spotswood, "Yes, you can. I know you were the Governor of Virginia."

Alexander, "Do you think we are related?"

Robert Spotswood, "I don't know . I never met my father. He died before I was born. My mother said she had met the family once when he was dying in the hospital right before I was born. She couldn't remember their given names.

Alexander, "Does the name Villiers mean anything to you?"

Robert, "No, but it is a popular name in England,"

Alexander, "Was your father a Mitchell?"

Robert, "I don' think so. My stepfather also died in a hospital when I was two years of age. He had suffered a wound in a war with France and never could get well."

Just then William Byrd came hustling in to Liddendales to get some coffee. He said, "Alexander, how is my ole friend?"

Alexander, "You mean ole enemy, do you not? This is Robert Spotswood and we were trying to figure out how he is related to me. Robert, this is Mr. Byrd, Assistant to the King of England. "

William Byrd chuckling, "I miss you, Alexander. You are more fun than Mr. Drysdale. I would say that this young man favors you enough to be your son. Nice to meet you, Robert."

Robert Spotswood, "Nice to meet you, too, Mr. Byrd."

Alexander looked again at the young man and the truth to whose Robert's father was may never be known.

Alexander to Robert, How would you like a job?" I will pay you fair wages if you check my property for me while I am in London on personal and commercial business. I have an overseer, Mr. Tyler who is charged with taking care of business, but you will be checking on the property and on Mr. Tyler for me. You will send me copies of the paperwork by mail and I will pay you from the sale of timber and tobacco. The mail system is so slow it actually makes me complain a little.

Robert, "I will glad to work for you, Mr. Spotswood."

Alexander, "You can call me, Colonel or Alexander. I see that your mother has taught you some good manners. "

Robert, "She has mainly taught me poetry and how to be a farmer."

Alexander, "I will explain what I want you to do. If I can't trust a Spotswood, who can I trust.? I will be in England for a few years. I will send you my address, but I believe it will be the Spotswood Trading Company, London, England. I will get a contract ready to show you your pay and what are the job duties. I will meet with you here tomorrow at the same time and place. I will buy you lunch, and you will get your first pay. I am leaving next week."

Robert said, "Great!" He shook hands with Alexander. Alexander left the tavern and went on to a room he had rented near the Palace. The young man ordered some more tea to drink and thought, "Virginia is for me. I have a feeling I will be rich and famous here." He left to walk out to the place on the edge of town that his mother and he had just signed for at the Courthouse.

The Journey to the End of Life.

After Alexander Spotswood got his business affairs settled, he was now ready to board a ship for England. He was almost 48 years of age in fine health and was well known as an effective and influential person in Virginia's past. Now he was thinking about the future and his regaining Butler's love for him. He had made up his mind that she was the only woman that he loved besides his mother, sister, and Aunt Bethia. They loved Alexander unconditionally and that he hoped Butler felt the same way about him as he did for her. That would be called an unconditional love. He had not been in England for 13 years but because of all his correspondence with family and Butler there, he could almost picture all the changes. He would board a ship at Yorktown. It would take an average of 10 weeks to get to Plymouth or London. They would sail with favorable winds and would take advantage of the gulf streams. The sailing rout and trip were routine, and it wasn't long that before they were at the docks in London. He stepped up on a carriage step and waited for the next carriage which would take them to St. John's Street in Westminster. On the way, the carriage rider came along and opened the door and Alexander told him where he wanted to go. The carriage rider asked Alexander how long he would be in London.

Alexander said, "Just long enough to get married and then we must get back to Virginia. "

Carriage driver, " That is where that Spotswood fellow is from isn't it?"

Alexander looking a little shocked that the driver knew about his name from Virginia, said "Yes. "

Carriage driver, "Everyone is still talking about his ride over the mountains of Virginia and making it possible for thousands of people from this country to have a house and land there and where a person can get rich. He was climbing all those tall mountains, killing rattlesnakes and bear, and eating all that elk, deer, and fish right out of the stream. He made all those toasts to good King George. He sounds like a good governor to me."

Alexander, " Spotswood is not the governor now. It is a Mr. Drysdale. Virginia is a good place to live."

Alexander did not want to identify himself as a rattlesnake killer or a bear hunter, so he remained quiet until he reached his destination.

It didn't take too long before the carriage carrying Alexander was at the destination's end on St. John Street. He saw a man walking down the cobblestone street and asked him if he knew where Mr. and Mrs. Richard Giles lived. The man pointed to what seemed to be a brand-new house, and there were some unfinished houses there on both sides of the Giles House. Alexander was impressed. It was almost as big as his former Palace. The house was built in the new Georgian style and had large lawns in the front and back. Alexander walked up to the door and knocked. The butler let him in and asked him who he was so he could be introduced to the Giles.

"Alexander Spotswood is my name. Please to make your acquaintance. " and he shook hands with the butler.

The butler went upstairs and left Alexander in the big hallway and Alexander began to look at all the paintings and sculptures to have something to do while he waited. Margaret came running down the stairs and asked, "Alexander, is that you? You look so old and thin. I am glad you are here, but did you write to me and tell me your coming?"

Alexander, "Yes, it is me. Thanks for being so honest. The pirates curse has been broken and I am no longer handsome. No, I did not write but I wanted to surprise you, and I thought you would be glad to see me. "

Margaret, "Oh Alexander, you know I am glad to see you. I am. I am. How was your trip? How long will you stay?"

Alexander, "My trip was actually enjoyable. It was so much better than the trip I had when I went to Virginia 13 years ago. I will tell you more about it later. I will stay awhile and find a place to rent in the old neighborhood."

Margaret, "Nonsense, you can stay here. You see that we have plenty of room."

Alexander, "Your house is very nice, but I want to get married and I need my own place. This is very nice. Maybe I should have been in the clergy instead of being a governor and in the land speculation business."

Margaret, "Well we have our income added together and I can't go into details, but my friend Sara Churchill helped us a little. If I had to make payments, I could not be happy here. "

Alexander, "I am sure you deserve every nice thing that comes your way. How is Richard?"

Margaret blushing, "He is nice and kind. You will like him when you meet him. "

Alexander, "I will not stay long. I have to find a place. "

Margaret, "So who are you marrying, Alexander?"

Alexander, "Butler Brayne, if she and her parents think it best."

Margaret, "Oh. Alexander, I hate to be the one that tell you this. She was upset because she didn't know if you wanted to marry her or not and she kind of got impatient. She was dating some different gentlemen, but she didn't seem to be happy with any of them. I have not talked to her in years."

Alexander, "I wrote her a letter several years ago and told her that I was madly in love with her. I got a curt reply so I prayed to God if he would reveal to me if she was the wife meant for me. I can't blame the mail system because I could have kept writing or I could have come to England, once or twice, and talk to her in person."

Margaret, " I am so sorry, but she told me she did not receive such a letter and asked why you quit writing to her. Don't get too upset if she is married or refuses to see you."

Alexander, "It was providence at work. I was still under the curse when I wrote her the letter. I always wondered why she did not answer the letter about how she truly felt. I knew that was not like her. And think that a lost letter may keep us apart. I will go and find her and talk with her. "

Margaret, "It is so good to see you Alexander, but I hate to see you hurting this way. Let me know if I can help you in any way. "

Alexander, "I will be back in several days. I have to get myself settled first. Good night."

Margaret, "Good Night, brother. Let me hug you." and they hugged.

Alexander left Margaret's house and walked down to the Golden Square to see if he could get a carriage driver to take him up to the business district near Oxford Street where his business was located. He finally got a horse and carriage to get him to the business, and he got down from the coach and walked into the office. He saw old and faithful Mr. Richard Brayne behind the desk working on the books.

Alexander, "Richard, I am Alexander."

Richard Brayne, "Alexander, is that you? You look so old and thin. I am glad to see you. I must not have received a letter, yet, telling us you were coming, or we could have had a big welcome for you. You have had such a good life and are so famous. I thought you would be too busy to ever come back to England."

Alexander, "Richard, I just wanted to come. You know that I have always loved your daughter. I want to marry her if you and Mrs. Brayne agree.

Richard Brayne, "I always thought that would come to pass, but Butler has a mind of her own and old enough to make up her own mind. "

Alexander, "Is she married or in love with anyone?"

Richard Brayne, "Not that I know of. Alexander, you seem so different and so anxious."

Alexander looking a little more relieved as if there was hope for him and Butler, "I want to see her."

Richard Brayne, "She will be here in a little while. She has to pick me up from work and take me home. I don't get around that good since I am getting old. "

Alexander, "You look just fine to me. "

Richard Brayne, "Alexander, you look so thin. Are you sure you are eating enough?"

Alexander, "Just the same as usual. I didn't eat that well coming over on the ship. When I get my new place, I will invite the Brayne family over for dinner. "

Richard Brayne, "That would be nice. Are you planning to stay here in London?"

Alexander, "That depends on Butler 's wishes."

Richard Brayne, "Why does that depend on Butler?"

Alexander, "I want to marry her, and I will be happy wherever she wants to live. "

Mr. Brayne, "She has been seeing other gentlemen, so I don't know what she wants to do. Her sister, Dorothea is engaged to Mr. Beninger and they will move to Virginia when he gets his business established there."

Alexander said impatiently, "I have to talk to her."

Mr. Brayne, a little tired and confused , " Who? Dorothea? She is already engaged."

Alexander anxiously, " No, I meant Butler. I have to marry Butler."

Mr. Brayne, "That would be a good thing , Alexander. You know we would support that the best we could. "

Alexander began pacing the floor and a few minutes went by. Mr. Brayne was busy organizing his files and preparing to leave for the evening.

Butler walked into the office and said, "Father, are you ready to go?" She looked around and saw Alexander. She looked faint as if she was seeing a ghost. The smile she had for her father now had turned into a scowl as she stared at Alexander.

Butler asked, "Alexander, is that you? You are so old looking and thin! Are you taking care of yourself? Now that you are famous in England and Virginia, I guess you are so busy that you forget to eat like you have forgotten to write me." She was so mad she was trying to hold back her emotions, and she almost started crying.

Alexander, "Butler, please don't be angry. I love you and wanted to surprise you. I sent you a letter where I stood with you and that I loved you. I don't think you got the letter. "

Butler in an angry tone of voice, "I never got any such letter. I will admit that I am angry with you, Alexander. I waited year after year for you to tell me that you loved me, but I never heard anything from you. I don't know what to say." She looked at her father and began crying. Mr. Brayne went on outside and waited in the carriage while Butler and Alexander talked. He respected their privacy and wanted them to work out their differences.

Butler stopped crying and moved closer to Alexander," I met a man that I thought I wanted to be with, but he is too controlling. And he is not generous and kind like you are. Alexander, you have put me in a predicament. I have to think about all of this. I am not used to surprises. "

Alexander, "Are you engaged? Do you love this man? Before you answer, can I say one thing? I will say that I fell in love with you, the first time I saw you. I am still in love with you. I knew that you would be the future, Mrs. Alexander Spotswood. How that would happen and when that would happen, I would not have been able to tell you. I do know that I didn't want to take you out to a strange land and have you raise several children in a rugged environment until we could afford some nice things. I did not know how my job would work out in Virginia. There are a few schools and only a few doctors. Sometimes it is hard to get good water, food, and other supplies if some of the supply ships get lost at sea. There is always a possible danger with the Indians and servants. I was fortunate that I had a staff of 25 servants, but I never knew how long that would last and that was a rare exception. I could have not afforded that all on my own. I want to give you all the time and attention I have. I know you have had a comfortable life here in London. I love you, Butler."

Butler, "No I am not engaged. And I do not love the other man. I know if you were too busy to write me, you were too busy to love any other lady. At this moment in my life, I can honestly say I don't know if I honestly love anybody but my family. "

Alexander, "I was afraid you would not want to see me if I wrote you ahead of time. If you said an absolute no to me, it would kill me. I cannot bare the thought of never seeing you again. I honestly love you. I hope you can see that in me."

Butler looking more relieved, " Oh, Alexander, you know me better than I know myself. Will you let me think about this? I have felt that I have not been that important in your life, but I have not heard how you feel until now. I want to pray about all this. Do you remember where we live? Will you come Sunday at 9 in the morning and take us to church like you used to?"

Alexander, "Yes, I remember where you live. I understand how you must feel. I will be there at 9 and we will go to church. "

Butler turned around and headed for the door and said, "The church is now called St. Marleybone Parish Church instead of St. Mary's . I will explain the name change to you , later. I have to take father home. I will see you Sunday. I have to sort it out. Good night, Alexander. "

Alexander, " I see. Good night! I will lock up."

Butler walked to the carriage. She was no longer the young girl with sparkle in her eyes waving goodbye to a friend at the docks when Alexander had left for Virginia. She was now a beautiful woman and had filled out but had a small waist. She had fire in her blue eyes, and she was attractive. Her blond hair was now curly and halfway down her back. She was stylish in her dress and still polite in her manners and had a sweet voice.

 Alexander found an apartment at the Golden Square. He had not brought that many clothes, but he would wear his best suit on Sunday, and he thought this would be the most important sermon that he would ever hear. Sunday finally came and Alexander met the Brayne family at 9 am sharp. Butler looked radiant and was very composed. She did not appear to be still angry with Alexander. Alexander grabbed her small hand and held her hand as they walked to St. Mary's Church or St. Marylebone's Parish Church where they had been attending for years. John Wesley was now of age to be a preacher and he was a fiery preacher at that. When the Bryans and Alexander entered the cathedral, John announced that they were going to receive a blessing from a sermon on forgiveness when the service began. The Braynes sat down on some of the back pews in the main auditorium. Alexander and Butler went up the aisle closer to the pulpit at the front and sat down in the fourth row from the front. Alexander and Butler listened intently and glanced at each other occasionally.

After opening benediction, opening prayer, and a after singing of some Anglican hymns, the sermon began. Wesley's remarked, "I am asking you today, has anyone ever hurt you in any way? Some people may say that another person would not hurt me unless the person did not care to be with me in the first place. That is not always true. It could be said that some events in our life cause us to do things which results in consequences. Sometimes it may be showing love for someone or something. Sometimes we make bad choices and people we love get hurt unintentionally, but they still feel hurt and we feel we need forgiveness. When we break God's laws, we may not intentionally think we are hurting the Lord, but we need forgiveness. Forgiveness from our sins. The Lord will be quick to forgives us and love us. In fact, the Lord loves us unconditionally . Why can't we forgive those who hurt us so the Lord can forgive us. The main topic today is from the Lord's Prayer in Matthew 6:14. "For if you forgive men their trespasses, your heavenly Father will also forgive you." A trespass is a misdeed. A deed of action that is done that is wrong and could hurt someone physically, emotionally, or spiritually. We have all failed God in some way and have fallen short of his glory. This is why we need His forgiveness and we need to seek him. Everyone needs to understand and come to terms with forgiveness because it is a central theme of understanding God's plan for us. If we can understand it, we will understand God's justice and feel his love. God's justice and love is always just and fair. Our sermon today is taken from Matthew 18:15 "If thy brother shall trespass against thee, go and tell him his fault between thee and him alone. if he shall hear thee, thou have gained thy brother. Verse 18 reads as follows: "Verily I say unto you, Whatsoever ye shall bind on earth, shall be bound in Heaven; and whatsoever ye shall loose on earth shall be loosed in Heaven. These are words spoken directly by Jesus. Forgiveness is not a compromise of morality. God's justice will not let the murderer get away with murder. If you sin, yes, you can be forgiven of your sins. If we keep on sinning after we are forgiven, is that compromising morality with forgiveness. If we Love God, then we will avoid the temptation of sin . God will love us as forgiven sinners. God will never compromise his justice. Forgiveness is not the absence or avoidance of conflict. Husbands do not provoke your wives and children to anger. If, as fathers, we do not say anything that would correct the situation we feel sometimes, we are missing an opportunity to improve that relationship. If you say that you are misunderstanding her remarks about you and ask for understanding and clarification, you are on the way to correcting the misunderstanding. If you stay silent, is that showing love? Some of us do not like confrontation or conflict. We hope that the situation will get better and that the other person knows our character and knows we mean well when we are trying to correct them. The simple avoidance of conflict is not the same as forgiveness. Fathers, ask your wife, ask your children every once in a while, how you can help them with their anger and their struggles.

The word forgiveness in Greek testament is aphesis. In English, it is the word release. When you forgive someone, you are releasing them from being obligated to you. If you have been holding resentment against someone, forgiving them means you are releasing their obligation to you. They are free. Let's pray that they learn why they have been given forgiveness or how they have been given forgiveness. They are still accountable to God for their actions and have to face the justice of God. Continuing in Matthew 18, the disciple Peter asked the Lord, "How many times shall I forgive my brother? Up to 7 times? Jesus gives a parable, a short practical story with a truth. A certain man owed a king 10,000 talents and was forced to sell all he owned to pay his just debt. He would soon have to sell his wife and children to slavery. He, too, would at last be at the mercy of the king . The man pleaded and pleaded with the king and that he wanted his family spared. The king forgave him of his misdeed and canceled his deed. He released him from his debt.

Now , think of a person's name. You have been thinking about your relationship to them for a long time. It may be a strained feeling or misunderstanding with that person. They have not met your expectation. Have you met their expectations? Maybe they did not have enough information from you so they would know how to properly respond. Maybe you were trying to avoid conflict because you really loved that person, and you didn't want to hurt them, and you didn't want to be hurt. Can you at least try to understand what they were trying to do? Maybe they were trying to respond and seek forgiveness. Be faithful in your service to the Lord and remember his words. If ye shall forgive the trespasses of your brother, then the Lord will be faithful in forgiving you. He will not only forgive you; He will shower you with blessings untold. I will close with Luke 6: "Bless those who curse you. Pray for those that hurt you." Is there anyone here today that would say, I need to be forgiven and I need to forgive my brother? If you want to renew your faith and have a closer walk with the Lord, please come forward at this time.

Alexander and Butler got up from the pew and walked up to the altar. He told the pastor, "I want to be forgiven for causing grief to Butler."

Butler, "I want to be forgiven by Alexander by misunderstanding his intentions for our relationship."

Alexander said, " I would like to renew my faith."

Butler, "I would like to renew my faith and ask forgiveness from the Lord."

The pastor, "The Lord has heard your petitions and will answer your unspoken prayers and your spoken testimony."

The pastor said, "Pray for this couple that they grow in a closer walk with the Lord and that their love, trust, and faith grow in each other. Bless their home and may they go in peace and prosperity. Amen"

Butler and Alexander looked at each other and smiled. Alexander's commitment to the Lord was real. He believed that Butler looked at him the same way as she once did when she was a young lady growing up in the church.   After the service, Mr. and Mrs. Brayne came up to the altar and congratulated the couple on their commitments. The pastor congratulated them on their decisions.

Alexander, "Mr. and Mrs. Brayne, "I would like to walk with Butler up to Regent's Park if she agrees and you agree. It is such a lovely fall day to take a stroll in the park. Butler, smiling, nodded in agreement.

Mr. Brayne, "It sounds like a splendid idea. If you can, be at our home at two o'clock for teatime."

Alexander and Butler were already walking towards the entrance gate to the park. Alexander turned back and looked at Mr. and Mrs. Brayne and Butler's sisters ,and Alexander was smiling and said, "Oh Yes , Mr. Brayne, we will be there for tea."

Butler, as they were walking down one of the long walkways in the park, asked, "Alexander, do you remember the first time we came to church here and then came here to the park? My parents were so worried that we would elope, and they thought I was too young to be married."

Alexander, "You are old enough now, will you marry me?" But you would have to agree to one other thing. You would be my second love, because the Lord has to come first in my life now. "

Butler, "Yes, Alexander, I will marry you and be a faithful wife, but I have to tell you something."

Alexander looked very happy on the one hand but was extremely curious about her next statement.

Butler, "If you had said anything else about me being first in your life and not the Lord being first, I would have had to say no."

Alexander, "Fair enough, my lady."

Alexander and Butler sealed their commitment to each other by kissing each other for several minutes. They were so much in love.

Alexander finally got to say, "We have a lot to talk about."

Butler, "I say, for one thing that we cannot do much about your looks, although you look distinguished. We do have to get some weight on you. "

.229

Alexander chuckling, " I have waited so long for this moment. You have made me very happy and there is nothing wrong with your looks. Let's walk a little longer and by the time we turn around and get to your house it will be two o'clock."

It was fall in London and the leaves were changing colors and looked spectacular in Regent's Park. It was a beautiful time of year to be in the park. The harmony of the color of the leaves of the trees in autumn brings harmony to everyone and everything. The tall trees that were along the sides of the walkways had a combination of splendid golds, pumpkin oranges, and heartwarming scarlet leaves. These colors are good for the soul. Also, the bushes and flowers along the lake looked like a candy store with chartreuse, pomegranate red, yellow, tans, rusts, and brown colors. The park was definitely a part of God's majestic handiwork. It was magnificent like a painting, but full of people, laughter, and life.

Alexander, "Do you want to get married in the Spring?"

Butler, "That would be fine."

Alexander, "After we get married, we could go to Scotland and Ireland for a holiday if you so desire."

Butler, "Yes dear. I would like that."

Alexander," Do you want to live in London?"

Butler, "I do, but what about your business in Virginia?"

Alexander, " It can wait. I have overseers to look after the mines and the plantations. I have built a big house in Germanna on a hill above a horseshoe shaped bend in the river below. I have acquired a large parcel of land by the home and maybe we can move there someday. I am in no hurry to get back there. One of the rooms in the house is used by the county for a courthouse until a new one is built. "

Butler, "I would say that someday is fine. But what about children? I am 34 and will not be able to have that many children. I would like to see little boys and girls playing around the house. It will be such a happy home!"

Alexander, "Sounds wonderful! We will love them and protect them."

Butler, "What about my sister, Dorothea staying with us in Virginia? She is waiting on her fiancé to get his business up and running well before he gets married."

Alexander, "Sounds familiar. I hope it won't take 13 years like it did for us. When we get back to your house, we will look at the calendar and set a date. Then we will announce our wedding plans to family and friends. " Alexander pulled a little box from his pocket. Butler was fascinated by the box. Alexander pulled out a jewel covered pin that was in the shape of a horseshoe.

 Butler asked, "Can I see it?"

Alexander, "Certainly. It is my gift to you. I gave one like it to each one of my Knights of the Golden Horseshoes and a few other special people. Only 50 of them were made to celebrate the journey over the Blue Ridge. Do you like the pin?"

Butler, "It is wonderful. I like the Irish four-leaf clover, English rose , and Scottish thistle engraving between the pretty stone covered nails of the horseshoe. Thank you for a beautiful gift. I thought it may be a wedding ring. It made me think, when seeing the box, that you must have been pretty sure of yourself, and that I would say yes to the marriage proposal. You knew ahead of time, that we would be together after the worship service. The one thing we do have is our love together, forever. "

Alexander, "True! "

Butler, ""We can get married here at Marleybone where we had our first date. It is said to be only second to St. Paul's Cathedral down by Tower Hill in importance to the Church of England according to Mr. Browning and Mr. Dickens, two of the more prominent members. No one can adequately explain why the name was changed from St. Mary's Marleybone to St. Marleybone Parish Church. "

Alexander, "Splendid! You have made me very happy!"

Butler, "You have made me very happy. "

If we get out of sorts with each other again, we should mend our differences quickly. We will never be separated by years again. I have yet to see why it was my fate to go to Virginia and go over the mountain in the first place."

Butler, "Agreed, my love. I like you anyway that you are an older looking gentleman. You just need to add some weight."

Alexander, "Even if you weren't the most beautiful lady in the world I have seen, I will still love you anyway!"

They embrace each other and kissed again and walked back up to the church where they would marry. They wanted to get to Butler's home quickly because they couldn't wait to tell the Brayne family they were getting married. They told the Braynes they would marry at St. Marleybone's Parish Church on March 11, 1724. The Braynes were happy with that decision. The Braynes had always admired Alexander as a learned, disciplined, and ambitious fellow. When the vows were exchanged in the chapel, Mr. Brayne had one of his friends, a painter named Hogarth, make a painting of the wedding and later placed it in the hallway of the Church.

The wedding day came after a few months of planning. The interior of the old church, St. Marleybone's, looked more majestic and grander than ever. The church of England had it dedicated for the Virgin Mary and a marble arch dedicated to St. John the Baptist was above the entrance to the churchyard. The couple were wished happiness by Minister Wesley and a small crowd of family and friends. Soon Alexander and Butler would be off to Ireland and Scotland for a holiday. Their married life had just begun, and they were so much in love.
.

The Spotswood first part of their journey took them to Ireland to the docks near Waterford . Alexander and Butler got off the sloop, which was a square-rigged warship with three masts, that they had taken from Plymouth, England. The sloop crossed by the Isles of Scilly, an archipelago off the southwestern corner of England known as the Cornish tip of England. The seaman would head up the Celtic Sea towards Ireland by going with the St. George Channel Current. The Spotswoods didn't seem to pay much attention to the beautiful English and Irish coastlines on the trip or didn't say much about the uncomfortable conditions on the sloop. They spent most of the time telling each other about the events in their lives before they were married. A lot of things had changed in the last ten or twelve years. There was a lot of catching up to do. They also had to plan their future together. Occasionally they would look over the decks and look for land. Most of the time, they just kept seeing cold blue water in front of them and light blue sky above the horizon. Sometimes they might catch a glimpse of a migratory sea bird wandering aimlessly towards some resting place on dry land. The Crystal Sea soon became part of the Irish Sea. The Irish fisherman had their little fishing boats out on the waters, and they were fishing for mackerels. In a few days they reached Waterford, Ireland and went to the churchyard where Alexander's mother was buried. She had been buried next to her third husband, George Mercer. Alexander went down on one knee and said prayer for giving him such a wonderful mother. Alexander told Butler that he truly loved them both and that he owed a great deal for the education and religious training he had received from his stepfather. The Spotswoods left the churchyard and then went on to Cork and Antrim. After a few days, they headed back to their apartment at the Golden Square in London. Here they would rest for a few days before they headed for Scotland. They rented a coach and driver at the livery stable on Oxford Street and started towards the village of Barnes, England. The drive followed and ole mail route along The Thames River. The origin of the route was close to St. James Park, walking distance from the Golden Square, called Charing Cross. Alexander had been to Charing Cross area many times. His favorite time was when Margaret had taken him there 40 years earlier at Christmas time. He told Butler about the little trip that Margaret had taken him and the Mercers on a journey around Westminster, Chelsea, Whitehall, and they ended up at the Tower. Butler had said that the Tower is a place where some people don't want to end up. They would go about ten miles southwest of Charing Cross to the village of Barnes lying on a hillside by a bend in the Thames River. The Spotswoods would stop here so that Alexander could pay his respects to his half-brother, Roger Elliott who was buried in the village's cemetery. Some of the villagers told Alexander that Roger's son was serving King George by being the Governor in Gibraltar. Alexander found that to be favorable news. Alexander told Butler that he really respected Roger and loved him like a brother. After they left Barnes, the driver got the couple on the Old North Road that went from the London to York to Edinburgh. It was a well-traveled road on the way north. It had been used by mail carriers for centuries to get mail from one part of England to the North part of England and further north to Scotland. There were lots of villages and inns all along this road so the Spotswoods had their choices. It was a scenic trip to Scotland. They saw some beautiful green covered lowlands and majestic barren mountain peaks of the highlands. In Scotland, the couple visited all the old Spotswood places, castles, and graves of their ancestors . This trip involved locating the cemeteries of the Morrisons and Maxwells and other related families. They stayed one night in Darsie Castle, an old Spotswood ancestral tower house. It was near the Eden River in Fife, Scotland. The next few days they traveled up the Fife of Fourth to get to St. Andrews . Here they told their carriage driver that he could go on back to London by himself and they were going to travel by boat back to London. At St. Andrews, Alexander saw the grave of his grandfather, Robert Spotswood, who had been beheaded by a swinging ax called the maiden. Robert had been loyal to Charles I, whose life ended by a similar death by the opposing political powers in England. The maiden was on display at one of the colleges in the village. The newly married couple took a romantic sailboat ride from St. Andrews and on the North Sea. They sailed the seas along the County Norfolk coastline with quaint little fishing villages all along the shoreline. They finally arrived at the Cliffs of Dover and the military village of Deal where Alexander had once lived. Alexander was eager to show Butler his barracks home and the garrison school where he had learned basic studies when he was in his youth. Deal had not changed much in the 40 years since he had been there. He took a walk down to the guildhalls where he spent a lot of his leisure time learning about farming and the feudal system. Alexander took Butler to one of the white cliffs of Dover where he once stood and watched William III of Orange sailing with his Armada in the English Channel on his way to defeat King James II. This day in Alexander's boyhood and a very important day in English history now seemed a lifetime ago to Alexander. Butler was holding on to Alexanders arm and was looking over the cliff to the blue sea water below and the blue sky across the channel. In the distance they could see the French shoreline. After many days of seeing pretty English countryside, the couple soon got back to London at their apartment to begin a happy life together.

In a few months, Butler told Alexander that she wanted him to take her to Regents Park and they could have a meal ready to take to the park. After lunch, she told Alexander some good news. She told him that they were going to have a baby. In 1725, a son was born to Mr. and Mrs. Alexander Spotswood. They would name him,

John. Alexander would work with his partners at the Spotswood Trading Company during the weekdays and rush home at night to be with his beautiful wife and young son. A few years went by and then the Spotswood had a daughter, Ann Catherine, who was born in 1728 and baptized 19th of October at St. Luke's Anglican Church in Chelsea. They were such a happy family. They often visited the Braynes' home and Richard and Margaret Giles home with their little family. Alexander enjoyed talking to Margaret's husband, Richard Giles about his popular and well received sermons. Alexander spent hours explaining the rustic and rural beauty of Virginia and about his experiences in the Virginia Colony.

One Sunday after church, Alexander decided to take his wife and family for a visit to Kensington Palace. Margaret had told him that it was being refurbished and available for visitors since there were no kings and queens living there after the death of Queen Anne, her sister, Queen Mary, and her brother-in-law , King William III. This is where Margaret's friend, Sarah had been serving in the bed chamber of Queen Anne. When Alexander drove his team of horses and carriage up to the to the south gate of the Palace, he noticed the beautiful architectural style of the south side of the palace. It had showed the grand architectural style of Christopher Wrenn. He opened the 12-foot-high metal gates to walk onto the grounds. On the gates was a brass plate that had the design of a daffodil, shamrock, rose, and a thistle, signifying the British realm of Wales, Ireland, Scotland, and Ireland. In the yard between the gate and the main house was a bronze statue of William III that had been recently unveiled. He went into the entrance and soon found him and his family walking up the Queen's Stairway to the drawing room and king's gallery. All around the walls and ceilings were paintings and tapestries of all the old master artists of England. Alexander noticed a round compass with the map of Europe and England. The compass showed the directions of where the other countries were located in relationship to England. It was mounted on the wall above one of the massive fireplaces. This room was approximately 40 feet by 80 feet . The ceilings also had beautiful paintings on them 20 feet above the pretty wood floors below. Also, the Spotswoods looked at the Council Chamber, the Privy Chamber, the Presence Chamber, and the Cupola room. They admired all the new furniture that Queen Anne had added to Kensington as she had expensive and good taste. She added many new pieces of fine furniture to the royal décor. The Cupola room had a dome ceiling and the room was circular and had a big cherry desk with four chairs pulled up to the desk in the middle of the room.

,Alexander saw the portrait painting of Queen Anne and she looked exactly like she did when he met her at her coronation service almost twenty-five years earlier. They got to see Queen Anne's bed chamber and her study. When the Queen first came to Kensington, she chose the King's Quarters of the palace to reside in, as it was more elegant and spacious than the Queen's Quarters. Alexander looked outside the window and saw the Queen's garden below. He might have briefly thought the Queen must have received some comfort and happiness by being able to see such a beautiful garden, lawn, and estate to the north of her bedroom and study. Queen Anne had her Royal gardener build an orangery in the garden to protect her orange trees. This turned out to be the most expensive greenhouse in history. The garden contained many exotic trees, Indian bean trees, fig trees, and hardwoods. There were many flowers arranged around a sunken garden that contained a small pond in the middle of the garden. One of the previous kings had stocked the pond with turtles because he would have the royal cooks prepare him turtle soup because of his fondness for the soup. The garden at Kensington Palace was well known and well visited because of its beauty and superb care. Alexander noticed from the former Queen's terrace a large pond north of the gardens about 500 yards from the Queens terrace. He noticed a wide variety of animals that looked like they were running wild unattended and unaffected by some of the other visitors who were walking by the pond and the park nearby. It was a strange sight indeed. There were deer drinking from the pond. Also, there were elephants, camels, buffalo, cattle and horses walking around as if they were in their natural habitat in the big park further north of the palace. He had always heard that King Henry VIII, James I, and Charles I had always hunted animals in the park for sport. Apparently, the animals were not afraid of any hunters now as they freely moved about. Alexander certainly did not want his family to get hurt by the wild animals wandering unnoticed amongst the people. His thoughts soon returned to the terrace. He must have imagined Queen Anne administering business for all of England and his former colony of Virginia, while she supped tea during teatime on the terrace overlooking Kensington Gardens. Alexander Butler took a look at all the pictures of Queen Mary and King William III. They both had died too soon. Mary had died from a bout with smallpox and William had died from injuries from a fall from a nervous horse. In the next room was a library and a room with some tables and board games that the royals used for entertainment. They soon walked down the Kings Staircase and entered into the long hallway by the servants' quarters and exited the palace and headed for home. Alexander had remarked to Butler how beautiful the palace was, but it seemed like the former owners had some happy and unhappy times there. No matter how much power and authority one can have in this world, it cannot be transferred to the next life. Alexander said that he prayed for their eternal happiness. Butler remarked that the Kings and Queens are only a defender of the faith. She also remarked that their earthly lives would always be remembered in the historical records of the country, but only God would know of their personal commitment to Him.

That same year, the word was quickly spreading around London and England that the architect, Christopher Wrenn had died, and his service would be at St. Paul's Cathedral which he had helped to design. Alexander told Butler that he must go and pay his respects. He told her that he had always admired his works since his stay at Chelsea Hospital that Christopher Wrenn had also designed. Alexander went to the service and watch the church laymen as they carried his casket down the steps to the crypt area under the Dome at St. Paul's Cathedral. This would be the final resting place for the 91-year-old man that had designed most of the largest cathedrals and palaces in London. Alexander thought about the days in Virginia when they were finishing the Wrenn Building at William and Mary College and Wrenn's influence on the belfry at Bruton Church in Williamsburg. Wrenn had been blessed by meeting some of the most important people in English history and blessed by living a long time.

On another occasion, Alexander, thought he would take his family to the Tower. The yeoman wardens expected visitors to come to see certain parts of the Tower. The Tower was one of the most formidable fortresses in the world and had been the home of King Henry III and his son, King Edward I of England. In fact, he showed his family the fireplace next to Edward's bed chamber. The fireplace was one of the first of its kind to be used in a building in history. Above the mantle on the fireplace was a painting of Henry III's royal shield which included artwork of the three leopards on the shield. Next to the bedchamber was an altar room where Edward used to pray. These two kings and William the Conqueror had spent considerable amount of the kingdom's money to improve the size and strength of the fortress. The tower consisted of 21 towers connected by a brick and stone wall that formed a fort like structure along the River Thames. Many visitors from other countries docked along the wharf by the Tower and would climb up the steps through the Queens Gate to get to the White tower which was like a hidden palace in the middle of the fortress. Alexander and his family came into the Tower through the West Entrance which was a beautiful entrance designed by Edward I and was a walkway and drawbridge over the moat that drained into the Thames. He told Butler not to be afraid because of the infamous reputation of the Tower. It was used as a prisoner and torture chamber. Many a royal traitor or enemy of the Queen or King had been beheaded or killed here. Alexander pointed out the tower that contained that contained the Royal Mint. Isaac Newton who he had met there almost 25 years ago had died about two years earlier. Also, Alexander pointed where the Board of Ordnance was located and how he had been shown how to get weapons and supplies for his troops at Blenheim. He pointed out one of the ravens, named George, was feeding on a rabbit. Alexander knew that Butler had heard about the Legend of the Ravens many times, Of interest to young John was the menagerie of wild animals that were roaming around on the north side of the North Tower behind the outer wall and between the inner wall of the Tower. There was a combination of tigers, lions, leopards, monkeys, camels, ostriches, birds, elephants, camels, owls, and many others. They required a lot of attention and money to take care of. These animals and their predecessors had been prisoners at the Tower for over 400 years. King James I had made a bottle with a nipple so he could nurse the baby lion cubs to help keep them alive. In fact, some of the kings would wrap the snakes in blankets and keep them warm by a fireplace. Lot of the animals were given as gifts to England from kings and queens of other countries.

Alexander preceded to the White Tower, and he remembered you can take an imposing spiraling staircase that went all the way from the basement to the top of the tower. They finally got to the middle floor where there was. some indoor plumbing. This was one of the first toilets to be used in England and was built long ago. They looked at all the swords and scabbards, orbs, and breastplates that were being stored in the White Tower. They soon grew tired of climbing the turrets spiraling staircase and went outside to eat their lunch. They had packed a lunch of some fried fish and chips. Alexander and Butler and the children soon went down to the wharf area and got on a small sailing vessel. They paid the owner a few pence and he took then for a trip up the Thames River to the docks at Charing Cross and the Savoy House. After their morning outing, they got off the boat and walked up to the Strand so they could get back quickly to their home in Westminster.

Alexander took his family one spring day for an outing to Blenheim Palace at Woodstock, England. This was the home of John Churchill, Alexander's former military boss and his wife, Sarah Churchill, the former boss of Alexander's half-sister, Margaret. Sarah Churchill greeted them at the Palace Gates. Her husband, John had died a few years earlier and had not lived that long after they had taken up residence at Blenheim Palace. The main structure had 9 state rooms and 39 other rooms and was one of the largest and most beautiful homes in England. It had a portico over the front entrance. It had a large tower on each corner of the house to hide the fireplace flues. The hallway that led onto the library of the Palace was 180 feet long. On the hallway walls were some of the finest art and paintings in Europe by well-known artists. The whole structure was surrounded by courtyards, pools, fountains, gardens, and a labyrinth maize covered the 7 acres. Alexander whispered to Butler that he was impressed by the home's architecture and style, and that he could be happy in any home as long as he was with Butler. She looked interested as if this was the type of home, she would like to live in. Alexander again whispered to Butler so Sarah could not hear and possibly be offended; that he had not seen any dining rooms or bedrooms. Alexander must have asked himself, "Where does one eat and sleep?" He thought to himself that Blenheim would make for a beautiful museum instead of a home. Butler was impressed by the architecture.

Sarah, "Do I need all these rooms ? I have one of the largest pipe organs on the English Island and more books in the library than any other person in England. The organ will seldom be played, and the books never read. Alexander, I hear you have been an admirable Lieutenant Governor in Virginia and used your studies in design to build government offices in Williamsburg."

Alexander answered, "Yes, I am quite proud of them."

"Sarah, "John tried to keep up with your journeys when he was still alive. He was proud of having led you at the Battle of Blenheim. He also kept up with your Knights of the Golden Horseshoes. He often talked about all the land west of the Blue Ridge. I always knew you would be successful leader in England. Do you remember his victories in the Wars? Blenheim 1704; Ramillies, 1706; Turin, 1706; and Oudernarde 1708?" Mrs. Churchill, now in her seventies was still beautiful and she now had fine white hair instead of the beautiful brown hair when Alexander first met her. Sarah kept looking at Butler and then would stare at Alexander and then again at Butler, to see if there was any reaction from Butler. I have enjoyed your visit, Mr. and Mrs. Spotswood. I am so proud that you named your toddler John after my husband. I hope he will be handsome like you, Alexander."

Butler in order to avoid embarrassment to her husband, said politely, "I hope he is handsome like his father."

Alexander, "Yes I did name our son John. I remember fondly, Major General John Churchill's victories. Why thank you Mrs. Churchill for the beautiful visit. I have enjoyed the day."

Mrs. Churchill now looking at young John and Ann Catherine being held in her mother's arms, "We think this home is beautiful, but some might think it is too large for one person. Have a safe trip back to London. Give my best wishes to Margaret and Richard."

Alexander said, " I most definitely will."

On the way home Alexander said to Butler, I believe she has to be one of the richest ladies in England, but I also believe that she might be the loneliest, too."

Butler said, " I think so, and I really believe she thinks you named our son after her husband."

Alexander laughing, " I did and also for my great-grandfather."

Butler, "Really. Maybe our John will have a nice home someday, too. It seems like Mrs. Churchill didn't forget you from long ago. "

Alexander, "I hope we don't have a home like that, because it would be too costly to maintain such a capacious mansion. As far as Mrs. Churchill goes, she is a beautiful person who is mostly misunderstood."

Butler smiling, "If you say so. I love you anyway."

When the Spotswoods got back home, there was a pile of letters in the doorway. Alexander began reading the letters which had been written at various dates. Some of the letters were a year old or older Alexander must have thought that there has to be something done about improving the mail service. The letters had described deteriorating conditions at Germanna. Alexander's plantation was experiencing a loss of crops and servants. The weeds and brush were overtaking the yards, orchards, and lawns. The German miners were not renewing their leases and leaving Germanna and going further west in the Virginia's Piedmont. The little village of Germanna was declining as well. Some of the citizens were moving to the fast-growing village of Fredericksburg because of its closer location to the shipping lanes and harbors. Out bound ships at the harbors took tobacco and other commodities to the rest of the world in exchange for supplies to the colony. Some of the citizens were moving to the growing adjacent counties of Spotsylvania, Fauquier, and Orange.

Alexander looked closely at one letter that had been sent by Robert Spotswood. Inside the envelope there was a letter which said, "Mr. Spotswood, I have enclosed a letter that is dated 1716. I found it in an old desk that housed the Spotswood Bible. The letter appeared to be used as a bookmark in the Bible. Since I did not know what was inside the letter or know of its importance to you, I decided to forward it to you in London so it would be in your possession. I trust your life in London is comfortable. I would like for you to come visit soon so you can show me how to improve the business. Sincerely, Robert Spotswood

Alexander, "Butler, please come here. You got some mail from Virginia. "

Butler, "Why, Alexander, what do you mean?" She looked at the old letter addressed to her from 1716. It was the letter that her husband had written years earlier that he said he had mailed and must have got lost somehow in the mail. It was the letter which declared Alexander's love for her, and he had asked Butler to state her feelings for him. It was the lost love letter that Butler had never received. It proved that Alexander was always in love with her and life may have been completely different if Butler had received the letter thirteen years earlier.

Alexander, "Now I know that you never could have received the letter, but how did it get in the Bible?"

Butler," It doesn't matter, now. It was meant for us to be together no matter who or what circumstances tried to keep us apart. God's timing is always right. He did not want me to move to Virginia then or I would have come. I knew you were telling the truth. I love you." She walked to Alexander and hugged him.

Alexander would now reflect on two things. One would be to improve the mail service and the other was that he had to get back to his properties in Virginia.

After living happily five years in England, Alexander and Butler decided they were very much needed in Virginia to keep their colonial businesses going and reverse the spiraling downward trend. The young couple took their young family and would move to the big house by the horseshoe bend in the Rapidan River. Alexander would again take charge of the plantation which allowed their overseers, Robert Spotswood and Mr. Tyler to pursue their own business interests. Alexander would call their new home; Porto Bello and it would take a few years to get the business in Virginia fully operational and profitable.

Alexander verily recognized Germanna after his absence for five years. The German miners had abandoned all their homes. The original 9 houses that had been built within the fort had deteriorated dramatically. Alexanders livestock was scattered all around the town. The tavern was the only business that had remained. There were only about half of the servants and farm workers still there. Most had either run away or moved on west to the new settlements west of the Blue Ridge Mountains. It looked like a hopeless situation, but Alexander made up his mind that he would restore Germanna to its original glory. It would take a few years to get everything beautiful and functioning again and increase the plantation's profitability. Butler was used to the big city of London and not used to seeing primitive conditions. She was not used to seeing cattle, deer, and forest animals living uncontrolled all around her. She was used to well-kept lawns and gardens. The front and back yard had no gardens and the grounds were overrun with brush, weeds, and saplings. They both knew that they had a lot of work and planning to do. Nevertheless, Butler was overjoyed at finally having a place of her own. She would miss seeing her family and friends in Westminster, but she now had a big house and 80,000 acres of land to help take care of. The children, John and Ann Catherine found a place to play on the porch on the big house. John was now 4 years old and Ann Catherine was now three years of age was oblivious to the challenging conditions facing their loving parents.

Butler certainly did like having a big house of her own. It was still in pretty good shape. The three-story house of stone and timber had weathered well in the last few years. Butler had always wanted to have horses and now she had plenty of them and land to ride them around Germanna. From the front portico of the main house, they had a beautiful view of large green meadows across the river below the house. The meadows were full of tall grass and beautiful wildflowers. The home was full of the finest furniture brought over from England. It was a comfortable spacious house. It was a far cry from what she had expected. She had imagined it would be a small cabin nestled in the woods. Porto Bello was a large elegant house modeled after the Palace in Williamsburg. Butler was so proud and happy and could see the potential to improve her new home as one of the finest in the Colony. She now had time to see that the gardens and orchards and lawns were all restored. She liked planting flowers and designing gardens. She loved the idea of having servants wait on her and the children. Butler's sister., Dorothea had reluctantly come along from England to help with the domestic duties, seemed happy with her new living conditions and went to see what her room would be like. It was elegant and spacious, also. Things improved with the property as the months went by. The family was growing, too. Alexander and Butler had another baby in 1731. They would name the little girl, Dorothea after her aunt. Dorothea and the servants would also look after the little girl so that Butler would have more time to be with Alexander. The family was happy and prosperous.

Because of Alexander's political ties and his popularity in England and Virginia, he finally got the chance to improve the mail service in the Colony of Virginia. He was appointed Deputy Postmaster General of the American Colonies. This was quite an honor and a demanding position. It would require him to travel from Porto

Bello to all the colonies in the New World. Butler would support him because she had known of Alexander 's frustration of getting his own letters to their final destination in a reasonable amount of time. He worked diligently so that a letter could leave Germanna and get to Philadelphia in the Colony of Pennsylvania in ten days . In the past it would have taken months to get a letter between the two places. While on one trip he met a young man, he couldn't wait to tell Butler about. It was one of his postmasters in Philadelphia. His name was Benjamin Franklin. Alexander told Butler that he stood out in his work and was a very interesting fellow. Alexander also said that when Benjamin was not working on improving the mail service, he experimented with lightning and worked on other science projects. Alexander told Butler that this young man was very witty and also wrote stories that he occasionally would get published. He surmised that Benjamin was extremely talented and truly had gifts from God. Alexander told his wife he predicted that Benjamin Franklin, postmaster would become a famous person.

In 1732, Alexander's political foe, Mr. William Byrd came by the plantation for a visit. William Byrd, handsome as ever, was still on the Assembly in Williamsburg. He had been on a business trip checking on some of his property in the new lands west of the Blue Ridge. Alexander came out of the main house to greet his old friend.

William Byrd was sitting in a handsome carriage waiting for his driver to get down to the ground first and then the driver would help Mr. Byrd down. Mr. Byrd walked up towards the main house and gave his old friend, Alexander a big handshake. He said, "Alexander, I don't know how you continue to be successful. You lost all your German tenants to the western frontiers. Your iron ore mines have produced no iron ore in years, Eighty percent of your servants and laborers ran off while you were away in London. Your tobacco crops failed a few times and yet you don't give up and you still are in business. In fact, your business is flourishing. You have turned your business around and you are making large profits. Is that not true, Colonel?"

Alexander, "I owe it to hard work, clean living, and my beautiful wife, Butler. As soon as my servant can get your belongings out from the carriage, we will walk up to our little home." The house was 120 feet by 40 feet and contained about 12,000 square feet of living space. Butler and her sister, Dorothea were coming down the stairs from the third floor. They had been busy looking out from the balcony and enjoying the view of the river and meadows to the west of the House. They were dressed in beautiful clothes. There were deer walking all around the great room downstairs, prancing from one piece of furniture to the next. The arrival of Mr. Byrd had startled the deer and they begin turning over the furniture and breaking the glassware in the china closet and all this commotion did not seem to bother the Spotswoods. Alexander was amazed that so few deer could cause that much clutter. One of the deer came over to Butler and she began petting the deer. One of the deer stared at Mr. Byrd. Alexander had a flashback to the time. Roger had told him about a beautiful princess who was a sultan's daughter. When her parents had got captured and taken to the neighboring sultan's camp, she hid in the woods and lived in the woods with the deer and the gazelles. Eventually she was caught and taken to the neighboring sultan and she married the prince, the sultan's son and they lived happily eve rafter. Butler could have been a beautiful princess and Alexander wanted her to be happy ever after. Alexander also remembered Byrd's prediction in 1710 about him marrying a beautiful English lady and there would be wild animals in his mansion house in Virginia.

Mr. Byrd said, "You have more than a little home! You possess an Enchanted Castle." He continued to look at all the activity and Butler and addressed her, "You must be the beautiful Ms. Spotswood. The deer seem to be fond of you. I had visions of you twenty-two years ago when I first met Alexander. I said that he one day he would have the most beautiful wife in Virginia and that she would be entertaining forest animals which seemed odd to me at the time. You are beautiful and more charming than anyone could imagine. "

Butler blushing art Byrd's boldness, " Yes, I am Butler Spotswood. Our children like to play with the deer. They mean no harm but sometimes get in the way. You are most kind about my appearance, but I am very blessed to have Alexander as my husband."

Mr. Byrd, "I am William Byrd. Your husband's best friend." He smiled at his own remarks and looked at Dorothea. "You must be Ms. Theky soon to be Mrs. Beninger. I knew a beautiful girl once who called herself Miss Theky. I will call you that if you don't mind."

Dorothea giggled, "I would not mind."

Butler, "I have heard my husband speak about you several times but always in a respectful way."

William Byrd, " I couldn't help but notice all the white flowers that are planted around the base of your enchanted castle here. The house and flowers are beautiful and elegant for a beautiful lady."

Butler, "Thank you for the compliment. There is an old superstition that if you plant white mums around the house, you will always be faithful in your marriage, and you will live a long time. For traditions sake, I have put a horseshoe above the door for good luck and coins under the doorstep so we will always have money coming into the house." "

Alexander, "Butler reads a lot. In fact, she probably knows the Bible and can recite the Bible verses as Mr. Thompson up at the Parish Church."

William Byrd, "Lady Spotswood, I have heard that Reverend Thompson is very handsome and is very learned in his preaching. Would you agree?"

Butler hesitantly, "Why yes I agree," She glanced at Alexander as if she knew that William Byrd was trying to provoke a debate and get Alexander jealous. "Mr. Byrd, I love only my husband and really do not think about other men that way."

Alexander was smiling as Butler was handling herself very well with Mr. Byrd. William who didn't miss a chance to charm the ladies.

Byrd continued, "Yes I see that your wife is a very attractive and an educated lady. She is very beautiful, Alexander. Why, she is more beautiful than Ms. Thornton and she was considered the most beautiful woman in Virginia. "

Alexander quickly identified Ms. Thornton, "Ms. Thornton was my aide, when I was Lieutenant Governor."

William Byrd, " She had cold black hair and the bluest eyes. She was smart as a fox, too. She left Williamsburg in 1722 and hasn't been seen or heard of since. She was last seen headed for the Atlantic Ocean. It was the strangest thing. She always seemed so full of life and was so polite. She said that she had only loved one man in her life and that man would not ask her to marry him. She had told the man that she would wait forever for him. Anyway, how do you like it here at the Castle? You do know that I am impressed with your husband's skill and judgment. He has a heart of gold and good business sense."

The deer ran outside the door to the garden.

William Byrd, "Don't the deer bother you when they are running through the house? Long ago, I told your husband that he would live in a beautiful castle with a beautiful wife and with many animals."

Butler answered, "Not really. I don't mind the animals. They are God's creatures, too. They don't usually stay long when they are around."

Byrd, " Alexander, you may not know that I married again in the same year that you and Butler were married. In 1724, I married Ms. Maria Taylor who was one of the most beautiful ladies in England. I met her parents in London, and they gave their permission right away for us to marry. I don't know if it was because she was 18, and they thought she might become an old maid if they didn't get her married right away. Anyway, she has pretty dark hair and beautiful dark eyes and some man would say that she was a good catch. She reminded me a little of Ms. Thornton. I always wondered why more men didn't notice Ms. Thornton's beauty and why she did not make advances towards me after my first wife died. My young wife speaks French and Greek and is submissive like most English wives. She loves Virginia and we have three daughters and a son William III now to look after. Lucy, my child by my first wife, is grown, out on her own and successful like me."

Alexander, "I am glad you are happy, William. We would be glad for you and your family to come here as our guests. "

William Byrd, "I did want to see you and meet your family. I also came to look at the iron ore furnaces . It is a miracle that they are producing anything at all. I also want to thank you for the land patent of 22,000 acres you put in for me on the Dan River. I will have Peter Jefferson or Robert Brooke survey it for me so I can sell it. "

Alexander, "You are welcome. I was just thinking that it was 16 years ago that we went over the Blue Ridge Mountains. In another 4 years we will have our reunion in Williamsburg.

William Byrd," I am going to write a story about our journey. I read John Fontane's diary of events , and I will write my own version of the journey. It will be very romantic."

Byrd spent a few days visiting the Spotswoods at Porto Bello. They had dinners of game and plenty of food. There were many servants available to make the stay comforting for Mr. Byrd. Byrd and Alexander reminisced about the good ole days in Williamsburg. Several of their friends had passed away, Robert Beverly had died and had left a journal about Williamsburg, his wine making operation at his home, Beverly Park, and his glorious time as being one of the Knights of the Golden Horseshoes. They also talked about their old friend, Hugh Jones, a minister who said that when he died, he wanted to be buried facing west and he wanted all the parishioners when they died to be buried facing east which was customary. Byrd said that his wishes had been complied with. Byrd said that James Blair was still on the Council and that he was still the Rector of Bruton Parish Church and he was active at William and Mary College. Byrd said that even though Blair was in his seventies, and in declining health, he still would supervise projects at the college by expanding the Library and Indian School. The college was still building a new wing adjacent to the old building. Both Byrd and Alexander believed him to be a dedicated pastor and was one of the most influential men in Virginia in promoting the Church of England. He was well respected for trying to improve the educational training of the children of the wealthy planters. Byrd also said that Blair had never said any disparaging words about Alexander and respected him for getting money for the college, Williamsburg, and the church. Alexander kept thinking about his personal dismissal as lieutenant governor and why it happened. For a while he was bitter and had bad feelings about the removal. In time he would accept it as the Lord must be calling him to do something else. It did allow him to pursue a gentleman's life in the country with a beautiful wife and children. He thought that all the arguing and debating in the Assembly had happened for good reason. It had made for a better Colony by getting different points of view from Byrd and Blair and accepting some of their ideas. Alexander told Byrd that this was the best time in his life when he moved to his estate. Byrd said that he could tell by the way Alexander seemed to enjoy life and by the way he was playing with his young children.

After breakfast one morning, Byrd said, "I had better get back to Westover. Alexander, I will see you in 4 years at the reunion of The Golden Horseshoes, God willing. I will write favorably about you and about your administration and your business acumen. I will say that I was impressed with your leadership in the home and how you teach your children," Byrd pulled out a bag of gold before he left and handed it to the Colonel. "Here is a pistole of gold for everyone in the household and every one of your servants can get a little piece of gold. Let's say I need to pay an old debt and you may consider it as a housewarming gift. "

Alexander, " I will graciously accept your generous gift on behalf of my family and my servants." No one would probably figure out why Mr. Byrd had performed another act of kindness. He soon got back in the handsome carriage and left for his plantation.

Butler said, "Well if I didn't know better, I think he was trying to make you and me jealous."

Alexander, "I knew you were going to ask me about Ms. Thornton. I never had any kind of relationship except a proper working relationship. "

Butler, ""I believe you. The way Mr. Byrd described her; she was not meant to be with you."

Alexander said, "This is why I love you so much." He kissed her on her hand as she sat by the fireplace.

In 1733, another son was born to the Spotswoods. They named him Robert after Alexander's father and Grandfather Spotswood. This family now contained 4 children. The children played well together and enjoyed learning from their mother and father.

Four years after Byrd's visit to Germanna, the Golden Knights of the Horseshoes had their reunion in Williamsburg in 1736 as planned back in 1716. They met at Liddendale's which was still a popular place to eat and drink. Alexander started the meeting by saying how fast the last 20 years had gone by since the trip over the Blue Ridge Mountains. He said that he was still thankful that he had such a talented group of distinguished and merry gentlemen to help make that journey twenty years earlier. He began to read a list of the explorers and knights. Alexander stated that John Fontaine has written a book about the journey. He had married Mary Sabaterre and lives in Wales. Mr. Beverly who also published some stories about the journey and died in 1722. He however will be most famous for his book, *The History of Virginia* written in 1705. George Mason III has just gone on to be with the Lord and his son, George Mason IV is already a great orator. Augustine Smith died in 1726 but helped his father and brother develop Temple Farm in Yorktown. He also is one of the founding fathers of Fredericksburg. James Taylor died at Hare Forest in Orange County in 1729. He continued to read several other names of knights dead or alive and whether they were present or unable to attend. Alexander said, "Now we will begin by re-introducing ourselves to those of you who are still alive and well, and we will entertain a brief speech from each one of you."

William Todd began, " I am William Todd of Toddsberry. It is debatable whether I am alive and well." The knights chuckled. "I think we killed every rattlesnake in Virginia on our trip." More laughter. "I was very honored to have one of the journey's camps named after me."

Jeremiah Crowder. "I am Jeremiah Crowder who did not get a camp named after me. I am a trustee for the City of Fredericksburg. I enjoyed the company and stories around the campfire every night of the Journey. I did get a creek named after me. "

William Robertson, "I don't have to introduce myself because I was Clerk of the Council and I can't remember if I had a camp named for me. I did have a rich experience and thanks for helping me get richer. I am a trustee at

William and Mary College."

Robert Brooke, " I am Robert Brooke. I am still a proud surveyor like my father. I have obtained 200.000 acres of land thanks to Alexander Spotswood and King George. I am in competition with Mr. William Byrd as one of the largest landowners in Virginia. I have revisited the place where we crossed the mountain several times and I think we had one of the biggest claims of land in the Colonies in the New World. "

John Robinson, " I am John Robinson who was the quiet one on the trip. I have enjoyed being on the Council and for making the expedition over the mountain. My cousin, Christopher also made the journey 20 years ago and he died in 1727 and left his plantation, Hewick. to his children. I like the fact the Robinson River was named for us during the journey. "

William Byrd, " I am probably the largest landowner in Virginia, and I was very proud to take part in the journey. I have been accused of being the founder of the city of Richmond in the Royal Colony of Virginia. As I have not as yet been called on to serve as the Colony's Governor or President of the Council. I did find favor with Governor Gooch and was commissioned by him for two great missions. I led the Commission for The Dividing Line between North Carolina and Virginia. I also was on the Commission of the Northern Neck of Virginia surveying the millions of acres around Maryland and Virginia and around the Potomac River and Rappahanock River. I also assisted Governor Gooch to get The Tobacco Act of 1730 passed. Some of you may remember that I argued strongly against this act when Alexander Spotswood originated the same idea in 1713. It took me 17 years to see that Governor Spotswood was correct on this. I will admit I was wrong. In the diaries and books, I write, I will identify myself as a senior counselor for the colony of Virginia. I was born in Virginia and I will die in Virginia. I am one of the most respected men in the room because I helped keep us in stock of food and drinks for the Knights of the Golden Horseshoes so we could toast our leaders."

Jeremiah Crowder, " I don't remember you being on the journey but if you say you were, it must be true. It was just too long ago to remember. I do remember that you are never at a loss for words. I didn't mention it earlier, but I also remember the pretty view from Mt. George and Mt. Alexander. We made history that day and I am proud of that. "

Alexander," I personally thank all you gentlemen for your contributions to Spotswood Journey. It would be a good time to toast our King George I who died a few years ago and may God rest his soul."

All the men raised their glasses, they all cheered, "Here's to King George I."

Alexander, "Let's toast to the present king, King George II. God, save the King so he reigns a long time over us. God save the King. "

All the men raised their glasses and said, "Here's to King George II. God, save the King."

Robert Brooke, "Let's toast to Gertrude, the daughter of King George I and sister to King George II as the prettiest monarch in England."

All the men raised their glasses, "Here's to Princess Gertrude."

Robertson, "Let's toast the entire Royal Family."

All the men raised their glasses and said, "Here's to the Royal Family. "

William Byrd, "Let's toast the Knights of the Golden Horseshoes."

All the men raised their glasses, "Here's to the Knights"

William Byrd, " I propose a toast to the Leader of the Knights and one of the best royal governors we have had, Alexander Spotswood. When we go outside, lets fire a round of volleys for Col. Spotswood like old times."

The men raised their glasses and said, "Here's to Alexander Spotswood." The men all put down their glasses and picked up their rifles and guns and went outside and fired a round of shots to honor their leader. After the salute was finished, they came back into the tavern.

Col. Alexander Spotswood, "I enjoyed being the Lt. Governor of Virginia but at the same time, I had bad feelings and bitterness for a while that I was removed from that office by my friend, Mr. Byrd and Mr. Ludwell, an ambitious Burgess. Actually, they did me a favor. I could not go to my grave unless everyone forgives me of my bitterness at the time of my removal, and I forgive those trying to discredit my hard work. I only wanted the best for Virginia. After being removed from office, I was able to marry and begin a family and enjoy the life of a country gentleman. Thank you again for the nice toast and salute."

William Byrd, "I respect the fact that you were able to see a brighter and better future for Virginia after the Journey. When Alexander came into office, there were only a handful of people in Virginia. Twenty years later, there are over 180,000 citizens. This is a big increase and is due to the expansion of Virginia's land west of the Blue Ridge Mountains. I propose another toast to Governor Spotswood. He is deserving."

The men raised their glasses and said, "Here's to Alexander Spotswood." And as on the journey twenty years earlier, they had many drinks at Liddendales to choose from. They drank of Virginia red wine, white wine, rum, cider, champagne, subsequah, ale, and water.

William Todd, " I would propose we meet again in 20 years, but the only ones who will probably be alive are Robert Brooke and John Fontaine. We should be thankful to Fontaine, Beverly, and Hugh Jones, William Byrd, and a few others for writing in their letters, diaries, and books the story of a merry band of gentlemen and its strong leader to conquer the Blue Ridge Mountain and claiming all the land for England. It will be up to history books and descendants to tell the true story of what happened on September 5th, 1716. They enjoyed the evening and the later the evening went, the taller the stories and the tales grew. They all left the meeting proud of what they had accomplished, and they had a memorable evening.

Alexander's plantation was doing well, and his crops were consistently successful. His business in England was also profitable. He spent a lot of time with Butler and they discussed the children and how they could be educated and what their careers might be. Robert seemed like he wanted to be a soldier as he tried to get his older brother John to play soldiers and war games with him. Ann Catherine and Dorothea would go to a private school and probably would marry into well to do families. John, the eldest would probably take over the estate and be the overseer, but he would still need a good education.

One day, he received a letter from the Admiralty Office in England. Apparently , he was getting news about an upcoming war between England and Spain. At the age of 63, he felt he still could lead his men as they wanted him to be a Brigadier General in the English Army. He would get instructions to go to Annapolis in the Colony of Maryland and get a briefing on what to do about leading his men to Cartagena in South America where the Spanish had a stronghold. Apparently, there was someone in England who knew of his military leadership skills during the battle of Blenheim 36 years earlier. He would welcome the challenge.

Alexander made some important decisions in his life. For changes in his personal life and his business life. Before he would depart for Cartagena, he would prepare as if he would not come back from war. He would resign his job as Deputy Postmaster. He would get his last will and testament in order. He would list all his debts and assets. He went to the Orange County Courthouse, the newest and closest courthouse to his land holdings, and prepared the will so that his executors would know his wishes on financial manners if he was killed in the war. He ran ads about selling his iron ore furnaces and personal property. He listed his land, his home, his carriages, horses, and livestock in all the largest cities' newspapers. He wrote a letter to the Admiralty Office and said he wanted to serve his country again. He said that he could not be considered a Christian if he held a grudge against the government for taking his governorship away. He said that the government had always treated him fairly, otherwise. He knew he had to tell Butler about his decisions and that she would ask him if he had prayed about all this and let the Lord lead.

Butler, "You know I love you and the children. I have been asked to be a Brigadier General in the British Army to make a land invasion in Cartagena, South America. I do not know if I will be killed in the war and return to you. I will always love you. I have written a will and it is in the Orange County Courthouse to explain how you and the children will be provided for. If I get killed in the war, I want you to feel free to remarry and live your life fully. I will try to not to upset the children now with this and hope that I can come home again. I have also written to Margaret about my affairs. I will have her promise to look after you and the children. I forwarded her some letters of instructions that I want her to faithfully to hand to John when he becomes of age. She knows about some of the legal and business holdings, too. Margaret only wants the best for you and the children."

Butler, with fright in her eyes, "Please don't talk like that Alexander. You will come back to me and the children. "

Alexander, "The faithful star, Sothis has followed me all my life. It has had the same journey that I have had. It has not been in the sky for a while now. I have had this vision and this feeling that I would not be here on earth that much longer. It may not be the war that causes my demise. The vision made me think how I have lived my life. I must prepare for my death. I am not afraid to die. I want you tell our children that if I do not return, how much I love them. I remember seeing my father's face when he was lying on his death bed and trying to smile at me . He was trying to make me think that everything would be fine, and he did not want me to worry. He eventually died and I felt sad, but I felt better thinking he had gone on to a better place. I have not slept well for nights. I keep having visions of Blackbeard's ghost. His father was the one that put the curse on me when I was a young boy. In these visions, Blackbeard asks me if I killed him to get revenge for his father's curse that he put on me. He also asks me if I found all the buried treasure that is buried up and down the coasts of Virginia and Carolinas. Then I picture his head sitting on a pole at Hampton Roads. Then I snap out of it as if I am having a nightmare."

Butler, "You have a fever. You are rambling with your words and stories. I love you; Alexander, and I know you believe all this, but it is hard for me to believe these stories. Are you happy with me and the children?"

Alexander, "I love you more than you will ever know. I have been the happiest in my life after the pirate's curse was broken years ago. These last years have been my happiest. Butler, you are so patient, kind, and loving. I adored you from the first time I saw you. I adore our children. I feel like I am being called away. I think the curse kept me away from serving the Lord like I should have. He will be just and forgive me. I have been on this journey of highs and lows in my life. You meet good people and you meet some bad. I have only had one main journey and that was down the path of righteousness to everlasting life. The journey to Toubkal in Morocco, the journey to England, the journey to Virginia, and the Journey over the Blue Ridge Mountains were small in comparison."

Butler, "Alexander, please stop with this talk. You are scarring me with your fever. I don't want to lose you. Please don't leave me. We will take care of you until the fever is gone. Surely, someone else can lead the men in the war. You need rest." Alexander put his arms around her to comfort her and then he kissed her on the forehead.

Alexander, "I have to be going soon. It will be fine. We have had a good life and for this I am thankful. I believe it is not how long you live but how well you live your life that is important. I have tried to live a life pleasing to my Heavenly Father and have been grateful to him for forgiving my sins. When I saw the star the other night, it was almost like it was guiding me to do this. It is like it has followed me since Toubkal. I can't even explain it. I believe it to be from the Lord and not from the Devil. The star has carried me through ever difficulty on my journey. Please take care of our children and continue to teach them what matters. They will need the Lord to guide them. I love you. I love you. I will always be with you. "You need rest." Alexander put his arms around her to comfort her ands then he kissed her on her forehead.

Alexander weakly said, "Do not worry. I am in God's hands. I do need to rest. I will go to our bedroom and rest for a while." He feebly walked up the stairs towards the upstairs bedrooms and living quarters. Butler dropped her head and had a concerned and worried look on her face and a faraway look in her beautiful tear-filled eyes. She went into the parlor and gazed at the warm fire in the stone fireplace. It was therapeutic. For a moment in time she felt as though the Lord was speaking to her by using Alexander's reassuring words to make her feel that everything would be all right.

The older son, John was now 15 and inquisitive like his father. He came into the big house from the big yard by the parlor. He had been overseeing and entertaining his brother and sisters. John saw that his mother had chosen one of the tapestry covered chairs to rest from her household duties. John sensed something was wrong because she would always smile when he came into her presence. This time she was looking away from him as if spellbound by the fire from the burning logs in the fireplace.

John delicately asked his mother, "Mother, is everything all right? Is it because father is leaving for war? He has fought in many battles and he will return to us safely."

Butler turned around to look directly at John and smiled, "You know that we love you, your brother, and your sisters and we want the best for you. It is not the war I am worried about. I feel your father needs to see a doctor and is not well enough to leave the house and go to South America. He has a high fever and is sweating profusely."

John asked, "May I go see him?"

Butler answered, "Why yes. I think he would like that, but don't wake him if he is asleep."

John said, "I will do as you say." John went up the stairs to the bedroom where his father had retired to check on him. John entered the room and his father was staring out the bedroom window. On hearing John's footsteps coming into the room, Alexander was looking at his son and smiling."

John asking, "Father, are you well? Are you sick? Maybe you can postpone going to war until you feel better."

Alexander, "I will be fine soon." He kept smiling as he was very proud of the good manners of his son. "I want you to know that I will always be proud of you and I love you and that is all you need to know for now. If anything happens to me, I want you to be the leader of the house and take care of your mother, Ann, Dorothea, and Robert. Will you promise me you will, John?" Alexander was obviously in pain and still had fever and was sweating.

John promised, "As I am a Spotswood, you have my word and my honor on that, sir. You can count on me." Alexander was pleased on hearing this and drifted back to sleep. John went downstairs and told his mother that his father was resting and didn't mention the conversation that he and his father has just had on the family's future. John did not want to upset his loving mother.

Letter to Margaret Giles and husband, Reverend Richard Giles on The Golden Square in Westminster, England

May 25th, 1740,

My beautiful and dearest sister,

I have not written much lately, but I felt it necessary to inform you of some upcoming events in my life that may affect my family's future. And I also want to tell you of my love and admiration for you. You have meant a lot to me and I want to thank you for always supporting me and looking out for my best interests. You and Richard mean everything to me.

I am, getting older with the uncertainties of good health. I will also be leading 2500 men into battle with the Spanish in South America. I do not want to appear pessimistic, but you are aware of the risks to life on the battlefield. In case of my death on the battlefield, I am sending you some instructions on what to do about assisting Butler and my four children. I have amply provided for their financial and business needs as best as I can. My will is in the Orange County Courthouse in the Colony of Virginia. My executors will be Butler, my cousin Elliott Beneger, and the Reverend Robert Rose of St. Anne's Parish in Essex County, Virginia. The will adequately explains what should be done with the business and personal property. I have had a great life and may live a long time. I regret that we have not had the opportunity to visit as much as I have wanted. I am not scared of death. I believe Jesus died for our sins and he is the only way we can be saved from eternal damnation. I hope we can see each other again. Sincerely, Your loving brother, Alexander Spotswood

---

After a few hours' sleep, Alexander woke up and came downstairs. He saw Butler in the parlor. He said, "I have to be going soon. It will be fine. We have had a good life and for this, I am thankful. I believe it is not how long you live your life but how well you live your life that is important. I have tried to live a life that is pleasing to the Heavenly Father and I have been grateful to Him for saving me from my sins. I am very grateful that you are my wife. When I saw the star the other night. It was almost like it was guiding me to do this. It is like it has followed me from Toubkal. I can't even explain it. I believe it is from the Lord and not from the Devil. The star has carried me on every difficulty on my journey. Please take care of our children and continue to teach them to be faithful, obedient, and to have good manners. They will need the Lord to guide them. I love you. I love you. I will always be with you." He then hugged and kissed Butler.

The day came when Alexander stood at the balcony of his enchanted castle overlooking the Rapidan River. The water was swiftly carrying the water towards the ocean. His thoughts may have been of past times and places.

He had thoughts of his father and mother and Aunt Bethia and all the great stories they had told him. He had thoughts about Roger and Margaret and her husbands. He thought about the Braynes and the all the people he had met in London. He though about Queen Anne. He remembered fondly John and Sarah Churchill. He had pleasant thoughts of Tangier, Williamsburg, his trips to Toubkal and the Blue Ridge Mountains. He thought about Byrd and Blair and the Assembly Men. He remembered his hospital stay and wondered about what happened to Barbara Villiers. He wondered if Ms. Thornton had ever got married. He thought about his voyages with Edward alias Blackbeard, Tancred Robinson, and the other Captains. He remembered about the curse that hat been put on him by Redbeard and then getting his sword back into his possession from Blackbeard when the curse was broken. He remembered his church services with George Mercer, Rev. Wesley, Reverend Tinsley, James Blair, and John Thompson and all the others. He had a flashback of his 16 years serving in the British Army and all the deaths he had seen on the many battlefields. It had been for the most part a blessed life in Africa, England, and Colonial Virginia. He had been respected by friends and foes for his hard work and honest labors. In the front yard he could see his four beautiful children, and they were his pride and joy. Ann and Dorothea were playing with their dolls and showing each other how to care for them. Robert was pretending that he was a soldier and using a limb from a tree that had blown off from the wind and was using it as a make-believe sword in battle. He was also pretending that John was his French enemy. It appeared to Alexander that his children were not worried about anything. He knew deep down inside that they would have a successful life. He did not know what awaited ahead for him. He had prepared his belongings so he could make the trip from Germanna to Annapolis to get his commission and orders for the war in Cartagena. He called the family together in the great ball room. Butler is trying to appear happy. The children are asking why they all can't go to Cartagena. He smiles and tells them he will see them again real soon.

He kissed Butler and said, "I promise to write you this time. You know that I have helped improve the mail service." She smiled a wry smile because the delivery of mail had always been a concern of his.

Butler and the 4 children watched as he mounted his horse. He started to gallop toward the wagon road eastward towards Williamsburg. Butler and the children waved to him as long as they could see him, and he soon went over a hill where they couldn't see him anymore. In a few days he arrived at the Army post in Annapolis.

Alexander traveled to the Army Post in Annapolis and waited for his orders so he can leave for Cartegena. He received his assignment but one of the generals told him to lie down because he looked feverish. He laid down but had already came down with a case of malaria and died on June 7, 1740. The general sent a messenger to Alexander's family and tells them of the sad news. The news of Alexander's death spread rapidly. The coroner would not have enough time to get his body back to Germanna before it would deteriorate in the hot summer heat. They managed to get his body on a sailing vessel and take the body by boat to Yorktown. The body soon arrived at the dock at Yorktown. The undertaker was greeted by Robert Smith. He told them that they could use the Smith Family cemetery on Temple Farm to bury Alexander after the memorial service. The farm was only a few miles from Yorktown and one of the places that the Governor liked to stay when he was not in Williamsburg or Porto Bello. Robert explained that his brother, Augustine was a friend of Alexander and had been one of his Knights of the Golden Horseshoes.

Mrs. Spotswood and the children soon arrived in Yorktown for the memorial service with the help of Pastor Thompson. He had brought them by carriage from Porto Bello. The service began. The pastors did not even know where to start in explaining the many noble achievements of Alexander Spotswood. Butler and the four children ranging in age from 3 to 15 were crying uncontrollably. Their sudden loss was Heaven's gain. A great explorer, military man, governor, planter, architect and man of letters who had been a child of God had come to the end of a journey that had begun in a remote garrison in Morocco, Africa. The family would see better days, but they had just lost a great family man. Many in the service came forward to offer their praise and eulogies.

The last speaker to come up and speak was William Byrd, the respected Councilor.

William Byrd said, "For the first time in my 66 years on earth, I am speechless. I thought I would be able to speaks hours about this great man. I don't know where to even begin to tell how many great things he has accomplished in his journey in life. I agree with all the previous speakers and their statements of gratitude and appreciation for this man. I met him 30 years ago in a drug store in Williamsburg. While we drank tea and chatted, I could tell that we differed greatly in our politics but I generally thought of him as a likeable, handsome, young man full of vigor and enthusiasm in his new job as lieutenant governor of the Colony of Virginia, a very prestigious position. I liked his passion for ideas and learning and his stubbornness for his beliefs. I could tell that he was a brother in Christ, and I would have been proud if he had been a blood brother to me. I have already written many favorable stories about Alexander in my writings, so you already know of my admiration for him. He good make and take a good fight or debate. He showed no fear as a leader. Yet, he loved people and especially his family. The only true love of his life was his wife, Butler. That is the only lady that he confided to me that he loved, and he wanted her to be his wife. They were blessed by having four children. One of his lifelong goals he obtained. He crossed over the Blue Ridge Mountains and improved the western expansion of his beloved colony of Virginia. The other lifelong goal he obtained was that he again restored the name of Spotswood as important in historical events. The name Spotswood will never be forgotten. The one gift he had that most people do not have is the ability to go from humble beginnings on his journey to being one of the most respected men in England and the Colony of Virginia. This was caused by his determination to be directed by the paths of the Lord. He also knew that earth was a temporary home and he would have an eternal home in the Heavens. He knew about the power of the stars and the moon, but his first love was the Lord. My hope that his descendants will be many, as many as the stars in the sky. God knows that the earth needs more people like him and exhibit his outstanding qualities. Alexander, I miss you as the others miss you, and many of us and I will see you again one day in Heaven. May you rest in peace , friend, till we meet again."

William Byrd then put a bouquet of flowers consisting of white mums on top of the casket and nodded at Ms. Butler Spotswood to signify that her marriage had been faithful. He also put a blue ribbon on the English flag that had draped the coffin. The blue ribbon had the words, "Leader of the Knights of the Golden Horseshoes" embroidered on the cloth as it lay draped on the casket. He looked over the crowd and he looked like he seen a ghost. Byrd saw a lady sitting in the crowd that looked like Ms. Thornton but she had gray hair. Could it be her? He had not seen her for 18 years and he was not sure if that was her. Also, he thought he saw Alexander sitting in the crowd. He later found out this was Robert Spotswood, whom he had met in 1722 at Liddendale's and also had been the overseer of The Enchanted Castle or Porto Bello while Alexander was in London finding his bride. After the service, Butler thanked William Byrd for his kind remarks and introduced him to Rev. John Thompson who was the pastor at her church and had brought the Spotswood family to Temple Farm for the memorial service.

The undertaker quickly made a tombstone which simply said, "Governor Spotswood, 1676 to 1740," by the freshly dug grave at Temple Farm. When the mourners and family got to the graveyard, the sky began to flash with lights and the sun would get dark and then get bright again and this went on for a few minutes. Alexander's children became scared. The ceremony continued and some Soldiers performed the customary gun salute. Colonel Spotswood was dressed in his military uniform. After some closing remarks at the graveside by Pastor Thompson, a rainbow with brilliant colors appeared in the sky and it seemed as though it started at one end of Yorktown and the other end went in the direction of Williamsburg, several miles away. Butler found comfort in that she believed this was a sign her husband had made it to his eternal home. She could see a brilliant light shining down towards her and the crowd. .

When they got home later that evening, Butler got the children to sleep even though they were still upset about all the days' activities. Butler went to the balcony of her enchanted castle and looked up into the nighttime sky.

Lights started to cross the sky from one corner of the horizon to another corner of the horizon. It looked like meteors going from corner to corner of the skies. The light shows quickly stopped almost as quickly as it started. Next to Sothis now a constellation of stars had appeared in the form of a horseshoe with the stars looking like the nails in a horseshoe formation. Butler wondered if she was seeing things . She asked herself, "Am I the only one that can see this? Is it a signal saying that everything is fine at the end of our journey? I will always love you, Alexander. I will be there, soon."

The journey of life for Alexander Spotswood had begun in humble and modest surroundings in a naval garrison and ended in an army barracks far away from home. He had restored the name of Spotswood to prominence. His earthly life had just ended, and his eternal life was just beginning.

Spotswood's Journey by Robert G. Taylor

I had a vision in my sleep,
That at my grave no one would weep.
The mourners would be glad for me
That my lifelong journey had ceased to be.
They believed I was in Jesus's swaddling arm,
As the bier laid gently deep in Temple Farm.

I had been ill for many days and nights,
And fever and cures caused supernatural sights.
And I will explain unknowns best I can,
what lead to my demise, my view, firsthand?
My journey had many highs and lows,
Old age the cause and stress of earthly foes.

My visions continued as I slept,
A feeling came to me that no one wept,
Cause my friends knew I was home at last.
Only good times now, the bad left in the past.
The joy and laughter at Heaven's door,
Matched only what Jesus has in store.

I began my spiritual life at birth,
And in Tangier , I grew up on earth.
I was an English doctor's son and had to be
at the naval garrison by the sea.
My mother was a loving and caring one,
Taught me about God's love and then some.

Half-sisters and Half-brother were always there

to help me learn and had stories to share.
The life we had behind the Mole,
Was happy, carefree and full of whoa.
Till one day a pirate put me under a curse,
and I thought my life would be the worst.

The curse given to me seemed tame,
That I would be rich, handsome, and have fame.
For while this seemed to be my lot,
and trouble and misery were all I got.
The curse was broken later in life,
After schooling and work, but before the wife.

When I got married, I took on a new life,
Plenty of Expenses and very little strife.
Four children I reared and loved so much,
were God's blessing that kept me in touch
with all that is real, were my treasures on earth.
We'll never know what their love to me was worth.

Butler and I had enjoyed Enchanted Castle, our home;
We loved the journey to mountains I once had roamed.
We spoke of all the things we had done in the past,
And knew this way our heritage would always last.
The Scottish, The English, the Virginians we learned;
And the Lord, The Word, and Grace we would yearn.

I had a dream that I soon would die.
The journey ended and no tears to cry.
The Knights of the Golden Horseshoes arrived
to bid Farewell and keep heraldry alive.
Life is an adventure and journey all its own,
The journeys end is Heaven, to all it is known

The best good news I can share with you,
That my love for all is forever true.
I hope you think of me sometimes,
when gazing at the starry sky that shines;
That Circinus in southern skies there, too
 With me holding the golden horseshoe.

The Lord has taken me under his wing ,
and flown me where the angels sing.
Seven nails, seven stars, and seven lights
Make a horseshoe shaped star group bright.
I'll be waiting here for those who make
The journey with the Lord and for his sake.

Appendix

Section 1
The readers of "Spotswood Journey" novel should view the characters as fictional characters in a novel. The reader should not assume that they are the same historical figures by the same names in English and Virginia history. Many of the events may be similar to what may have happened in history, but the story, "Spotswood Journey" is not historically accurate. People in history.

Alexander Spotswood, (1676-1740)   Lieutenant Governor of Virginia
Robert Spotswood, (1631- 1680)   Father of Alexander, English navy doctor
Katherine Maxwell, (1632-1709)   Mother of Alexander Spotswood, m. (1) George Elliott, m. (2) Robert Spotswood (3) George Mercer, d. in Waterford, Ireland

Robert Spotswood, (1597-1649)   Grandfather of Alexander; Scottish Knight and Royalist
Bethia Morrison, (1597-1639)   Grandmother of Alexander Spotswood
John Spotswood, (1565 -1639)   Archbishop of St. Andrews, great gf. of Alexander
Bethia Spotswood, (1637- after 1683),   Aunt to Alexander
George Elliott , (1636 -1668)   m. Katherine Maxwell at St. Olav Church on Hart St., London

    In 1654, father of Roger Elliott
Major- General Roger Elliott,   half-brother of Alexander; Governor of Gibraltar
    (1665-1714)

Katherine Elliott, (b. ca1660-unknown)   half- sister of Alexander
Margaret Elliott, (b. ca1663-unknown)   half-sister of Alexander
Richard Andrews,   husband of Margaret Elliott
Richard Giles   (2) husband of Margaret Elliott
George Mercer   (3) husband of Katherine Maxwell
Lt. Gen. Percy Kirke, (1646-1691)   Col of 2nd Tangier Regiment, Gov. of Tangier 1682
John "Salamander" Cutts, 1661-1707   British soldier and author
King Charles II, (1630-1685)   King of England 1649-1685
Catherine Braganza, wife of King Charles II,

introduced tea to the English citizens
Andrew Rutherford, 1st Earl of Teviot,
d. 1664 Tangier, Lt. General of France,
 Gov. of Dunkirk

Charles FitzCharles, Ist Earl of Plymouth, (1662- 1680) in Tangier 1680

Gen James Scott, Duke of Monmouth, (1649-1685) Monmouth rebellion

Thomas Coryat of Odcombe, Eng. Writer, 1611," Coryat's Curdities," Introduced forks to the English

Moulay Ismail ibn Sharif, (1645-1727) King of Morocco 1672-1727, retook Tangier from the English in 1684, known as Warrior King. He ordered that 10,000 heads of his slain enemies would be placed on the walls of his capital city. He commanded 150.000 men in his elite Black Army. He fathered 888 children, most of any man in recorded history.

Admiral Edward Montagu, Ist Earl of Sandwich (1625-1675) House of Commons, Regiment of Foot,

Louis Almeida, Last Portugese ruler of Tangier

Henry Mondurant, 2nd Earl of Petersborough, Governor and Captain General of all British forces in Tangier

Henry Shere and Hugh Chomeley, English engineers who designed mole in Tangier and Whitby, Eng.

Earl Sochelles, Governor of Tangier

King James II of England, (1633-1701) brother to King Charles II, married (1) Mary of Modena (2) Anne Hyde

John, Lord Culpepper, 3rd Baron of Thoresway, (1640-1719) uncle of Katherine Culpepper

Katherine Culpepper, daughter of Thomas Culpepper. 2nd Baron of Thoresway and Dutch heiress, Margaret Van Hesse. Wife of Thomas Fairfax, 5th Lord

Thomas Culpepper, 2nd Baron of Thoresway, 1635-1689, Colonial Governor of Virginia 1677-1683) interested in Northern neck development in Virginia,

Thomas Fairfax, 5th Lord Fairfax of Cameron, (1657-1710)

Thomas Fairfax, 6th Lord Fairfax of Cameron, administrator of 5.2 million acres of land grants in . Northern Neck part of VA between Potomac and Rappahannock Rivers

Charles, Lord Marquess of Winchester, 2nd Duke of Bolton, Lord Lieutenant of Ireland, (1661-1722}

Rev. John Wesley (1703-1791) Anglican preacher, with brother Charles, and others founded Methodists

Rev. John Thompson, minister at St. Marks Parish, "Salubria" (2) husband of Butler Brayne Spotswood

Anne Thompson, b. 1744, d. 1815, dau. of Rev. John Thompson and Butler Brayne Spotswood, m. Francis Thornton

William Thompson, b. 1745, son of Rev. John Thompson and Butler Brayne Spotswood, m. Sarah Carter of Cleve

Blackbeard, (Edward Teach) (b. ca. 1680. d. 22 Nov. 1718) , a notorious pirate that wreaked havoc on coasts of the Americas

Col. William Dandridge, British naval officer, (1689-1743) owner of "Elsing Green"

Mary Dandridge, (1727- 6 Dec. 1798), daughter of William Dandridge and Unity West. Wife of John Spotswood, b. 1727

Capt. Tancred Robinson, 3rd Baronet (1685-1754) English Rear Admiral. Captain of the ship, "Deptford". Lord Mayor of York, England. Author.

Dr. William Cocke (1672-1720), Secretary of the Virginia Colony (1712-1720), physician

Grace O'Malley, {1530-1603), notorious pirate, inherited a large shipping business, trader, and Chieftain of Maillot Clan in Ireland. Said to have spoken Latin with Queen Elizabeth I of England.

John Churchill, (1650-1722) lst Duke of Marlborough, statesman and general in British Army. Served 5 monarchs, One of richest men in England during Queen Anne's reign. Knight of the Garter.
Lead the Allied Forces against the French in the War of Spanish Succession

Sarah Jennings Churchill, (1660-1744) one of the most influential ladies in the reign of Queen Anne of England, wife of Gen, John Churchill, heavily involved in the designing of Blenheim Palace. Changed her will 27 times and owned much property in England

William Shakespeare, (1564-1616) English playwright, poet, actor

Joseph Addison, (1672-1719) English essayist, play wright, poet, politician

King George I, (1660-1727) King of England 1712- 1727 m. Sophia Dorothea of Celle

King George II, 1683-1760) King of England 1727-1760 m. Caroline Ansbauch

Children of Alexander Spotswood and Butler Brayne

1• John Maxwell Spotswood, (1725-1758) m. Mary Dandridge

2• Anne Catherine Spotswood, (1727-1802) m. Bernard Moore

3• Dorothea Spotswood, (1733-1773), m. Nathaniel Dandridge

4• Capt. Robert Spotswood, (1737-1758), killed near Ft. Duquesne during French and Indian War, while serving under George Washington as a scout.

Dorothy Brayne, b. ca, 1692, d. ca 1759. sister to Butler Brayne, wife of Alexander Spotswood

Elliott Beneger, husband of Dorothy Brayne, cousin of Alexander Spotswood, executor of Alexander Spotswood's will, died May 16th, 1751, Postmaster General of the British Crown for North America and the West Indies

Reverend Robert Rose, pastor of Vawter's Church, 1725-1743) b, ca 1705 in Scotland, d. 1751, executor of the will of Alexander Spotswood

Augustine Moore, owner of Temple Farm, near Yorktown, VA

William Byrd, (1674-1744) planter, VA Colonial Statesman, author, founder of Richmond, VA

Rev. James Blair, 1656-1743, 1st President of William and Mary College, VA Colonial Statesman

King William III (1650-1702) and wife, Queen Mary II, (1662-1694} of England

George Hamilton, (1666-1737) First Earl of Orkney, Field Marshall in Spanish Succession Wars

John Flamstead, (1646-1719) English Royal Astronomer, catalogued 3000 stars

Isaac Newton (1642-1726) English physicist, built 1st refracting telescope, assisted in development of calculus, Gravitation studies, studied the speed of sound, Warden and Master of Royal Mint

Edmond Halley (1656-1742) Astronomer, physicist, studied orbit of Halley's comet

William Livingstone, b. 1682, son of William the Merchant of Aberdeen, started 1st theater in Colonies which had British plays

John Lederer, German physician and explorer, became the first explorer to see the Blue Ridge in 1669

William Kidd, (1654-1701) one of the most famous pirates in history

Section 2

Some of the German Settlers that settled Germanna
John Joseph and Maria Katherine Martin
Melchior and Elizabeth Brumbach

John and Mary Spillman
Jacob and Margaret Holtzclaw and sons, John and Henry
Tilman Weaver and his mother, Ann Weaver
John and Kathrina Hoffman
John and Agnes Fishbach, (progenitor of 5 governors)
Joseph and Kathrina Coons and son, John and daughters; Annalis and Kathrina
Herman and Kathrina Fishback
Jacob and Elizabeth Rector and son, John.
Peter and Elizabeth Hitt

Section 3
Colonial Governors at Tangiers

Henry Mordaunt, 2nd Earl of Petersborough	1662-1663
Andrew Rutherford, 1st Earl of Teviot	1663-1664
Sir Thomas Bridges	1664-1664
John Fitzgerald	1664-1665
John, Baron Belasysne	1665-1666
Sir Henry Norwood	1666-1669
John Middleton, 1st Earl of Middleton	1669-1670
Sir Hugh Chomondeley	1670-1672
John Middleton, 1st Earl of Morton	1672-1674
Budget Meakin, acting governor	1674-1675
William O'Brien, 2nd Earl of Inchiquin	1675-1680
Palmer Fairbourne	1680-1680
Thomas Butler,6th Earl of Ossery	1680-1680
Charles FitzCharles	1680-1680
Edward Sackville	1680-1681
Sir Percy Kirke	1681-1683
George Legge	1683-1684

Section 4

Rulers of England during Alexander Spotswood
Journey through Life

King Charles II	1660-1685
King James II	1685-1689
King William III	1689-1702
Queen Mary II	1689-1694
Queen Anne	1702-1714
King George I	1714-1727
King George II	1727-1760

Section 5
Knights of the Golden Horseshoes

.

James Taylor II, (1674-1729) of Caroline County, Burgess of King and Queen County

Augustine Warner Smith (1666-1736 s. of Lawrence) Trustee of Frederick, VA

Capt. Christopher Smith (d. ca. 1740) Owned land near Rapidan and Anna River

William Todd, (ca.1685-ca, 1736) member of the quorum of King & Queen County

Capt. Jeremiah Crowder, one of founders of Frederick, VA. Justice of Pennsylvania

Christopher Robinson (1681-1727) Burgess from Middlesex County, naval officer

John Robinson, (1683-1749) brother to Christopher, Burgess from Essex County

William Robertson (ca. 1657, Edinburgh, died. 1739)Clerk of Council, Trustee of William and
Mary College

Robert Brooke II (1700-1744) Surveyor, wrote a book," Plan of the Potomac River" in 1737

George Mason III (1690-1735) Sheriff of Stafford County

Robert Beverly (ca.1667-1722) historian, Burgess 1706, Clerk of Council of VA

John Fontaine (1693-1767) Lt. In British Army, wrote journal of the Blue Ridge Journey

Some of the other names that might have been Knights of the Golden Horseshoes.
These are some of the most distinguished and prominent names in Virginia History

Peter Berkeley	Henry Lee
Charles Ludwell	William Beverly
Charles Mercer	Theodore Bland
Bernard Moore	Thomas Bray
William Moseley	William Byrd
John Munroe	Kit Carter
Alexander Nott	Nathaniel Dandridge
Mann Page	Dudley Digges
Edmund Pendleton	Dr. Evelyn
John Peyton	Thomas Fairfax
John Randolph	John Fitzhugh
Edward Saunders	Henry Hall
Peyton Skipwith	George Hay
John Washington	Joe Jarvis
Ralph Wormley	Rev. Hugh Jones
George Wythe	Charles Ludwell
Oliver Yelverton	Francis Lee

Section 6

Some of the Ancestors of Alexander Spotswood

1. Adam (B. C. 4000-3070), Eve.
2. Seth (B. C. 3869-2957), Azura
3. Enos (B. C. 3764-2859),Noam
4. Canaan (B. C. 3674-2895), Mualeleth
5. Mahalaleel (B. C. 3604-2709), Dinah
6.Jared (B. C. 3539-2577), Bera
7. Enoch (B. C. 3377-3012), Edna
8. Methusaleh (B. C. 3312-2344), Edna
9 ,Lamech (B.C. 3125-2349), Ashmua

_____10. Noah (B. C. 2943-2007), Emzara_____.

{   {   {
11. Shem (B. C. 2441-1841). Sedeqetelebab   11. Ham -Ne'elatama'uk 11. Japeth,   Adataneses
12. Arphaxad (B. C.2341-1903). Raseju   12. Magog
13. Selah (B. C.2306-1873) Hua Mu'ak bint Kesed   13. Boath
14. Heber (B. C. 2276-1812) Azarad   14. Phoeniusa Farsaid,
15. Peleg (B. C. 2241-2003) Lomna   15. Niul
16. Reu (B. C. 2212-1973) Ora Chaldees   16. Gaodhal Gas, the
Egyptian
17. Serug (B. C. 2180-2049) Melka   17. Asruth, (Easru)
18. Nahor (B. C. 2050-2002) Jaska   18. Sru (Syruth), b. Egypt,
19. Terah (B. C. 2221-1992) Amtheta.   19. Heber Scut
20. Abraham (B. C. 1992-1817), Sarah.   20. Beouman, King o
Scythia
21. Isaac (B. C. 1896-1716), Rebekah.   21. Oghaman, King o
Scythia
22. Jacob (B. C. 1837-1690), Leah.   22. Tait, King of Scythia
23. Judah (b. B. C. 1752), Tamar.   23. Aghenoin, King Scythia
24. Pharez, Barayah   24. Lamhfinn Glunfionn
25. Hezron, Abia   25. Heber Glunfionn
26. Aram, Abiah bat Machir   26. Agnan Fionn, King of Gothia
27. Aminadab   27. Febric Glas, King of Gothia
28. Naasson. Sinvar   28. Nenuall, King of Gothia
29. Salmon, Rahab   29. Nuadhad, K.of Gothia,b. Getulia
30. Boaz (B. C. 1312), Ruth.   30. Allaid, King of Gothia
31. Obed, Abalit   31. Earchada (Arcadh) King of Gothia
32.Jesse, Natzbath   32. Deaghat, King of Getulia
KINGS OF JUDAH AND ISRAEL   KINGS of GETULIA (LIBYA)
33. King David (B. C. 1085-1015), Bathsheba.   33. Brath, K. of Getulia,Gothia Galicia
34. King Solomon (B. C. 1033-975), Naamah.   34. Breoghan, King of Galicia
35. King Rehoboam (b. B. C. 1016, d. 958), Maacah.   35. Bille, K.Galicia and Spain m. Baun
36. King Abijah (B. C. 958-955), Ana de Naftali   36. Milesios Gallam, King of Braganza
37. King Asa (B. C. 955-914), Azubah.   }
38. King Jehoshaphat (B. C. 914-889), Atila Bat Omri
39. King Jehoram (B. C. 889-885), Athaliah.   {
40. King Ahaziah (B. C. 906-884), Zibiah.   {
             }   {

41. King Joash (B. C. 885-839), Jehoaddan.   .}

42. King Amaziah (b. B. C. 864, d. 810), Jecholiah.
43. King Uzziah (b. B. C. 826, d. 758), Jerusha.
44. King Jotham (b. B. C. 783, d. 742).
45. King Ahaz (b. B. C. 787, d. 726), Abi.
46. King Hezekiah (b. B. C. 751, d. 698), Hephzibah.
47. King Manasseh (b. B. C. 710, d. 643), Meshullemeth.
48. King Amon (b. B. C. 621, d. 641), Jedidiah.
49. King Josiah (b. B. C. 649, d. 610), Mamutah.
50. King Zedekiah (B. C. 599-578).
51. Queen Tea Tephi (b.c.565 BC.)   marries   37.Eochaidh   KINGS OF IRELAND
52. King Irial Faidh (reigned 10 years), son of Eochaidh Heremon (note 1)
53. King Eithriall (reigned 20 years).
54. Follain.
55. King Tighernmas (reigned 50 years).
56. Eanbotha.
57. Smiorguil.
58. King Fiachadh Labhriane (reigned 24 years).
59. King Aongus Ollmuchaidh (reigned 21 years).
60. Maoin.
61.King Rotheachta (reigned 25 years).
62. Dein.
63. King Siorna Saoghalach (reigned 21 years).
64. Oholla Olchaoin.
65. King Giallchadh (reigned 9 years).
66. King Aodhain Glas (reigned 20 years).
67. King Simeon Breac (reigned 7 years).
68. King Muirteadach Bolgrach (reigned 4 years).
69. King Fiachadh Toigrach (reigned 7 years).
70. King Duach Laidhrach (reigned 10 years).
71. Eochaidh Buailgllerg.
72. King Ugaine More the Great (reigned 30 years).
73. King Cobhthach Coalbreag (reigned 30 years).
74. Meilage.
75. King Jaran Gleofathach (reigned 7 years).
76. King Coula Cruaidh Cealgach (reigned 25 years).
77. King Oiliolla Caisfhiachach (reigned 28 years).
78. King Eochaidh Foltleathan (reigned 11 years).
79. King Aongns Tuirmheach Teamharch (reigned 30 years).
80. King Eana Aighneach (reigned 28 years).
81. Labhra Suire
82. Blathucha
83. Easamhuin Famhua
84. Roighnein Ruadh
85. Finlogha
86. Fian
87. King Eodchaidh Feidhlioch (reigned 12 years).
88. Fineamhuas
89. King Lughaidh Raidhdearg
90. King Criomhthan Niadhnar (reigned 16 years).
91. Fearaidhach Fion Feachtnuigh
92. King Fiachadh Fionoluidh (reigned 20 years).
93. King Tuathal Teachtmar (reigned 40 years).
94. King Conn Ceadchathach (reigned 20 years).
95. King Arb Aonflier (reigned 30 years).
96. King Cormae Usada (reigned 40 years).
97. King Caibre Liffeachair (reigned 27 years).
98. King Fiachadh Sreabthuine (reigned 30 years.)
99. King Muireadhach Tireach (reigned 30 years).
100. King Eochaidh Moigmeodhin (reigned 7 years.)
101. King Nail of the Nine Hostages.
102. Eogan.
103. K. Murireadhach.
104. Earca.
105. King Fergus More   KINGS OF ARGYLESHIRE
106. King Dongard
107. King Conran
108. King Aidan (d. 604).
109. King Eugene IV. (d. 622).
110. King Donald IV. (d. 650).
111. Dongard
112. King Eugene. V. (d. 692).

113. Findan
114. King Eugene VII. (d. A. D. 721), Spond
115. K. Etfinus (d. A. D. 761), Fergina
116. King Achaius (d. A. D. 819), Fergusia
117. King Alpin (d. A. D. 834)
118. King Kenneth I. (842-858).   SCOTTISH KINGS
119. King Constantin I. (862-876).
120. King Donald II. (889-900).
121. King Malcolm I. (943-954).
122. King Kenneth II. (971-995, d. A. D. 995).
123. King Malcolm II. (1005-1034, d. A. D. 1034). .
124. Bethoc, married to Crinan, Mormaer of Atholl and lay abbot of Dunkeld.
125. King Duncan I. (1034-1040, d. A. D. 1040), Sybil.
126. King Malcolm III. Canmore (A. D. 1058-1093), Saint Margaret of England.
127. King David I. (1124-1153, d. A. D. 1153), Matilda of Huntingdon.
128. Prince Henry of Huntingdon (d. A. D. 1152), Ada Warrenne of Surrey.
129. Earl David of Huntingdon (d. A. D. 1219), Matilda of Chester.
130. Isobel m. Robert Bruce, 4th Lord of Annandale
131. Robert Bruce 5th Lord of Annandale. m. Isobel of Gloucester and Hertford
132. Robert Bruce 6th Lord of Annandale m. Marjorie, Countess of Carrick.
133. King Robert I. (The Bruce) (A. D. 1306-1329), Isobel, daughter of Earl of Mar.
134. Marjorie Bruce m. Walter Stewart, 6th High Steward of Scotland
135. K. Robert II. (b. 1317, 1371-1390, d. A. D. 1390), Euphemia of Ross (d. A. D. 1376).
136. Elizabeth Stewart, Countess of Crawford m. Sir David Lindsay of Glenesk, 1st Earl of Crawford
137. Alexander Lindsay, 2nd Earl of Crawford m. Lady Marjory Dunbar
138. David Lindsay, 3rd Earl of Crawford m. Marjory Ogilsvey
139. Walter Lindsay of Beaufort, Lindsay, and Edzell m. Isabel Livingstone
140. Sir David Thomas Lindsay of Edzell m. Katherine Lindsay
141. Walter Lindsay of Edzell, 8th Earl of Crawford m. Elizabeth Falconer
141; Alexander Lindsay of Edzell m. Rachel Barclay
142. Dr. David Lindsay, Bishop of Ross m. Jonetta Lindsay
143. Rachel Lindsay m. Dr. John Spots wood, Archbishop of St. Andrews
144. Sir Robert Spotswood, Knight, m. Bethia Morrison
145. Robert Spotswood, Surgeon m. Katherine Maxwell
146. Lt. Governor Alexander Spotswood (1676-1740) m. Ann Butler Brayne
147. John Spotswood m. Mary Dandridge
148. Ann Spotswood m. Col. Lewis Burwell
149. Armistead Burwell m. Lucy Crawley
150. Ann Spotswood Burwell m. Richard Taylor
151. Ravenscroft Taylor m. Martha Mills McCulloch
152. Richard Spotswood Taylor m. Mary Pulley
153. Robert Edward Taylor m. Vinita Anderson
154. Robert G. Taylor, Sr. m. Elnora Kuykendall
155. Robert G. Taylor, Jr. (author)

Note 1. It is assumed by many genealogists and historians that Tamar Tea Telphi was a daughter of King Zedekiah of Judah and his wife who was said to be a daughter of the prophet, Jeremiah. This is one of the mysteries of Jeremiah if he traveled to the English Isles as reported by some of the historians. It is generally accepted that the line of descent from Adam to the historical Alexander Spots wood is through The Irish line of descent through Eochaid Heremon and is accurate. More study or proof is needed to prove the identity of Eochaid's wife. Some believe her to be Tamar an Irish Princess from an Irish family. The Bible proves the Judean descent from Adam to King Zedekiah.

Section 7
TEMPLE FARM.
Major General Alexander Spotswood, when on the eve of embarking at the head of another journey, destined for Cartagena in South America, died at Annapolis, Maryland, on the 7th day of June 1740. It is supposed that he may have been interred at Temple Farm on York river. A mile or two below Yorktown, on the south bank of the majestic York, extending from a bluff a mile back from the river, is the old Temple farm. An aged tombstone there suggests that it was one of the earliest settlements on the river. From the bluff by the farm, the view is unbroken down the York river to its mouth, where it merges in the waters of the Chesapeake Bay. The mansion house still survived during the revolutionary war and was known as the Moore House, a name which was derived from a widow, Lucy Smith Moore, whose husband was Augustine Moore. Augustine Moore had purchased Temple Farm from his brother-in-law, Robert Smith who owned it. Augustine Moore was killed by a stray bullet from a Revolutionary War Battle while he was working the fields on Temple Farm. Many people think his ghost still haunts the Moore House from the cemetery behind the house. Robert Smith was a grandson of the former owner, Mayor Lawrence Smith. Major Lawrence Smith would name this land "Temple Farm", possibly after a previous owner, Peter Temple. Upon the death of Major Lawrence Smith, Temple Farm was passed to his son, Colonel Lawrence Smith and was then passed on to Colonel Lawrence's son Robert. Robert sold the land to Augustine Moore, husband of his sister, Lucy Smith. The deed was acknowledged February 20, 1769. Major Lawrence Smith also had a son Col. Augustine Smith who was one of the Knights of the Golden Horseshoes who had accompanied Colonel and Lt. Governor Alexander Spotswood on the Journey over the Blue Ridge Mountains. The Moore House would become a very important historical house as this is where the surrender papers were signed by

Lord Cornwallis of the British Army and given to General George Washington to end the Revolutionary War. Lord Cornwallis chose the Moore House as the place to surrender and his real reason for choosing this particular house are unknown. After numerous owners, the Moore House became property of the National Park Service and was dedicated in 1934. The National Park Service has restored the Moore House to its original and glorious colonial appearance.

Dr. Shields, owner of the Moore house in 1834, found broken pieces of a tombstone at Temple Farm. When he got the broken pieces together the words on the tombstone were that of Governor Spotswood

Section 8
Some of the House of Burgesses Members during the Administration of Alexander Spotswood

Charles City County: Littlebury Eppes and Samuel Harwood
Elizabeth City County: Nicholas Curle and William Armistead
Essex County: James Baughan and John Hawkins
Gloucester County: Peter Beverly and Ambrose Dudley
Henrico County: John Bolling and William Randolph
Isle of Wight County: Arthur Smith and Joseph Godwin
Jamestown: Nathaniel Burwell
James City County: Thomas Cowles and Henry Soane
King and Queen County: William Byrd and John Holloway
King William County: John Waller and Henry Fox
Lancaster County: William Ball and Henry Fox
Middlesex County: John Robinson and Chris Robinson
Nansemond County: Thomas Godwin and Francis Milner
New Kent County: Nicholas Merriweather and John Stanup
Norfolk County: John Wilson and George Newton
Northampton County: Benjamin Nottingham and Charles Floyd
Northumberland County: Christopher Neale and Peter Presley
Prince George County: John Hardiman and Robert Bolling
Princess Ann County: Max Bousch and Henry Spratt
Richmond County: William Robinson and William Tayloe
Stafford County: George Mason and John Waugh
Surrey County: William Gray and John Simmons
Warwick County: William Howard and William Cary
Westmoreland County: George Eskridge and Willoughby Allerton
York County: Thomas Ballard and William Barber

Some of the Burgesses during the time of Alexander Spotswood period as Lt. Governor.
Willoughby Allerton, Westmoreland County
George Anderson, Stafford County
Anthony Armistead, Sr. Elizabeth City, County
Robert Armistead, Elizabeth City County
Henry Ashton, Westmoreland County
Major James Ball, Lancaster County
Col. William Ball, Lancaster County
Charles Barber, Richmond County
William Barber, Jr. York County

Some of the Burgesses during the time of Alexander Spotswood period as Lt. Governor.
Willoughby Allerton, Westmoreland County
George Anderson, Stafford County
Anthony Armistead, Sr. Elizabeth City, County
Robert Armistead, Elizabeth City County
Henry Ashton, Westmoreland County
Major James Ball, Lancaster County
Col. William Ball, Lancaster County
Charles Barber, Richmond County
William Barber, Jr. York County
Capt. Harry Beverly, King and Queen County
Robert Beverly, Knight of Golden Horseshoe, Essex County
William Byrd, King and Queen County
John Buckner, Gloucester County
Richard Buckner, Gloucester County
Thomas Buckner, Gloucester County
James Burwell, York County
Archibald Blair, James City County
John Bolling, Henrico County
Robert Bolling, Prince George County

Maximilian Borush, Princess Ann County
George Braxton,
Col. William Bridger, Isle of Wight County
Rev. James Blair,
John Blair,
Capt. William Cary, Warwick County
John Clayton, Sr.
John Carter
Robert Carter
John Custis,
Hancock Custis
William Cole, Warrick County
Edwin Conway, Lancaster County
Gawin Corbin, King and Queen County
Mordecai Cooke, Jr.
William Crawford, Norfolk County
Nicholas Curle, Elizabeth City, County
William Dandridge,
Cole Digges
Dudley Digges
Robert Dinwiddie
Henry Duke
Col. Francis Eppes, Henrico County
Solomon Ewell, Accomac County
Col. George Eskridge, Westmoreland County
William Fairfax
William Fitzhugh
Richard Fitzwilliam
George Fitzhugh, Stafford County
Charles Floyds, Northhampton County
Henry Fox, King and Queen County
Joseph Godwin, Isle of Wight County
Thomas Godwin, Jr.
William Gray, Surrey County
Thomas Griffin, Richmond County
John Grymes
Philip Grymes
Benjamin Harrison
Henry Harrison
Nathaniel Harrison
Robert Hall, Prince George County
Peter Hack, Nothumberland County
John Hamlin, Prince George County
Francis Hardeman, Charles City County
John Hardiman, Prince George County
George Harmanson, Northampton County
William Harwood, Warwick County
Joseph Harwood, Charles City County
Samuel Harwood, Sr. Charles City County
Samuel Harwood, Jr. , Charles City County
John Hawkins, Essex County
John Holloway, King and Queen County
Edmund Jennings
Thomas Lee, Stafford County
John Lewis, Gloucester County
Philip Lightfoot
Matthew Maury
Daniel McCarty, Richmond County
Nicholas Meriweather, New Kent County
Augustine Moore, King William County
Christopher Neale, Northumberland County
Richard Neal, Northumberland County
Benjamin Nottingham. Northampton County
Peter Presley, Northumberland County
Thomas Randolph, Henrico County
James Ricketts,
James Reddick, Nansemond County
William Robertson, Clerk of the Council, Knight of The Golden Horseshoes
James Roscow, Warrick County
John Simmons, Surrey County
Arthur Smith, Isle of Wight County

Lawrence Smith, York County
Henry Soane, Jr, James City County
Philip Ludwell, Jr.
Mann Page
John Robinson,
Hancock Custis, Richard Drummond, Accomack County
John Tayloe of Mt. Airy
Bartholomew Fowler John Stamp, New Kent County
John Stith, Charles City County
James Taylor, King and Queen County, Knight of the Golden Horseshoes
Samuel Thompson, Surrey County
John Thornton, New Kent County
William Thornton, Richmond and King George County
Thomas Todd, Toddsberry
Anthony Walker, Princess Anne County
John Waller, King William County
William Waters, Northampton County
John Waugh, Stafford County
Col. Henry Willis, Gloucester County
Miles Wills, Warwick County
Willis Wilson, Norfolk County
William Woodbridge, Richmond County
Horatio Woodhouse, Princess Anne
William Wright, Nansemond County
William Young, Essex County